The Mask

He rose to his feet and moved over to the table by the door and was surrounded by the pool of light cast by the oil lamp. She tried not to look at him, but to no avail. Dear heaven, he was as beautifully exotic as a jungle animal and just as free from shame.

A faint smile touched his lips. "This must have been meant for you."

On the table was an extravagant feathered mask of brown, black, and turquoise peacock feathers. "Pretty thing. I'd like to see you in it." He held up the mask to his own eyes. "Would you care to oblige me?"

The exotic feathered mask covered the entire top of his face and a spray of sable peacock feathers jutted out on either side. His blue eyes shimmered through the almond-shaped holes and the close fit of the mask enhanced the beautiful molding of his cheekbones.

He looked wild, wicked, and completely male, a rare, splendid creature from an alien land.

BOOKS BY IRIS JOHANSEN

Stalemate
An Unexpected Song
Killer Dreams
On the Run
Countdown
Blind Alley
Firestorm
Fatal Tide
Dead Aim
No One to Trust
Body of Lies
Final Target
The Search
The Killing Game
The Face of Deception
And Then You Die
Long After Midnight
The Ugly Duckling
Lion's Bride
Dark Rider
Midnight Warrior
The Beloved Scoundrel
The Magnificent Rogue
The Tiger Prince
Last Bridge Home
The Golden Barbarian
Reap the Wind
Storm Winds
The Wind Dancer

The Tiger Prince

IRIS JOHANSEN

BANTAM BOOKS

NEW YORK TORONTO LONDON SYDNEY AUCKLAND

THE TIGER PRINCE
A Bantam Book

PUBLISHING HISTORY
Bantam mass market edition published January 1993
Bantam mass market reissue / March 2007

Published by Bantam Dell
A Division of Random House, Inc.
New York, New York

ISBN 978-0-553-59039-5

Printed in the United States of America

www.bantamdell.com

OPM 10 9 8 7 6 5 4 3 2 1

The Tiger Prince

Prologue

Promontory Point, Utah
November 25, 1869

"Wait!"

Dear God, he hadn't heard her. He was still striding across the wooden platform toward the train. In a moment he would be out of reach.

Panic soared through Jane Barnaby and she broke into a run, the faded skirts of her calico gown ballooning behind her. Ignoring the pain caused by the ice shards piercing her feet through the holes in the thin soles of her boots, she tore through ice-coated mud puddles down the wheel-rutted street toward the platform over a hundred yards away. "Please! Don't go!"

Patrick Reilly's expression was only a blur in the post-dawn grayness, but he must have heard her call, for he hesitated for an instant before continuing toward the train, his long legs quickly covering the distance between the station house and the passenger railway car.

He was leaving her.

Fear caught in her throat, and she desperately tried to put on more speed. The train was already vibrating, puffing, flexing its metal muscles as it prepared to spring forward down the track. "Wait for me!"

He kept his face turned straight ahead, ignoring her.

Anger, fired by desperation, flared within her and she bellowed, "Dammit, do you hear me? Don't you *dare* get on that train!"

He stopped in midstride, his big shoulders braced militantly beneath the gray-checked coarse wool of his coat. He turned with a frown to watch her dashing toward him down the platform.

She skidded to a stop before him. "I'm goin' with you."

"The hell you are. I told you last night at Frenchie's you were to stay here."

"You gotta take me."

"I don't have to do nothin'." He scowled down at her. "Go back to your ma. She'll be looking for you."

"No, she won't." She took a step closer to him. "You know all she cares about is her pipe. She don't care where I am. She won't mind if I go with you."

He shook his head.

"You know it's true." Jane moistened her lips. "I'm goin' with you. She doesn't want me. She never wanted me."

"Well, I don't want you eith—" A flush deepened his already ruddy cheeks, and his Irish brogue thickened as he said awkwardly, "No offense, but I don't have no use for a kid in my life."

"I'm not so little, I'm almost twelve." It was only a small lie; she had just turned eleven, but he probably wouldn't remember that. She took another step closer. "You gotta take me. I belong to you."

"How many times do I have to tell you? I'm not your father."

"My mother said it was most likely you." She touched a strand of the curly red hair flopping about her thin face. "Our hair is the same, and you visited her a lot before she went on the pipe."

"So did half the men of the Union Pacific." His expression softened as he suddenly knelt in front of her. "Lots of Irishmen have red hair, Jane. Hell, I can name four men on my own crew who used to be Pearl's regulars. Why not pick on one of them?"

Because she desperately wanted it to be him. He was kinder to her than any of the other men who paid her mother for her body. Patrick Reilly was drunk more than he was sober when he came to Frenchie's tent, but he never hurt the women like some men did and even treated Jane with a rough affection whenever he saw her around. "It's you." Her jaw set stubbornly. "You can't know for certain it's not you."

His jaw set with equal obstinacy. "And you don't know for certain it is me. So why don't you go back to Frenchie's and leave me alone? Christ, I wouldn't even know how to take care of you."

"Take care of me?" She stared at him in bewilderment. "Why should you do that? I take care of myself."

For an instant a flicker of compassion crossed his craggy features. "I guess you've had to do enough of that all right. With your ma sucking on that damn opium pipe and growing up in that pimp's hovel."

She immediately pounced on the hint of softening. "I won't be a bother to you. I don't eat much and I'll stay out of your way." He was beginning to frown again, and she went on hurriedly. "Except when you have something for me to do, of course. I'm a hard worker. Ask anyone at Frenchie's. I empty slops and help in the kitchen. I sweep and mop and run errands. I can count and take care of money. Frenchie even has me time the customers on Saturday night and tell them when they've had their money's worth." She grasped his arm. "I promise I'll do anything you want me to do. Just take me with you."

"Hell, you don't under—" He was silent a moment, gazing at her pleading face before muttering, "Look, I'm a railroad man. It's all I know and my job here is over now that the tracks have been joined. I've got an offer to boss my own crew in Salisbury and that's a big chance for an ignorant mick like me. Salisbury's way across the ocean in England. You don't want to go that far away."

"Yes, I do. I don't care where we go." Her small hand tightened on his arm. "Try me. I promise you won't be sorry."

"The devil I won't be sorry." His tone was suddenly impatient as he shook off her grasp and rose to his feet. "I won't be saddled with no whore's kid for the rest of my life. Go back to Frenchie's." He started toward the train again.

The rejection frightened but didn't surprise her. She had been rejected all her life by everyone but the inhabitants of Frenchie's crib and had learned long ago she wasn't like the children of the respectable wives who followed the railroad crews from town to town. They belonged in a world of clean crisp gowns, Saturday night baths, and church on Sunday mornings while she . . .

Jane felt suddenly sick as memories flooded back to her of the lantern-lit haze of Frenchie's tent, where the cots were separated only by dirty blankets hung on sagging ropes, the sweetish smell of the opium her mother smoked from the funny-looking glass bowl by her cot, Frenchie's hard palm striking her cheek when she wasn't quick enough to do his bidding.

She *couldn't* go back to that now that escape was so near.

Her nails dug into her palms as her hands clenched into fists at her sides. "It will do you no good to leave me. I'll only follow you."

He reached the train and placed his left foot on the metal step.

"I *will.* You belong to me."

"The hell I do."

"I'll follow you to this Saddlebury and—"

"Salisbury, and you'd have to swim the goddamn ocean."

"I'll do it. I'll find a way. You'll see that I'll find a way to—" Her voice broke and she had to stop.

"Dammit." His head lowered, his gaze fixed on the ridged metal of the step. "Why the hell do you have to be so damned stubborn?"

"Take me," she whispered. She did not know what else to say, what to offer him. "Please. If I stay, I'm scared someday I'll be like her. I . . . don't like it there."

He stood there, his shoulders hunched as moment after moment passed. "Oh, what the hell!" He whirled, jumped back down on the platform. His big, freckled hands grasped her waist and he effortlessly picked her up and lifted her onto the train. "Jesus, you're tiny. You don't weigh anything at all."

Had he given in? She was afraid to believe it. "That doesn't matter. I'm small for my age, but I'm very strong."

"You'd better be. I guess you can trail along, but it don't mean anything. I'm not your father and you'll call me Patrick like anybody else."

"Patrick," she repeated obediently.

"And you'll damn well earn your keep."

"If you say so." She held tight to the iron guardrail as the relief pouring through her made her dizzy with delight. "You won't be sorry. I'll make it up to you. There's nothing I won't do to make it—"

"Wait here and I'll talk to the conductor about letting you on board." He turned away from her. "Christ, he'll probably make me buy a ticket for you. I spend years building this damn railroad and now they make me pay hard cash for—"

"Two tickets."

He stopped and slowly turned back to her. His tone was ominously soft. "Two tickets?"

She braced herself. "Li Sung." She lifted her arm and waved it at the small, thin young man who had been following her and now stood waiting in the shadow of the station house. "He's goin' too." At her signal the Chinese boy limped forward, carrying a knapsack and a worn, dilapidated carpet bag. "He's my friend. He won't be any trouble."

"No trouble? He's a cripple."

"He can cook," she said quickly. "You know he can cook. You had some of his stew once at Frenchie's. And he's smarter than almost anyone I know. He's teaching me to read and cipher and knows all about herbs and—"

"No," Patrick said flatly. "I ain't draggin' no cripple along. The chink goes back."

"He has to go with us." He was scowling again. What if he changed his mind and sent her away too? Yet she couldn't leave Li Sung. She went on urgently. "You're letting me go along and Li Sung is seventeen, almost a man. He'll be able to help you more than—" Patrick's expression wasn't softening. "He won't bother you. I'll take care of him."

Patrick looked at her incredulously.

"I can do it. Just buy him a ticket." She whispered, "Please."

"You think I'm made of money?"

"I can't leave without him. Frenchie does terrible things to him."

Li Sung stopped beside them, his glance going from Jane's face to Patrick's. "I am going?"

Jane gazed pleadingly at Patrick.

"Dammit to hell." Patrick whirled and started down the platform toward the uniformed conductor who was talking to the engineer in his cab. "Only as far as Omaha. I'll be damned if I tote him with me any farther."

Jane's breath escaped in a little rush. "It's all right. Get on the train, Li Sung."

"Where is this Omaha?"

"A long way, I think." Jane was a bit vague about that too. "And by that time I'll think of a way to make him keep you with us all the way. He's not a hard man."

Li Sung smiled bitterly. "But he is Irish and the Irish do not like my race."

"I'll find a way," Jane repeated. "Just stay out of his sight for a while."

As she opened the door to the passenger coach, she felt the floor suddenly vibrate beneath her feet and froze in alarm. The motion felt . . . odd. Though she could not remember a time when she had not been dragged with her mother from tent city to tent city as Frenchie followed the construction crews who laid the tracks, she had never actually been on a train before.

Li Sung nodded understandingly as he met her gaze. "Much power. I can see why they call it the iron horse."

She shook her head. "It's more like the dragons you told me about, breathing fire and smoke and swishing their tails." She went on down the aisle ahead of him. "We'll get used to it."

Li Sung nodded as he set the knapsacks on the rack above her head and the carpet bag beside her. "If it is possible to become used to dragons."

"It's possible." She sat down and folded her hands in her lap. The air smelled of stale cigars and the fresh-cut wood and coal in the fuel box by the stove at the front of the car. She must become accustomed to the vibration, the scents, the noise that was to make up this new life. "It's going to be all right, Li Sung. You'll see, we're going to be—"

A mournful whimper suddenly issued from the carpet bag.

"Oh, damn, I hoped he'd stay asleep." Jane glanced furtively out the window and saw Patrick still arguing with the conductor. She quickly opened the carpet bag. Immediately a brown and white muzzle poked into view. She gently stroked the soft fur on the head of the scrawny beagle pup. "Hush, not now. No noise."

"I told you not to bring the stray."

Her head lifted and she glared fiercely at Li Sung. "Sam's only six weeks old. Frenchie would have let him starve like he did his mother and the other pups. I had to bring him."

A small smile lit Li Sung's sallow face as he nodded resignedly. "I know, it is your nature. Still, your father will not be pleased."

"He doesn't know . . . yet." She quickly closed the carpet bag and thrust it at Li Sung. "You'd better take him up to the front of the car and stay there until I come for you."

Li Sung shrugged and took the carpet bag. "He will probably throw me and the pup off the train."

"No, he won't. I won't let him. I'll just convince him we'll need a guard dog in—" She paused a minute, trying to remember the name of the town for which they were destined. "Salisbury."

"And how will you do that?"

"I'll just keep at him and never give up." She set her jaw. "If you want something bad enough, you can make it happen. You just keep on going until everybody else gets tired of fighting."

"Let us hope he grows weary before we reach this Omaha." Li Sung limped down the aisle toward the far end of the car.

Her father had finished his discussion with the conductor and was striding down the platform, his expression distinctly displeased.

Father. She must remember not to call him that, she thought wistfully. He would not acknowledge her as kin, and it would only anger him. Perhaps, if she worked very hard, if she made herself useful enough, someday he would let her use the word.

The piercing blast of the whistle made her jump and then grab hold of the wooden seat as the train lurched forward.

She heard Patrick's obscene exclamation as he loped the last few yards, jumped for the steps, and pulled himself on the train.

Steam frosted the cold air outside the window as the black dragon began to glide slowly away from the hastily erected shacks and weather-stained tents that was Promontory Point.

Fear caught and held Jane as she saw the scenes flying by and realized everything she had ever known was vanishing before her eyes.

"Want to go back?"

She looked up to see her fath—Patrick standing beside her, his expression hopeful. "I can send you home once we reach the next stop."

"No."

"Last chance."

Promontory Point vanished from view as if it had never been, and suddenly her fear also vanished. "No." She did not really know much about homes, but she was sure Frenchie's had never been one. Her father was a railroad man who moved from place to place, so perhaps this puffing, roaring dragon they were riding would be her home from then on. If so, she must learn everything about it and make it her own. Yes, that was what she must do; her father loved the railroad and it must become as much a part of her as it was of him.

She settled gingerly back on the hard seat and deliberately tried to relax her tense muscles. "I'm not goin' back. I was just a little scared for a minute, but I'm all right now."

He muttered something beneath his breath and dropped onto the seat next to her.

She closed her eyes and listened to the rumble of the wheels on the iron track. Slowly, gradually, she became aware of a rhythm in the metal clatter like the beat of a giant heart, a cadence in the hissing of the steam that was vaguely soothing. Perhaps the dragon wasn't so fierce after all. Perhaps, in time, he would let her befriend him and learn all his secrets. . . .

Chapter 1

Krugerville, Africa
April 3, 1876

Ruel reminded Ian of a beautiful tiger set to pounce.

Ruel's right hand gripped a bone-handled knife with deadly competence, and an eager smile curved his lips. Stripped to the waist, his muscles gleaming gold-bronze in the lantern light, blue eyes blazing with fierce joy, he circled the huge mulatto holding the machete.

Shock jolted through Ian MacClaren as he peered through the smoke layering the air of the bar at the two men squaring off across the room. Somehow he had not expected Ruel to look so lethal. Yet the reports he had received over the years should have given him some warning, and even as a boy Ruel had never been tame. Certainly no trace of tameness lingered in his brother now.

Tiger pad softly, tiger burn bright . . .

The scrap of an old verse popped into Ian's mind, underscoring the impression that had leapt into being the instant he had caught sight of Ruel. The boy had always burned with a restless, volatile energy, but now he cast out an almost incandescent vitality. Time had honed and hardened the faultless symmetry of the face Margaret had once described as having the beauty of a fallen angel, but it still held the riveting magnetism it had always possessed. Strands of tawny white-gold laced the dark brown hair he wore tied back in a queue, adding to the tigerish quality of his appearance.

The mulatto suddenly sliced out with the machete.

Ruel easily avoided the parry and gave a low, pleased laugh. "At last. You were beginning to bore me, Barak."

"Don't just stand there." The woman, Mila, grabbed Ian's arm. "You said if I brought you to him, you would help. Barak will kill him."

"He certainly appears to be trying," Ian murmured. He had been told when he had arrived in town a few hours earlier that she was only one of the gold camp's whores, but she was clearly emotionally involved with Ruel. The circumstance did not astonish him. Drawn by those wicked good looks and careless, joyous paganism, women had gravitated to Ruel's bed before he had reached puberty. However, Ian was surprised he felt no fear the woman's prophecy would prove true. This Barak towered almost seven feet and his bull-like musculature made Ruel's five-foot-eleven physique appear childlike in comparison. Yet Ian felt Ruel would have no more trouble defeating him than he had the bullies who had taunted his brother as a child. "I believe we'll wait and watch awhile. Ruel never liked me to interfere in these matters."

The giant mulatto made another lunge, and Ruel's

torso arched catlike as the blade just missed digging into his belly.

"Better," Ruel laughed. "But not good enough. God, you're clumsy."

Barak roared with anger and lunged again.

But Ruel was no longer there.

He had danced with lightning swiftness to the left, and a red slash suddenly appeared on Barak's side. "As clumsy with the machete as you are at dealing from the bottom of the deck. I could teach you a bit about both." He circled the huge man with the quickness of a mongoose with a cobra. "But I don't really think it would be worthwhile. I hate to waste my time, when you'll be dead soon anyway."

Ian stiffened, jarred back to the realization that this was no childhood fight that would end only with black eyes and scraped knuckles. He turned to the woman. "I think we'd better go get the local magistrate to stop this."

She gazed at him in bewilderment. "Magistrate?"

"The law," he said impatiently.

"There's no law here," she said. "*You* must stop it. Barak wants Ruel's claim. He cheated only to make Ruel angry enough to fight so he could kill him."

Ian muttered a curse as he looked around the crowded bar. God knows he was no more equipped to step into this battle than he had been for Ruel's boyhood frays at Glenclaren, but he could see no help would be forthcoming from any of the roughly dressed men sitting at the tables in this disreputable hovel; the miners were staring at the two combatants with only amusement and a curiously hungry look distinctly more sinister in nature.

Yet it was becoming evident Ian must do something. He could not permit Ruel to commit murder even in self-defense.

Barak lunged again and Ruel whirled away. A long, bloody cut suddenly appeared on Barak's upper arm.

"You're beginning to bore me, you son of a bitch," Ruel said.

Ian recognized the signs; Ruel was toying with Barak, but he was beginning to get impatient and would soon go on the offensive. He would have to do something—

Barak had drawn blood.

Ruel had been a tenth of a second too slow, and Barak's machete had grazed his rib cage.

"Excellent." Incredibly, Ruel nodded with approval. "You should always take advantage of an opponent's overconfidence. Perhaps your wits aren't as thick as I thought."

"You lied to me. You do *nothing.*" The woman beside Ian released her death grip on his arm. "Don't you understand? He *helped* me. He made them—and you will let him die while you stand there and watch Barak—" She darted across the room toward the two men circling each other.

"No!" Ian moved forward, grabbing a whiskey bottle from the table beside him. He heard a shout of protest from one of the miners at the table and murmured, "I do beg your pardon, but I may need this."

Ruel was laughing again, but Ian could detect the slightest hardening in his expression. He was not foolish enough to ignore the warning of Barak's pinprick and would move to finish it now.

"Barak!" Mila jumped on the giant's back, her wiry arms encircling his thick neck.

Ruel stopped, disconcerted, and then started laughing again. "Get off him, Mila. He's having enough problems."

Barak shook himself like a sodden bear and broke Mila's hold. She fell to her knees on the floor.

Barak whirled toward her, the machete raised.

"No!" The laughter vanished from Ruel's expression. "Me. Not her, you bastard. You want *me.*" He lunged forward and the tip of his dagger drew a thin red line on the back of Barak's neck. "Do I have your attention, you stupid ox?"

Barak cursed, whirled back to face Ruel, and took a step forward.

Ruel balanced on the balls of his feet, his blue eyes

glittering wildly, his nostrils flaring. "*Now*, you thieving son of—"

Ian stepped forward and said quietly, "No, Ruel."

Ruel froze. "Ian?" His gaze flew from Barak to Ian, his eyes widened in shock. "What the hell are—"

Barak sprang forward, and the machete sliced into Ruel's shoulder. The blade had been aimed at his heart. If Ruel hadn't spun away at the last moment, it would have cleaved his chest as it had his shoulder.

Ian heard the scream of the woman kneeling on the floor, saw Ruel's face contort with pain, and acted without thinking.

He took a step forward, lifted the whiskey bottle, and brought it down with all his strength on Barak's head.

Glass shattered; liquor sprayed.

The giant grunted, tottered, and fell to the floor.

Ruel swayed, his knees began to buckle.

Ian stepped forward and caught him before he could follow Barak to the floor.

"Why—" Ruel stopped, flinching as pain washed over him. "Dammit, Ian, why the hell are—"

"Hush." Ian shifted his hold and picked Ruel up in his arms as easily as if he weighed no more than a child. "I've come to take you home, lad."

As soon as Ruel opened his eyes he realized he was back in his own shack. He had lain looking at the stars through those cracks in the ceiling too many nights not to recognize his surroundings even through this haze of feverish pain.

"Awake?"

Ruel's gaze shifted from the cracks to the man sitting by his cot.

A long, aquiline nose, wide mouth, bright hazel eyes set deep in a face saved from homeliness only by humor and intelligence. Ian's face.

"You're going to be fine. You've had the fever, but you're mending nicely."

Ian's brogue fell pleasantly on Ruel's ears, and for an

instant he felt a sharp pang. He rejected the thought that it might be homesickness. Christ, it must be the fever. He had gotten over any maudlin yearnings for Glenclaren the first six weeks after he had left. He whispered, "What are you doing here?"

"I told you." Ian dipped a cloth in a bowl of water by the bed. "I've come to take you home."

"You almost took me home in a coffin. I've always told you to stay out of my way in a fight."

"Sorry. I thought it time I took a hand. You were in a temper, but you didn't really want to kill that lummox."

"Didn't I?"

Ian wrung out the cloth and laid it on Ruel's forehead. "Killing is a mortal sin. Life is much easier when you're not forced to carry around those kinds of burdens. Do you wish a drink of water?"

Ruel nodded, then studied Ian as he reached down and filled the iron dipper from the bucket beside his stool. Ian was in his middle thirties now, but Ruel could see little change brought by the years. The big, loose-limbed strength that had enabled Ian to lift Ruel as if he weighed no more than a feather was clearly still there, as was the neatly barbered black hair, the slow, deliberate way he moved and spoke.

Ian brought the dipper to Ruel's lips, holding it steady while he drank thirstily. "There's stew in the pot on the stove over there. Mila made it only a half hour ago, and it should still be warm."

Ruel shook his head.

"Later, then." Ian returned the dipper to the bucket and gently wiped Ruel's forehead. "This Mila appears to be very loyal to you."

"In a hole like this you cling to the people you can trust."

"I assume you're bedding her? She did try to take that machete for you."

Ruel smiled with genuine amusement. "I admit I have a certain talent in that direction, but even my conceit won't permit me to think a woman would risk being beheaded by a machete to keep me between her legs."

He deliberately changed the subject. "But she'll keep an eye on me until I'm better. You don't have to stay."

"Are you sure you won't have something to eat? It will strengthen you and I'd like to be able to travel in a fortnight."

"I'm not going with you."

"Of course you are. What do you have here? Mila tells me Barak has recovered and taken over your claim."

"Son of a bitch," Ruel muttered.

"Probably." Ian grimaced. "But I admit to being glad he occupied himself stealing from you instead of wreaking vengeance on me."

"You should have thought of that before you interfered."

"Possibly." He smiled faintly. "Particularly as you weren't able to fight my battle for me as you did when we were boys."

"You were never merciless enough. You could have bested anyone in the glen, but you never learned to go for the jugular. You can't let anyone—"

Ian interrupted. "I suppose the minute you're on your feet you're going to go after Barak and try to retrieve your property?"

Ruel thought about it. "No."

"Very sensible." Ian tilted his head to study Ruel's expression. "But not at all like you. As I remember, you always believed in taking an eye for an eye and a tooth for a tooth."

"Oh, I still do," Ruel said. "But these days, when the issue isn't important, I sometimes let fate exact vengeance for me."

"Which means?"

"The claim here was played out a week ago." He smiled with supreme satisfaction. "I'm going to enjoy thinking about that bastard breaking his back working that claim and getting no more than a pouch of gold dust for his trouble."

"I see." Ian paused. "Then your gold mine was another failure like Jaylenburg?"

Ruel stiffened. "What do you know about Jaylenburg?"

"Just that you staked a claim, stayed there for six months, and moved on." Ian dipped the cloth again and wrung it out. "You've moved on a good deal. Australia, California, South Africa . . ."

"You seem very knowledgeable."

"Not really. I paid a young man to find you, but he always managed to just miss you until Krugerville." He shook his head as he laid the cloth on Ruel's forehead. "You're not a boy any longer. You can't chase rainbows for the rest of your life."

"I've never chased rainbows." Ruel smiled faintly. "I was always after the pot of gold at the end of the rainbow, never the rainbow itself."

"Gold." Ian pulled a face. "You always told me that you'd find your gold mine and become the richest man in Scotland."

"And I will."

"You ran away from Glenclaren when you were only fifteen and haven't found it yet."

"How do you know?"

Ian glanced around the crudely furnished hut and then up at the cracks in the ceiling. "If you did, you've become more miserly than old Angus MacDonald."

Ruel found his smile widening. "And how is the charming Maggie MacDonald? Did you ever wed?"

Ian shook his head. "You know Margaret has her duty to her father. She will not wed while he needs her by his sickbed."

"Still? Good God, at this rate you won't be wed until you're both doddering on the grave."

"It will happen as God wills." Ian changed the subject. "What is Cinnidar?"

Ruel stiffened, his gaze flying to Ian's face. "Cinnidar?"

"It seems to be on your mind. You kept repeating it while you had the fever."

"Anything else?"

"No, just the one word . . . Cinnidar."

Ruel relaxed. "It's not important. Just a place I visited once."

"You've visited too many places. It's time you came home and put down roots." He paused. "Father's dead."

"I know. I got your letter."

"You didn't answer it."

"There was no point. He had stopped being important to me years ago." He added, "So had Glenclaren."

"And me?"

"You *were* Glenclaren."

"I cannot deny that." Ian smiled. "I love every pond, stone, and moth-eaten tapestry of the old place."

"Then go back there."

Ian shook his head. "Not without you." He looked down at the floor, and the next words came awkwardly. "It was not because I did not have love for you that I didn't come after you while Father was alive. I knew he was wrong and treated you badly. It just seemed . . . difficult. I have always regretted that—"

"Guilt?" Ruel shook his head. "For God's sake, I knew you always walked a fine line between the two of us. I didn't expect anything of you."

"I expected it of myself."

For an instant Ruel felt a rush of warmth as he looked at Ian. Affection? God, he had thought those gentler feelings had been burned out of him years before. Affection was dangerous, and it was far safer to skate on the surface of emotion than plunge into that quagmire. He said deliberately, "But then, you always were a fool."

"Aye." Ian smiled gently. "But foolishness or not, I mean to give you back your place at Glenclaren."

Ruel stared at Ian with exasperation mixed with helplessness. Ian had always felt guilty about their father's treatment of Ruel, and now it seemed he was determined to put things right. Ruel was too familiar with his brother's dogged obstinacy not to realize Ian, once set on a course, would not give up. "Why should I go back? There's nothing I want there." He could see no softening in the resolution hardening Ian's features, and for the first time realized Ian might actually become a problem. Christ, he had a hell of a lot to do in the next few months, and he didn't need Ian plodding behind him, trying to lure him away from his goal. "Dammit, I don't want you here."

"Unfortunate."

"You'll get in my way."

"Only until we board the ship. I'll leave you alone once we're on our way home."

"I'm not going to Glenclaren. When I'm well enough to travel I'm going to Kasanpore."

"Not to this Cinnidar?"

"Let's say Kasanpore is a way station on the way to Cinnidar."

Ian frowned. "I don't believe I've ever heard of this Kasanpore."

"India. The city of Kasanpore is the primary residence of the province ruled by the Maharajah of Savitsar."

Ian shook his head. "You'll be much better off at Glenclaren than traipsing off to another heathen country."

"I'm going to Kasanpore," Ruel said through his teeth.

Ian gazed at him for a moment before sighing in resignation. "You have sufficient funds for this journey?"

"The claim produced exceptionally well for over three months. After I give a small nest egg to Mila, I'll still have enough for my purposes."

"Good, then you can afford my company. Unfortunately, Glenclaren is still as land-rich and pound-poor as it was when you were there. I'll go with you and wait until you tire of this foolishness."

"And if I don't?"

"I'll wait some more."

"Ian, dammit, I have something important to do in Kasanpore. I don't have time to—"

"God will provide the time," Ian said tranquilly as he stood up and moved toward the stove. "But you can tell me all about your business in Kasanpore later. I'll get you a bowl of stew and you must stop this arguing and eat. As I said, you'll need your strength for the journey."

Kasanpore, India
May 6, 1876

"A good evening to you, Miss Barnaby. Has no one told you that foreign ladies should not be in this section of town after dark without protection?"

The tone was low, smooth, but an underlying menace darkened the words. Jane's heart lurched and then sped to breakneck pace as she glanced over her shoulder. Only a few yards behind her she saw Prince Abdar and the beautiful young man, Pachtal, who had accompanied him when he had come to question her at the site. Dear God, she had thought she was being so careful, and yet tonight she hadn't even realized she was being followed!

She responded instinctively, breaking into a run, flying down the dark, deserted street.

It was too late. They'd been too close. Before she reached the corner, a powerful hand gripped her shoulder and spun her around.

Abdar stood before her. His handsome young companion moved behind her and grabbed her arms, forcing her to drop the knapsack she carried as he pulled both her arms up behind her.

"It's not courteous to run away when I wish to speak to you," Abdar said as he set the lantern he carried down on the ground. "I think we must chastise her for that discourtesy, Pachtal."

Jane bit her lower lip to keep back a scream of agony as Pachtal lifted her left arm and twisted it. Prince Abdar's smooth, childlike face framed beneath the white turban swam through the tears stinging her eyes.

"You were most uncommunicative when we had our little discussion a few days ago. I thought it best we have a more private interview. Now, where is Kartauk?"

"I don't know any Kar—" She broke off as her arm was thrust still higher.

"You can see Pachtal is growing impatient," Abdar said softly. "He prefers the joys of the palace and was not at all amused to spend these last three evenings trying to follow you. Particularly when his efforts proved of no avail."

She tried desperately to think of a way to reach the dagger sheathed in her boot. "Which should have proved to him I can't give you what you wish."

"It proved only that you know our bazaar quite well for a foreigner and can be very elusive. Where is he?"

"I don't know. I told you—" She gasped as Pachtal thrust her arm higher, at the same time giving it a sharp twist that sent another bolt of agony through her. The flame of the lantern in Abdar's hand seemed to waver and dim. Why, she was going to faint, she realized with a dim sense of outrage. No! She had never fainted in her life, and this bastard would not be the one to make her start.

"Again," Abdar ordered the man behind her.

For a long moment, Jane's whole world was pain.

"Why are you so stubborn?" Abdar asked. "You will tell me anyway. You are only a woman and too weak and stupid to resist for long."

Even through the haze of anguish she felt a vague sense of resentment at his words. Though she had been stupid not to realize she had been followed from the bungalow, she was *not* weak.

"Why suffer like this? What is Kartauk to you?" Pachtal whispered in her ear as his grip tightened on her forearms. "You've gotten what you want from him. Now give him back to His Highness."

"I don't know any Kartauk."

"Is he your lover?" Pachtal whispered. "His Highness believes he must give you great pleasure for you to risk so much. But you will have to give him up. His Highness has need of him."

Abdar's well-shaped hand reached out and cupped her breast through her cotton shirt. "You are not uncomely and will find another man to please you. I would not even be averse to letting you come to my couch."

She wondered what he would do if she spat in his blank, childlike face.

The prince leisurely studied her features. "Yes, she is not all bad. The cheekbones are too high, but the mouth is quite lovely. Let's have a look at her body, Pachtal." He unbuttoned the loose shirt and spread the edges back to reveal her breasts. "Ah, those grotesque mannish garments hide treasures. You are so thin, I would never have guessed these would be so beautifully full." He cupped her naked breasts, weighing them as if they were melons. "She reminds me a little of Mirad, Pachtal."

"Let—me—go," she said through her teeth.

"Very nice." Pachtal ignored her command as he drew closer and peered over her shoulder at Abdar's hands cradling her breasts. "It's difficult to tell in this light, but the nipples are rosier, I think. Mirad's were like huge purple grapes."

She started to struggle.

"No!" Pachtal's grip tightened with bruising force on her arms. "You will not refuse His Highness when he honors you with his touch."

"I have never had a foreign woman in my bed. I believe you could amuse me for quite a long time." Abdar smiled as he brought her single thick braid over her shoulder and quickly unfastened it. "Of course, these hideous trousers and shirt will not be permitted. I will have you perfumed and given proper womanly garments." He ran his fingers through her loosened hair that now flowed halfway down her back in a wild stream. "Dark red. It looked closer to brown when in the braid. Interesting." His hands returned to her breasts as his voice lowered to honey softness. "I would like to see you bound naked and helpless in my bedchamber at the palace. And why not? No one would ever know if I decided to take you back to my palace and teach you the submission due me."

A chill went through her as she remembered the tales Kartauk had told her of Abdar. "I'm not one of your subjects. I would be missed. Your father will not permit this."

Abdar raised his brows. "He will not object to my amusing myself. Women have little value for my father."

She had no argument to give him on that score. In his own way, the maharajah was as arrogant and self-serving as his son. She said quickly, "But his railroad does have value for him. And my father needs my help to complete the railroad."

"I have observed that you seem to aid him. Perhaps I will reconsider." He lifted his gaze to meet her own. "If you give me your lover, Kartauk."

The combination of pain and revulsion at his touch was making her stomach churn. "I don't know any Kartauk."

He nodded at Pachtal, and she had to grit her teeth to keep from crying out as another agonizing pain shot through her.

"You're beginning to anger me. I have waited too long already, and I want Kartauk tonight. Now, tell me the truth."

She tried to block out the pain and panic and think. Obviously it would be useless to continue to deny any knowledge of Kartauk. Abdar would continue to torture her until he got what he wanted. "Very well. What do you want to know?"

"That is sensible. You admit you know Kartauk?"

She nodded jerkily.

He nodded to the man behind her and she was suddenly released. "Better and better. You see how we reward cooperation? We have no desire to cause you discomfort."

He was lying. She had seen too many men who liked to prove their power over women with pain and subjugation when she was at Frenchie's not to recognize the breed when she encountered it.

"You've left your bungalow three nights in a row to come into the city. You've been meeting Kartauk?"

"Yes."

He glanced down at the knapsack she had dropped on the ground. "And taking him food?"

She nodded again.

"That is good. It would displease me if Kartauk suffered harm or deprivation." He reached out and gently grasped her throat. "Now, you will tell me where he is so that I may place him again under my protection."

"He's hiding in one of the shops that border the river."

"Which house?"

"Yellow sod. With a dirty striped awning."

"You describe half the shops in Kasanpore." He frowned. "You will take me there."

"You don't need me. I've told you what you wanted to know."

"But is it the truth? I think I will make certain before I permit you to leave us. You carry the lantern, Pachtal. I will escort the lady."

Pachtal released her arms and moved around to stand beside Abdar before reaching down to pick up the lantern from the street.

Jane's lids lowered swiftly to veil her eyes as sudden hope spiraled through her. Pachtal's action left her back unguarded, and she doubted if she would get a better opportunity to escape.

She meekly dropped her eyes as she whimpered, "Why won't you let me go back to my bungalow? I've told you what—" In midsentence she lowered her head and launched herself at Abdar.

The top of her head crashed into his mouth.

He screamed in pain, his hand releasing her throat and flying to his bleeding lower lip.

She whirled and tore down the twisting, cobbled street.

"Get her!"

She heard the pounding of running steps behind her and Abdar's venomous cursing.

She turned left at the corner, almost tripping over a beggar huddled in the shadows.

She caught her balance, avoided the beggar's outstretched grasping hands, and ran on.

The beggar hurled obscenities after her and then let out a shrill screech of pain. She risked a glance over her shoulder and saw the beggar doubled over in the street, clutching his stomach as Pachtal and Abdar ran past him. They were gaining on her, swiftly closing the distance between them.

Panic choked her, and for an instant she couldn't remember which way to turn. Left. Right led to the river. She must go left and try to lose herself in the bazaar. The day after she had decided to help Kartauk she had spent the entire morning in the bazaar, familiarizing herself with every stall and corner of the huge marketplace. Darkness had just fallen, and the bazaar would still be crowded. She could hide among the stalls until Abdar gave up the chase.

She turned the corner and burst into the crowd of people in the large square.

The bazaar.

Copper lanterns hanging on awning-covered booths. A camel burdened with rolled carpets moving with ponderous gait through the throng.

Noise. Beggars whining. Merchants calling out their wares.

She heard Abdar cursing behind her, but she was already darting through the throng and between the stalls. She passed a leather vendor, a pink-turbaned cleaner of ears wielding his small silver spoon in the orifice of a customer seated on a low stool, a gold merchant, a kiosk hung with wicker cages containing raucously squawking parrots. She glanced behind her again and her heart sank. As people recognized Abdar, they were making way for him.

Then, to her relief, she saw a small female elephant burdened with copper pots and pans and her master on the aisle that bordered the western edge of the bazaar. It was common knowledge Abdar hated elephants and avoided them at all cost. If given a choice of direction, he would surely choose another aisle. She ran ahead into the thick crowd of people gathered around a vegetable booth to lose herself from Abdar's view, turned left at the next booth, ran past the elephant, and then dove behind a fishmonger's stall. She crouched low, moving far back into the shadows.

The overpowering stench of fish, elephant dung, garbage, and a heavy Oriental perfume drifting from the stall next to the fishmonger's nearly gagged her. She tried to hold her breath, her eyes straining as she peered through the small opening between the stalls. She could see only the lower portion of bodies and tried frantically to remember what Abdar and Pachtal had been wearing. Dear God, all she could recall was Abdar's smiling, childlike face and the vicious beauty of Pachtal's well-shaped lips as he twisted her arm. The memory started her heart pounding so hard, she was sure it could be heard even above the clamor of the bazaar.

"Would you care to enlighten me why we are both in this extremely uncomfortable position?"

She whirled to peer into the shadows to the left of her.

Li Sung sat a few yards away with one leg folded beneath him and his bad leg stretched before him.

"What are you doing here?" she whispered.

"I saw you dart behind this disgustingly aromatic stall and thought it best to join you."

"I told you to wait at the city gate."

"And I chose to wait at the mouth of the street from which I knew you generally entered the bazaar. I decided I was too conspicuous at the gate. You know they do not like the Chinese here in Kasanpore, and I believe my pigtail was in great danger of being lifted from my—"

"Hush." She turned back to scan the street. "Abdar."

Li Sung went still. "Himself?"

She nodded, her gaze searching the flow of people passing the small opening. "With the same man who came to the site three days ago. They followed me from the bungalow, but I think we're safe. If he'd seen me run back here, he would have come by now." She scowled as she settled back on her heels. "But I lost the knapsack with the food."

Li Sung's gaze wandered over her wild, tousled hair and the glimpse of pale breasts revealed by her unbuttoned shirt. His mouth tightened grimly. "And is that all you lost?"

She knew that expression very well. If she wasn't careful, Li Sung's protective instincts would be aroused, and that must be avoided at all costs. "No." She grinned. "I also lost my temper. I butted my head against Abdar's lip and split it like a walnut and then ran like the wind." She quickly buttoned her shirt before reaching into the deep pocket of her denim trousers and pulling out a small chisel. "Give this to Kartauk. I bought it in the bazaar yesterday, and I'll bet he'll like it better than food anyway. I'll try to get another knapsack to you tomorrow."

Li Sung shook his head. "From now on, stay close to either the site or the bungalow. It's too dangerous now that Abdar suspects you. We still have a little bread and cheese left, and I'll come and get the supplies from now on."

"Very well, I'll leave a knapsack behind the pile of rails at the supply yard every other evening." She reached into her pocket and slipped a key from a small brass ring. "I'll keep the gate of the supply yard locked from now on to make it safer for you. Be careful."

"And you also." Li Sung took the key before rising with difficulty and limping toward her. "Turn around."

"Why?"

"I'm going to rebraid your hair. This disarray displeases me."

"Here?"

"You do not want to call any more attention to yourself than you already have. If you had a fine black mane like my own, there would be no problem, but your hair is too gaudy not to be noticed."

"It's not gaudy," she protested.

"Ugly, then. Hair was meant to be black, not red. God clearly made the Chinese and then grew weary and careless with his palette. I cannot see why he lacked the discrimination as to experiment with yellow and red and . . ." He trailed off, his fingers quickly plaiting the bright strands into their usual thick single braid.

Over the years Li Sung had performed this task a thousand times, and the familiar ritual calmed her. She could feel her heartbeat steadying and the panic gradually leaving her.

"Have you been well?" Li Sung asked. "No more fever?"

"Not for over two weeks."

"But you're still taking the *quinghao* I gave you?"

"I'm not a foolish child, Li Sung. I know I have to keep well. I lost almost a month of work when I was ill."

"And almost died. You forgot to add that unimportant detail." He paused. "You are foolish to protect this man, you know. He is no stray puppy."

"You know you like him."

He thought about it. "He is amusing, but it is dangerous to like Kartauk."

"Well, I like him."

"Because you think him without defense, but he is not without weapons. Get in his way and he'll pass over you like a runaway locomotive."

He was probably right, but she knew she still could not give Kartauk up to Abdar. "He did me a favor. You know I was desperate."

"He did himself a favor. He was hungry and you fed him." He finished the braid and then took a scrap of string from his denim trousers and secured it. "If Patrick finds out about Kartauk, he will be angry."

She tensed. "He won't know."

"Unless Abdar decides he wishes to involve him."

"He won't do that. Kartauk said Abdar doesn't want his father to know he's looking for him." Jane tossed back her braid. "And Patrick won't ask questions. He's too busy building this blasted railroad."

"You mean he is too busy drinking and whoring and letting you build his railroad."

She didn't bother to deny the charge as she would

have done with anyone else. "He'll be better once we've left Kasanpore."

"You said that about Yorkshire." He turned her around and began to button her blouse. "And with every passing day you grow thinner and more weary and Patrick grows lazier and does not see." He added softly, "Or does not care."

"He *does* care." She jerked away from him. "He just doesn't know what to—the heat affects him."

"It certainly gives him a great thirst."

She could not deny that fact either, she thought wearily. These days Patrick started drinking in the afternoon and didn't stop until he staggered off to bed at midnight. But surely his escalating drinking was being caused by this inferno of a country. Heaven knows, the difficulties they had faced in England seemed minor compared to suffocating heat, unskilled workers, and a maharajah whose impossible demands and pettish threats had driven them to the brink of bankruptcy. "I don't want to talk about it." She glanced cautiously out into the aisle before rising to her feet. "I have to get back to the bungalow and get some sleep. We're starting to lay the track on the bridge over Sikor Gorge tomorrow."

"And Patrick will be nowhere within a mile of the site."

"He will. He promised me that—" She stopped as she met Li Sung's steady gaze and then burst out, "And if he's not, I won't care. It's no hardship. I like it."

"You like doing the work and Patrick getting the credit?"

"He needs me."

"So you give and give until there is no more to give." Li Sung raised his hand as she started to speak. "But why should I complain? I take as much as Patrick."

"Nonsense. You've always worked harder than anyone on the line." She stood up and moved cautiously out of the shadows toward the aisle.

"What if Abdar is waiting for you at the bungalow?"

"I'll circle and go in the back way." She paused to smile gently at him over her shoulder. "Stop worrying about me. Just keep Kartauk safe and tell him I'm trying to find a way to slip him out of Kasanpore."

"He is not impatient." He looked down at the chisel she had given him. "Sometimes I wonder if he is even conscious of the passage of time."

She knew what he meant. She had also seen Kartauk in that oblivious state. "He can't stay here forever with Abdar searching for him. We'll have to get him away." She hesitated as a sudden thought occurred to her. "You weren't waiting here in the bazaar because you'd just come from Zabrie?"

Li Sung gazed at her impassively. "Why would you assume that?"

She persisted. "Did you?"

He shrugged. "A man has needs."

"Abdar saw you at the site with me. It's not safe for you to be seen in the city."

"I will make sure I do not lead him to Kartauk."

"That's not the question. It's not safe for you to—"

"It is not your concern."

She could feel him closing against her, drawing back into himself, and felt a surge of helplessness and frustration. Sometimes Li Sung appeared as old as Buddha and at other times he was only a sensitive, prickly, proud young man. She could not tell him it was very much her concern and that what had started as an act of compassion might now be a magnet drawing him into a net. "Will you at least promise to be careful?"

He smiled. "Always."

It was the only concession she was going to be able to wrest from him, but if the danger continued, she knew she would have to do something about Zabrie. "See that you are." She didn't wait for an answer as she glided from behind the stall, looking cautiously both ways before beginning to make her way swiftly through the bazaar.

Chapter 2

Savitsar Palace
Kasanpore, India
May 30, 1876

"I've never seen anything like it." Ian stared in revulsion at the four-foot statue on the carved teakwood table. "What the hell is it?"

"A superb work of art." Ruel reverently touched the golden drops of blood dripping from the dagger brandished by the sari-clad woman who was the central figure before he circled the table to view the statue from every angle. "By God, look at her expression. I wonder how he caught the malevolence. . . ."

"I have no desire to look any longer at that heathen idol. This Prince Abdar must be a very peculiar man to have such an object in his reception room, and

I cannot see how you can call it—" Ian broke off and grimaced ruefully. "Yes, I do. Gold. You would think Satan himself beautiful if he wore a cloak of gold."

Ruel grinned over his shoulder at him. "Not just a cloak, but perhaps if he were fashioned as splendidly as this fascinating lady." His gaze returned to the statue. "I wonder who the artist was."

"Probably some twisted soul dead these many centuries." Ian suddenly frowned. "And you're not to ask Prince Abdar about this atrocity. I've heard these heathens are a bit sensitive about their gods and goddesses, and I have no desire to be thrown to the crocodiles."

"You'd have nothing to worry about. They'd choke on you," Ruel murmured. "That stiff backbone and rigid moral fiber would strangle them." He squatted to get a better view of the statue. "Now, me they'd gulp down with no trouble. Sin is always more appetizing than virtue."

"Stop mouthing nonsense," Ian said gruffly. "You're not as wicked as you—"

"Oh, but I am." Ruel smiled mockingly. "As you should know, considering that hellhole you dug me out of a few months ago. I have no more moral fiber than a tomcat and no desire to develop it. You'd best leave me and go back to Maggie and bonnie Scotland."

"Margaret." Ian's correction was automatic. "You know she hates to be called Maggie."

"Margaret," Ruel substituted solemnly. "You really should go back to Margaret, cool misty hills, and sanity. You don't belong here, Ian."

"Neither do you." Ian paused. "This heathen country isn't a decent place for any civilized man to live."

"It's more civilized than most of the places I've lived for the past twelve years. You should have been at the gold camp at Zwanigar." He shook his head. "On second thought, you probably shouldn't. The crocodiles there were human, and you're much too honorable to have survived it."

"You survived it."

"Only because I became king of the crocodiles." His

smile gleamed white. "And learned how to use my teeth."

"All the more reason for you to come home. This damnable Eastern savagery isn't good for you."

"It's only a place like any other." Ruel's smile faded as he saw Ian's unhappy expression. He knew Ian hated being away from Glenclaren, but his brother had been surprisingly patient and helpful since they had arrived in Kasanpore. He said quietly, "But I promise I won't offend his royal highness with flippant remarks after all your trouble to obtain this audience for me."

"I have no faith you will get what you wish from this prince, but I knew you wouldn't give up without at least an interview."

"You're right, I wouldn't."

"Besides, my efforts will probably be of no help," Ian said. "The colonel said Prince Abdar has no fondness and little to do with his father, the maharajah."

The last trace of mockery faded from Ruel's expression. "You still have my gratitude for making the attempt. I know you think this venture is foolishness."

"Gratitude?" Ian looked startled, and then a slow smile lit his craggy, homely features. "Careful, Ruel, gratitude is one of the softer emotions. Therein lies the path to virtue."

"I'm in no danger." Ruel's stare returned to the statue. Something about it was making him uneasy. No, it wasn't the statue itself, he realized, but its place of prominence in this chamber of the palace, a position that indicated its importance to the man who possessed it. He said impulsively, "You've done your part. I can handle the matter now. Why don't you go back to the hotel and wait for me?"

"You may need me."

"Look, I've been batting around this part of the world for a hell of a lot longer than you have. I know how—"

"We'll see."

"I promise I won't let Abdar feed me to the crocodiles, dammit."

Ian didn't answer.

"All right, stay, but let me do the talking. I have an idea Abdar and I will have no problem understanding each other."

"I'm the elder. It's only fitting I put through the request."

Dear God, he actually meant it, Ruel realized. Ian didn't realize those seven years meant nothing. Ian's life at Glenclaren had plodded steadily on its tranquil course while his own had whirled as if caught up in a monsoon.

"God forbid you do anything that isn't fitting." He reached out and followed the dagger with his index finger. "And me from doing anything that is. Have it your own way. It was just a fleeting thought."

"A kind, protective thought." Ian's stern expression softened. "Another step."

"It wasn't a prot—" Ruel threw back his head and laughed. "Dear God, you'll not to be satisfied until you have me wearing a halo. How many times do I have to tell you that I'm not—"

"Good afternoon, gentlemen. I see you're admiring my statue. Is she not a thing of beauty?"

Ian and Ruel turned to see an Indian dressed in a knee-length dark blue silk jacket, white silk trousers, and white turban. Tall, slim, graceful, the man moved lithely across the mosaic floor toward them. "I am very proud of my goddess. She is very dear to me." He stopped before them. "I am Abdar Savitsar."

The prince's face was plump, unlined, almost boyish, but his large dark eyes gave a curious impression of flat blankness, like an onyx that has never been faceted.

"Your Highness." Ian bowed slightly. "It is very kind of you to receive us. I am Ian MacClaren, Earl of Glenclaren, and this is my brother, Ruel."

"English?"

"Scottish."

Abdar waved a casual hand. "It is all the same."

"Not to a Scotsman," Ruel murmured blandly.

Abdar turned to face him and Ruel stiffened with sudden wariness. In spite of the childishness of that face, he felt the same uneasiness as when he had regarded the statue.

After studying Ruel for a moment, the prince returned his gaze to Ian. "You do not look like brothers. I see no resemblance."

"We are only half brothers," Ian said.

Abdar's glance dropped to Ruel's hand resting on the golden dagger of the statue. "You should not touch her. For a foreigner to touch the goddess is sacrilege."

Ruel's hand fell away from the statue. "My apologies. The texture of gold begs to be touched, and I've always found the temptation irresistible."

Abdar's gaze suddenly narrowed on Ruel. "You have a fondness for gold?"

"It's more of a passion."

Abdar nodded. "Then we have found a meeting ground. I, too, have such a passion." He moved across the room and seated himself on the turquoise cushions of a finely carved peacock chair. "Colonel Pickering told my secretary you wish to ask a boon of me. I have little time. State your request."

"We wish an audience with your father, the maharajah," Ian said. "We've been in Kasanpore over two weeks trying to secure a meeting with him."

"He sees few people these days. All he cares about is his new toy of a railroad." Abdar's lips curled in a bitter smile. "But I am surprised you did not succeed in your quest. My father believes the British are his true brothers and even sent me to Oxford to be educated. He cannot see how the British queen seeks to make a puppet of him and Kasanpore."

"We have a business proposition for your father that has nothing to do with the politics of either India or England," Ian said. "All we ask is ten minutes of his time."

"It is still too much." Abdar stood up. "I cannot help you."

Disappointment rushed through Ruel before he caught a flicker of expression on Abdar's face that caused his disappointment to vanish. He was too good a poker player himself not to realize this was no dismissal but an attempt to intimidate them. "Cannot or will not?" he asked softly.

"Insolence," Abdar said. "You are very arrogant for a second son."

"Forgive me, Your Highness, but it has always been my philosophy that a man shouldn't be afraid to lose what he doesn't have." He paused. "And that he shouldn't ask for anything he isn't willing to pay for."

"And what are you willing to pay for my influence on your behalf?"

"What do you want?"

"Why should I wish anything from you?" Abdar smiled contemptuously as he threw out his hand to indicate the splendor of their surroundings. "Look around you. Do I appear to be in need?" His lips twisted. "The jewel I wear on my little finger could probably buy your Glenclaren."

"Possibly." Ruel leaned against the table. "But wanting sometimes has very little to do with need. Why did you agree to receive us, Your Highness?"

"As a courtesy to Colonel Pickering."

Ruel shook his head. "I don't think so. You've displayed no overwhelming fondness for the British."

"Then why should I permit you to come?"

"Why, indeed?"

Abdar hesitated before allowing a slight smile to touch his lips. "It may be that we can negotiate. There is something I desire that you may bring me."

"And that is?"

"A man." He nodded at the statue on the table. "A goldsmith named John Kartauk."

"He created this?" Ruel's gaze returned to the goddess. "Superb."

"A genius. My father brought him from Turkey six years ago and bestowed on him our royal patronage. Kartauk created many beautiful objects to grace our palaces." Abdar's lips tightened. "And then the ungrateful dog spurned our generosity and ran away from us."

"Ran away?" Ruel's brows lifted. "How curious.

Why should an artist so favored find it necessary to run away?"

Abdar glanced away and did not answer at once. "I am not good with English. I merely meant he had left us with no farewells."

Abdar's English was better than his own, Ruel thought cynically, and the prince had meant exactly what he had said. "And gave no reason?"

"Great artists are often unstable and given to fancies." Abdar shrugged. "However, I am willing to forgive him and take him back."

"How kind."

Abdar chose to ignore the irony in Ruel's tone. "Yes, it is. But I must find him in order to persuade him to return."

"Perhaps he's no longer in Kasanpore," Ian said.

"He is still here. I've recently seen an example of his work."

"Where?"

"You are aware of the railroad my father is having built from Kasanpore to our summer palace in Narinth?"

"We could hardly miss it," Ian said dryly. "Everyone in the city appears to be laboring on it."

"My father is like a child with a new toy. He imported this Patrick Reilly, a construction engineer, from England, to build it, and talks of nothing else. He is concerned only with engines and whistles and velvet-covered seats that—" He broke off and drew a deep breath. "I do not like these new ways. This railroad is an atrocity. Anyway, my father decided he desired a golden door carved with wondrous designs to grace his private car and insisted Reilly provide one."

"Rather an extravagant demand."

"Not for a maharajah." Abdar lifted his chin haughtily. "It is our right to demand what pleases us from those beneath us."

"And did Reilly provide what your father demanded?"

"Eventually. My father told him if he did not furnish

the door, he would pay him nothing and find another construction engineer to finish the railroad."

"I can see how that might have proved an incentive," Ruel said dryly.

"The door was carved by John Kartauk."

"You're certain?"

"I know his work well." Abdar's lips thinned. "The door is an exquisite abomination."

"Exquisite abomination," Ruel repeated. "It would seem to have to be either one or the other."

Abdar shrugged. "My poor English again."

"The solution seems simple enough. Ask Reilly where your artist is to be found."

"Do you think me a fool? I did ask and he claimed he had no knowledge of Kartauk. He said his ward found a man in the town to do the work, and when I questioned her she would tell me nothing. She said he was only a local goldsmith and had left for Calcutta directly after he finished the door."

"She? A woman?"

Abdar nodded jerkily and his words were suddenly heavy with venom. "Reilly calls her his ward, though the slut is undoubtedly his whore. Her name is Jane Barnaby, a bold piece with no manners and an unbridled tongue. She frequents Zabrie's house of shame, where she mixes and sleeps with foreigners and low-caste workers and shows no—"

"Bribe her," Ruel cut into the tirade.

"I do not offer money to whores and liars."

"Pity. It's such a useful tool."

"However, I have set watch on her and she has not met with Kartauk in the past two weeks."

"Perhaps she told the truth and he did leave for Calcutta."

"He could not have left the city! Kasanpore is *mine.* No one draws a breath here without my knowing it."

"And yet Kartauk managed to hide himself and fashion an entire door without you knowing it."

A faint flush tinted Abdar's olive cheeks. "I begin to

find your insolence intolerable. Perhaps I do not need your help after all."

Ian said quickly, "What is it that you wish us to do?"

"I told you, find Kartauk and bring him to me. His mother was Scottish and he has the same fondness as my father for those of your nationality. Perhaps he will trust you when he would hesitate to give faith to a man of my race."

"And how do you suggest we find him?"

"The woman. The Barnaby slut must occupy Kartauk's bed as well as Reilly's, or she would not run such risk." He shrugged. "It is not surprising. Reilly is no longer in his first youth, and Kartauk is a man in his prime."

Ruel's gaze narrowed on Abdar's face. "And what risk does she run?"

Abdar smiled blandly. "Why, the risk of displeasing my father by her deceit, of course. What other risk would I be speaking about?"

"And in return you'll arrange a meeting with your father?"

"Yes."

"And offer what influence you possess to gain us what we seek?"

"Just what do you seek from him?"

Ruel shook his head. "I believe we'll not discuss that at the moment."

"You expect me to promise blindly?" Abdar didn't wait for an answer. "Oh, very well, it doesn't matter. Bring me Kartauk and I'll give you whatever you wish." He turned and strode across the room. At the door he paused, glanced over his shoulder at Ruel, and for a moment a curious smile curved his lips. "I believe I would like you to pose for Kartauk."

"What?"

"The molding of your features has a certain beauty that rather reminds me of the sun god the Greeks favored. When I get Kartauk back, I'd like you to pose for a golden mask for the wall in my study."

"I think not."

"I can be very persuasive. We will discuss it later." The next moment the door had closed behind him.

"Arrogant bastard," Ian said.

"Yes." Ruel's tone was absent as he gazed at the carved panels of the door. "But he just may be able to give me Cinnidar."

"You're going to look for this Kartauk?"

"No." He started toward the door. "I'm going to find Kartauk."

Ian frowned as he followed him across the room. "I'm not sure we should have dealings with this Abdar. Kartauk may have had good reason to leave the court."

"I'm sure he did. But no better than I do for finding him."

"You're obsessed."

"Possibly."

"Even if you do find him, you won't turn him over to Abdar."

"Don't bet on it. I'll make that decision when I find him."

"I'll bet on it," Ian said placidly. "You intend to watch and follow the woman?"

"Probably."

"But Abdar said she hadn't met with Kartauk in two weeks."

"Which should make her very frustrated and eager to bed him at the earliest opportunity."

"Even if it places him in danger? What could justify that?"

Ruel's lips twisted cynically as he murmured a single obscene Anglo-Saxon verb.

Ian immediately shook his head. "Carnal pleasure isn't that important."

"Perhaps not to you." Ruel inclined his head in a mocking nod. "But to self-indulgent voluptuaries like Jane Barnaby and myself, it can cause a temporary fever that makes it seem worth quite a few risks."

"You don't know if he's telling the truth about her either."

"True. I admit he painted her a little too black. Even

the most lustful of whores usually has some discrimination when choosing a bed partner. We'll have to see."

Ian shrugged as he glanced back at the statue. "Any man who can worship that monstrosity is capable of any falsehood."

"Probably." Ruel smiled recklessly as his glance followed Ian's. "But Abdar was right. His Highness and I do have a great deal of common ground. His lady isn't my favorite goddess, but I've dealt with her before and I know her ways well."

"Which goddess is she?"

"Kali."

"That doesn't mean anything to me. You know I pay no attention to these heathen practices."

"She's the wife of Siva." Ruel strode quickly down the hall past two turbaned footmen and out the front entrance of the palace. He paused a moment on the top step, the wet heat robbing him of breath as he looked down at the muddy river Zastu winding snakelike past the palace. A scrawny, half-naked beggar crouched by the river shaded by a palm-leaf umbrella as he dispensed blessings on the passersby who tossed him rupees, and curses on those who did not.

Kasanpore. Christ, what a miserable place. Hot, stinking, overrun by disease and snakes that crawled on the ground and walked on two legs.

As Ian joined him, Ruel started down the hundred stone steps leading to their waiting ricksha outside the palace gates. "But that's not Kali's only distinction," Ruel said. "The diety Abdar admires so much is also the goddess of destruction."

Jane Barnaby wasn't what he had thought she would be.

Ruel leaned back against the rock and pulled his felt hat forward to shade his eyes as he gazed down at the crew laboring on the track in the valley below. From Abdar's description, he had pictured a strident, Junoesque virago, but Jane Barnaby was none of those things. Small and fine-boned, she appeared almost childlike in the baggy denim trousers, loose blue chambray shirt, and brown suede boots she always wore. A tan straw coolie hat shaded her head from the merciless rays of the sun as she moved down the row of track, stopping now and then to examine a fitting or speak sharply to a worker who was carelessly hammering a tie. Today her every step, every slightest movement, was charged with energy and vitality, but it was not always so. Often at the end of the day, when the workers had been dismissed and she thought no one present to witness her weakness, Ruel had seen her lean her forehead on the saddle of her mare, Bedelia, her shoulders sagging with exhaustion before gathering enough strength to mount her horse for the long ride back to Kasanpore.

Jane stopped, her gaze zeroing in on a wiry Indian whose pace in pounding the steel into the ground was almost leisurely. Ruel grinned as he saw her shoulders square and jaw tighten. He recognized those signs of annoyance and determination as he now recognized every gesture and motion she made. It was odd how quickly he had learned to read the woman. He had thought the surveillance would bore him, but instead he found himself caught, intrigued, and often amused.

She strode down the track toward the Indian and stopped before him. Ruel couldn't hear her words, but he could tell by the scowl on the Indian's face that the spate blistered. She turned and walked away and the Indian gazed after her, an ugly expression twisting his features. However, he kept his place, and it was not because of the brawny overseer, Robinson, who watched from the side of the road. He knew about the knife sheathed in Jane Barnaby's left boot.

And so did Ruel.

After a moment the Indian picked up his huge hammer and started pounding the spike with slightly more enthusiasm.

"Why don't you give it up?"

Ruel glanced over his shoulder to see Ian climbing the hill from the grove where he had tied his horse beside Ruel's. "Why should I? She's the key to Kartauk."

"You've been watching her for four days and she's done nothing but work like a galley slave." Ian crouched down beside Ruel. "Can't you see Abdar was lying to you? She couldn't be Kartauk's mistress. Just look at her, the lass isn't much more than a child."

"Appearances are almost always deceiving. Remind me to tell you about a whore I once had in Singapore. Mei Lei had the face of a baby angel and the delightfully corrupt talents of Delilah." His gaze returned to the woman below. "What did you find out from Colonel Pickering about Reilly?"

"Not much. Reilly's uneducated but good-natured enough and drinks like a sot. He had a fairly good reputation in Yorkshire, and after he finished building a line between Dover and Salisbury, he entered a bid for this job."

"And the woman?"

Ian shrugged. "No one ever sees her. She never goes to the club with him. Reilly keeps her pretty much to himself."

"And their relationship?"

Ian looked uncomfortable. "There are rumors . . . but no one knows for sure." His gaze shifted down to Jane in the valley below. "I believe it's all nonsense and she is Reilly's ward."

"Because you want to believe it."

Ian tilted his head as he looked back at Ruel. "And you don't. Why not?"

Ruel realized to his surprise that Ian was right. He wanted Jane Barnaby to be the promiscuous harlot Abdar had described, and the reason lay in the odd fascination she held for him. It couldn't be lust, he thought impatiently. How could he feel lust for this bony, big-eyed waif? Nor was it pity. Even exhausted she displayed a strength of purpose and an endurance that defied sympathy. Yet, somehow, she *moved* him.

The acknowledgment caused his defenses to instantly rise. God, the sun must be addling his brains. He allowed no one to touch his emotions, and certainly not a woman whom he might have to use to get Kartauk. He turned to Ian and smiled cynically. "I haven't your faith in human nature. We're all what life makes us, and I'd wager Jane Barnaby's life has been as turbulent as mine."

"I still think that—" Ian shrugged as he met Ruel's gaze. "You've been out here for hours in the sun. Would you like me to watch her for the rest of the day?"

"No." Ian's brows lifted in surprise at the quick refusal. Ruel tempered his tone. "I'm used to the heat. You'd probably get sunstroke after an hour."

"You're probably right. I can't see how you can bear it." Ian's voice became wistful. "It never gets this hot at Glenclaren. Remember how the cool mists on the hills rise in the morning?"

"No, I don't remember."

Ian smiled. "Then it will come as a delightful surprise when you come back to us." He rose to his feet. "If you won't let me help now, I'll take my turn watching the bungalow tonight."

"We'll see."

"You never know when to stop. You're becoming as obsessed about watching that child as you are about your Cinnidar."

"She's not a child." The words came too sharply again, and Ruel forced himself to smile carelessly. "If you want to help, go back to the Officers' Club and see if you can find out from Pickering if the maharajah has any passions besides his new toy of a railroad."

Ian nodded as he took out his handkerchief and wiped his perspiring brow. "I won't argue with you. A cool drink on the veranda while being fanned by one of the club's servants seems like heaven right now." He turned and started down the hill toward the horses. "I'll see you back at the hotel."

"Yes." Ruel's tone was abstracted as he turned to look down at the woman again. Jane had stopped by the water bearer and took the dipper of water he held out to her. As she drank, she tilted back her head, and he could see the graceful line of her throat and the dark lashes curving against her tan cheeks as she half closed her eyes against the glare of the sun.

He waited, anticipation stirring. After she drank she would splash a little water on her cheeks and throat and run her damp palms under the heavy braid covering her nape.

She returned the dipper to the bearer, who smiled, filled it again, and poured the water into her cupped hands.

Ruel leaned back against the rock, watching as she cooled her cheeks and forehead and then her throat and nape. It was ridiculous to feel this absurd sense of satisfaction just because she had done what he had expected her to do. Yet the satisfaction persisted, escalated, as she returned the dipper back to the bearer.

Now she would retrace her steps back to the point where the new track started and examine the ties, measure the distance between the rails to make sure it was exactly four feet eight and a half inches.

Jane whirled and walked briskly back along the newly laid track.

He laughed softly and tilted his hat until it rested on the back of his head. By God, he *knew* her. He felt as if he had never known anyone in his entire life as well as he knew Jane Barnaby. He knew every gesture, every reaction, almost her every thought.

His smile faded as he realized the pleasure that knowledge brought him, the pleasure a man might feel in exploring the gaits of a fine horse he had just acquired or the first sensual discoveries of the talents of a mistress.

The pleasure of possession.

Nonsense. He had no desire to own anyone and had a passion only for what awaited him on Cinnidar. He was merely bored and it amused him to predict the girl's next moves. Besides, it would be only sensible to familiarize himself with the way she thought if she could lead him to Kartauk.

"The work is going too slow." Patrick stretched his long legs out before him under the dinner table and lifted the glass of whiskey to his lips. "The maharajah paid me a little visit this afternoon and the bastard says he wants the railroad finished before the monsoon season."

"Well, he's not going to get it." Jane looked dully down at the rice and chicken on her plate. She felt too tired to eat but knew she must. Food brought strength and she had to keep strong. She picked up the fork and attacked the rice. "The rains start in two weeks and we've just finished the bridge across Sikor Gorge."

"That leaves only another twenty-five miles of track to lay before you join with the track we laid from Narinth. At six miles a day we—"

"We're not doing six miles a day. We're lucky to do two."

Patrick muttered a curse. "Then push them, dammit."

Jane's hand tightened on the fork. "I'm doing the best I can. You know the workers won't listen to me." She smiled mirthlessly. "Those who don't regard me as a freak look on me only as a woman and therefore unworthy of attention."

"The crew listened to you on the Yorkshire job."

"Because most of the time you were on the site. They thought I was only mouthing your orders." She met his gaze across the table. "It might be the same here if you'd just make an appearance every day."

He flushed. "This infernal heat gives me a headache. You have Robinson to back you up."

"Robinson is only an overseer. Come just for an hour or so. Then you can go back to Kasanpore."

He was silent a moment and then a smile lit his ruddy face with warmth. "You're right. From now on I'll be there every day until the job is done." He studied her face. "You're looking a bit ragged. Why don't you stay in bed tomorrow and get some rest?"

"I'll be fine after a night's sleep." She took another bite of rice. "But it really would help if you'd come with me tomorrow."

He frowned. "Good God, you sound like a nagging fishwife. I said I'd come, didn't I?"

"Sorry." She finished the rice on her plate. "You're not eating."

"It's too hot to eat." He refilled his glass from the bottle on the table. "And even if I were hungry I couldn't stomach this slop. I don't see why you had to send Li Sung to Narinth. I haven't had a decent meal since he left."

She hurriedly glanced down at her plate. "Sula isn't a bad cook. I needed someone in Narinth to make sure the work on the station was going well."

"No one would pay any attention to the orders of a chink." He flushed defiantly as he saw the expression on her face. "Well, they wouldn't."

"No more than they would a woman," she agreed. "But he can watch and report if we're being cheated by the subcontractor you hired to do the work." She stood up and began to stack the dishes on the table. "Try to eat a little, or you'll have a bad head in the morning."

"Later." Patrick lifted the glass to his lips and she knew he'd leave the meal untouched. "That friend of the prince's came with the maharajah."

She stiffened. "Pachtal?"

Patrick nodded. "Seems a pleasant enough fellow. He said to give you his regards."

"Really?" She tried to make her tone noncommittal. "Did he say anything else?"

"No." Patrick made a face. "The maharajah said it all. He wanted to know where his locomotive was and when we'd finish laying the track."

"You told him the locomotive would arrive in a few days?"

"If the damn boat doesn't sink to the bottom of the river with it," Patrick said gloomily. "It would be just our luck. Nothing else has gone right on this job." He brightened. "At least, he'll be pleased with the locomotive. It's going to sport so much brass, he'll well nigh be blinded by it."

Her gaze flew to his face. "How could we afford to do that? We barely had enough cash left to afford the engine itself."

"I managed to cut a few corners." Patrick didn't look at her as he sipped his whiskey. "The maharajah likes a little flash and glitter, and we need to keep him sweet-tempered."

"That's true enough." She stood looking at him, frowning. "What corners?"

He waved a vague hand. "I just eliminated a part here and there. Nothing important."

"You're sure?"

"I said so, didn't I?" Patrick's tone turned testy. "I've been a railroad man since I was a lad of fourteen, Jane. I think I know what I'm doing."

"I just wanted to be—"

"It's too hot in here." Patrick pushed back his chair, stood up, and grabbed his glass and bottle. "I'm going out on the veranda, where it's cooler."

And where there were no troublesome questions to make him uncomfortable, Jane thought as she watched him walk toward the door leading to the screened veranda. His step was a little unsteady, but he wasn't staggering, which meant he probably hadn't been noticeably inebriated during his interview with the maharajah and Pachtal.

Pachtal. Both his presence and his message were obviously meant as a warning that she had not been forgotten by Abdar. During the past two weeks she had been scrupulously careful not to leave the encampment. Abdar must be seething with frustration, she mused. She smiled with grim satisfaction as she carried the dishes to the kitchen adjoining the dining room.

The tall, sari-clad servant woman was in the process of scraping bits of chicken into Sam's bowl and straightened with a guilty smile as Jane entered the kitchen. "I know the dog is not supposed to be in here, but I thought only this once?"

"It's all right, Sula. Just don't let the sahib see him."

Sula nodded. "The meal pleased you, memsahib?"

"Very good." Jane gave her an abstracted smile as she set the dishes on the countertop. She then bent and patted the dog's silky head. Perhaps she shouldn't be so complacent about Pachtal's visit, when it might have signaled the end of the waiting game Abdar had been playing. She had meant to visit Zabrie before this and ask her to set up a way for Kartauk to leave the city, but the pressure of work had caused her to ignore everything but the laying of the track. She should really go see the woman tonight.

No, not tonight. She could feel the cold lethargy of exhaustion dragging at every limb. Why did she care anyway? Li Sung was right; Kartauk was using her as much as she had used him. But it made no difference; she did care. She had never been able to bear the idea of cruelty to the helpless—though the idea of Kartauk being helpless was ironic. Yet while Abdar held the power in Kasanpore, Kartauk was without—

Dear heaven, her mind must be as weary as her body to meander like this. She would wash up and go to bed and try not to think of Abdar, his father, Kartauk, or the monumental pressure of the work waiting for her tomorrow.

As she crossed the living room on the way to her bedroom she heard Patrick humming to himself on the veranda. For a moment she felt a flicker of fierce resentment. He was happily drowning his worries in his bottle of whiskey, leaving her to solve their problems.

"Jane?" Patrick called.

She stopped but did not turn toward the veranda. "Yes?"

"I meant it about you staying in bed tomorrow." His tone was soft, caressing, almost affectionate. "We can't have you falling ill again. Whatever would I do without you?"

Jane's resentment vanished. He *did* care about her and God knows he needed her. "I won't be ill. I'm just a little tired."

"Well, take care of yourself."

Easy to say but almost impossible to do when the work never ended, she thought ruefully. "I will." She started quickly toward the bedroom door again, but a little of the lethargy and discouragement had dissipated in the surge of warmth she had felt for Patrick. He might use her, as Li Sung claimed, but he had rescued them both from Frenchie's and given them freedom and a roof over their heads. For that alone she would always be passionately grateful.

She lit the oil lamp on the table beside her narrow mosquito-net-draped bed and started to unbutton her loose shirt. She felt better now and would feel still better when she had washed away some of the sweat and dirt of the day. It would be foolish to put off going to see Zabrie when Abdar was clearly becoming an active danger again. The bath would revive her. Then she would be restored enough to set out for the city and deal with Zabrie.

"What is this place?" Ian whispered, peering at the large two-story sod house across the street.

Ruel's gaze never left the doorway through which Jane Barnaby had just passed as he answered. "Zabrie's. The Kasanpore version of a house of ill repute. Not exactly the kind of place a respectable lady visits."

"Zabrie . . . ah, yes, Abdar mentioned the place, didn't he?" Ian frowned. "Abdar could have lied about its purpose."

"He didn't."

"How do you know?"

"I spent two nights here last week."

"You didn't tell me."

Ruel murmured, "I'm hardly accustomed to consulting with anyone when I visit a whorehouse."

"I don't suppose you found out anything about Kartauk?"

"No, I could hardly go from whore to whore asking questions."

"Then why did you come here?"

"Before you dig for a rich vein you have to survey the claim," Ruel said. "And this particular survey was not without its pleasures. Zabrie is an ardent student of the Kama Sutra."

"What's that?"

"The eighty-eight positions of pleasure."

"Heathen debauchery." Ian was silent a moment before he was unable to restrain his curiosity. "How many did you try?"

Ruel chuckled. "Six. What else could you expect when I paid the lady only two visits?" His smile faded as his gaze went back to the house. "I wonder how well versed our Miss Barnaby is in the joys of Kama Sutra. It seems you were wrong about her."

"Not necessarily. Perhaps this is where Kartauk is hiding."

"Perhaps." Ruel smiled. "But not likely."

"Why not?"

"Abdar knew she came here, and I doubt if he would have neglected to search the place. No, it's more reasonable she's missing her lover, needed an outlet for her appetites, and chose to make herself available. Zabrie told me a few of the so-called prim and proper wives of the officers of the fort come here on occasion. She furnishes them with fanciful masks and a dimly lit room, and a diverting time is had by all." He kept his tone deliberately light to cover the chaotic mixture of outrage, satisfaction, and disappointment he was experiencing as he thought about Jane Barnaby lying naked in one of those dusky rooms. Satisfaction that he had been right and she was fair prey, outrage somehow connected with the sense of possession he had been fighting. As for the disappointment . . . Enough of this soul-searching, he thought impatiently. He started across the street.

"Where are you going?"

"Why, to offer my services." He smiled recklessly over his shoulder. "I'm tired of watching and waiting. It's time I took a more personal interest in the lady."

"You're going to ask Zabrie to send her to you?"

"Not by name. It's not necessary. I doubt if there will be more than one white woman at Zabrie's tonight."

"Wait. I'll go with you."

"And sacrifice your chastity for my benefit?" Ruel

asked mockingly. "I wouldn't even consider it. Maggie would never forgive me."

"Margaret," Ian corrected him. "And I have no intention of indulging my carnal urges."

"I was joking." Ruel gazed at his brother curiously. "You've been affianced to her since she was a lass of sixteen. You're saying you're still faithful to her after all these years of waiting?"

"Of course."

"There's no 'of course' about it. I'm not sure you weren't destined for the priesthood." He smiled. "And a priest would stick out at Zabrie's like the proverbial sore thumb. Stay here and wait for me."

"You are not welcome here." Zabrie scowled at Jane across the room. "You have brought me too much trouble."

"I've also given you a substantial amount of rupees to lighten those troubles."

"True." Zabrie's scowl vanished as she turned back to look at herself in the mirror of her vanity. "And it pleases me to make things difficult for His Highness. I suppose you may sit down while I prepare myself for the evening."

Jane sat down on the satin-cushioned divan. "Has Abdar been back since he searched the house?"

Zabrie shook her head. "I told him you came only to make yourself available to my clients." She smiled slyly. "I said it was the only way you could enjoy yourself without exposing yourself to shame. Was that not clever of me?"

"Very clever." Jane came across the room and seated herself in the chair beside the table. "We must talk."

"Li Sung?" Zabrie straightened warily. "He has complained?"

"No, on the contrary, he visits you too often."

"Because I am very, very good." Zabrie smiled complacently as she dipped her brush into the pot of kohl on the vanity. "After all, is that not why you came to me?"

"Tell him you can't see him so often. It's dangerous for him to come here now."

"Very well." She carefully drew a line around her left eye. "The fee will be the same, however."

Jane nodded. "I didn't expect anything else, but make up a good excuse. I won't have him hurt."

Zabrie drew a line around the other eye. "He thinks he is a fine lover. He wouldn't believe anything else now." She looked up with a satisfied smile. "I have done well with him. Is that all?"

Jane shook her head. "Kartauk."

Zabrie's smile faded. "It's too dangerous."

"You said Pachtal and His Highness hadn't been back."

"That does not mean I am not watched." Zabrie painted her lips vermilion. "You will have to think of another way of getting him out of Kasanpore. I will not risk bringing His Highness's anger down on my head."

"I thought you enjoyed the thought of foiling Abdar."

"On a small scale. But he gains more power every day and it will soon be too dangerous to displease His Highness."

"It's not a danger if—"

"I beg pardon to interrupt." The same doe-eyed young girl who had brought Jane to Zabrie's chamber stood in the doorway. "But there is a man here, Zabrie. You said—"

"I'm busy, Lenar. Give him another woman."

"But you told me to tell you when he came back."

Zabrie turned quickly to look at the girl. "It's the Scot?"

The girl nodded. "He says he's in the mood for something different. He wants a white woman. . . ."

"Oh, does he?" A tiny smile touched Zabrie's lips. "I believe I might have to change his mind." She nodded to a door across the dressing room. "Take him to the chamber next door and get him settled. Tell him I'll be with him in a few moments." As the girl left the room she turned to Jane. "You'll have to leave. I have a customer."

"I'm also a customer. Let him wait."

Zabrie smiled as she picked up her silver-backed brush and began to run it through her long dark hair. "But I don't want him to wait. He is . . . unusual. A challenge. I've never before met a Westerner who had the knowledge and experience to dominate me. At times I was not sure whether I was really in control."

"You have British blood, that makes you half a Westerner yourself."

Zabrie's vermilion lips thinned. "The British officers who come here to use me would not agree. They see only an alien with dark skin that excites them and they condescend to try me." She stood up and straightened the flowing saffron-colored drapings of her gown. "And once they've had me, *I* have them."

"You hate them?"

"I do not like them any more than I like my own people who consider me untouchable because of my mongrel birth. However, it does not matter. Soon I will be so rich I will not need either of them." Zabrie smiled mockingly at Jane in the mirror. "We are both outcasts in our fashion, are we not? You come here in your men's clothes, sometimes so weary you can scarcely stand. There is a simpler life than the one you lead. Why not give up that foolish railroad and come here and let me show you where the easy riches lie?"

Jane shook her head.

"You should do well enough." Zabrie regarded her critically. "You're young and not unattractive. Sometimes the British tire of the exotic and wish to indulge themselves with one of their own race."

"Like your Scot?"

She frowned. "He meant only to tease me. He would be disappointed if I sent someone else." She stood up, her henna-tinted fingers smoothing the sheer material veiling her breasts. "What do you say?"

"No."

She shrugged. "I'll wait. You'll change your mind. When a woman is alone and without protection, there is only one road for her to take."

The certainty in Zabrie's tone sent a lightning bolt of fear through Jane. "I said no! I'm not alone, and even if I were, I don't need anybody else. I can protect myself. I'm not a whore. I'll *never* be a whore."

Zabrie drew herself up haughtily. "It seems you, too, think a whore is beneath your touch."

Jane drew a deep breath, trying to regain control. Her fierce response to Zabrie's words had caught her by surprise. "I didn't say that."

"You did not need to say it."

"I didn't mean to hurt you and certainly not condemn you. My mother was a harlot and in a far worse place than this. You must make your own choices, but . . ." She hesitated and then burst out, "I would rather die than sell myself."

Zabrie's gaze narrowed on her face. "You are afraid. Why?"

"I'm not afraid." Zabrie gazed at her in disbelief. Jane explained haltingly, "Such a life takes away your freedom, you become a slave."

"It is all how one looks upon the act. If a woman is good enough, it is the man who becomes the slave." Zabrie turned away from the mirror. "You must go now."

"Kartauk."

Zabrie smiled as she saw Jane's determined expression. "You don't give up, do you? We may disagree on many things, but it's one quality we have in common."

"Will you at least provide a shelter for Kartauk in the city if I need it?"

"If you can arrange it so that there is no danger to me, I will consid—"

The door was flung open and the young girl Zabrie had called Lenar rushed into the room. "Pachtal! He came in a few minutes ago. He demands to see you."

"What?" Zabrie whirled to face Jane. "You fool!"

"He didn't follow me." Jane stood up. "I know Pachtal and would have noticed him. He must have been watching this house."

"And saw you come in. What difference does it make how he came to be here? He's *here.*"

Jane felt a thrill of fear as she remembered Pachtal's vicious expression, the agony as he had twisted her arm. "How can I get out of the house without him seeing me?"

"It's too late." Zabrie grasped her wrist and dragged her toward the door across the room. "He'll probably search the place for you, but I'll try to keep him away from here."

"How?"

"The usual way. Pachtal and Abdar didn't hesitate to use me when they were here before. I'll call you when it's safe." She opened the door, pushed Jane into the adjoining room, and slammed the door.

Chapter 3

Even in the dim lamplight Ruel recognized the gleaming auburn of Jane's hair as she hurriedly entered the room.

The muscles of his abdomen clenched and his loins immediately hardened in response. Easy, he told himself, he was here for a purpose other than what his body demanded. Easy? The thought was ludicrous; at this moment both calmness and reason were out of the question.

She was here.

Soon he would know more about her than ever before.

Soon he would touch her for the first time.

• • •

Jane heard the key turn in the lock of the door behind her. Another click sounded in the lock on the only other door across the chamber.

She was a prisoner.

Her chest was tight with fear. The caged feeling reminded her of the helplessness she had experienced when she had stood sandwiched between Pachtal and Abdar on that lonely street only a few weeks before.

Darkness hovered over the chamber lightened only by a single oil lamp on the table beside her, and the heavy scent of musk and incense pressed down on her.

"At last. Come here and let me look at you."

She froze, her glance flying across the room to the man lying on the bed.

In the dimness she could tell only that he was naked and lying on his side facing her. His cheek rested on his hand as his gaze slowly ran over her. "Unusual. It seems Zabrie took me at my word."

This time she caught the slight brogue in the words. The Scot, Jane remembered, the man whom Zabrie had ordered brought here, the man who had wanted something different. "Zabrie will come to you later. She's busy now."

"But she sent you to entertain me?" He crooked his finger, motioning for her to come to him. "Don't be nervous. I don't mind. I told her I was in the mood for an English lass."

He had mistaken her panic for nervousness at his displeasure. She would have laughed if she hadn't been so frightened. "I'm not English and I'm not nervous. You don't understand."

"I understand I'm going to be a little annoyed if you don't come over here and let me see what you look like." She moved reluctantly to stand beside the bed. "I'm sure Zabrie will not be—"

Dear God, he was the most beautiful human being she had ever seen. He was all lion colors, golden skin, tawny hair pulled back in a queue to reveal a bone structure that was close to perfect. But his eyes were blue, not a catlike green or yellow, a deep, piercing blue. . . .

He lifted a brow. "How long before Zabrie arrives?"

She had forgotten what she had been about to say. She swiftly gathered her composure. "Just be patient."

He chuckled. "This isn't a situation where patience comes easily." He gestured to his lower body. "As you can see."

Her gaze followed the gesture and she inhaled sharply as she saw bold, pulsing arousal, splendid dimension. She quickly looked back to his face. "Zabrie will be here soon."

"It's not Zabrie who made me like this. You walked in the door and I wanted you."

She stared at him in disbelief.

"It came as a surprise to me too. I didn't expect it. In those masculine clothes you certainly don't look very appealing." He reached out and grasped her wrist. "Take them off," he said softly.

Her flesh under his grasp felt strange, hot, tingling, and she was experiencing a queer breathlessness. "No."

"You prefer that I do it?" He pulled her down to a sitting position on the bed beside him. His light eyes narrowed on her face, holding her gaze. The scent of him surrounded her, soap and spice and something deeper, darker, blending with the incense-laden air. "Why not?" he murmured. "I might find it interesting changing a boy into a woman."

"I didn't say that I wanted—"

He started unbuttoning her shirt.

She instinctively jerked back.

He quickly grasped both her wrists in one hand. "Shh, it's all right." His other hand moved from the buttons to pet her breasts through the material. "I just want to see you." He smiled as he looked down at the protrusion of her nipples against the material of her shirt. "Ah, isn't that pretty." He rubbed his palm slowly back and forth over her breasts.

Jane felt heat ripple through her and a tingle begin between her legs. Why wasn't she struggling? She was strong enough to break his grip if she made the effort. Pachtal. She grasped desperately at the only sensible reason occurring to her. She must be afraid Pachtal would come if she made a disturbance, or perhaps it was this incense that was making her dizzy and weak. "I . . . I don't want this."

"Of course you do." He undid two more buttons. "Why else are you here?"

She swallowed. "You don't understand."

"You said that before. You're wrong. This is something I understand very well. Ask Zabrie." He undid another button. "We can—"

"Stop it!"

"You don't want me to undress you? Whatever you say." His hand fell away from the buttons and gathered up both her hands in his own. "See, I've stopped." His thumb rubbed slowly, exploringly, over her palm. "Calluses." He turned her hand over and gazed down at it. "Hard and rough. You didn't get these planting flowers in an English garden."

She tried to draw her hand away from him, but his grasp tightened.

"I meant no insult. I like them. They make us akin. I have calluses too." He rubbed his palm over the top of her hand. "Feel them. You see? I know what it is to work so hard I'm tottering on my feet with exhaustion. I understand weariness and discouragement. I understand how you can try and try and still never reach a goal. It's not easy to have to fight every single day, is it?" His voice was caressing, his words weaving silky bonds around her emotions. "That's why we have to reward ourselves when we get the chance."

"I don't have to reward my—"

"Shh . . ." He leaned forward until his mouth hovered over her breast. "I want to see you but perhaps this is better. It's quite arousing seeing what your nipples do to that shirt. Is that why you wear men's things instead of a mask when you come here?"

His breath was warm on her nipple, and the tingling increased between her thighs until it was close to pain.

She felt drugged, disoriented . . . yes, it must be the incense. . . .

His head was bent, and she could no longer see those light, glittering eyes, but his sun-streaked hair shone in the lamplight and she had the odd impression of sensual savagery, hovering, about to strike . . . or stroke.

His warm tongue touched the tip of her breast through the thin cotton of her shirt.

She gave a low cry, her back arching in a spasm of sensation.

"That's right," he whispered. "Feel me. *Need* me."

She did need him, she realized dazedly. She had always thought it was men who needed women, that the soft, whimpering cries of pleasure and subjugation she had heard from her mother and the other whores were pretense. Now she had to bite back those same cries as she felt the warmth of this stranger's lips. Dear God, perhaps it wasn't the opium pipe that had seduced her mother and made her a slave, but this same pleasure.

No! She wouldn't be caught like this. She would not be a whore. She would not be a slave. "Let me go!" She broke his grip and leapt to her feet. She fastened her shirt with trembling fingers. "Don't *touch* me. I'm not a whore."

He didn't try to stop her, nor did he make any attempt to cover his nudity. He merely lay and watched her, graceful, catlike, aroused. "I didn't think you were. I understand from Zabrie that a number of the British wives of the officers from the fort come here to amuse themselves."

"I told you, I'm not English." Her voice was shaking, and she tried to steady it. "It's a mistake. I don't want to fornicate with you."

"I beg to disagree." His gaze lingered on her engorged nipples clearly outlined against her shirt. "You most certainly do."

"It was a mistake," she repeated with sudden fierceness. "I was frightened and off guard."

"Frightened? Of me?"

"No." She backed away from the bed toward the

door and then stopped. She couldn't leave until Zabrie came back and unlocked the door. "Not of you."

He sat up and swung his feet to the floor.

She stiffened. "Don't come near me. I have a knife."

"Do you? How very uncivilized." He didn't move from the bed. "I wasn't going to attack you. I can wait for my pleasure since you are apparently reluctant to provide me with it. Won't you sit down?"

Her gaze flew back to his lower body.

"Oh, yes, it's still there." He smiled faintly. "But I can control myself." He studied her strained expression. "Why didn't you run out of here?"

"Zabrie locked the doors."

"Interesting. Was it supposed to make the situation more exciting?"

"No, there's someone here I don't want to see."

He went still. "Who?"

She didn't answer.

"Never mind. It doesn't matter." He rose to his feet and moved over to the table by the door, where he was surrounded by the pool of light cast by the oil lamp. She tried not to look at him, but to no avail. Dear heaven, he was as beautifully exotic as a jungle animal and just as free from shame. His brown hair, bound in a queue, was full of tawny streaks set ablaze by the light. She watched the way the lamp highlighted the arch of his spine and the tightness of his buttocks, the compactness of the muscles of his shoulders. For the first time she noticed the white bandage that was tied around his left shoulder.

He picked up the bottle on the table and poured wine into a goblet. "Would you like a glass?"

"No."

He lifted the glass to his lips. "Who are you afraid of? Is it your lover?"

She didn't answer.

An object lying on the table caught his attention, and a faint smile touched his lips as he picked it up. "This must have been meant for you."

The object was an extravagant mask of brown, black, and turquoise peacock feathers. "Pretty thing. I'd like to see you in it." He held up the mask to his own eyes. "Would you care to oblige me?"

The exotic mask covered the entire top of his face, and a spray of sable peacock feathers jutted out on either side. His blue eyes shimmered through the almond-shaped holes, and the close fit of the mask enhanced the beautiful molding of his cheekbones. The tawny feathers of the mask were the identical shade as the triangle of hair on his chest and surrounding his manhood, and he looked wild, wicked, and completely male, a rare, splendid creature from an alien land. "No, I'd look foolish in it."

"What a shame." He tossed the mask down and half leaned against the table, his mocking gaze fixed on her face. "Now, who could be pursuing you? A husband? Let's see if I can guess. An aging husband who can't please you so you're forced to come here for satisfaction." He lifted the back of his hand melodramatically to his forehead. "But, alas, the husband follows you and hence—"

"Nonsense. I have no husband." She frowned. "And if I did, I would not betray him. Promises should be kept."

"Agreed." He sipped the wine. "Then we're back to the lover." He straightened away from the table and moved over to the bed. "What's his name?"

How long had she been in this room? she wondered desperately. The air seemed thick and hard to breathe and the situation unbearably intimate. Surely Zabrie would come for her soon.

He lay down on the bed and settled himself comfortably against the headboard. "Talk to me. Since it seems we're to be imprisoned together for a while, the least we can do is pass the time as pleasantly as possible."

"I don't have to entertain you."

"Ah, yes, the knife." He smiled as he lifted the wine to his lips. "But I'm strong and quick, and why risk failure when I can be appeased with a little conversation?" He waved at the chair across the room. "Sit down. My name is Ruel MacClaren."

"Ruel. That's a strange name."

"Not in Scotland. It's a very old name. Sit down," he repeated. "Aren't you going to return the courtesy? What's your name?"

She crossed the room and sat down gingerly on the chair he had indicated. "Jane."

"Jane what?"

She didn't reply.

"You're right, of course. Under the circumstances, last names are a formality that are a bit bizarre, but I find myself wanting to know more about you." His brow creased in concentration. "Jane . . ." The frown vanished and he snapped his fingers. "Jane Barnaby. Patrick Reilly. The railroad."

Her eyes widened in surprise.

He chuckled. "You didn't think I'd make the connection? Your accent is neither English nor Scottish and, though Reilly's never brought you to the Officers' Club, there're not that many Americans in Kasanpore. You'd be surprised how much gossip is floating about town about Reilly and his 'ward.' "

She flinched. "You're wrong, I'm not surprised."

"Is it Reilly you're hiding from?"

"Of course not."

"Then why are you—"

"And why are you in Kasanpore, Mr. MacClaren?"

"Ah, the offensive," he murmured. "I was expecting that move earlier." He took another sip of his wine. "I'm trying to get an appointment with the maharajah. I've had little luck as yet."

"Why do you want to see him?"

"He has something I want." He paused. "Perhaps you could intercede for me. I hear he comes often to examine your progress on the railroad."

"Which never pleases him." Her hands clasped together on her lap. "I'd be the last one to influence him."

"Too bad." He casually lifted one leg, and the sole of his foot began to rub back and forth on the flat surface of the mattress. "I suppose I'll just have to look for help elsewhere."

Her stare was drawn by the motion of his foot, the flexing calf muscles, the contrast of warm, golden skin against the white of the sheet. She quickly shifted her glance up to the bandage she had noticed earlier. "How did you hurt your shoulder?"

"I allowed myself to become distracted and received a severe lesson for my carelessness. It won't happen again." He suddenly set the glass on the table by the bed and swung his legs to the floor. "I'm becoming restless, aren't you? Let's get out of here."

"We have to wait for Zabrie."

"I don't like waiting." He strolled over to a chair in a shadowy corner of the room and picked up a white linen shirt. "I don't like locks." He was dressing quickly as he spoke. "And I particularly don't like the idea of a vengeful lover rushing in to skewer me. Under the circumstances, I believe we should both leave the premises." He sat down on the bed and pulled on his left boot. "Pity. It's not at all what I had in mind for the evening."

"How are we supposed to get out? Both doors are locked."

"We still have a window."

"We're on the second floor."

He drew on his right boot. "A circumstance which can be overcome."

"I have no intention of breaking a leg trying to jump to the ground."

"I would have expected you to be more determined."

"I'm determined to get the railroad built, and I can't do that by becoming a cripple."

"The railroad." He smiled as he rose to his feet. "I forgot about your railroad." He moved toward the window. "Don't worry, I'll make sure you don't injure yourself irretrievably." He sat down on the windowsill and swung his legs out the window. "As far as I can make out, this room must face to the rear. There seems to be an alley below." He wrinkled his nose. "Yes, definitely an alley. The odor is the same the world over."

She followed him and peered over his shoulder. Moonlight revealed the narrow alley he had mentioned, but it seemed very far down. "Are you mad? How are you—"

He jumped to the ground, landing with knees bent and immediately went into a somersault and roll. Then he was springing lithely to his feet and moving to stand beneath the window. "Jump."

She stared at him with open mouth. "How did you do that?"

"Never mind that now. Jump. I'll catch you."

She looked at him uncertainly.

"You won't be hurt. Trust me." When she still hesitated, he explained impatiently, "When I was a lad in London I earned my living as a street acrobat for a while."

The agility she had just witnessed certainly bore testament to his claim. She hesitated, but with freedom in sight she had no desire to sit and wait for Zabrie or be discovered by Pachtal. She sat on the windowsill, her legs dangling over the edge as he had done.

"Good," he said. He held up his arms. "Now come to me."

The ground was looking farther away every second.

"What are you waiting for? Just remember to push away from the windowsill when you jump so you won't hit the wall."

She took a deep breath, closed her eyes, and pushed away from the sill.

For an endless moment she was falling through space.

Ruel plucked her from the air. "Got you."

Then he staggered, cursed, and fell in a heap to the ground.

"Ouch," he grunted. "Damn, that hurt."

It took a moment for her to get her breath back. Then she rolled off him and struggled to her knees. "I thought you said you were an acrobat."

He scowled. "I didn't say I was a *good* acrobat. That was when I was fifteen and I never could catch worth a tuppence." He rose painfully to his knees. "That was why I quit after six months and became a running patterer."

She glared at him. "You bloody fool. I could have broken my neck!"

"But you didn't." He grimaced. "I'm the one who fell on my nether parts into a pile of Lord knows what."

"How could you take such a—" She broke off and started to laugh helplessly at the foolish sight they must have presented, kneeling there facing each other among the garbage and dung. It was as if a weight had been lifted from her and she realized for the first time how intimidated she had been by the man. She had never before met anyone quite so splendid or enigmatic as Ruel MacClaren and it was a relief to see the human side of him.

He tilted his head, and a slow smile lit his face. "I've never heard you laugh before."

"That shouldn't surprise you since we've known each other less than thirty minutes."

He got up and helped her to her feet. "I don't think you laugh over-frequently." He turned away and moved down the alley toward the corner of the building. "Let's get away from here before your lover appears. I have no desire to incur any more bruises on your behalf."

She was immediately jarred back to reality by his words. Sweet Mary, how could she have forgotten the danger Pachtal posed? Yet, for an instant she had forgotten it. She had felt young and happy . . . and strangely safe.

"I told you I wasn't hiding from a lover." She quickly followed Ruel down the alley, rounding the corner just behind him. "You didn't listen to— Look out!"

A knife descended out of the shadows, arching toward Ruel's unprotected back.

No time to think. Instinctively she threw herself between Ruel and the dagger, trying to push him aside.

Agony took her breath away as the dagger sliced through her upper arm. As she staggered to the side she caught a blurred glimpse of the assassin. Tall, thin . . .

the white folds of a turban. Pachtal, she thought dazedly, it had to be Pachtal.

She dimly heard Ruel mutter a curse as he whirled on the man, one hand darting out to grasp the wrist holding the knife, the other closing on the man's throat.

Darkness. She could no longer see Ruel's face.

She was slipping down the wall. No, she must stay on her feet and help Ruel. The knife . . . Pachtal would . . .

She was being lifted.

Her lids flew open to see Ruel's grim face above her. "Are you . . . hurt?" she asked faintly.

"Why should I be hurt?" he said roughly. "I didn't take the knife."

"I thought Pachtal . . . where—" She broke off as she saw their attacker on the ground a few feet away. His mouth was stretched wide in a silent scream; his eyes were open and bulging from their sockets, staring straight ahead. She had never seen him before. "It's not Pachtal," she whispered. "Is he dead?"

"Very." He started to move quickly across the street. "But not in time to help you. Now, be quiet until I get you away from here."

Something warm and wet was flowing down her arm. "Bleeding."

"I know you're bleeding, dammit. I'll fix it as soon as I can, but I—"

"Good God, what did you do to her?" Another voice with the same Scottish brogue. The owner of the voice stepped out of an alcove and looked down at her.

Abraham Lincoln, she thought hazily as a long, homely face swam into focus. No, this face was clean-shaven, not the bearded visage she had seen in pictures in the newspaper. Besides, Lincoln had been shot, hadn't he?

"I didn't do anything to her," Ruel said curtly. "She took a dagger in the arm meant for me."

"Dear me, another Mila? You do seem to inspire self-sacrifice in the female gender."

"I'm glad the situation amuses you, Ian. Are you going to continue to chuckle while she bleeds to death?"

All amusement instantly vanished from the expression of the man Ruel had addressed as Ian. "Is she seriously injured? Put the lass down and let me take a look."

"She says someone else is after her and I want to get her away from here. Tie your handkerchief around her arm above the wound to lessen the bleeding."

"Aye." Ian obeyed, his gaze fixed on her face. "It's going to hurt a bit, lass."

It hurt more than a bit. She gasped as he tightened the bandage carefully about her arm.

"Tighter," Ruel said. "Now isn't the time to be gentle. The blood's still flowing, dammit."

Ian tightened the bandage. She bit her lower lip to keep back the cry of pain, but Ruel must have heard her sudden intake of breath, for his gaze flew to her face. "I know," he said hoarsely. "But we have to stop it. I'm not going to let you die." He turned to the other man. "Let's get her away from here."

"I'll carry her," Ian offered.

"No." Ruel's arms tightened possessively around her. "I'll take care of her. You watch the rear."

She opened her eyes to see Abraham Lincoln sitting beside her bed.

No, that was wrong, she thought hazily, she had made that mistake before.

"You're going to be fine, lass. It's hardly a pinprick, though you bled quite a bit." He smiled. "I don't believe we've been introduced. I'm Ian MacClaren, Earl of Glenclaren. Ruel's my brother."

She glanced down at her arm. She was still fully dressed, but the sleeve of her shirt had been cut away and a neat clean bandage encircled her upper arm. Her gaze flew around the room. "Where—"

"The Nayala Hotel. This is Ruel's room. When you fainted we decided to bring you here. Ruel said it was closer than your bungalow."

"I never faint," she protested.

"Of course not," he said gravely. "Let's just say, then, that you were sleeping very hard indeed."

"Where is Ruel?"

"He was a trifle bloody from carrying you and smelled atrociously, so I sent him next door to my room to change. I was afraid you might be alarmed if you woke and saw him."

He spoke of sending Ruel off as if he were a naughty little boy, and yet she could not imagine the man she had met at Zabrie's tamely going off at anyone's command. Her gaze flew to the darkness beyond the window across the room. "What time is it?"

"Almost one o'clock in the morning. As I said, you had yourself a bit of a nap."

She struggled to a sitting position. "I have to get back to the bungalow."

"You can stay here tonight. I'll bunk in with Ian." Ruel stood in the doorway. He had changed his clothes and was wearing tan breeches, brown boots, and a crisp white linen shirt. He strolled toward her and she was again aware of that lithe grace of movement she had noticed at Zabrie's. "I'll send a message to tell Reilly where you are."

"No!" she said instantly. "I mean, thank you, but I don't want to worry him."

"And you don't want Reilly to know where you were tonight." He asked softly, "Who is Pachtal, Jane?"

She didn't answer.

"May I remind you I killed a man in that alley tonight?" He shrugged. "Not that I'm objecting. I have no use for killers who wait in the dark, but I believe I deserve to know if there are going to be any repercussions."

Her hands clenched on the coverlet. "No repercussions. I think he must have been one of Pachtal's servants."

"And who, I ask again, is Pachtal?"

"Pachtal serves Prince Abdar." She went on quickly. "But you needn't worry about the maharajah becoming involved. Abdar doesn't want him to know about any of this."

"About what?" Ruel asked.

It had been only fair to assuage his concern, but he didn't have to know any more. She tossed back the covers. "I have to get back to the bungalow. I need to be up at dawn."

"Your railroad can do without you for a day or two. You can use a little time to recuperate from losing all that blood."

"A day or two?" She looked at him as if he had gone mad. "The monsoons start in two weeks. I can't afford to lose even an hour."

"Reilly can take over for you. It's his railroad, isn't it?"

She didn't answer as she struggled out of bed to her feet.

Dizziness. The room swung around her.

"Dammit, what are you trying to do to yourself?" Ruel took two steps, reached out, and grabbed her arms, steadying her. "Lie down."

"No, it's better now." She spoke the truth. She still felt weak, but the room was no longer swaying. "I have to get—"

"Back to your blasted railroad," he finished. "The hell you will."

"You shouldn't curse in the presence of a lady," Ian said reprovingly. "But I admit the sentiment is valid. You should rest, lass."

"I'll be fine." She backed away from Ruel. "Thank you for your concern."

"Concern?" Ruel exploded in exasperation. "Why should I be concerned just because you were stupid enough to jump in front of a dagger meant for me?"

"It couldn't have been meant for you. It must have been a mistake." She shook her head. "I don't understand. You're not involved in this."

"I appear to be very much involved," he said grimly. "I owe you a debt, and I pay my debts."

"You don't owe me anything."

A sudden smile lit his face, melting away the grimness as if it had never been. "I've heard the Chinese believe if you save a man's life, it belongs to you." His voice was velvet-deep, the tone wheedling. "Now, you can't just toss me away, lass."

Dear heaven, he was as beautiful and seductive as the whistle of a train in the night traveling to wondrous places. "Li Sung says that proverb is a fallacy made up by white men."

"And who is Li Sung?"

"My friend."

"I prefer my own version of the Oriental philosophy," he said, that radiant smile basking her once more. "Won't you do as I ask?"

He knew exactly what he was doing, she realized suddenly. He knew down to the last glowing ounce of that strong, beautiful body how to seduce and persuade and bend a woman to his way of thinking and had probably learned it through a thousand encounters such as the one that had taken place at Zabrie's.

"No." She felt an instant of satisfaction as she saw the flicker of surprise on his face, but she knew she hadn't the strength to argue with him any longer. She must put an end to this discussion. "Thank you for taking care of my arm. You needn't worry anymore about this. I'm sure you won't get in trouble for—"

"Oh, no, you don't." Ruel moved in front of her, blocking her passage to the door. The grimness had returned to his expression. "Get back in that bed." When she didn't move but stood there looking at him, he said impatiently, "All right, blast it, I'll let you go slave on your wonderful railroad, but a few hours rest won't hurt. Get some sleep and we'll be on our way at first light."

"We?"

"Your railroad's hired nearly everyone else in Kasanpore. Why not me? After tonight, I'd say you need someone to guard your back."

"I don't need anyone to protect me. I can take care of myself."

"Then, at least, I can watch over you and see you don't kill yourself with overwork."

Watch over you.

The phrase held a sweet, wistful fascination for her. Not that she needed anyone to watch over her, she thought quickly. "Laying tracks isn't the kind of work you'd want to do."

"A few days of it won't hurt me."

She glanced around the tastefully furnished hotel room. "You'd be of no use to me."

"Because I don't occupy a hovel? Ask Ian where he found me in Krugerville. When you're seeking an audience with a maharajah, you don't spare the rupees. I assure you I can make myself useful in most circumstances and I'm not afraid of hard labor."

She recalled the hard roughness of the calluses on the hand that had stroked hers.

"Lie down," Ruel repeated. "I'll wake you at dawn and we'll ride out to the site together."

She turned and lay back down on the bed, drawing the covers over her. She was accomplishing nothing but draining her strength by fighting him. One day of pounding spikes should assuage his conscience. "I'll need a clean shirt to cover this bandage. No one must know I've been hurt."

"I believe I can supply one."

"No." She nodded at Ian. "Him. He's bigger and I want it loose."

Ian smiled. "It will be my pleasure."

"And be sure to wake me at dawn." She closed her eyes.

"Should I send word to Reilly that you're here?" Ruel asked.

"No, he won't miss me. I'm usually gone by the time he wakes up in the morning."

"How charming," Ruel said caustically. "I must remember to—"

"Go away," she said without opening her eyes "You're keeping me awake."

She heard Ian's delighted chuckle. "Are you properly

put in your place, Ruel? Let's retire to my room and have a glass of whiskey. I've had enough of this soggy air for one night. I'll be glad to get home to Glenclaren."

"So you tell me every day."

"I decided it would do no harm to remind you. I've always believed in fortifying my position."

Her eyes remained shut after the door closed behind them. What a strange contrast the two men made, Ruel as volatile and glittering as quicksilver, and his brother sturdy and homely as raw granite. Yet, in spite of their differences, she could sense a strong bond between them.

She must stop thinking of Ruel or his brother. Scottish lords and beautiful exotic young men had nothing to do with what was important in her life. She must get to sleep and gain strength to fight off this weakness.

"I like her." Ian handed the glass of whiskey he had just poured to Ruel. "She's a brae lass."

"You like her because she's just as obstinate as you are."

"I admit I enjoyed seeing a woman say no to you. I'm sure it's very good for your character." Ian took his own glass and moved to the window. "It appears the threat to the girl Abdar spoke about is more than the maharajah's displeasure."

"Yes."

"But you always suspected that, didn't you?"

"I told you I was familiar with crocodiles."

A few moments passed before Ian spoke again. "You were gone a long time. Did you—" He hesitated.

"Are you trying to ask if I had a carnal romp with our guest?"

"I suppose I am."

"I have not." Ruel took a sip of whiskey. "Yet."

"You still believe this Kartauk is her lover?"

Ruel's lashes lowered to veil his eyes. "Why should I have changed my mind? She's risking a good deal for him."

"You think the assassin in the alley was waiting for her?"

"It makes sense. When I showed up with her, he decided the first blow should be for the more dangerous target."

"But you're not certain, are you?"

"You're beginning to read me too well. No, I'm not sure. This particular crocodile may have cunning as well as teeth." He shrugged. "But it does make the search more interesting."

"The lass could have lost her life tonight." He frowned, troubled. "Everything is changing. I want you to give up this nonsense of using her to find Kartauk."

Ruel didn't answer.

"Ruel?"

"Nothing has changed except I'm now in a far better position to receive confidences and find out information than I was earlier this evening." He smiled sardonically. "Don't look so appalled. I tried to tell you what I am."

"You just like to shock me." Ian added quietly, "She saved your life. You won't betray her trust."

"She doesn't trust me. She probably doesn't trust anyone, unless it's this Kartauk."

"And that bothers you, doesn't it?"

"Goddammit, it doesn't bother me!" Ruel crashed his glass down on the table and sprang to his feet. "The only thing that bothers me is your infernal probing. I've had a bellyful of it." He strode toward the door.

"Where are you going?"

"I need some air. I'm suffocating in here." He glared back at Ian. "And I don't give a damn about you, or Glenclaren, or that blasted girl. All I want is Cinnidar."

The door slammed behind him.

Ian smiled slightly as he lifted his glass to his lips.

Tiger pad softly, tiger burn bright . . .

At the moment, the tiger was not padding at all softly but he was definitely burning. Even in that moment in the barroom when Ruel had been goading Barak, Ian had not seen him this savage. Still, it was not a bad sign. Sometimes a flame could purify as well as destroy. He could only hope all those nonsensical dreams of Cinnidar would be burned away in its wake so they could go home.

Home.

Though he constantly held Glenclaren up before Ruel as a beacon, when he was alone he tried not to think of it. It made the yearning for home only deeper and more hurtful.

Instead, he would think of Margaret. Margaret was not his own in the same way Glenclaren belonged to him, and he had waited so long for her, the anticipation had lost all bitterness and become sweetly wistful. Margaret, cool and brisk, yet with a heart as warm as a winter bonfire.

Yes, he would think of Margaret. . . .

"He's dead." Zabrie looked up at Pachtal from where she knelt beside the body. "From the bruises on his throat it looks as if he was strangled. Will this interfere with your plans?"

"Not at all," Pachtal said. "Resard's death is of no importance." He gazed without expression into the staring eyes of his servant. "Not if he first accomplished his task."

"There's blood on the knife and more drops leading across the street. You wished the Scot only wounded?"

Pachtal nodded. "Events were moving too slowly for His Highness. He wished the Scot placed in a position of intimacy with the girl." A faint smile touched his lips as he gazed down at the bloody knife on the pavement. "I believe I can tell him his wish has been granted."

Zabrie suppressed a shiver as she looked down at the dead man. It should not have surprised her that Pachtal regarded the man's death as weighing nothing against Abdar's whims. She had known from the first time she had met Pachtal he could be either a danger or a boon to her, depending on how she handled him.

She rose to her feet, picked up the lantern, and moved toward the arched door. "Then His Highness should be pleased with us both. Did I not send for you the moment the girl crossed my threshold? How did you know he would follow and ask for a white woman?"

"We could not be sure, but we knew he was watching her." He smiled. "And the Scot is not a patient man. It was only a matter of time until he made his move."

"So, I set the trap and you sprang it."

"You set the trap, but the Scot did not respond as you thought he would. You said he wouldn't trust the word of the girl and would try the door leading to the hall, find you hadn't really locked it, and take the girl to the alley that way. Yet no one was seen going out this alley door. How did they get out?"

"How do I know? The Scot is not predictable." She experienced a moment of regret as she remembered how delightfully unpredictable he had proved in their bouts together. Then she dismissed the emotion and asked, "What difference does it make as long as the end was accomplished?"

"No difference. You'll be adequately rewarded for your services. The bitch made no mention of Kartauk?"

"I told you she had not. She was concerned only about her friend Li Sung." She had learned it was always better to tell a little bit of the truth when you told a lie and she had decided it would not be wise to reveal all she knew to Abdar. "She's afraid he comes here too often and will anger Reilly by neglecting his duties in Narinth."

His lips curled. "How can you bear to bed that mongrel Chinese dog?"

Mongrel. Pachtal regarded all but his own caste as unclean. She had to smother the sting of rage his words brought. "I must earn food for my table, and all men do not bring me as much pleasure as you and His Highness. I hope you found me skillful?"

"Adequate. His Highness told me he found you very pleasant to look upon."

"He did?"

He smiled. "He also said when we found Kartauk

perhaps he would have a golden mask made of your face."

"I am honored."

"But you would be more honored if he made you one of his concubines at the palace," he said softly. "His women have fabulous jewels and rich golden trinkets that would make your eyes shimmer with delight."

She felt a leap of hope. "Has he spoken of this?"

"No, but I have great influence on His Highness. I could remind him how talented you were the one time we both enjoyed you."

"And would you be so generous as to do this for me?"

"It's a possibility." He paused. "If you please me."

It was the answer she had expected. "I will please you." She smiled at him. "Come along to my chamber and I will show you what we experienced before was only the beginning."

He shook his head. "No, here."

Her eyes widened as she looked around the alley and then to the dead man a few yards away. "You jest. There is stink here and your servant . . ."

"It excites me," he murmured. "Turn around and lean your hands against the wall."

"We would both be more comfortable in my bed. I have cool silken sheets that feel wonderful against your skin."

"I don't want comfort." He took the lantern from her hand and carefully positioned it on the ground beside the dead man's head. "I want to take you while he lies there staring at us. I want to show him how good it is to be alive." His nostrils flared, his eyes glittered wildly. "But perhaps you do not wish to please me, whore?"

She swallowed and then turned around and leaned her palms against the rough sod wall. It did not matter, she told herself. She had performed many acts almost as twisted as this with less to gain.

Her skirt was pushed up and the next moment she felt him plunge deep within her. He grunted, his breathing quick, heavy, excited as he began to rut with brutal animal ferocity.

It *did* matter. He was taking her as if she were of no more value than a bitch in heat. The smell of garbage and refuse churned her stomach, and she was horribly conscious of the dead man staring at them only a few feet away.

But she was no mongrel and, when she had the riches and power Abdar would heap on her, she would show them all.

Jane stopped in surprise as she and Ruel were walking out of the hotel the next morning.

Her mare, Bedelia, was tied to the hitching rail beside a chestnut stallion.

"How did you get Bedelia?"

"I couldn't sleep, so I found out from the desk clerk where the Sahib Reilly's bungalow was located and rode Nugget over to fetch her. By the way, that dog you have at the stable is less than useless. The only threat he could pose is if he licked you to death."

"I know, I tried to teach Sam to be a guard dog, but he's not too bright and much too friendly. I keep him in the stable only because Patrick won't have him in the bungalow." She spoke absently as she stroked Bedelia's nose. "But how did you know which horse was mine?"

For an instant an indefinable expression flickered over Ruel's face. "It wasn't difficult. There were only two horses in the stable and the other one was larger, not in good condition, and showed a lack of exercise. I thought you'd probably work your horse as hard as you do yourself. I'm glad I chose correctly." He moved to the mare's left side. "We'd better get on our way. Let me help you up."

She hesitated before allowing him to boost her onto the mare. She couldn't remember the last time she had been given this courtesy, and it felt odd and vaguely pleasant. She watched him mount. "Why couldn't you sleep?"

"It was a stimulating evening." He smiled sardonically as he turned his horse, Nugget, and kicked him into a fast trot. "I trust you had no problem sleeping."

"None at all. I couldn't allow myself to do anything else." She looked away from him. "I'm much better this morning. You needn't go with me."

"We had this discussion last night."

"You didn't listen to me last night."

"And I'm not listening this morning. How far away is this site?"

"About five miles. We started the track in Narinth and worked our way back to a point twenty miles out of Kasanpore while the bridges were being built."

"Bridges?"

"There are two deep gorges about ten miles apart that had to be bridged. The Zastu River flows from the north and then splits into two tributaries that join together about a mile before it reaches Kasanpore. We had to build a bridge before we could lay the track."

"And that's finished?"

"The track across Sikor Gorge has been completed, but we've got another seven miles before we come to the bridge across Lanpur Gorge."

A silence fell between them that lasted until they were a few miles outside the town following the railroad track toward Sikor Gorge.

"What's a running patterer?" Jane asked suddenly. At Ruel's blank look she added, "You said you became one because you weren't good as an acrobat."

"Oh, a running patterer is a street seller who peddles stories. He stands on the street corner and tries to make the stories in the papers he's selling more exciting than the ones the other running patterers are hawking."

"And you were good at that?"

"Not at first, but I learned fast. An empty belly can lend the melody of a nightingale to the voice of a crow."

"Why were you hungry if your brother is an earl?"

His expression became shuttered. "Because I'm not Ian."

Clearly questions on this particular subject were not welcome. "What other work did you do in London?"

"Rat catching." He glanced slyly at her from under his lashes. "Shall I describe my adventures in the sewers?"

She made a face. "That won't be necessary. I had no idea such things went on in London. Not that I know much about it. I was there only a few days before we went to Salisbury, and it seemed a crowded, confusing place."

"Aye, it's that all right. You must just sort out the confusion and make it your own. So you never went back to London?"

"No."

"Why not?"

"There was the railroad to build."

"Apparently there's always a railroad to build."

"Yes," she said simply. "Always."

"Some people would say it's no task for a woman."

She bristled. "Then some people would be fools. Why not? Because I don't have huge, bulging muscles? It takes more than physical strength. It takes care and measuring and knowing when to blow through a mountain and when to go around. It takes making sure every tie and rail is laid safely and well. I can do that as well as a man. Better."

"Easy. I'm not arguing with you." He paused. "And who taught you to do it better?"

"I taught myself. When we got to Salisbury I followed Patrick everywhere and listened and learned."

"And where did you live before you came to Salisbury?"

"Utah." She quickly changed the subject. "The gorge is just around the bend." She reined in and gestured to the bluff ahead. "We'll have to dismount and walk across the ties from here."

"If you can walk without falling down on your face. You're still paler than a tombstone."

"I won't fall down. I told you I was quite well this morning." She got down from the mare. "If you don't think about discomfort, it goes away." She could feel his gaze on her as she unsaddled Bedelia and tied her to a banyan tree in a grove a few yards from the track.

"No, you won't fall down." An odd note in his voice made her glance over her shoulder at him, but his expression was as mocking as ever. "Tell me, does Reilly appreciate what he has in you?"

"Of course."

"But not enough to let you keep a dog you care about in the bungalow?"

"Patrick thinks animals are good only if they perform a function." She rushed defensively on. "Lots of people feel that way about keeping pets. I bet you've never had a pet yourself."

"You'd lose. I did have a pet once."

She looked at him in surprise. "A dog?"

"A fox."

"What a peculiar pet."

He shrugged. "I was a peculiar lad."

"What was his name?"

"I never gave him one."

"Why not?"

"He was my friend. It would have been an imposition. Besides, I had only him. There was no question of getting confused."

"Strange . . ." She started down the track crossing the gorge. "I have an entire crew to protect me a half mile from here. You don't have to come any farther with me."

"Stop trying to get rid of me." He dismounted, unsaddled his horse, and tied him to a tree a short distance away. "There are other threats than Abdar. What if you fell off the bridge?" He glanced down at the narrow yellow-brown ribbon of water trickling through the gorge as he followed over the railway ties. "Well, maybe you wouldn't drown, but the fall could hurt you. Besides, why should I leave? Now that I'm here, I might as well learn a new skill."

"There's no skill needed in laying track," she said dryly. "You only have to have a strong back."

"Oh, I've got a strong back."

A sudden memory of Ruel lying naked on the bed, all sleek tendons and power, came back to her. "I don't doubt it," she muttered.

"Then I assume I'm hired?"

"What about your wound? You have no business working with a hurt shoulder."

"That's what I tried to tell you," he murmured. "The pot calling the kettle? My shoulder's almost healed. I keep the bandage on only because Ian insists."

She met his gaze. "Why are you doing this?"

"You don't believe I want only to keep a benevolent eye on you?"

She frowned, trying to puzzle out his motives. "You're not like your brother."

"I'm cut to the marrow. I must get Ian to have a talk with you. He believes I have a noble soul."

"I don't know anything about souls, but I know you're not what you seem."

"Very perceptive. But then, few of us are what we appear to be. Actually, I'm more honest than most when it doesn't hurt me too grievously." He added softly, "And I do pay my debts, Jane."

"But that's not the only reason you're here, is it?"

For an instant the mockery disappeared from his expression. "No, that's not the only reason, but I have no intention of sharing the others with you. You'll have to take me as you find me."

And she found him a disturbing, glittering enigma. "I don't have to take you at all."

"But you will, won't you," he said, looking steadily into her eyes.

She should reject him. He didn't belong here and she didn't need the distraction of his presence. Yet she was curiously reluctant to say the words that would banish him. In some mysterious fashion he had lent a shimmer and color to the last hours that she had never known before. Perhaps it would do no harm to let him linger for a little longer. "Working in this heat is no pleasure. One day should be enough to make you give it up."

"Oh, no." He smiled. "I never give up a job until something more interesting presents itself."

Chapter 4

He didn't give up.

The only reason her gaze was drawn to him so constantly during the day, Jane assured herself, was her concern for his hurt shoulder. But the wound didn't seem to hamper him, for with every blow of the hammer the muscles of his back and abdomen slid as smoothly as the gears of a locomotive. The rhythmic force with which he struck each wedge-shaped spike sank it deep and true. At the end of the day he was still swinging the huge hammer with the same strength and determination he exhibited when he had started ten hours before.

"You can stop now." She walked over to him. "Didn't you hear Robinson call a halt? The others left five minutes ago."

"I heard him." He swung the hammer and the spike plunged deeper. "But I'm not like the others. I had to prove myself, didn't I?" He tossed the hammer aside. "Do I come back tomorrow?

She gazed at him, baffled. "I can't understand why you'd want to."

"Sometimes I like this kind of work. You don't have to think, you just feel."

He had shed his shirt only minutes after he had accepted the hammer from Robinson. His golden skin now gleamed with a patina of sweat and dust, and his chest was moving harshly with his labored breathing. She felt a tingling in the palms of her hands, and she realized with astonishment that she wanted to reach out and touch him to see if the ridged muscles were as hard as they looked. She quickly clenched her hands into fists and stepped back.

He picked up his shirt from the ground beside the track and slipped it on. "Invite me to your bungalow for dinner."

"What for?"

"I want to meet your Patrick Reilly." He started up the track across Sikor Gorge. "I want to see you together."

She started to put another question to him, but his expression had taken on the shuttered look she was beginning to recognize. "You wouldn't get along. You're not at all alike."

"Invite me."

She hesitated and then said formally, "Will you be so kind as to join us for dinner?"

"Delighted. I'll go to the hotel first and wash off this sweat and be at your bungalow at eight." He shot her a shrewd look. "And don't worry, you won't have to be protective of your friend Reilly. I'm no threat to him."

She had a sudden memory of the bulging eyes of the man lying dead in the alley. Ruel MacClaren might not be a threat to her or Patrick, but there was no doubt he could be extremely dangerous when aroused.

"He deserved it." Ruel's gaze was fixed on her face and she had the uncanny impression he had read her thoughts. "I always return what's given to me, Jane."

"Well, then I have nothing to worry about." She smiled with an effort. "Once you're convinced I'm quite well again, you'll be about your own business." She turned to look at him. "By the way, what is your business?"

"At the moment I'm involved in investing." He laughed at her incredulous expression. "Do I look too rough to be a man of commerce? It's true I'm not comfortable with the business world, but I learned a long time ago everything is forgiven royalty."

"Royalty?"

"With enough money a man can make himself a king."

"Is that what you want to be?"

His eyes twinkled. "Well, perhaps I'd be satisfied with being crown prince as long as I had prospects. Isn't that what everyone wants? It's a hell of a lot better than being crushed under someone else's heels."

She shook her head. "I don't think I'd be comfortable in a life like that. It would be . . . strange."

"You'd rather slave on your railroad?"

"It's not always like this. It's been bad here, but sometimes the work is easier."

"And worthwhile?"

She nodded eagerly. "Oh, yes."

"Why?"

"I can't explain." She thought for a moment. "A train is . . . freedom. You step on a train and it takes you away and lets you leave all the bad things behind."

"And what if the track leads you somewhere that's worse than what you left behind?"

"Then you get off before you get to that somewhere. It gives you a choice."

"And escape." His gaze narrowed on her face. "What are you trying to escape from, Jane?"

"I've already escaped and I'm never going back," she said quietly.

"And your Patrick helped you make your escape?"

She smiled. "Yes, Patrick helped me."

"Another whiskey, Mr. MacClaren?" Patrick asked.

"I don't believe so, thank you."

"I believe I'll have a dollop." Patrick poured the last of the whiskey in the bottle into his glass. "I know they're putting less in these bottles. I think that servant at the club is shortchanging me. You know you can't trust these Indians, MacClaren."

"Has that been your experience?" Ruel asked politely.

"Sula!" Patrick called. "Where is that woman? Jane, run to the kitchen and tell her we need another bottle."

"I took the last one from the kitchen cabinet last night," Jane said.

Patrick scowled. "She's probably been selling the liquor to someone in the bazaar. It was never like this when Li Sung was handling my whiskey. I want you to get him back here where he belongs, Jane."

Jane looked quickly down at her plate. "I told you I needed Li Sung in Narinth."

"This is the Li Sung you mentioned to me?" Ruel asked.

She glanced up to see his gaze narrowed on her face and anger flared through her. It wasn't enough that Patrick was under that merciless scrutiny all evening. Now it seemed it was her turn. "Yes, Li Sung works for us."

"Good man for a chink. Not like these cheating Indians." Patrick rose to his feet and weaved toward the door leading to the veranda. "Be right back, MacClaren. I think I left a full bottle on the table on the veranda."

"Pleasant fellow," Ruel commented as Patrick disappeared from view.

Jane whirled fiercely on him. "Why don't you leave?"

Ruel's brows rose. "Have I done something to offend you?"

"You sat there all through dinner and watched him, taking him apart with—" She stopped and drew a deep breath. "You watched both of us. I didn't like it."

"I like watching you." He smiled slightly. "I thought I knew everything about you, but I'm finding out new things all the time."

"You don't know me at all and you have no business judging Patrick when you know nothing about him."

"You wound me." His blue eyes gleamed in the lamplight. "And I thought I was being both charming and informative. I'm sure Reilly thought so. Providing he could think at all through that haze of spirits surrounding him. Is he always drunk by the time you come home from laboring on his behalf?"

"It's the heat."

"Indeed?" He rose to his feet and placed his napkin on the table. "Since I seem to have overstayed my welcome, I will take my leave." He bowed slightly. "Thank you for dinner. I trust the presence of this Sula assures you don't have to act as a kitchen skivvy as well as day laborer?"

Her hands clenched into fists beneath the table. "Good night."

Abruptly the mockery vanished from his expression. "For God's sake, go to bed," he said roughly. "You're dead tired and he won't miss you. I'll see you tomorrow on the site."

"You're coming back?"

"Oh, yes, I found it a most interesting experience." He moved toward the door. "It's always intriguing learning new things. That's why I had such an enjoyable dinner."

"And what new things did you learn here tonight?" she asked warily.

He slanted her a glance over his shoulder. "That you're incredibly loyal and genuinely willing to work yourself to exhaustion for that likable sot."

"He's not a sot. I told you—"

"It's the heat," he finished. "I've met any number of men out here who blame their self-indulgence on the weather. The heat makes them thirsty, the monsoons make them depressed, and the sandstorms give them headaches. But I'm not really interested in Patrick Reilly now that I've found out what I want to know about him."

"And what," she asked scathingly, "would that be?"

He met her gaze. "That whatever lies between you, the rumors are wrong. He doesn't share your bed."

"Well?" Ian asked as Ruel walked into his hotel room an hour later. "Was your day productive?"

"Productive enough." Ruel stripped off his coat and shirt and strode across the room toward the washstand. "I met Patrick Reilly."

"And?"

"He's not involved with Kartauk. I'd judge he isn't involved with anything but his bottle."

"Poor lass."

"She wouldn't appreciate your sympathy." He poured water into the bowl and began splashing his face. "And anyone who can take on Abdar is too strong to deserve it."

"I still feel sorry for her. She reminds me a little of Margaret."

"Our pure and proper Maggie would not be pleased at the comparison with a woman who frequents brothels and struts around wearing men's clothes." He grabbed a towel and dried his face. "Believe me, they're nothing alike."

"You never really knew Margaret." Ian smiled. "And I don't believe you know that child."

"I'll know her soon." He cast him a glance over his shoulder. "And Kartauk." He began unbuckling his belt. "This Li Sung she mentioned is supposedly in Narinth. Why don't you take a ride tomorrow and see if he's really there?"

"You think he has something to do with Kartauk?"

"Maybe. I know she lied about where he is." He threw his belt on the chair and began unbuttoning his trousers. "She doesn't lie well."

"Which means she's an honest lass."

"Suppose you get out of here so I can get some sleep?"

"You're going to work on the track tomorrow too?"

"As long as it takes." He began to strip off his trousers. "Good night, Ian."

"I get the feeling I'm being dismissed." Ian rose leisurely to his feet and moved toward the door. "If I can help with anything else, let me know."

"You'd help me deceive that 'poor child'?" Ruel asked mockingly.

"You won't deceive her. You're a decent man and you're already softening toward the lass," Ian said tranquilly. "But the sooner we get this Kartauk business out of your system, the sooner we can go home."

"I'm not soft—" Ruel stopped in midsentence as Ian closed the door behind him.

Five minutes later Ruel blew out the oil lamp on the nightstand beside the bed and lay back, staring into the darkness. He should be tired but he was too tense to sleep, and Ian's words hadn't put him in any more gentle mood.

He was *not* softening toward Jane Barnaby, dammit. The fact that he had a debt to pay complicated matters, but he still had every intention of using her to find Kartauk. After he had accomplished his aim, he would make the decision whether to turn Kartauk over to Abdar or kill the bastard himself and—

Kill Kartauk? The violence of the thought had come out of nowhere. He didn't even know John Kartauk and certainly had no reason to kill him.

But he knew Jane Barnaby cared enough about the son of a bitch to risk her life for him.

And he knew enough to know she had probably taken him for her lover.

The fury the thought brought sent a shock through him.

Lust. Not casual lust but obsessive, overwhelming desire for possession. He had allowed himself to fall into the trap of becoming intrigued and admiring even before his body had responded to her at Zabrie's. Now it was all tied together in some twisted, painful fashion.

He had to rid himself of emotion and think coldly and clearly. There was no reason to let this feeling he had for Jane interfere with his pursuit of Cinnidar. He must keep the two goals entirely separate and find a way to accomplish both of them. She had shown a response to him at Zabrie's, and he would play on that response. He was not unskilled, and if he could show her more pleasure in bed than Kartauk, perhaps—

Jane in bed with Kartauk, writhing beneath him as he plunged in and out of her body . . .

Rage tore through him. His hands clenched into fists at his sides. God, what was happening to him? He had never felt jealousy over any woman. Passion had always been a pleasant game to be indulged and then forgotten. Yet now he was in a fever over the thought of a faceless stranger plundering the body of a woman he had never even possessed.

Perhaps he *would* kill the bastard.

"Colonel Pickering told Ian the maharajah's private railway car is supposed to be quite something to see," Ruel said casually as he helped Jane onto Bedelia. "Will you show it to me?"

She looked at him in surprise. She was nearly stumbling with weariness, and she had not been pounding spikes all day as Ruel had done. Yet he appeared as tough and energetic as when he had started work that morning. "Now? Aren't you tired?"

"I've been more tired." His eyes twinkled as he mounted his horse. "As someone recently told me, if you don't think about it, it goes away. Will you show me the car? The new station is on the way to the bungalow, isn't it?"

"Yes, there are two cars at the station. One is the

maharajah's private car and the other is a passenger car for his guests."

"But it's the private car that has the golden door?"

Her gaze flew to his face. "You've heard about the door?"

"I'd have to be deaf not to have heard about the door that's the talk of Kasanpore. You don't run across golden doors every day."

"I guess not." She hesitated. "Wouldn't you rather wait? I received word last night the locomotive is on its way downriver and should be delivered tomorrow afternoon. You could see them both."

"The locomotive doesn't interest me." He raised a brow. "Unless it has a golden boiler?"

She laughed. "No, though we made sure it has plenty of flash." She paused. "The maharajah will be there and has invited practically everyone in Kasanpore to see it."

"That changes the situation. Will you be able to introduce me to the maharajah?"

She shook her head. "I can't risk annoying him. He's not going to want to concentrate on anything but his new locomotive."

"Too bad. Then I'd rather see the door now, when I have leisure to study it. I have a great fondness for gold in any shape or form."

"I know someone else who feels the same way." Her smile faded. "Actually, I know two people who—" She kicked her horse, and the mare sprang forward. "If you want to see it, let's hurry and get it over with."

The sun had almost gone down by the time they came within sight of the station, but the last weak rays caught the brightly burnished brass adorning the two scarlet railway cars and set them ablaze.

"The maharajah is clearly not a retiring man," Ruel said as he reined in before the station and dismounted. "I imagine all that brass is fairly blinding in full sunlight."

"Yes." She got off Bedelia and followed him across the platform toward the cars. "As I said, he likes a bit of flash."

"And where is this famous golden door?"

She gestured toward the second car.

He moved quickly past the first car and up the four metal steps of the second car. "The sun's almost gone down. I can't see it properly. . . ." He took down the lantern hanging on the hook beside the door, lit it, and held it high. He gazed at the door in silence for a moment. "Magnificent."

"It's supposed to represent the Garden of Paradise. The door itself is bronze that's been heavily gilded with gold." She frowned. "But it still cost us far too much money."

The blasted door had caused her a mountain of trouble as well as money, and lately she had not been able to look at it with the appreciation it deserved. Now she found herself seeing it through Ruel's eyes.

Two flowering trees framed either side of the door on which intricately carved tropical blossoms draped the branches and burst in luxuriant profusion over the entire golden surface. Through the screen of flowers glimpses could be caught of a tiger and gazelle romping playfully together before a sari-clothed woman. The woman was gazing at herself in a hand mirror and completely ignoring the beasts.

"The workmanship is superb. Who did it?"

"Just a local craftsman." She asked quickly, "Have you seen enough?"

"No." His gaze suddenly focused on the bole of the tree on the left side of the door. "What's this?" He started to laugh. "Good God, it's a serpent."

She had hoped he wouldn't notice the serpent coiled around the bole of the tree. "Isn't there always a serpent in paradise?"

"So I've heard." He smiled curiously. "But never one this cleverly presented."

His absorption in the snake made her uneasy, and she tried to distract him. "I thought the tiger was done quite beautifully."

"Very nice." His gaze was still on the serpent. "An exquisite abomination," he murmured.

"What?"

"Nothing." To her relief, his stare finally left the serpent and shifted to her face. "May I see inside the car?"

"Of course." She quickly pulled out the ring of keys from her pocket, then hesitated as she remembered what lay beyond that door. "There's nothing unusual about the furnishings. Haven't you seen enough?"

He studied her. "What's in there that you don't want me to see?"

"I'm tired and hungry." She gestured impatiently. "You wished to see the door and you've seen it. This is a waste of time."

"Why?" he asked again.

"Oh, for heaven's sake." She unlocked the heavy door and flung it open. "Look, if you like. I don't care."

"Thank you, I shall." He entered the car. "Coming?"

"I've seen it all before." When he merely stood looking at her, she moved reluctantly forward to stand beside him. "Hurry."

"Oh yes, I remember, you're hungry." He lifted the lantern and glanced around the car. The light played over crimson-velvet-cushioned divans, polished teakwood tables, tasseled curtains draping mother-of-pearl inlaid windowsills. He lifted the lantern higher, and his gaze fell on the eight pictures gracing the walls. He whistled long and low. "I think I'm beginning to develop an appetite myself."

"They were the maharajah's choice," she said quickly. "He had the paintings brought from the palace."

"The concubine quarters, no doubt. Kama Sutra . . ."

"Kama what?"

He stepped closer, examining the painting directly in front of him. "These are really quite well done. Zabrie showed me some paintings in a book, but they were all concerned more with inciting than depicting emotion. Notice the tender expression on the man's face?" He raised the lantern nearer to the painting. "And the texture of the woman's buttocks looks as smooth and plump as peach halves. This position is fairly pleasurable if the angle is done right. . . ."

She found she wasn't looking at the painting but at the play of light on the finely molded line of his cheekbones. Though they weren't touching, she could feel the heat of his body and was acutely aware of the earthy fragrance of salt, soap, and sweat surrounding him. She was finding it hard to breathe. The intimacy of the car seemed to be smothering her, weakening her. "Shall we go now?"

He glanced curiously at her. "Are you blushing? I wouldn't think a woman who frequents Zabrie's would find anything shocking in these paintings."

"I'm *not* blushing." She knew the heat in her cheeks belied the words and deliberately made her tone brusque. "I don't find them shocking, merely unbelievable. Men don't . . . There's no gentleness. It's not like that picture."

His gaze narrowed on her face. "No? What is it like?"

"Hard and fast," she said baldly.

He chuckled. "I can't deny it's hard. You should—"

"I don't want to talk about it."

"Why not? I'm finding the discussion fascinating. Tell me more."

"You're making fun of me."

"Perhaps. Your experience must be somewhat limited."

"You're wrong," she said fiercely. "I spent the first twelve years of my life in a whorehouse. I know all about—" She stopped abruptly. Then she turned on her heel and strode toward the door. "I've had enough of this nonsense."

"A whorehouse?" The strange thickness in his voice caused her to glance at him over her shoulder. All humor had disappeared from his expression and he was tensed, arched like a cat about to spring. "Is that where Reilly found you?"

"Yes."

"It seems I misjudged him. I wouldn't have guessed his tastes run to children. I'm beginning to find the sot not quite so tolerable."

"It wasn't like that— I have to get back to the bungalow."

"That's right, you mustn't be late." Stinging ferocity underlay the silken tone, and his light eyes glittered through half-closed lids. "I'm sure your Patrick is desolate if you keep him waiting for even a moment."

"Be quiet!" Her hands clenched into fists. "Patrick may not always be sober, but he doesn't mock or try to hurt people. He's not cruel like you are." She turned and threw open the door.

"Jane!" He muttered a curse and was suddenly beside her, his hand grasping her arm.

She tried to pry his fingers from her arm. "*Damn* you, let me go."

He immediately released her and held up his hands. "See, I'm not touching you. Now may I say something?"

She glared at him.

"I admit I did try to hurt you. I felt the flick of the whip and instinctively struck back."

"I wasn't striking out at you. I don't even know what you're talking about."

"I'm trying to apologize." He grimaced. "And obviously doing it very badly. I suppose that's to be expected since I can't remember the last time I so humbled myself. God knows, we all have to do what we must to survive. I had no right to judge you. Will you forgive me?"

She felt her anger ebbing away. "You're a strange man."

"Without doubt." He took a step back and gestured for her to precede him. "Go on. I'm feeling a little savage at the moment and it would be better if you weren't around me. I'll see you in the morning."

"Is there any point in suggesting once again that you give up on laying track for the railroad?" she asked haltingly.

"None." He didn't look at her as he moved past her

and down the steps to the platform. "It's too late for that. We have to get on with it and finish it."

"On with what?"

"I used to know," he said harshly. "Now I'm not so sure anymore."

A moment later he had mounted his horse and trotted off toward town.

"Li Sung isn't in Narinth," Ian said. "He hasn't been there since he visited the town some two months ago with Jane Barnaby."

"Then the next question we ask is why she lied?" Ruel murmured. "And where the gentleman is at present."

"And why you've had three whiskeys in a row since you walked in the door," Ian added mildly.

"I was thirsty." He smiled recklessly. "And it's good Scotch Whiskey. You should approve. Isn't everything even remotely touching on Glenclaren worthwhile?" He threw himself in the chair. "Wonderful, splendid Glenclaren. Tell me, have you heard from Maggie lately?"

"You know I have not."

Ruel lifted his glass to his lips. "No doubt she's still nursing her father and being the dutiful daughter. As I remember, MacDonald made Maggie's life hell on earth. I always thought he was malingering just to tie Maggie to his bedposts and keep her slaving."

"So did I. He has no liking for the idea of giving Margaret to a man with little means."

"Haven't you ever been tempted to push the old bastard over the edge?"

"Frequently."

"And?"

"It's a mortal sin. We can wait."

"Shall I do it for you?"

Ian's eyes widened.

"Shall I?" Ruel repeated.

"You're joking."

"Am I?" Ruel wondered himself if he had made the

offer only to shock Ian or if he actually meant it. He was in a mood for violence, and MacDonald's nagging, torturous enslavement of his daughter seemed to him to be far worse than the mortal sin of which his brother spoke. "How do you know?"

"I know you."

"Not anymore."

"It's only the liquor speaking." Ian shifted his shoulders uneasily. "Now, stop talking nonsense."

"As you like." Ruel took another drink. "Tell me if you change your mind."

"Why are you like this tonight?"

"Like what?"

"Wild."

"It's the nature of the beast."

Ian shook his head. "You're on edge. Why?"

"I'm not on—" Why deny it when Ian wouldn't believe him anyway? He had hoped the liquor would dull the sharpness of the jealousy, anger, and pity Jane's words had aroused and had not lessened since he left her. He wanted to strangle—who, for God's sake? Patrick, Kartauk, those men who had made her childhood a nightmare? Oh, what the hell. He poured another drink. "I saw the gold door tonight."

"And?"

"It's a splendid depiction of the Garden of Paradise . . . with Abdar's face as the head of the serpent."

"What? Are you sure?"

"It's very subtly done, but you can't miss the resemblance."

"An exquisite abomination." Ian chuckled. "I believe I'm beginning to like this Kartauk. The man has a sense of humor."

Ruel's reaction had been the same, and he had been fighting it since the instant he had seen that devilishly sly serpent. "The maharajah must not be overly fond of his son if he permitted that particular bit of humor."

"That was Colonel Pickering's opinion, if you remember."

"They're delivering the locomotive to the station tomorrow, and Jane said the maharajah will be there. Why don't you go down with the colonel and see if you can't get an introduction?"

"An excellent idea. You're giving up looking for Kartauk?"

"I didn't say that, but it's always wise to explore every avenue." He started toward the door, taking his glass with him. "Though, from what I saw of his taste in art in his car tonight, I sincerely doubt if the maharajah and you will have much in common."

"This must be a great day for you."

Jane turned to see Ian MacClaren standing a few feet away and felt her spirits rise as she saw his warm smile. "Good afternoon, Lord MacClaren."

"Ian." He took a step closer, his tall figure blocking out the crowd of chattering men and women milling around the small station house. "What are you doing hiding in here? I would have thought you'd want to be out on the platform, basking in the maharajah's approval."

"I did my part by supervising the transfer of the locomotive from the boat." Her glance went to Patrick, who was standing on the platform beside the maharajah and gesturing to the brass cowcatcher on the front of the locomotive. "Patrick's better at this kind of thing than I am. Is Ruel with you?"

"No, he's laboring on your behalf at the site. I came with Colonel Pickering." Ian nodded at a big man with steel-gray hair and an impressive array of medals decorating his uniformed chest. "Have you met him?"

"No, but Patrick has mentioned him. He's been very helpful using his influence with the maharajah."

"That's what Ruel hoped would happen today, but I don't believe we're going to have any luck." He smiled. "Getting that behemoth of a locomotive here must have been no easy task. You deserve a reward. Come with me to the buffet table and let me get you a glass of fruit juice."

"No!" She took an involuntary step back. "I mean, I'm not thirsty."

"In this heat? You have to be thirsty." Ian took her gently by the elbow. "Come along and we'll . . ."

"No." She jerked her arm away. "I said I wasn't thirsty." He was staring at her with such bewilderment she finally said, "Can't you see? I don't belong there. They all look at me as if I were some strange creature." She lifted her chin. "Not that I care."

His gaze went over the loose shirt and denim trousers she wore. "You appear neat and clean. I'd be honored to escort you."

"Cleanliness isn't enough. They can see I'm different." She turned on her heel. "I can't waste any more time here. I have work to do. Good day, Lord MacClaren."

"Ian," he said again. "I don't believe formality is appropriate when I've given you the shirt off my back."

She looked at him, stricken. "Oh, dear, I forgot. I meant to return it. I'm sorry, Lord—" She stopped as she met his gaze. "Ian. I'll give the shirt to Ruel tomorrow to return to you."

"No hurry." He fell into step with her as she left the station house, effortlessly cleaving a path for her through the crowd on the platform. "You're not going to the site today?"

She shook her head. "It's too late now. It would be sundown by the time I reached the gorge. I'm going to the supply yard and check to make sure a shipment of rails came in with the locomotive."

"Then permit me to escort you." He made a face. "I'm clearly not going to be able to arrange an introduction to the maharajah in this mob, and I may not be as ferocious as my brother, but my sheer size sometimes deters aggressors."

"I don't need protection." She paused. "And I'm not certain Ruel's purpose is really to protect me. Sometimes he reminds me of a great cat ready to pounce."

"Tiger pad softly, tiger burn bright," he murmured.

"I beg your pardon?"

"It's a line from an old Scottish poem. It rather suits Ruel, don't you think?"

"Yes." She smiled. "A Scottish poem? I didn't think there were any tigers in Scotland."

"We have our share of the two-legged variety. My illustrious ancestor, Alexander MacClaren, was one of that ilk. The rascal could have given Ruel lessons." Ian glanced at her soberly. "And I believe you're wrong. I'm sure Ruel does wish to protect you. Even if he doesn't realize it himself."

"I've never met anyone who appears to know more what he's doing than your brother," she said dryly.

"He's had a hard life. It gets in his way sometimes, and he can't always see himself clearly."

"But you do see him for what he is?"

"Oh, yes, I've always known."

"And what is he?"

"A giant," he said simply.

"What?"

"He's one of the heroes of the world. I've always believed the world is gifted with a small number of heroes in every generation. Men who are capable of tremendous acts of self-sacrifice. Men who have the strength and boldness to take life by the horns and conquer it. Ruel is a hero. But he refuses to accept his fate."

She chuckled. "And are you also a hero?"

"Oh, no, I'm very boring. I just plod along, doing my duty and trying to live a good life."

"I don't believe that's boring," she said gently.

"You're very kind." He grimaced. "But I'm a dull fellow. It's a wonder Margaret even looked at me."

"Margaret?"

"Margaret MacDonald. We're affianced."

"Then she's very fortunate."

"I'm the one who is fortunate." His smile made his homely face almost handsome. "As you'd know if you met her. She's a remarkable lass. I told Ruel you reminded me a little of my Margaret."

"Me?" She looked at him in astonishment before shaking her head. "No, I couldn't be like her."

"Why not?"

"Because I'm not . . ." She waved a hand at the station house. "Because you're a lord and she's probably like them."

"In what way?"

"I don't know." She thought about it. "Gowns with bustles and lace at her throat . . . soft hands. She wouldn't like me. I'm different."

He burst out laughing. "That's not Margaret. And God made us all different. You mustn't be ashamed of what you are."

"I'm not ashamed." She could see he didn't understand. "I'm proud of what I am. None of those women could do what I do and not many men either. It's just wiser not to force myself in where I'm not wanted."

"Because you meet cruelty and intolerance when you do?" he asked quietly.

She nodded jerkily. "And your Margaret would be the same."

"You're wrong. Ask Ruel. Ruel was always considered an outcast, and she never treated him with anything but fairness."

"Why was Ruel—" No, she didn't want to know any more about Ruel than she did already. She had spent an uneasy night after he had left her yesterday evening, and he was occupying far too much of her thoughts. She smiled with an effort. "Then I must be wrong and your Margaret everything you say she is." They had arrived at the supply yard and she pulled out her key ring. "Thank you for accompanying me. I won't keep you any longer. I know you want to get back to the other guests."

"It was my pleasure. I find your 'difference' far more interesting than their 'sameness.' "

Warmth surged through her as she realized there was no mockery in his tone. He was not like Ruel, whose every word must be examined and weighed for hidden meaning. "You have unusual tastes." She unlocked the gate. "I'm sure you—"

"Do you always keep your supply yard locked?"

"Yes."

"Why?" he asked curiously. "I wouldn't think anyone would dare steal anything from a project for the maharajah."

She quickly glanced away. "I suppose I became accustomed to guarding our supplies in England."

"I see." He bowed slightly. "Well, I'm sure you do it very well. Margaret believes in guarding her own too."

She gave him a tentative smile as she opened the gate and strode swiftly into the supply yard.

"You're right, she doesn't lie well," Ian said slowly.

Ruel shot him a glance as he turned away from the washstand. "Something happened today at the station?"

"Not exactly."

"Ian."

"She feels very much alone, you know."

"We're all alone."

"She thinks she's different from other women."

"She is different."

"No . . . I believe she's been hurt a good deal."

"Are you going to tell me what happened today?"

Ian didn't answer for a moment, and then said reluctantly, "The supply yard. She keeps it locked at all times and I don't think it's because of thieves."

"You think Kartauk—"

"I didn't say that. She just seemed uncomfortable when I mentioned her locking the gate." He grimaced. "I didn't want to tell you. I feel as if I've betrayed her."

Ruel frowned thoughtfully. "Kartauk can't be there. It would be taking too much risk when rails have to be moved from the yard to the site every few days."

"Good," Ian said, relieved. "Then I must be wrong."

"Perhaps. Watch the yard for a few evenings to make sure."

"I'm not comfortable with this, Ruel."

"I know." Ruel smiled. "You're afraid your soul is going to be damned to perdition."

He shook his head. "I'm afraid I'm going to hurt the lass."

Ruel's smile faded. "We're not going to hurt her, only find Kartauk."

"It may be the same thing."

He stripped off his shirt. "Get out of here. I have to get some sleep."

Ian rose to his feet with a sigh. "I'll watch the yard, but I hope I'm wrong." He moved toward the door. "And I believe you do too."

"The hell I do."

Ian smiled and left the room.

Ruel muttered a curse as he stared at the closed door. He wouldn't give up searching for Kartauk because of some idiotic twinges of conscience, nor would it stop him from taking what he wanted from Jane. Christ, if he'd had any sense, he would have eased this blasted lust in the railway car yesterday. He couldn't go on like this much longer, heavy and hurting whenever he was with her.

Why the hell shouldn't he take what he wanted? He was no saint like Ian. Dammit, he was through waiting and biding his time.

"Where are the rails?" Jane demanded of Patrick when he walked into the bungalow that evening.

"I think the maharajah was pleased, don't you?" Patrick strolled over to the cabinet and poured himself a drink. "He was preening like a peacock over those brass lanterns."

"The rails were supposed to be delivered with the locomotive. Where are they?"

"I had to delay the shipment until I could arrange another loan from the bank." He took a long drink. "God, it was hot out there in the sun."

"I need those rails."

"And we'll get them. In three days. I took care of everything."

"I thought you told me the bank wouldn't give us any more credit."

He scowled. "I told you, I took care of it. Now, go see if that lazy Sula's bothered to make us any dinner."

He wanted to put an end to her questions, but she couldn't permit it this time. "We'll be at Lanpur Gorge in a week. I'll need those rails."

"You'll have them." He dropped down on the easy chair and closed his eyes. "Trust me."

She had no choice. She would have to trust him, she realized with frustration. "I'll tell Sula we're ready to eat."

She turned and walked away from him. God in heaven, sometimes she didn't think she could go on. She was weary of fighting these constant battles with Patrick and the maharajah, and now Ruel MacClaren had appeared on the scene to disturb and perplex her. She quickly shied away from the thought of Ruel. She had enough problems without remembering the expression on his face as he had looked up at that blasted painting.

She noticed a subtle difference in Ruel at the site the next day. He scarcely looked at her and betrayed no hint of the sensuality he had exhibited in the railway car, and yet there was something . . .

The first time he spoke was when they were walking back to their horses at sundown. "You've been nervous all day. Would you like to tell me why?"

"I'm not nervous. I just have work to do. You may have time to indulge your whims, but this railroad is no joke to me."

"Stop attacking and tell me what's wrong. I may be able to help."

"You can't help."

"How do you know? I'm a very resourceful fellow. I find answers to most questions."

She whirled on him. "Can you stop the monsoons from starting next week?" she asked fiercely. "Can you find me a hundred workers willing to work free? Can you keep the maharajah from plaguing me with demands to get the blasted railroad completed? Can you—"

"No, I can't do any of those things," he broke in. "And neither can you, so why not accept it and tell the maharajah he's not going to have his railroad completed on time?"

"Because he won't pay us, dammit." She smiled bitterly. "He, too, indulges in whims. If we don't perform to his satisfaction, he could ruin us."

"Don't you have a contract?"

She nodded. "But it's not worth anything in Kasanpore. We're helpless to enforce any contract against the maharajah."

"Then why did you take the job?"

"Patrick thought it was—" She untied the mare and mounted. "Why should I bother to answer your questions? You don't care about my problems. I don't even know why you come back here every day."

"Do you really want to know why I labor so devotedly at your side?"

"I've asked you often enough."

"I'll give you one reason." He paused and then said deliberately, "I plan on trying that position we saw in the painting in the railway car with you."

Her gaze flew to his face. His expression was impassive, his tone so casual she wasn't sure she had heard correctly. "*What?*"

"Oh, yes, it's become something of an obsession with me in the past few days. I think about it all the time. How I'd position you on your hands and knees, how I'd cup your breasts in my hands. How I'd slowly slide in and feel you tighten around me." His voice hoarsened. "How I'd start easy and then push harder, deeper, how I'd make you scream when I—"

"Stop! I don't want to hear this," she interrupted, moistening her lips. "Go back to Zabrie if you need a woman."

"I don't want a woman." He paused. "I want you."

"One woman is as good as another for what you want."

"That's what I used to think. I've changed my mind."

"Well, change it back again. I don't want . . . that."

"I could make you want it. I believe you discovered at Zabrie's that we were very compatible." His gaze suddenly shifted to her face. "Perhaps too compatible. Did I frighten you?"

"You?" She tried to make her tone scoffing. "You've never frightened me."

"Perhaps not in the usual way, but then, you're not the usual woman. You're used to your independence. Are you afraid you might not be able to control me?"

"I don't think about you at all. I don't have time for wondering about such foolishness."

"We often respond without thinking in this kind of situation."

"Not you. You're always thinking and plotting and planning." She added grimly, "And you have the arrogance to believe you know everything about me."

"Not everything. I find out new things every day. I've also discovered the longer I study you, the more disturbed I'm becoming. That's why I've finally decided I have to do something about it." He smiled recklessly. "Shall I tell you what?"

"I thought you'd already told me."

"Oh, that's only the beginning."

"Zabrie," she said desperately.

"Jane," he said softly. "Only Jane."

"You're not listening to me." Her hands clenched on the reins. "I want you to go away. I should never have let you start work on the line to begin with."

"Why did you?"

"You were amusing." Having Ruel near had been more than amusing. It had been like staring in fascination into the glittering depths of a magician's crystal ball waiting breathlessly to see what new vision would appear. She felt an odd wrenching pang at the knowledge that that excitement was about to end. She would get over it, she quickly assured herself. The emotion he made her feel was too intense, the fascination too dangerous.

"I won't be used by you, Ruel."

"Yes, you will. We're going to use each other and enjoy every minute of it." He saw her start to protest and held up his hand. "And there's no way I'm going to rush when I finally have you. You won't find me 'fast,' Jane."

The raw words evoked a picture of Ruel lying naked on the bed at Zabrie's, his foot rubbing lazily back and forth, testing the textures of the sheet. Her chest felt suddenly tight, her breath constricted. "I won't enjoy any—"

"Dammit, you *will.*" His coolness was suddenly gone, his blue eyes blazing at her. "I won't be made to feel I'm brutalizing you. I'm not one of those men in that stew where you grew up and I'm not a stranger in a darkened room, waiting to give you what you need and be dismissed. I'm Ruel MacClaren, and you'll know who I am every minute I'm with you."

Another picture—tanned muscular legs braced against the white counterpane as he pushed slowly forward . . .

She felt the heat sting her cheeks. "I don't want to talk about this."

"Then we won't talk about it." He looked straight ahead, and his words came hard and fast. "But I'll be thinking about it and so will you. You'll know I want you so badly I hurt most of the day. You'll know every single time I position a spike I'm thinking about you. Every time I give it that first gentle tap to get it started I'm thinking about coming into you. Every time I swing that hammer I'll think of it as a thrust sinking deep and warm inside you." His voice thickened. "And I'll hit each stroke with every bit of my strength and power because I want to go very, very deep." He kicked his horse into a gallop that sent it springing ahead of her. "You might keep that in mind, Jane."

The spike bit deep into the wood.

Jane felt a shock go through her body. It was the vibration of the pounding of the hammer against wood, she told herself. She had felt it a thousand times before, so many times she had ceased to notice it.

Dear God, but she was noticing it now. Her breasts were swelling against her loose shirt, the nipples achingly sensitive as they touched the cloth.

Ruel swung the hammer again. The muscles of his arms rippled, gleamed gold in the sunlight.

The spike sank deeper.

The muscles of her stomach clenched.

The hammer exploded against the head of the spike.

What was happening to her? She was burning up, the blood pounding beneath the skin.

Heat. It had to be the strong sun that was causing this reaction.

She tore her gaze away from Ruel and strode quickly toward the water bearer.

She shook her head as he extended the dipper and cupped her hands. An instant later she was splashing the cool water over her face and cheeks and then over her nape and throat. That was better. She had been right, it had been the sun, not Ruel who had caused the unusual heat.

Not Ruel . . .

He had stopped work and was staring at her, his legs slightly astride, the huge hammer held balanced in both hands, his gaze on her throat. She was suddenly conscious of the drop of water gliding slowly down her throat, beneath her shirt and over her upper breasts.

Cold liquid against hot flesh.

Searing blue eyes watching her.

The drop of water reached her nipples, pooled, darkening the light-blue chambray and delineating her engorged nipple.

Ruel's tongue moistened his lower lip.

A shudder went through her.

He smiled and his gaze went deliberately to his lower body.

Stark, heavy arousal.

He swung the hammer again.

The spike dug deeper into the wood.

• • •

"You didn't wait for me yesterday," he said softly. "How can I protect you if you run away from me?"

"How many times do I have to tell you I don't need you to protect me." She didn't look at him as she moved quickly over the ties of Sikor Gorge. "And I wasn't running away."

She could feel him staring at her and her breasts tautened, responding mindlessly as they had when she had watched him wield the hammer.

"Why are you fighting it? It will be easier once you let me have you."

"Be quiet," she said jerkily.

"You'll like it." His voice thickened. "And God knows we both need it. I think I'm going crazy."

Her pace quickened until it was almost a run, her boots stumbling on the ties.

He muttered a curse. "Be careful, dammit," he called after her. "Do you want to stumble into the gorge?"

"No, you wouldn't want me to do that, would you?" she said through her teeth. "A crippled woman would be of no use to you."

He suddenly chuckled. "It would hinder things a bit, but we could make a few adjustments and make it work for us. Shall I tell you how?"

"No!" She ran the last few feet to the end of the gorge to the banyan grove where Bedelia was tied. She glanced over her shoulder, but he was still strolling across the gorge, making no attempt to pursue her. She hastily saddled the mare. "If you come tomorrow, I'll tell Robinson to throw you off the site."

"No, you won't. Because I'd become annoyed and that would mean you'd have to do without an overseer." He smiled. "Did I ever mention how nasty I am when I'm annoyed?"

Dead eyes staring sightlessly in the darkness of the alley.

"You'll have to solve the problem yourself," he said softly. "It's so easy. Why are you making it difficult?"

Sunlight shimmered on the tawny streaks in his hair,

and he seemed bathed in light as he moved lithely toward her. She stared, as helpless to keep her eyes off him as she had been all day as he swung that damned hammer.

"No!" She finally managed to tear her gaze away, mounted, and kicked Bedelia into a trot and then, desperately, into a full gallop.

"I believe Li Sung came to the supply yard tonight," Ian said.

Ruel stiffened and turned to look at him. "You're sure?"

"Fairly sure. He had a key. Jane came to the supply yard early this evening carrying a knapsack and left without it. A Chinese man with a limp came two hours later and picked up the knapsack. I followed him but lost him in the bazaar."

"On purpose?" Ruel asked sardonically.

"God works in mysterious ways."

"Convenient ways also."

"Shall I continue to watch the yard?"

Ruel hesitated. "Not now. We know what we need to know. The rest can wait."

"That's not at all like you. You're usually more impatient."

Impatient? Christ, he was so impatient and on edge, he felt like a volcano about to erupt.

But his impatience had nothing to do with Kartauk.

Chapter 5

The rains started early in the morning two days later.

The skies opened and a deluge poured from the heavens. The rain was like everything else in this blasted country, Jane thought with frustration—heavy, warm, and near impossible to fight. During the first few hours she actually welcomed the struggle against the elements because, for the first time in days, she was able to ignore Ruel's presence and concentrate on the task at hand.

By noon the water had pooled on either side of the track and the workers were slipping and sliding with every step. By three o'clock the sheets of rain were falling so hard and fast, it became difficult for the workers to even see the heads of the spikes they were hammering. At four o'clock Jane called a halt and told everyone to go home and come back at dawn tomorrow.

"It's about time," Ruel muttered as he threw his hammer into the tarpaulin-covered wheelbarrow beside the tracks. "I thought you were going to wait until we drowned in this muck."

"Don't come back if you don't like it," she said fiercely. "No one asked you to stay. I'm not going to let the rain stop us. I have fifteen more miles to go before the rails are joined, and we'll be here every day until the job's finished."

"Or you're finished." Ruel stood looking at her, rain dripping off the brim of his hat and running down his cheeks. "You're barely able to stand on your feet."

"I'm fine. You're the one who's complaining." She moved toward the bridge over the gorge. "Perhaps you'd better not come back tomorrow."

"You don't get rid of me that easily." He suddenly smiled. "I don't like this damn weather, but I can get used to it."

The demon could probably get used to burning in hell, she thought despairingly. Dear God, it was happening again. He had only to look at her in that certain way and her body began readying, ripening. "Why bother? It can't be worth it to you."

"It's worth it."

She could feel his gaze on her back as she walked quickly over the bridge. The river was no longer a sickly trickle but a muddy torrent racing through the gorge. The supports were holding firm, she noticed with relief. That's right, think about the railroad. Forget about how Ruel had looked standing in the rain with his shirt clinging to the ridged muscles of his chest and belly. Think about her weariness and discouragement, not about this strange, aching emptiness between her thighs.

"Why not wait until the monsoons are over?" Ruel

asked quietly. "You can't make much progress in this rain."

"We'll do what we can." She ducked beneath the heavy canopy formed by the branches of the banyan trees and picked up Bedelia's saddle. "The maharajah doesn't make exceptions because of the weather, and that means we can't either."

"What a charming man. I can hardly wait to make his acquaintance."

"Well, it won't be through me." Why was he just standing there watching her? Her fingers fumbled with the cinch as she quickly saddled Bedelia. "If that's what's holding you here, then you might as well give it up."

"That's not what's holding me. You know why I'm here."

"I don't know why—"

"Then stop avoiding looking at me and find out."

"I don't want to look at you. Why should I want—" Her gaze met his and she quickly closed her eyes. "No," she whispered.

But she still saw him standing there, the rain molding his clothes to his body, muscles tense, gaze intent.

"Aye," he said. "It's time, Jane." His tone was soft, coaxing. "You don't want to fight me any longer. You're tired and discouraged, but I can help you forget all this. You want it—take it. If you don't like me, I won't bother you again."

But she knew he would make sure she liked him. He was like one of those powerful ancient mandarins Li Sung had told her about, effortlessly casting spells, mesmerizing his subjects.

Yet she was no helpless simpleton. She had the strength to fight him . . . if she wished.

If she wished? It was the first time she had admitted to doubt, and a sudden stream of relief cascaded through her. He was right, she was weary of fighting him. Why not let him have his way? One time, and he would no doubt grow bored, as men always did when their needs were assuaged, and she would be done with him.

He was unbuttoning her shirt.

Her eyes flew open.

"Shh." His face was only inches from her own, his fingers deft and quick on the buttons. "I want only to see you. I didn't get the chance at Zabrie's, but I believe today you may be in a mood to be more generous." He parted the edges of her shirt and looked at her. "Oh, yes, very generous." He bent forward, his breath feathering her engorged nipple. "Now, let me—"

She cried out, arching back against the mare's saddle, her hands clenched into fists at her sides as sensation after sensation poured through her.

He sucked slowly, sensuously. "Good," he muttered. "So good."

His hand slid beneath her belt and found the curls surrounding her womanhood, petting, tugging. "Part your legs. That's right, now a little more."

Her knees almost gave way as he found the nub for which he had been searching.

Her neck arched. A primal cry tightened her throat as he began pressing, plucking.

He lifted his head. Beautiful, she thought dazedly, she had never seen any sight as beautiful as Ruel at this moment, his cheeks flushed pomegranate-bright, his blue eyes glittering.

"Not here in the rain." His hand left her and he quickly buttoned her shirt. "We need to go somewhere." He lifted her onto Bedelia and quickly saddled and mounted Nugget. "And, for God's sake, don't change your mind."

She wasn't sure she had a mind to change. She felt blank, dazed, responding only to touch, like an animal in heat.

He gave Bedelia's rump a slap to urge her into a gallop. "Only a little while longer," he said hoarsely. "Hold on."

Hold on to what? she wondered. She was without a mooring, floating helplessly on the tide Ruel had ignited.

"Wait." He nudged his horse closer, his hand reaching out to slide up her thigh and cup her womanhood.

His nostrils were flaring, his cheeks hollowed as if from a terrible hunger. "I didn't have enough. I have to touch you. God, I want *in.*" He squeezed slowly and then released, squeezed again. "Do you know what I'd like to do? I want to drag you down in the mud and strip off your clothes. I want you naked and wanting, holding up your hips, asking me for more."

The rawness of the words should have offended her. They did not. A thrill of heat shot through her.

His hand fell away and he muttered something she couldn't hear. "Let's go, I can't wait much longer."

The rain was falling as heavily as ever, but it didn't cool her. She felt as if nothing could ever cool her again. "Where are we going?"

"The railway station." He spurred ahead. "It's closer."

It didn't seem close. By the time they reined in at the station platform, she was trembling and shaking, as if with the fever.

"Hurry," he said jerkily as he lifted her down. "Where are the keys?"

The maharajah's car. He wanted the keys to the railway car. She fumbled in the pocket of her sodden denim trousers as he propelled her across the platform toward the maharajah's private car. He grabbed the keys, unlocked the gold door, and pulled her inside. He slammed the door behind them.

The car was in half darkness, the light streaming through the window gray and bleak, the raindrops running down the glass veiling the interior from the outside world.

"Hurry." Ruel stripped off his shirt and threw it on the carpet. "God, just listen to me. I promised you it wouldn't be fast and I'm like all the others. But I'll try . . ." He turned and saw that she hadn't moved. "Why aren't you undressing?"

She couldn't seem to move. She was aching, still hot with the same fever, but found herself unable to look away from him. She had never seen anyone so alive, so charged with emotion. She could feel his need and passion. He blazed like a thousand burning candles in the pearly dimness.

"Don't tell me you've changed your mind. I couldn't . . ." He stepped closer, his fingers unbuttoning her shirt, his tone velvet-soft, almost crooning. "Did I frighten you? I promise you'll like me. We have only to get past the first time, and I'll keep my word."

His brown hair was wet, and she couldn't distinguish the golden threads she knew ran through it. His magnificent face was alight, his eyes shimmering as he exerted a magnetism so strong, she could only stare at him, mesmerized.

He peeled the wet shirt off her and dropped it on the floor. He slowly bent forward and his warm lips brushed the hollow of her left shoulder.

A shudder went through her. The touch was much less intimate than the ones that had gone before, but somehow was more boldly sensual.

"I'm hurting so much, I don't think I can hold on for very long until—" He broke off and laughed harshly as he looked down at his hands. "Christ, look at me. I'm trembling. You'll have to do the rest yourself."

His confession of weakness broke the spell. Her hands were also trembling as they went to her belt. She felt weak, helpless, wax-pliable, her heart pounding as hard as the rain on the metal roof. Dear heaven, she wanted his hands on her again. She had to rid herself of these clothes, rid herself of barriers so that he would touch her.

"That's right." His tone was coaxing, encouraging, as he sat down on the divan and took off his boots. "It's going to be fine. You know we both want this." He paused, half undressed, his gaze on the fleece surrounding her womanhood. "Soft," he whispered. "I remember how soft. . . ."

Heat moved through her, and she clenched as if his hand were still there between her thighs, searching, caressing.

He saw the movement and a muscle jerked in his cheek. "Come here."

She moved toward him, obeying without question, vaguely aware of the softness of the carpet under the soles of her bare feet. She stopped before him.

He gently parted her thighs, and his hand cupped her as he had before.

Pleasure, need, hunger.

"You want me?" His finger rotated, pressed.

She shuddered. "Yes."

"You want to draw me in and hold me?"

"Yes."

"Fast? Hard?"

"Yes."

He pushed her gently down on the divan and was between her thighs. "Then take me," he said hoarsely as he nudged into her womanhood.

She gasped as she felt the intrusion, warm, smooth, club-hard.

He frowned. "Don't fight me. I'm not going to hurt you. Let me in."

"I'm not fighting you," she said. If anything, she was fighting to take him, accept more.

"Too tight," he muttered. "You have to be fight—" His hips thrust powerfully forward.

At the sudden pain, her teeth sank into her lower lip to keep from crying out.

His head snapped up and he looked down at her. "No!"

He was sheathed deep within her, a part of her yet not part of her.

His light eyes blazed down at her. "I can't stop, dammit. It's too late now. I have to go on."

"I know you do." She swallowed. The pain was going away, leaving only an ache for completion in its wake. "I know. . . ."

"You don't know anything," he said harshly. "I wish to God you did." He drew a shuddering breath. "Jesus, this is going to—*kill* me." He drew out and then thrust gently forward.

Gentleness, care, skill. She could sense the stormy

violence brimming beneath the surface, and yet every move was controlled, disciplined.

"Ruel . . ."

"Be quiet," he grated between his teeth. "I have to think about what I'm doing." He laughed desperately. "And not doing. Are you all right?"

"Yes."

"Then I'm going to take the next step." He flexed, drew out, and then sank fast, hard like a sword thrust.

She gasped, her gaze flying to his face.

His eyes were now unseeing, his lips heavy with sensuality, his expression revealing the same mindlessness as she felt.

"Good," he said hoarsely. "Now hold me, I'll try to have it over fast. Ride it out."

He exploded in a flurry of motion, thrusting, plunging.

Her fingers dug into his shoulders as she held on as he had bid her. Dear heaven, what was happening to her? Total possession. She felt chained to him in body and response. She couldn't stop herself from taking, yielding to his every move, his every command. She was held captive by the pleasure, the need that kept soaring higher and higher. . . .

The pleasure mounted, crested and then . . .

Was she screaming? She wasn't sure of anything through the heat haze enfolding her.

He tensed, his back arching, and an expression of unutterable pleasure stamping his face. Then he was collapsing on top of her, trembling as if he had the shaking sickness.

Dangerous . . . The thought emerged through the mist of languor and exhaustion enfolding her. She had been right to resist Ruel, wrong to yield. It was too powerful. *He* was too powerful.

She became vaguely aware of Ruel shifting off her, rising to his feet and moving toward the far end of the car.

"Where are you going?" she murmured. Dear

heaven, she felt as limp and weak as if she had been ravaged by the torrent pouring through Sikor Gorge.

"Lighting the stove." He knelt beside the pot-bellied ceramic stove and opened the door.

"Are you cold?" she asked wonderingly. Her own body had never felt warmer, more heavily ripe.

"No." He lit the coal and swung the door shut again. "But we may be here awhile and I don't want you chilled. God knows I feel guilty enough without that burden." He stood up and strode toward her. "How do you feel? Are you sore?"

"A little." She sat up and brushed a tendril of hair back from her temple. "It was . . . more than I expected."

"You were more than I expected too." He grabbed a paisley silk couch throw from the divan and draped it around her. "And I have no liking for it."

Even through the mellow haze surrounding her she became aware of the grimness of his tone. "You're angry."

"I didn't want this." He dropped down on the rug, his hands tightly linked around his knees. "It's a complication. You weren't supposed to be a virgin, dammit. I don't want the responsibility."

Hurt spiraled through her, jarring her back to reality. She said haltingly, "It's not your responsibility. No one forced me to come here. It was my choice."

"The hell it was," he said roughly. "I seduced you. I wanted you and I set out to get what I wanted."

"That's right, you did." That first flush of heat was leaving her. She shivered and drew the throw closer around her. "And I'm sure you were very good at it. But I let you do it and now it's over. I'd . . . better get back to the bungalow."

"To Patrick." He smiled bitterly. "Do you know I've been very close to paying dear Patrick a visit? I kept thinking about him and his fondness for little girls and decided I wanted to cut his heart out."

She believed him. Ruel sat motionless, looking like a splendid statue of a naked gladiator, but the repressed ferocity she sensed beneath his stillness bewildered her. "It was never like that with us."

"Obviously. Why the hell did you let me do it?"

"I thought if I let you . . . men go away afterward. They don't want it anymore."

"Don't they?"

She gazed at him and her breath left her.

"Oh, yes, I still want it. I wanted it again almost the minute I left you and I'm mad as hell I can't have it. Are you going to tell me why you deliberately misled me?"

"I didn't mislead you. It was none of your concern."

"Well, it is now. Who is Patrick Reilly to you?"

"My father." She saw his surprise and rushed on. "There's no proof, you understand. He was only one of my mother's customers, but I know he's my father."

"But he doesn't?"

"He doesn't like responsibility either," she said simply.

"Christ."

"Someday he'll tell me he believes it's true," she said quietly. "But you don't have to worry. I don't expect anything from either of you."

"Even I have a code of sorts. I took something from you and now I have to give it back."

She smiled tremulously. "I believe that's considered physically impossible."

"Then I'll give you something else. What do you want?"

She realized he actually meant it. "You didn't take anything of value from me. I'm not like those women at the fort who believe a woman is lost to shame because she doesn't go to her wedding bed a virgin."

"Ian told me," he said sardonically. "You're 'different.' I doubt if your bridegroom would approve of this particular difference."

"I shall probably never wed, so it's foolish to continue this discussion." She looked around for her clothes and found them strewn across the carpet where he had tossed them. "Would you please pass me my shirt?"

"No, but I'll put them closer to the fire to dry out."

He scooped up the garments and crossed back to the stove. "You're not leaving until we finish this. Now, what do you want?"

Sweet Mary, why wouldn't he give up? She was tempted to tell him she wanted only to escape from this strange pain that continued to grow the longer she stayed with him. "You don't owe me anything," she repeated. "Why won't you listen to me?"

"Because I'm having uncomfortable twinges of conscience. I guarantee it doesn't happen often." He turned from spreading her clothes out before the stove. "But then, I've never been in this particular situation before. First I cause a woman to be knifed, then I take her innocence. It's a bit much even for me."

"I wasn't innocent."

"The hell you weren't. Growing up in a whorehouse doesn't make you a whore."

She stiffened. "I know that," she said fiercely. "I'll never be like her."

"Who?"

She could have bitten her tongue. "My mother."

"And she was a whore?"

"Yes, but I *don't* want to talk about it."

"Oh no, you're not closing me out again. We've come too far for that. If I'd probed a little deeper before, I wouldn't be in this predicament. Why does the idea of being like your mother frighten you?"

"Living like that . . . it's a nightmare. She became a slave. I'll *never* be a slave. I'll never let anyone do that to me."

"If you have such a revulsion for whorehouses, why did you go to Zabrie's?" He smiled grimly. "Since I know it was definitely not for the purpose I originally envisioned."

She looked down at the carpet. "I had business with her."

"Railroad business?"

"No."

"Kartauk?"

Her head snapped up. "What do you know about Kartauk?"

"More than I did an hour ago. I know he's not your lover either."

"Of course he's not." Her tone was abstracted as she stared warily at him. "Where did you hear about him?"

"Abdar." As he saw her go rigid with shock, he added roughly. "Don't look at me like that. If I was still a threat to you, do you think I'd be talking about Kartauk or Abdar? The game's changed, and I'll have to find some other way to get what I want."

"And what do you want?"

"An audience with the maharajah and pressure brought to bear to influence him in the direction I want him to go." He paused. "That's what Abdar promised me in return for finding and turning Kartauk over to him."

"And you were going to do it?" she whispered.

"I hadn't made a firm decision. It was a possibility."

"You went to a great deal of trouble just for a possibility." She shook her head uncomprehendingly. "How could you? He's a monster."

"I suspected as much, but then, we've already discussed my lack of scruples. I don't believe we have to probe any further into my iniquities."

Her shock was rapidly being replaced by anger. "And is that why you brought me here? Did Abdar tell you to—"

"Don't be foolish. Abdar has nothing to do with this."

She suddenly remembered something. "Not even our meeting at Zabrie's? Was that man you killed in the alley a part of your plan?"

"I hate to disappoint you, but I don't kill without good reason." He frowned. "His presence there was none of my doing, but Pachtal's arrival was a little too convenient for my taste. I've been wondering—where do you think you're going?"

"I'm leaving." She threw the wrap away and jerked

on her damp shirt. "Providing you haven't stationed Pachtal or one of his men outside to stop me."

"No Pachtal. No Abdar," he said curtly. "That's over. I know I've hurt you, but try to think reasonably."

She whirled on him. "You haven't hurt me. I don't let men like you and Abdar hurt me." She pulled on her trousers and snatched up her belt. "And reason dictates I'd be very stupid to trust you again."

"You never trusted me. You let me take you because it gave you pleasure, not because you had faith in my honesty." He held up his hand as she started to speak. "And I never expected anything else. You'd be a lunatic to trust me. Now that we've established that truth, let's get on with the matter at hand. Abdar wants Kartauk. You don't want him to find him. I assume that means you also want him out of Kasanpore?"

She didn't answer.

He shrugged. "Very well, I'll get your Kartauk out of Kasanpore and find a place for him where he'll be safe from Abdar. Then we're quits, all debts paid."

"What?"

"You heard me. I'm certainly not going to repeat this idiocy." He began to dress. "Christ, I can't believe I said it to begin with."

"Neither can I. Nor that you'd think I'd believe you."

"You want proof that I'm not in Abdar's pocket?" He pulled on his right boot. "Li Sung."

She went still. "What about Li Sung?"

"He's not in Narinth. He paid a visit to your supply yard night before last and departed with a knapsack you'd left earlier. I assume he was taking it to Kartauk. Ian followed him but lost him in the bazaar."

"Your brother is helping Abdar too?"

"My brother is helping me . . . with the greatest reluctance." He pulled on his other boot. "I didn't have to tell you any of this, you know. I could have staked out the supply yard myself and waited until Li Sung came back. There's a good chance I'd have found Kartauk. I'm better at stalking prey than Ian."

"Yes, I imagine you are. You have the hunter's instinct."

He ignored the bitterness in her tone. "I'm not ashamed to admit to that instinct. It's helped me to survive any number of times. It can help me save your Kartauk."

"What if I don't want your help?"

He said curtly, "You've got it anyway. I want this debt paid and out of my way."

"How honorable."

"I'm not honorable, but I'm usually honest." His lips thinned. "But with you something went wrong and I don't like it."

"You said that before."

"It's true. It's dangerous when a man starts lying to himself."

"It's me you lied to."

"No, I just didn't tell you the entire truth. But I lied to myself. I was in a fever to have you and so I convinced myself. . . . I'm not stupid and I know people." He smiled crookedly. "But I never explored any path that would lead me where I didn't want to go. I was careful never to dig very deep into why you went to Zabrie's. You threw out all kinds of signals you weren't what I wanted you to be, but I didn't let myself believe them. Hell, even Ian told me I was seeing what I wanted to see."

"Are you finished?"

"Almost. Abdar has to be watching my progress with you with interest. If you let me help you, we'll get Kartauk out of Kasanpore, but if you send me on my way, Abdar will think I've failed and probably initiate a move himself." He smiled. "Can you afford the time to contend with Abdar with your railroad to finish?"

"Better than I can afford to trust a man who might betray me."

"I won't betray you. You'll realize that if you look clearly at me and judge me as I am. Can you do that, Jane?"

Sweet Mary, the man was impossible. He had dominated her body until she had felt as possessed as a concubine in the maharajah's harem and then turned around and told her he had used her. How did he expect her to think coherently through this haze of hurt and anger?

"I don't know." She smiled bitterly. "But I agree you've made sure I know exactly what you are." She turned on her heel and strode out of the railway car.

"I received word the rails will arrive tomorrow." Patrick smiled triumphantly at Jane over the dinner table. "Right on time. I told you everything would be fine."

"You'll have to supervise the transfer from the dock to the supply yard. I can't spare the time away from the site. We laid less than a mile of track today."

Patrick nodded understandingly. "The monsoon. Poor darlin', my heart fair ached for you when you came in this evening."

Her heart had ached too, after those blunt revelations from Ruel in the railroad car that afternoon. No, it wasn't her heart, she assured herself quickly, it was her pride that had been stung. "Maybe it will go faster tomorrow."

"Not likely." Patrick poured another whiskey. "I've been thinking about what you said about my place being at the site. You're right, Jane. I've been a selfish bastard, but I'm going to mend my ways."

"It doesn't matter," she said dully. "The job is almost finished now."

"And it's fine work you've done too." He sipped the whiskey. "But these monsoons are a nasty business, and I'm not having you out there in that rain and mud. You could fall ill again. Give me one more day to transfer the rails, and then I'll take over on the site and you can stay home and take the rest you deserve."

She slowly raised her head to look at him. He sounded as if he meant it, but she mustn't get her hopes up. He had made promises before and they had come to naught. "It would help if you'd come," she said cautiously.

"Then it's done." He beamed. "And in nine days we'll finish up the job and bid his high muckity-muck and this blasted country farewell."

"I don't need a rest. With both of us at the site the work will go fast—"

"Nonsense. I can handle it myself. If you want to be helpful, you can take on those pesky accounts in the top desk drawer. They haven't been done since Li Sung's been gone."

She was beginning to believe him. Hope leapt within her as she realized that without the burden of supervising the work on the site, she could spare the time to find a way to get Kartauk out of Kasanpore. "You really mean it?"

For an instant a flicker of compunction crossed Patrick's face. He leaned forward and covered her hand with his. "I really do. God knows, it's time I did some of the work around here. Sometimes I wonder why you stay with me."

Because you're my father, she wanted to tell him. Because someday, if she proved she was worthy of it, he would tell her so.

She knew she couldn't say those words yet, but hope was growing stronger, brighter. "I made you a promise, didn't I?" She threaded her fingers through his. "And it will be good to rest a bit. Thank you, Patrick."

He withdrew his hand and reached for his glass. "Speaking of rest, you'd better get on to bed. You have one more day of dealing with that muddle before I take over."

"You're right, I'll do that." She stood up and moved toward her bedroom. "Good night, Patrick."

Now that she had the opportunity, how was she going to get Kartauk out of Kasanpore?

Ruel. She instantly rejected the thought and then brought it back and examined it. He had promised her not only escape for Kartauk but to find a sanctuary for him. She could find a way to the first requirement but had no means to furnish him a permanent safe haven. No one could doubt Ruel was a forceful, clever man and would probably be a match for Abdar. His words in the railway car had made sense and had also seemed sincere. His brother was an honorable man and believed in Ruel's basic integrity.

Dear God, she didn't *want* to be involved with Ruel MacClaren again. She wanted only to be quit of him. She had been berating herself for her foolishness since the moment she had left him. She had told him it had been her choice, but she had yielded him something she had never given before and she felt hurt and betrayed. Her body still ached from his possession and her emotions were raw as an open wound. The mere idea of seeing him again frightened and angered her.

Frightened? It was ridiculous to fear him now that she was aware of how he had manipulated her. She had a mind as well as a body and from now on would make certain her mind was fully in control. He was no longer an enigma, and now the only decision she must make was whether she could trust Ruel enough to use him as he had used her.

Two hours later Ruel opened the door of his hotel room in answer to a brusque knock.

Jane stood in the hall.

"What a pleasant surprise. Would you care to come in?"

"No," she said coldly. "I just came to tell you Patrick is taking over the site day after tomorrow which leaves me free to try to work on getting Kartauk out of Kasanpore. Be sure to be at the site on time tomorrow. We don't want Abdar to suspect anything is wrong."

He became still. "Then I take it this means you're going to accept my help?"

"Why not? As you said, it's not often you offer it."

"Quite true." He paused. "You don't have to worry, Jane. I'm capable of doing any number of self-serving things, but you can be sure of two things about me. I always take revenge for any injury done me and I never break my word."

"I will worry but I'll be watching you." She turned and strode back down the hall toward the steps. "And getting Kartauk out of Kasanpore is worth the risk."

"Wait. How did you get here?"

"What difference does that make?" she asked impatiently. "I walked. I wasn't about to take Bedelia out in this weather again." She disappeared around the landing.

He was tempted to follow her and offer to escort her back to the bungalow, but he knew she would reject his protection. She distrusted him and perhaps, though she wouldn't admit it, even feared him. A fear that was more justified than she realized, he thought grimly. He had expected his lust to abate after the afternoon, but having her had only whetted his appetite. The moment he had opened the door and seen her tonight he had hardened.

She had probably reached the street now and was starting toward the outskirts of Kasanpore.

There had been no sign of Abdar and Pachtal in the past weeks, but who knew when Abdar would grow impatient? The streets were dark and in this heavy rain someone could hide unseen in one of the shop alcoves. . . .

He slammed the door and hurried down the hall, cursing himself. Since when had he become enamored of rescuing females? Jane knew how to care for her own well-being and, if she saw him following her, would probably draw that knife in her boot and gut him. He was bone-tired, dry for the first time all day, and did *not* want to go out again.

But he knew he wouldn't sleep until he knew the blasted woman had safely reached the bungalow.

Chapter 6

The rain fell just as heavily the next day, and again Jane was forced to stop work by late afternoon. After she called a halt, she turned and started in the opposite direction from Sikor Gorge.

"Where are you going?" Ruel asked as he fell into step with her.

"I have to inspect the supports of the bridge over Lanpur Gorge." She added curtly, "Go back to your hotel."

"I'll toddle along." He strolled beside her. "How far is it?"

"A quarter of a mile around the bend." She

looked straight ahead. "And I don't want your company."

"You'll have to become accustomed to it. We have to talk sometime. Where have you hidden Kartauk?"

"You don't need to know that yet. When you have a plan, tell me about it and I'll decide if it's necessary for you to meet him."

"It's necessary now."

"Too bad. I don't agree."

"Jane, listen to me." His hand fell on her arm. "I intend to—"

"Don't *touch* me!" She jerked back away from him, her eyes blazing.

"Why not?" he asked softly. "Do you like it too much?"

"I hate it."

"No, you may hate me, but you don't hate my hands on you. Never lie to yourself. I made that mistake, and look where it's brought me."

"I'm not lying to myself." Sweet Mary, could he be right? She felt sick her body could betray her so easily, and yet she had felt something besides anger when he had put his hand on her arm. No, she would not permit it to be true. She whirled away from him and trudged on through the mud. "Why do you want to see Kartauk?"

"The most selfish of reasons. I want him to help me."

"You're supposed to be helping him."

"I will help him, but after you left last night I considered the situation and decided there may be a way we can help each other." His lips tightened. "I'll be damned if I'll give up my plans for this quixotic idiocy."

"No one could accuse you of being quixotic."

"I'm glad you understand me at last. Though, you must admit, I've never aspired to virtue."

No, he may have used her, but he had never pretended to be anything but what he was. "What can Kartauk do for you?"

"According to Abdar, Kartauk lived at the palace for years and had the favor of the maharajah before he decided to leave so precipitously. He must know him very well, perhaps well enough to tell me the way to persuade him to my way of thinking."

"You wish only to question him about the maharajah?"

"I wish to know everything there is to know about His Imperial Majesty."

"Why should I help you? I don't care if you get what you want." She added fiercely, "It would serve you right if you didn't."

"But we seldom get what we deserve in this world," he said mockingly. "And almost always get what we're capable of taking. As to why you should help me, it will keep me happy."

She stared at him in astonishment. "You're mad if you think that matters to me."

"Oh no, if I'm happy with the way my own plans are proceeding, then I'll be less likely to regret abandoning Abdar's cause for your own. Since you obviously don't trust me, wouldn't it be wise to make sure there are boons to keep my loyalty intact?"

"I'll think about it."

"Tomorrow."

"I said I'll think about it," she said curtly. "Stop pushing me."

"I have to push. I've wasted too much time already." His mockery had been replaced by bleakness. "When I get your Kartauk out of Kasanpore, the odds are Abdar will make certain I don't get another chance at the maharajah. I have to have that bill of sale before we leave."

"Bill of sale?"

"I'm going to buy a piece of property from the maharajah."

She stared at him incredulously. "You did all this for a piece of property?"

"A very special piece of property. I want to see Kartauk tomorrow and ask him—"

They had rounded the bend. The roar of the water racing through Lanpur Gorge drowned out the rest of his sentence.

The water was running even faster here than in Sikor Gorge, she noticed anxiously. This branch of the Zastu received the drainoff from the hills, and yellow-brown water was exploding through the gorge past the flat rocks bordering the steep banks as if shot from a pistol.

"They seem to be holding firm enough," Ruel shouted over the roar, his gaze on the two steel posts supporting the bridge over the gorge. "You must have built strong foundations to resist this flood."

"Of course I did."

"Then why were you worried?"

"I wasn't worried. I just wanted to check to be sure. Patrick should reach the gorge and start laying the track on the bridge in the next two days."

"Then what happens?"

"We join the track from Narinth ten miles beyond the gorge."

"And you're finished?"

"Patrick will ride horseback along the track from the gorge to Narinth, examining it for any damage. Then we do a trial run in the train to Narinth and back again. The next day we officially turn the train over to the maharajah." Her lips tightened grimly. "And get our money at last." She turned away and started back the way they had come.

"Tomorrow?" Ruel asked as he fell into step with her. "I need to see Kartauk."

He was persistent as the devil and would probably continue to plague her until he got his way. Why was she wasting her strength resisting? she wondered impatiently. As he had said, it would be safer to assure his loyalty with self-interest. "Be at the bungalow tomorrow morning at nine."

"Am I mistaken, or have we been going around in circles since we left the city gates?" Ruel asked.

"You're not mistaken," Jane said as she pushed aside the wet foliage overhanging the path. "Your friend, Pachtal, may still be watching me, and if we didn't lose him in the bazaar, I want to make sure he won't be able to follow us."

"Or that I would never be able to find my way back here," Ruel added shrewdly. "Are we going to go through this maze again on the way back to the city?"

"Of course." She gave him a level glance. "I'm not a fool to take you at your word until you prove yourself. I have no intention of sacrificing Kartauk to your ambitions."

He suddenly chuckled. "Good for you. When you agreed to take me here yesterday, I was a little disappointed in you. It always pays to be cautious of Greeks bearing gifts."

"Or Scots," she said dryly. She glanced hurriedly away from him and strode ahead into the underbrush at the side of the path. "The temple is just ahead."

"Temple?"

"An abandoned Buddhist temple." She added deliberately, "One of many in the area that were left deserted hundreds of years ago."

"You're warning me that I couldn't describe it accurately to Abdar if I chose?" He nodded solemnly. "Kind of you to save me the bother."

"You find this amusing?"

His smile disappeared. "Actually, I'm taking all this with great gravity, but it never hurts to laugh at little things. You'll find that out as you grow older."

"I'm not a child."

"That's what I told Ian, but I find myself in a position of trying to relegate you to a status where you'll be safe from me."

"I am safe from you," she said defiantly.

"No, you're not." He met her gaze. "Not if I choose to make it so. I'm very good at making the forbidden seem irresistible." He glanced away from her and said lightly, "My experience as a running patterer, no doubt. I spent a great deal of time and effort learning that trade. At any rate, I refuse to rob you again, so I believe we'll try to keep you in the realm of childhood."

"You have no—"

"May I ask what you're doing here?" Li Sung stepped out of the bushes and limped toward them. "Besides making so much noise, I was forced to tramp through this mud to find out who was approaching."

"This is Ruel MacClaren. He's going to help us get Kartauk away from Kasanpore." She handed Li Sung the knapsack she carried and turned to Ruel. "This is my friend, Li Sung. He'll take you the rest of the way to the temple. I'll join you later."

"Where are you going?" Ruel asked.

"I'm going to retrace my steps to be sure we weren't being followed."

"After all that weaving to and fro? Aren't you being a little too careful?"

"No," she said baldly.

A flicker of indefinable emotion crossed his face. "I believe I may have to take measures to rid you of that distrust. It's becoming tiresome and may get in the way."

"He's not to be trusted?" Li Sung asked Jane.

"Within limits. Take him to Kartauk."

She turned and walked away from them.

"How far is it to this temple?" Ruel asked as he followed Li Sung through the jungle.

"Not far."

"Why hide in a temple?"

"Kartauk wanted it."

"Why?"

Li Sung didn't answer.

"Why?" Ruel repeated.

Li Sung glanced over his shoulder. "You ask many questions."

"Because your answers don't reveal very much."

"They're not supposed to. Jane doesn't trust you."

"And is her judgment infallible?"

"No, she has a loving nature and wants to believe in people. It has often caused her great hurt."

"Then, since she doesn't believe in me, I'm no threat to her."

"Unless you've already hurt her."

"And what would you do if I had?"

"Find a way to punish you." Li Sung smiled coldly. "We Chinese are very good at causing pain. Do you think because I am a cripple I am less than a man?"

"I would never make that mistake again." Ruel grimaced. "I was once in a barroom brawl in Sydney and a sailor named Hollow Jack kicked me with his pegleg and nearly emasculated me. Then once he had me down he took the damn thing off and clubbed me on the head with it."

"How interesting." Li Sung's face was expressionless. "Perhaps I should trade this crushed limb for a more practical appendage. What did you do to the sailor?"

"What could I do? When I woke up he had already hopped a ship for New Zealand."

Li Sung studied him. "You are lying to me," he said flatly.

"Why should I do that?"

"You seek to win me over and think by glorifying this crippled sailor you will make me feel better about my own infirmity."

Ruel threw back his head and started to laugh. "You're a clever lad."

"It will do you no more good to flatter my mind than my body. Though that last statement held far more truth than the tale about the sailor."

Ruel shook his head, his face still alive with laughter. "But that story was true."

Li Sung raised his brows.

"Well, most of it," Ruel amended. "I was a trifle irritated, so I followed the sailor to New Zealand."

"And?"

"It's enough to say that he won't be using that pegleg to rob any other man of his virility."

"Yes, quite enough to say." Li Sung's lips twitched. "I believe you and Kartauk may get along very well."

"Why do you say that?"

"You will see." He increased his pace and a moment later they emerged from the jungle.

Across the clearing Ruel glimpsed the ruins of a large, weather-stained stone temple. A tide of green vegetation flowed around the building, creeping halfway up the broken steps as if the jungle were trying to devour the square, columned structure. At the apex of the steps was a statue of Buddha whose serenity was seriously compromised by a shattered head and a missing foot.

"Quite a splendid domicile," Ruel murmured.

"It keeps the weather out," Li Sung said. "Or it did before we were afflicted by the monsoons. Now these stones seem to breathe in the damp." He shrugged. "But Kartauk likes it here. He says if he cannot live in a palace, a temple is almost as fitting an abode for him."

"Indeed."

"Watch your step. This place is teeming with snakes. There is a poisonous tree snake that is almost the color of the vegetation and moss growing on the steps."

Ruel stiffened. "Snakes?"

Li Sung smiled. "You do not like them?"

"I hate them."

"Kartauk!" Li Sung called as he negotiated the high temple steps with difficulty. "We have a visitor."

"Tell him to go away . . . unless it's Abdar," a deep voice boomed from within the temple.

A ripple of shock went through Ruel. He called, "You *want* to see Abdar?"

"Of course, it is my dearest wish. I want to see Abdar . . . dead." Laughter boomed again. "I suppose you may come in. You've disturbed my concentration anyway. Who is he, Li Sung?"

"Ruel MacClaren. Jane says he is going to help you leave Kasanpore," Li Sung said as they entered the temple.

"Ah, what a noble soul."

In the center of the temple a wood fire burned in a huge bronze brazier. Other than the brazier, the chamber appeared barren of furniture except for two cots set against the far wall and a long trestle table by a window facing toward the north.

"You come to save my glorious gift for posterity?" John Kartauk stood at the table, his hands deftly molding clay around a form before him. He appeared to be in his late thirties, a man whose size was as big as his laugh, dressed in loose trousers, long white cotton tunic, and sandals. As Ruel drew closer, he seemed to grow even larger in dimension as he noticed the bulging biceps of Kartauk's arms and massive shoulders. His dark brown hair flowed free to his shoulders, and an equally silky brown beard accented the goldsmith's strong jawline, but his other features were undistinguished except perhaps for deepset brown eyes and slashing black brows.

"Are you a priest or a saint that you—" Kartauk looked up from his form and stiffened, his eyes widening as he looked at Ruel. "Good God, what a face. Come here in the light, where I can see you."

Ruel moved forward to stand next to the window. "Is this good enough?"

Kartauk nodded and took a step nearer. "Turn your head to the right."

Ruel obediently turned his head.

"Magnificent," Kartauk murmured. "The symmetry is nearly perfect."

"May I move now?" Ruel asked politely. "The rain is coming in the window and I'd like to get rid of this slicker and dry off."

"I suppose so." Kartauk reluctantly stepped back and watched Ruel step away from the window. "Superb . . ."

"It warms my heart to be appreciated."

"Are you a sodomite?" Kartauk asked suddenly.

Ruel blinked. "No, I'm afraid you'll have to look elsewhere for your pleasure."

"Oh, I'm not of that persuasion." Kartauk made a face. "God knows how many times I've wished I were, stuck out here in the jungle all these weeks." He cast a sly smile at Li Sung. "However, Li Sung is no doubt grateful. The poor crippled rascal couldn't have gotten away if I'd seen fit to vent my lust on him."

"I'd have managed," Li Sung said calmly as he sat down by the brazier and held his hands out to the fire.

Kartauk's gaze shifted back to Ruel. "The reason I thought you might be a sodomite is that most men don't accept their own physical beauty so readily."

"A pleasing face is only a tool to be used, like a strong back or a keen mind." Ruel shrugged. "Sometimes it works to my advantage, sometimes to my detriment."

"But you still use those tools?"

"Of course, that's what they're here for." He smiled as his gaze went to an ivory-handled chisel on the table beside the clay model. "Would you keep a useful tool like that in a cabinet just because it was fashioned to please the eye as well as the hand?"

Kartauk's laugh boomed out. "I like him, Li Sung."

"Jane said we must use care with him."

"But of course, anyone interesting can always be a threat. I knew that the moment I saw him and I will learn more as time goes on. I have the keen eye of a great artist and can rip aside the outer trappings and bare your very soul."

"It sounds a trifle chilly," Ruel said mildly.

"I want to model a head of you." He frowned. "Unfortunately, I have no proper medium. I've been using wood and clay, and you deserve better."

"Are you asking me to pose for you?"

Kartauk nodded briskly. "I'm going mad here with nothing to do."

Ruel's gaze went to the objects on the table. "You appear to be keeping yourself busy. That monkey is very fine."

"You have a good eye. I like it myself." He reached under the table and brought out another wooden bust. "You might appreciate this."

Jane, her hair loose and flowing, not tightly braided as he was accustomed to seeing it. She was smiling, vibrantly alive, and looked younger than he had ever seen her. He reached out and gently traced the curve of her cheek with his index finger. "I'm surprised she consented to pose for you."

"Oh, she didn't. She said she was much too busy. I did this from memory . . . and imagination. It was a great challenge. All that strength and yet no one is more vulnerable than Jane."

Ruel's finger moved down to trace the line of the statue's lips. "You must know her very well." Kartauk didn't answer, and when Ruel raised his eyes from the statue, it was to see the sculptor's gaze fixed intently on his face. His finger dropped quickly from the statue. "Of course, your statue of Kali is a good deal more powerful."

Kartauk shrugged. "Abdar liked it."

"But I prefer the serpent on the golden door."

He chuckled. "A tiny jest I couldn't resist. Our Jane was not pleased."

"She knew it would cause her great trouble," Li Sung said.

"Yes, I know, and I was properly repentant . . . for almost a quarter of an hour." He shrugged. "There was little danger. I knew the maharajah wouldn't care even if he noticed the resemblance."

"But Abdar noticed," Ruel said. "He called it an exquisite abomination."

"Truly? I can't tell you what pleasure that brings me. You know Abdar?"

"I've met him."

Kartauk's smile faded. "He *is* an abomination, you know. He claims he worships artistry but twists it to his own purposes."

"Like the Kali statue?"

"No, that's not what I meant." He was suddenly grinning. "But he also has an excellent eye. I imagine he told you that you'd be a splendid addition to his collection."

"He did mention something to that effect."

"A statue?"

"A mask."

"How . . . interesting. What do you think of him?"

"Not much. He found me equally unpleasant. I can't imagine why."

Kartauk slapped his thigh. "By God, I *do* like him."

"I knew you would," Li Sung said. "I recognized several deplorable similarities in your characters."

Kartauk's glance shifted back to Ruel. "Well, will you pose for me?"

"Can't you do me from memory as well?"

He shook his head. "Too many layers. Will you do it?"

"Perhaps." Ruel took off his slicker and strolled over to seat himself on a large square stone across the huge brazier from Li Sung. "If we can come to an agreement."

"He is here to rid me of the burden of your presence, not to pose for you," Li Sung said.

"It will take only a day or so," Kartauk said. "Time doesn't matter."

"Jane would disagree. She wants you safe."

"I'll be safe," he said abstractedly, his gaze dissecting Ruel's features. "What do you say?"

"If you pay my price."

"And that is?"

"How well do you know the maharajah?"

"I created a statue of him when I first came to the court. No one knows him better."

"Ah yes, you stripped him bare also?"

"To the bone. It wasn't difficult. There wasn't much there beyond what you see."

"I need something from him."

"And you want to know the key to getting it?"

"Yes, can you help me?"

"Oh yes, I can help you. I can tell you the way to get anything you want from the maharajah."

Ruel felt a leap of hope. "How?"

"After I get my statue." Kartauk smiled. "How do I know you won't flit away?"

"How do I know you can really help me?"

"We'll just have to trust each other, won't we?"

"I seem to be the only one required to trust," Ruel said dryly.

"Which is only fitting. My work is worth more than any prize you can hope to win from the maharajah."

"How do you know?"

"Because my art is worth more than anything in heaven or hell," Kartauk said simply.

"I see." Ruel gazed at him a moment before nodding. "Three days?"

"Four." Kartauk smiled. "Come early tomorrow morning and be prepared to spend all day."

At that moment Jane entered the chamber and moved toward them. "No sign of Pachtal. I went back two miles and I think I would have seen him."

"Does that mean I've been washed clean of the suspicion of perfidy?" Ruel asked.

"No, it means Pachtal didn't follow us . . . this time." She took off her coolie hat and slicker and dropped them on the stone floor before stepping closer to the fire. "Hello, Kartauk."

"Jane." Kartauk nodded. "You've grown thinner since I last saw you. Are you well?"

"Of course." She didn't look at Ruel as she addressed Kartauk. "He has something to ask of you."

"We've already come to an understanding," Kartauk said.

"Already?"

"Fortunately, I discovered I had an unexpected prize with which to bargain," Ruel said lightly. "Kartauk likes my face."

She nodded with instant understanding. "I should have known."

Kartauk laughed. "Yes, you should have. It's a cheap price to pay for a face like his."

"Perhaps not so cheap." She turned to look at Ruel. "I believe it's time you told us just what property you want to buy from the maharajah."

He tensed. "Why is that important?"

"It's not important in itself, but you know everything

about us and we know nothing about you. That knowledge gives you an advantage I don't want you to have."

He was silent a moment and then said, "I want to buy an island called Cinnidar from him. It's about two hundred miles off the coast in the Indian Ocean."

"And why do you want to buy this island?"

He hesitated again. "Gold."

"You're mistaken," Kartauk said instantly. "If there were gold on any island owned by the Savitsars, Abdar would have known about it. He's mad for gold and scoured the entire province for deposits."

"I'm not mistaken. It's *there.* A mountain of gold, the richest strike I've ever seen."

"Then why has no one found it before?"

"It's not accessible. The mountain is on the north end of the island and sheer cliffs make it impossible to breach from north, east, and west. A deep canyon over a hundred miles wide intersects the center of the island and cuts it off from the south."

Kartauk's brows rose skeptically. "It's impossible to get to but you know it's there?"

"I've seen it."

"How?" Jane asked.

"I believe I've said enough for your purpose." Ruel smiled crookedly. "Now you know enough to pique Abdar's interest in Cinnidar and destroy my plans if I betray you."

"If you're telling the truth."

"He's telling the truth," Kartauk said slowly, his gaze fastened on Ruel's face. "Tell me, have you ever heard the story of El Dorado?"

"Yes."

"That gold was supposedly at the bottom of a fathomless lake. Your Cinnidar gold may prove just as elusive and your money wasted."

"Cinnidar is no El Dorado. If I can get the maharajah to sell me the island, I'll find a way to get the gold out."

Kartauk suddenly smiled. "I hope you do. There can never be too much gold in the world for me."

"Since I'm laboring to provide you with material for your art, I suppose you wouldn't consider waiving payment for your information?"

"Certainly not. If Abdar finds out what you're trying to do, he'll undoubtedly cut your throat, and then where would I be?" Kartauk turned to Jane. "So you must bring him here for the next four days so I may capture his likeness while his neck's still intact."

"Unless you'd care to give me directions on how to get here," Ruel added.

"I'll bring you."

"I thought that would be your choice," Ruel said. "You'd be much more comfortable out of the rain in your cozy little bungalow."

"No, I wouldn't." She shivered and drew closer to the brazier. "Though it's much chillier in here than out in that warm rain. This fire is dying down. We need more wood, Li Sung."

"Soon. First you need to dry off." Li Sung got up and limped toward the cot in the corner. "I'll get a towel."

"I don't have time. I've wasted half a day already," she said. "And when I get back to Kasanpore, I need to go to the site and—"

"Make sure Patrick is doing his job," Li Sung finished for her as he grabbed a towel and came back toward her. "Do you intend to spy on him every day?"

"I'm not going to spy on him. I want only to make sure the job is going smoothly and he knows everything I've been doing."

"And that he is truly working and not sitting under a tree guzzling whiskey." He knelt beside her and brusquely wiped her face before shifting to a position behind her. He lifted her heavy braid and closed it between folds of the towel to dry it. "It's a wasted effort. You can do little if he chooses that course."

"It's different this time." She started to turn her head to look at him. "He really is—"

"Sit still. How can I dry this ugly hair if you keep swiveling your head about?"

"I didn't ask you to dry my hair." She looked forward again. "And this is foolish. It will only get wet again when I leave."

"That is true, but it will make you feel better and I will know I did the proper thing." He continued to dry her hair. "Now be quiet and let me behave foolishly if I wish."

Ruel felt a queer pang as he gazed at them across the fire. The bond of affection between them could not be mistaken. Affection . . . and trust. Christ, what was wrong with him? For some reason the sight of them together filled him with anger and rejection. What did he care if she gave the Chinese boy the trust he had forfeited? Yet, he *did* care.

"No, you're no sodomite." Kartauk dropped down next to him.

Ruel turned to see the sculptor studying him again and was immediately on guard. "I told you that."

Kartauk spoke softly so the two across the fire would not hear. "You did not tell me you lusted after my friend Jane."

He felt a ripple of shock. "And if I had told you?"

"I would have warned you to take care. She has done much for me and I will not have her destroyed."

"I have no desire to destroy her."

"Desire and carelessness are two different things." He shrugged his massive shoulders. "But she is on her guard with you. Perhaps I will not have to act."

"Thank you," Ruel said dryly. His gaze returned to Jane and Li Sung across the fire. That nagging dissatisfaction was growing within him with every passing minute.

"They are very close," Kartauk commented. "It's natural that they take care of each other."

"So I see."

"It disturbs you."

"Why should it disturb me? God knows, she needs someone to look after her. Reilly appears to make a poor job of it." He changed the subject. "Why do you enjoy working in gold?"

"It's the metal of the gods, the only one fit for a great artist. That's why I stayed so long at the palace. Not many patrons can afford to furnish such rare materials."

"Then why did you leave?"

"I thought where my work was concerned the end always justified the means." He shrugged. "I was mistaken. To my infinite horror I found I possessed a conscience."

"What do you mean?"

"Abdar wished me to perform certain tasks I found distasteful. I refused him."

"And he was angry?"

"Extremely. He threatened to cut off my hands if I did not obey him. Naturally, I could not permit such sacrilege. When I left, he persuaded my weasel of an apprentice, Benares, to do what he wished, but Abdar knows there is no comparison." He raised his voice and called across the flames in the brazier. "I hope you brought something in that knapsack other than rice, Jane. I've eaten so much rice my eyes are starting to slant like Li Sung's."

"What a fortunate miracle," Li Sung murmured. "That is how all eyes should be shaped."

"I brought beef and beans." Jane smiled at Kartauk. "I hope by the time they're gone, you will be too."

"But where?" Kartauk grimaced. "Great artists must have patrons, and patrons enjoy displaying their treasures. Inevitably, Abdar will hear of one of my magnificent creations and find me."

"Yes, where?" Jane turned and challenged Ruel. "You said you'd find a safe haven for him."

"Which now includes a patron who keeps his work secret," Ruel said testily.

"You're the one who said you'd give me anything I wanted."

His lips tightened. "And I will." He turned to Kartauk. "What about returning to your home in Turkey?"

"I left only jealousy behind when I left. It's no safer than anywhere else for me."

Ruel frowned. "Then I'll have to think about it."

"Think first about how to get him out of here," Jane said.

"I've already decided about that."

Her eyes widened. "You have?"

"The trial run to Narinth the night before you officially turn the railroad over to the maharajah. We station Kartauk on the line somewhere outside Kasanpore, pick him up when we're out of the city, and hide him on the train. We deboard him before we reach Narinth and from there he can make his way to the coast."

Kartauk chuckled. "Very clever. I can see why you decided to let him help us, Jane."

"It might work," she said slowly. "If Abdar doesn't suspect anything."

"Oh, he probably will suspect. It's our job to misdirect those suspicions."

"How?"

"I'll think of something. I'll have plenty of time to meditate while Kartauk is baring my soul." He stood up and reached for his slicker. "In the meantime, I think we'd better start on our way back to Kasanpore." Ruel smiled. "And not so I can rush immediately to the palace and reveal our friend Kartauk's whereabouts to Abdar. I thought I'd go see if Patrick is tending to duty."

"But I was going to—"

"And now I'm going instead." He picked up her slicker and put it over her head. "Call it a penance. Don't you think I deserve a penance?"

"Oh, yes, I'm sure you deserve anything anyone could think of to—"

He interrupted. "Then send me out in the rain after our charming Patrick." He picked up her wide-brimmed hat and put it on her head, carefully tying the cords beneath her chin. The service gave him an odd, deep, primitive sense of satisfaction, soothing the abrasive unrest he had known. Suddenly he realized Kartauk was not as perceptive as he believed himself to be. It hadn't been lust ripping at him this time. *This* was what he wanted when he had watched her with Li Sung. He had been fiercely resentful of the bond of affection and trust that allowed Li Sung to perform those services instead of him. He quickly turned away and said gruffly, "Besides, I'll get a chance to look over the terrain and decide on the best place to hide Kartauk while waiting for the train."

"How did Jane find you?" Ruel asked Kartauk.

"Hold your head still." The goldsmith carefully shaved the plane of the cheek of the wooden statue on the table in front of him. "She didn't find me. I found her. I was hiding in the bazaar at the time and, when I heard she was inquiring about a goldsmith to execute the door, I went to her bungalow."

"You took a big chance."

"I was desperate," he said simply. "I hadn't been able to work for nearly three weeks and I felt as if I were starving to death. I'd had to leave my tools at the palace when I bolted and couldn't carve so much as a chess piece. I couldn't stand it any longer." He turned the model so more light would fall on the left side of the statue. "I might have been able to resist if the door was to be anything but gold. Jane tells me your passion for gold equals my own."

"What else did she tell you?"

"That you're ambitious, ruthless, and self-serving."

"True."

Kartauk laughed. "And honest."

"Did she say that?"

"No, that's my own judgment." Kartauk's gaze wandered across the chamber to where Jane and Li Sung sat on the floor playing cards. "She appears to be having trouble accepting you might also have a virtue or two. I didn't disabuse her. She's much safer believing only in your satanic qualities."

"You told her Abdar was searching for you and she still let you do the door?"

He nodded. "I didn't intend to tell her, but after we

met and I realized what she was, I decided the best course would be to throw myself on her mercy."

"And what is she?"

"A caretaker. She can't help herself from nurturing and caring for those in need. Didn't you realize that?"

"I've never thought about it."

Kartauk shot him a shrewd glance. "Or never permitted yourself to think about it?" He didn't wait for a reply. "Anyway, I cast myself under her wing and let her care for my needs in return for my labor on the door."

Ruel frowned. "You didn't care that your presence would endanger her?"

"I cared, but I had to work. I couldn't let anything stand in the way of that." Kartauk lifted his head. "You should understand. I'd judge you're also a driven man where your Cinnidar is concerned."

"Yes." His resentment and condemnation of Kartauk was completely unreasonable, but then, nothing about his attitude toward Jane made any sense. "Li Sung said you were the one who chose this temple as a hiding place."

"I found it suitable. A temple should always shelter beauty and greatness. Besides, I knew I could dismantle one of the interior walls for my furnace."

Ruel's eyes widened. "You tore down one of the temple walls?"

For the first time Kartauk's tone became defensive. "It had fine square stones and I needed a furnace to cast the door. No one ever comes here to worship anymore, and it's much better I put the wall to good use."

Ruel chuckled. "I'm sure it is." His smile faded as his gaze was drawn to Jane, as it had constantly been during the past days. He had told her he was going to try to think of her as a child, but that intention had gone up in smoke that first day at the temple. What the hell was wrong with him? It had never been like this with any other woman. He couldn't keep his eyes away from her. He wanted to *touch* her.

Jane's plaited hair shone deep red in the firelight, and an odd tingling started in his fingertips. He wanted to loosen the heavy braid, comb his fingers through the silken mass until it flowed wildly about her shoulders. He wanted to see her as naked and abandoned as she had been beneath him on the floor of the railway car. A surge of heat tore through him as he readied, thickening until he ached with the weight of it.

She stiffened and he knew she was aware he was watching her. She kept her gaze fixed on the cards in her hand but she knew, dammit. She reached up nervously to smooth a tendril of hair back from her temple, and the sleeve of her shirt fell back, revealing the smooth symmetry of her forearm. Another bolt of heat wrenched through him, bringing anger and frustration in its wake. All right, he would somehow keep himself from raping her, but he would *not* be alone in this. Look at me, he willed her. See what I'm feeling. Admit what we're feeling.

She darted him a flickering glance from the corner of her eye. Her spine went rigid as she met his gaze. Oh yes, she knew, he thought grimly. Her eyes widened and then her head snapped back around and she was once more staring down at her cards, deliberately ignoring him again.

He wished he could do the same. Christ, why the hell couldn't he look away from her?

"Yes, she's much safer believing you're Lucifer incarnate," Kartauk murmured. "It's getting worse, isn't it?"

Ruel jerked his gaze away from Jane. "I don't know what you mean."

Kartauk smiled. "I mean that if I were doing a full statue instead of a head, I might be forced to employ an extraordinary multitude of fig leaves to mask a certain portion of your anatomy."

Ruel carefully kept himself from glancing back at Jane. "Then it's fortunate you've confined yourself to a limited area."

"Particularly since the transformation occurs so frequently. At first I wondered if I should send her away." His attention returned to the statue. "The signs of desire aren't confined only to the nether parts, you know. The jaw tightens, the nostrils flare slightly, the mouth—"

"I regret to have caused you artistic difficulties."

"Oh, no difficulty. I would not have permitted that to happen. Actually, your lust gave the work an added shading of primitive beauty."

"And, of course, that's worth any amount of discomfort I might experience."

"Any discomfort," Kartauk agreed.

Ruel shifted restlessly on the stone block on which he was sitting. "When will you be finished with that blasted head?"

"Tomorrow." Kartauk added wistfully, "It's quite wonderful, one of the best pieces I've ever done. I'm truly magnificent. If I only had—"

"Gold." Ruel chuckled. "I'm beginning to think your passion may be even greater than mine."

"I have no doubt it is. To me, gold means beauty, to you, power; but beauty always triumphs in the end. Kings fall, empires fade, but art and beauty endure." He paused and then sighed. "I suppose you wish your reward?"

"It seems a small price to ask for contributing to your greater glory."

"Do I discern a note of disrespect?"

"You wouldn't recognize it if you did."

Kartauk's laugh boomed out. "I would recognize it. I'd just lose faith in your judgment." He went back to work. "Toys."

"What?"

"Send the maharajah a toy."

Ruel gazed at him blankly. "What kind of toy?"

"A child's toy. Trust me."

"I'm to give one of the wealthiest maharajahs in India a child's toy?"

"He *is* a child. That's the whole point of the matter. How do you think I survived his eccentricities for six years? He would have driven me mad if I hadn't learned how to distract him when I needed to send him off in another direction." Kartauk saw Ruel's doubtful expression and continued impatiently. "It's true. The maharajah has the mind of a child. The Savitsars are Hindu and have adhered strictly to the caste system for hundreds of years. Since there are not that many choices in the upper castes, they've been forced to inbreed. It's no wonder the maharajah and Abdar's minds are not what they should be."

"Abdar doesn't have the mind of a child."

"No." He smiled sardonically. "But I assure you, there is no one more twisted."

"Toys . . . you make it sound simple."

"Not simple, but possible. Go to Namir on the Street of the Palms, a brilliant craftsman. Tell him to sell you a toy like the ones he occasionally made for Kartauk. Maybe something with an elephant. The maharajah's mad about elephants."

Was it possible Kartauk was right about the maharajah? Eagerness began to surge through Ruel as he remembered what he had heard about the monarch's unreasonable demands, his tantrums and idiosyncracies.

He's not interested in anything but his toy of a railroad.

He likes a bit of flash.

Everything he had heard about the maharajah substantiated Kartauk's claim. The maharajah's self-indulgent behavior and unreasonable demands could certainly have been that of a child.

"Why isn't anyone else aware of this?"

"Perhaps they are, but it's not wise to question the sanity of a ruler who has the power of life and death. It's safer to assume he's merely spoiled than feeble-minded. Besides, not everyone has my great powers of perception."

"If I do send the maharajah a toy, what guarantee will I have he won't merely accept it and then forget I exist?"

"No guarantee. I gave you the key, it's your task to unlock the door. I'll be interested to see how you accomplish it." He scowled. "And stop frowning. I knew I should have waited until tomorrow to tell you. Now you'll be plotting and planning and I'll have a much harder time getting the forehead right."

Chapter 7

"I've decided the toy has to be in two parts," Ruel told Ian. "I owe one more day to Kartauk, so will you go to see this Namir tomorrow? I want one of the figures of the toy to be a maharajah, the other an elephant. Tell him he may use his own judgment for the rest as long as the first part of the toy is fascinating enough to intrigue and yet still whet the appetite for the second half."

"Quite a challenge. How much time will he have?"

"Three days. The tracks are due to be joined in another six, and I don't want excitement over the completion of the maharajah's big toy to distract from his interest in this one."

"Isn't it dangerous to withhold something he wants from the maharajah?"

"Probably, but I'm counting on him wanting the other half of the toy more than feeding me to the crocodiles. Besides, he likes the British and I'll make sure to involve Colonel Pickering in the final negotiations."

Ian nodded. "Very well, I'll go see Namir in the morning. I imagine you'll have to pay him fairly well."

"Anything he wants. Who knows? I may not have to pay the maharajah as much as I thought for Cinnidar. Kartauk had some interesting insights into his character."

"You like Kartauk?"

"He's a keen judge of character. I don't have to like him to appreciate his astuteness."

"But you do like him?" Ian persisted.

"Ian, dammit, I told you—yes, I like him."

"Good. And you like this Li Sung?"

"Well enough." He scowled. "All right, I'm positively brimming with warm and felicitous feelings. Satisfied?"

"Oh, yes, things are going quite nicely."

"I wouldn't have thought you'd be so overjoyed at the prospect of my possible success with the maharajah. If I persuade him to sell me Cinnidar, you know I won't go back to Glenclaren."

"If Cinnidar is best for you, then that's what I want." Ian smiled gently. "Lately I've begun to suspect there's more than gold waiting for you on Cinnidar. I'm not sure it's even the gold you really want. You need roots and a home that you'll love as much as I love Glenclaren. That's all I've ever wanted for you, Ruel."

Christ, Ruel felt as if something hard and tight were breaking up inside him as he looked at his brother. He wanted to reach out and touch him, clap him affectionately on the shoulder as he had done when they were boys together. Everything seemed to be shifting, changing around him since he had come to Kasanpore.

Or was Ian right and it was Ruel who was changing?

No, he couldn't accept that the lessons of a lifetime could be so easily discarded. He may have allowed Jane and Ian to touch him on a certain level, but once he had paid his debt he'd be able to dismiss them from his thoughts and go about his own business.

"I'm glad you're not disappointed," he said in a reserved tone. "Good night, Ian."

Ian smiled again. "Good night, Ruel."

"In four more days we'll be joining the rails," Patrick said. "Lord, and it's about time. I'll be glad to see the last of this foul country. This last week has almost killed me."

"I could come tomorrow and help you," Jane offered.

"I wouldn't think of it," Patrick said. "You just stay here and let me do the work for a change." He stood up and stretched. "I've got to get to bed. I'd forgotten how tired a man gets working the rails."

"But I really want to help, Patrick," she said eagerly. "Remember how it was in the beginning when we worked together in Salisbury?"

"You've done your share. Now let me do mine."

She was disappointed but reluctantly decided not to insist. Patrick had cut his drinking down to less than a quarter of a bottle a day since he had taken over the site from her. If it was responsibility that had made this change in him, she would be foolish to rob him of it. "Well, if you change your mind—" She paused and then said casually, "Since you won't let me help with the construction, I hope you won't mind if I make the trial run to Narinth?"

"Why should I mind?" Patrick yawned. "I'll be glad to stay home and rest my bones after the last week. I've got to take the maharajah and all those highbrow nabobs to Narinth the next day, and he'll probably find a hundred things wrong."

She hadn't expected any other answer but still felt

relieved. "Then it's settled. I'll bring Li Sung from Narinth to engineer and I'll ride the fireman seat."

"Whatever you like." Patrick moved toward the bedroom. "It's about time Li Sung came back and did some real work for a change. I bet he's not out in the rain working the rails." He glanced back over his shoulder. "And I noticed our friend MacClaren quit us the minute the rains started. I keep telling him I'm the only one who has the gumption to put up with this foul weather."

"You do? When did you last see him?" she asked with careful casualness.

"Oh, he drops in at the site every day or so for a cup of coffee or a word."

She hadn't known Ruel had gone back to the site after that first afternoon and for an instant felt a completely unreasonable flicker of gratitude. After all, Ruel was not keeping an eye on Patrick for her sake. He wanted the railway completed as fast as possible so that he could get Kartauk out of Kasanpore.

Ruel staring at her across the temple, his gaze searing, demanding, holding.

"Your cheeks are flushed," Patrick said idly. "Are you coming down with something?"

Her discomposure must be blatantly evident if Patrick, who never noticed anything about her, commented on it, she thought in exasperation. "No, I'm just feeling the heat. It seems worse since the rains came." She jumped up from her chair and bid Patrick good night.

She would get over this craving, she thought desperately. She was not an animal.

Yet her body's response to Ruel was like that of an animal in heat. There was not a moment in his presence she was not aware of him. When she had met his gaze in the temple she had felt a melting, a yielding that had frightened her.

She would ignore it and eventually this hunger would go away.

Dear God, it *had* to go away.

• • •

Ruel carefully placed the toy in a large box and then wrapped the package in bright crimson velvet and tied it with a flamboyant white satin bow.

An hour later he handed the package to the head footman at the palace, together with an extravagant bribe and the promise of an even bigger one if the maharajah received the gift at once.

He then went back to the hotel to wait for events to take their course.

The message came the next morning in the form of a summons from the palace to appear immediately for an audience with the Maharajah Dulai Savitsar.

An hour later he was ushered into the reception chamber to find the maharajah kneeling on the floor, the toy board on the carpet before him. The maharajah's small, plump frame was garbed in a brilliant red brocade tunic and white silk trousers, and he bore little resemblance to his son, Abdar. Gray peppered the ruler's bushy mustache and sleek black hair and, at that moment, there was no trace of Abdar's blank impassiveness about his father's demeanor. He was clearly displeased.

"You're this Ruel MacClaren?" The maharajah didn't wait for an answer but went on peevishly. "I'm very angry with you. It does not work. There's something wrong with it."

The four-foot board at which he was staring was a representation of a jungle with each tree, bush, flower, and animal exquisitely crafted and amazingly lifelike. The central figure on the board was a tiny maharajah wearing a gold tunic and tiny bejeweled crown. Ian had told Ruel that Namir had worked a year creating this elaborate toy and had found it necessary to substitute only a few of the figures to suit Ruel's requirements.

"You see?" The maharajah pressed the mechanism.

A lion sprang at the tiny crowned figure, appeared to just miss him, but really triggered another mechanism, causing the maharajah to rise in the air and be lost to view behind the foliage of the branches of a tree. This action in turn triggered another mechanism that caused a figure identical to the first maharajah to spring down on the other side of the tree to stand before a rhinoceros. The rhinoceros charged and the second royal figure rose to be lost to view in the next tree. The motion of attack and evasion continued across the board, using various animals and reptiles with the tiny maharajah always evading the threat until he reached the edge of the board which resembled a high cliff. The final mechanism sent the maharajah hurtling into the air and then stopped, suspended over the abyss.

"Look at that. He just hangs there like an overripe pomegranate," the maharajah complained. "Everyone knows a maharajah must always triumph against fate. It is most unsatisfying."

"That's because you don't have the other part of the toy."

The maharajah looked up quickly. "What other part?"

Ruel pointed to the almost invisible slots in the side of the toy. "The second half of the toy slides in here. The maharajah survives the fall from the cliff and lands before a tiger, then springs into another tree and then lands on the back of a magnificent white elephant, where he is safe at last."

The maharajah's eyes brightened. "An elephant?"

"A white elephant. What other animal is worthy to bear a maharajah?"

"That's what I told my High Adviser, but they cannot find a real one for me. They keep making excuses." He frowned with dissatisfaction at the figure hanging over the cliff. "I must have the other part of the toy. What kind of man are you to give me only half a gift?"

"But an extraordinary gift, one worthy of Your Majesty's cleverness. I saw it in the shop and knew instantly it was fit only for a man of your taste and intelligence."

"But I need the other part."

"I'm searching for it now. Unfortunately, I seem to have misplaced it."

The maharajah's gaze narrowed on Ruel's face. "And

what would it take to help you find it?" He sighed. "I suppose you wish me to give you a present in return? Everyone wants something from me. What do you want me to give you?"

"Sell, not give. You own a small island in the Indian Ocean called Cinnidar I wish to purchase. I'll give you forty thousand pounds for it."

"Cinnidar? I do not recall . . ." He impatiently waved a plump, dimpled hand. "It cannot be very important if I don't remember the place. I will ask my adviser if you offer a fair price. Meanwhile, you will continue to look for the other half of the toy?"

"Diligently. May I call on you tomorrow with word of my progress?"

"Yes, yes." The maharajah turned back to the jungle board, pressed the button to reset the mechanism, and watched enraptured as the lion rose in the air. "Tomorrow."

Hallelujah, Ruel thought jubilantly as he walked down the palace steps. It was only the first step but a damn big one. All the prospects looked bright. Even the rain that had been pouring down when he entered the palace had temporarily stopped. The murky sky would no doubt soon open up again, but it was still a good sign.

"The hotel, sahib?" the bearer asked as he climbed into the ricksha.

"Yes." Then on impulse he said, "No." He was brimming with hope he wanted to share but suddenly he knew it was not with Ian he wanted to share it. "Take me to the bungalow of Sahib Reilly."

The cobra wove back and forth, his onyx eyes fixed malevolently on the dog excitedly darting back and forth directly in front of him.

Dear God, don't let him strike, Jane prayed as she edged inside the stable door. She carefully set the bowl of scraps she'd brought for Sam on the floor and reached for the knife in her boot.

The snake was coiled in the middle of the stable directly in front of Bedelia's stall. If he didn't strike at the yapping dog dancing in front of him, he might turn on the mare.

"For God's sake, hush, Sam," she breathed.

The idiotic dog paid no attention to her, of course. His barking grew more shrill as the snake suddenly arched to a height of nearly four feet.

The blasted cobra must be at least ten feet long. If he launched that length at Sam, the dog would never be able to evade him. She glanced impatiently down at the knife in her hand and tossed it aside. A dagger would be no good as a weapon against the snake. To use it she would have to be too close. That pitchfork propped against the wall would be much more effective.

She froze as the snake's head swiveled in her direction. Her heart was thundering so hard it seemed louder than the uproar Sam was making. Though she was beyond the cobra's reach, fear still iced through her as she was pinned by those beady eyes.

Sam bounced to one side and the cobra's head swung toward him.

Jane's hand closed on the handle of the pitchfork.

"Back, Sam!" she cried desperately. "For heaven's sake, stop teasing him." She moved slowly in a circle until she was behind the snake.

"What the *hell* are you doing?"

She pulled her gaze from the cobra to see Ruel standing in the doorway. His skin was death-pale and gleaming with sweat. "Get away from him."

"Be quiet!" Jane said sharply, her gaze shifting back to the snake. "And stand perfectly still. If you scare him, he might strike at Sam."

"I don't give a damn about Sam," he said hoarsely. "Get away from that goddamn snake before he kills you."

Jane ignored him and took a step closer. Four yards from the cobra. Three yards.

Ruel muttered an obscenity. "All right, I'll get that crazy hound." He took a step toward the dog. "Just get out of here!"

The cobra caught the motion and reared higher, hissing.

"Don't move," Jane whispered.

Ruel froze.

The snake was confused, his attention divided between Sam and Ruel. He had forgotten about her. If she were quick, she might be able to—

She dashed forward, holding the pitchfork out in front of her. She caught the snake's body between the tines and slung it across the stable. His long body struck the wall. Stunned, he fell writhing to the floor.

Sam immediately darted after it.

"No!" she screamed.

Ruel cursed steadily as he ran after the dog and scooped him up only a scant foot away from the serpent.

"Hold him!" Jane pushed Ruel aside and brought the wooden handle of the pitchfork down on the snake's puffed head with all her strength. She struck again and again and again. . . .

She stopped, breathless, as she realized the snake was no longer moving. "I . . . think he's . . . dead."

Ruel didn't answer.

She poked at the snake with the pitchfork. No response. "It's safe to let Sam down now." She turned to look at Ruel. "He was a big one, wasn't he? I don't remember ever seeing one that size around here. They're usually much— Let me go!"

Ruel's hands were grasping her shoulders. "Damn you." He shook her, his eyes blazing in his white face. "*Damn* you!"

"Get your hands off me or you'll get this pitchfork in your belly," she said fiercely.

"Do you think I care? You and your damn pitchfork and your goddamn snake." He shook her again. "I could—" His hands fell away from her, and he staggered toward the door.

"Where are you going?" she asked, startled by the sudden abandonment.

"To throw up." Ruel's voice was muffled as he dashed outside.

She gazed after him in astonishment. She had been terribly frightened too, but Ruel's extreme response was completely unexpected. She impulsively started after him and then stopped. Li Sung hated to be seen in moments of weakness, and Ruel would probably be even more resentful. While she was still shaking with her own fear she didn't feel up to handling his bad temper. She turned back to Sam, who was sniffing at the dead snake. "All right, you troublemaker, let's get rid of him."

When she left the stable a few minutes later, Ruel was scooping water from the horse trough onto his face. His slicker lay on the ground beside him and his damp shirt clung to his torso. His face was still pale as he lifted his head to look at her. "Sorry," he said curtly. "I don't like snakes."

"Neither do I." She shrugged. "But I got used to them. I grew up in tents, and it wasn't unusual for one to come visiting."

"Why in the hell didn't you do what I said?" he asked harshly. "You could have been—"

"Sam," she interrupted. "The snake would have killed him."

"And that's worth risking your life for?"

"He belongs to me," she said simply. "You have to take care of what belongs to you."

He stared at her. "Christ."

She bristled. "It's none of your business. Sam's not very smart, but he's—"

"He's an asinine hound." He added grimly, "And a fitting animal for you. I couldn't believe it when I saw you charging that cobra with a pitchfork. I wanted to strangle you." His hands balled into fists. "God, I was scared."

She hadn't expected him to admit it. "So was I."

"But snakes don't make you freeze and break into a sweat." He smiled lopsidedly. "I didn't cut such a brave figure, did I? Hell, I was a sniveling coward. All I wanted to do was to turn tail and run away."

"But you didn't run away," she said quietly. "You told me to go. You were going to help Sam."

"Because there wasn't any other way to get you out of that damn place. I saw you there and I—" He broke off and drew a shaky breath. "Jesus, I hated every second of it."

She had never seen Ruel at a disadvantage, and this evidence of weakness filled her with curiosity. "Why are you so afraid of snakes?"

"We're all afraid of something." He picked up his slicker from the ground and pulled it over his head. Then as he saw her still watching him he shrugged. "I suppose I owe you an explanation for being such a damn coward." He was silent a moment and then admitted, "I was bitten once."

Her eyes widened. "By a cobra?"

"No, this was years ago at Glenclaren. An adder. I used to sleep in the hills sometimes." He spoke quickly, jerkily, as if he wanted to get through it. "I told you about my pet fox. I used to take him with me. It got lonely sometimes. I woke up one night with a stinging in my left leg and found the adder snuggled under my blanket. I killed him with a rock." His lips tightened. "But I found my fox dead a few yards away. The damn snake had killed him before he decided to crawl in bed with me."

"Oh no," she whispered.

"I took off my shirt and tore a strip off to bind my leg and went to find help." He lifted his shoulders. "I was never a lucky lad. My mother had decided to go to the village for the night. Ian found me unconscious the next morning and got help for me."

"Not before?" she asked, horrified. "Why didn't someone else—"

He ignored the question. "End of tale. I was on my feet in short order and none the worse."

Except he had lost a pet he loved and incurred a horror of snakes that would last him a lifetime.

His expression altered, closed. He said lightly, "You can see why I approved Kartauk rendering Abdar as a serpent on his golden door. I can't imagine a greater insult." He turned toward the ricksha waiting on the road beside the bungalow. "I believe it's time I made my way back to the hotel. Don't worry, I won't bore you with any more of my reminiscences."

"I wasn't bored," she said slowly. "It made me sad."

"Really? I can't understand why." He snapped his fingers. "Oh, yes, it must be the fox. Your heart is bleeding for my furry friend?"

"No." But she had an idea his heart had bled that night. Not that he would admit to such weakness.

"Then it must be for me," he said mockingly. "Tell me, do you want to take me under your wing as you have Kartauk?"

She stiffened as she realized how much of her resistance toward him had melted during the past moments. How stupid of her. Ruel was no more defenseless than that cobra she had dealt with in the stable. She hurriedly changed the subject. "Why did you come here? Is there something wrong?"

An indefinable expression crossed his face. "I just decided to drop by."

His answer surprised her. Ruel and she were hardly on terms that would invite such a casual visit. "How was your interview with the maharajah?"

"Good." All mockery completely disappeared as a sudden brilliant smile lit his face. "No, very good."

"You think you'll get your Cinnidar?"

He nodded. "I'm damn close." He glanced at Sam. "Keep that dog in the bungalow no matter what your precious Patrick says. You don't want another snake to pay him a visit. There are too many cracks in that stable floor."

"I'd already decided to do that."

"That's right. You don't need any advice from me, do you?" He took off his hat and bowed.

He was walking toward the ricksha when a sudden thought occurred to her.

"Ruel, how old were you when you were bitten by the snake?"

He glanced at her over his shoulder.

"I don't remember. About nine, I suppose."

She watched the ricksha roll away in a jingle of melodious bells.

It got lonely sometimes.

Nine years old. She had thought he had been speaking of a time when he was much older. What had a child that young been doing alone in the hills at night? And why had he not been found until the next day, after he had made his way back to the castle? She would probably never know the answers to those questions. Ruel had clearly slammed the door on any further confidences.

Not that she wanted to breach those barriers, she assured herself quickly. Just when she thought her own defenses impregnable, he had found a way to squeeze through them. The most exasperating aspect was that he had not even been trying. He had shown her weakness instead of strength, honesty instead of deception.

And in that vulnerability he was more dangerous to her than ever before.

"You've brought it?" the maharajah asked eagerly as soon as Ruel walked into the audience chamber the next afternoon.

"No, but I think I'm close to finding it." Ruel paused. "Unfortunately, I've been so distressed by this business of the purchase that my memory has completely flown away."

The maharajah scowled. "Why do you play this silly game? I know you could give it to me if you wished."

Ruel merely smiled and remained silent.

"Oh, very well, you may have the island, but not for forty thousand pounds. The High Adviser says it's worth at least ten thousand more."

Ruel tried not to let the tension show in his expression. "I'm not a rich man. I could perhaps afford another five."

"Done." The maharajah smiled craftily. "We'll sign the papers after you give me the—"

Ruel cut in quickly, "My brother and Colonel Pickering are outside in the anteroom with the proper agreements. Perhaps we could sign the papers now and then I could devote my entire attention to finding the other piece." He paused. "You might have it within the hour."

"Then let's have it over with," the maharajah said impatiently. "Call them in."

Forty-five minutes later Ruel tucked one copy of the legal agreements in his pocket and handed another to Colonel Pickering, who in turn gave a bank draft to the High Adviser.

"There, it's done," the maharajah said. "Now keep your promise."

"I have every intention of doing so." Ruel snapped his fingers. "The carriage. I've just remembered I left the other package in the carriage after I left the toy store." He turned to Ian. "Would you go out and fetch it for His Majesty?"

"Delighted." Ian moved toward the door with Colonel Pickering. "I'll give it to a footman and meet you at the front entrance."

The maharajah watched them leave the chamber before turning and smiling slyly at Ruel. "You think you've bested me, don't you?"

"Why would I think that?"

"But I'm the one who has cheated you. Cinnidar is worthless. My adviser said it's just a barbarian wilderness of jungle, mountains, and wild animals. Even the summer palace my great-grandfather built there has probably rotted away with disuse. The island's not worth a quarter of what I charged you for it."

"Then you've obviously made a fool of me."

He pouted. "You don't appear upset. I *wanted* you to be upset."

Ruel allowed himself a small smile when he felt like jumping in the air and shouting. By God, he *had* it! "No doubt when I've had time to think about my foolishness I'll be appropriately dismayed."

The maharajah brightened. "No doubt. I've been very clever, haven't I?"

"Very clever." Ruel turned and left the audience chamber.

• • •

"You had to give more than you planned for it," Ian said as soon as Ruel joined him.

"I still have three thousand pounds left. It will get me started."

"I wish I could help you," Ian said, frowning. "But you know there's never been any money at Glenclaren."

"I don't want your money, Ian," Ruel interrupted.

"It's your money too. I've always planned on sharing what little there is with you." He added gently, "Don't let bitterness stop you from accepting what's yours."

"I'm not bitter." Ruel realized to his astonishment that he spoke the truth. For the first time since he could remember, he felt entirely free of bitterness. It was as if the acquisition of Cinnidar had miraculously banished the weight of those painful memories and made him suddenly lighter . . . younger. "Keep your money, Ian. Glenclaren needs it worse than I do. I'll find a way to get what I need. I'll be fine."

Ian studied his face and then slowly nodded. "Yes, I believe you will. I guess it's time I went home." He cleared his throat and said, "Suppose we kill two birds with one stone? I'll arrange passage on a ship out of Narinth for myself and a servant and go with you on the trial run. Scotland should be as safe for Kartauk as anywhere else."

"But will Glenclaren be safe *from* him," Ruel murmured. "He might decide to tear down the battlements to make a furnace."

"What?"

"Never mind. I'm sure Maggie will be able to put a stop to any blatant desecration."

"Margaret," Ian corrected him automatically, then in a softer tone. "Margaret."

Ruel felt an overwhelming surge of affection as he looked at Ian's wistful face. Now that Ian was leaving, it was safe to lower the barriers he had raised against him so long ago. Even if it hadn't been safe, he didn't know if he could have stifled the emotion. In this moment the world seemed a bright and kind place, where no walls were necessary. "I'll try to remember," he said gently. "Margaret."

"Cinnidar," Abdar murmured. "You're sure it was Cinnidar?"

Pachtal nodded. "So the emir said. He was boasting about what a fool the Scot was to buy a worthless island."

"MacClaren is no fool. Cinnidar must have value of some sort. After we have Kartauk we may have to look into that purchase." Abdar shrugged. "And, now that MacClaren has what he wants, we've lost a weapon. Pity. I believe the Scot provided us with an excellent chance to get Kartauk back."

"And what now?"

"Now we must find Kartauk on our own . . . which means Jane Barnaby. Go to Zabrie's and find out if the Chinese boy has returned."

"I could approach the girl again and attempt to bring her here. Time has passed and she will probably not expect a move on our part."

"Not yet. She has already demonstrated she is both loyal and stubborn, and it would take considerable time and effort to get the information out of her." He reached out a finger and stroked the dagger in the goddess's hand. "The railroad is nearly completed and she and Reilly will leave Kasanpore soon."

Pachtal smiled. "Which means she will wish to leave Kartauk safe."

"It seems a reasonable surmise. So we stay very close and when the opportunity presents itself—"

"We scoop Kartauk up and bring him back to the palace."

"At last." His finger touched a golden drop of blood. "I cannot tolerate that fool of a Benares for much longer. Compared to Kartauk his skills are laughable." He smiled. "And since my father has no further use for the girl now that the railroad is completed, I believe we may also take her. Do you not think it fitting we let his little savior be Kartauk's first subject?"

"Scotland?" Kartauk frowned. "My mother told me it was a stark, cold country. An artist needs warmth and color to feed his soul. I like the sunlight."

"But I wager you like your hands better," Ruel said.

"True." He shrugged philosophically. "Perhaps I'll get used to the cold. Your brother will be my patron?"

"Ian can't afford to give you more than a roof over your head."

"No matter. I will find a patron for myself. Perhaps your Queen Victoria. I hear she has much gold."

"I'm sure she'll be delighted to know you have plans for it."

"Once she has seen my work, I'm sure she will also. Maybe I will even consent to do her head." He frowned. "Though I doubt it. Her face does not please me and I abhor double chins. I'll make her a salt cellar instead." He turned to Jane. "Where do you and Patrick go after you finish here?"

"Patrick doesn't have any offers of employment yet. He said we'll make a decision as soon as we get the money from the maharajah." She braced herself and turned to Li Sung. "I want your promise you won't leave the temple until the night we go to Narinth."

He gazed at her without expression. "No."

"Why not?"

"Why do you ask when you know the answer?"

"Li Sung, I *told* you what happened at Zabrie's."

"And I have not gone to her since that time."

"It's even more dangerous for you to go to her now."

"You do not know she betrayed you. She has given me gifts. It would not be proper for me to leave without saying good-bye." He didn't wait for a reply but walked out of the temple.

Jane's hands clenched into fists with frustration. She wanted to strike out at something.

"Li Sung is no fool. He won't betray us to the woman, Jane," Kartauk said quietly.

"Do you think I don't know that? I'm afraid for him. I wish I'd never given that woman one rupee."

"And why did you give her money, Jane?" Ruel asked softly.

"Because I was stupid. Because I never thought—"

"Because she has too much heart," Kartauk said. "She saw that Li Sung was hurting and tried to ease his hurt. Because of his race and his crippled leg, he was shunned by women, even the whores in houses like Zabrie's."

"So you went to Zabrie and paid her to make sure he was made to feel like a man, not a cripple," Ruel said.

"You're not to tell him," she said fiercely.

"I respect Li Sung. I wouldn't hurt him, Jane."

"Wouldn't you?" She strode across the room toward the temple entrance. "We'll leave the station for Narinth at seven two nights from now, Kartauk. Ruel thinks the safest place for you to wait for the train is on the other side of Lanpur Gorge. I'll come for you in the early afternoon of that day and take you to the gorge."

Ruel followed her out of the temple. "I'd better be the one to come for Kartauk. If Abdar's found out I've managed to buy Cinnidar from the maharajah, he'll know you're his only route to Kartauk and will be keeping a closer watch on you."

"You can't come here alone. You don't know the way."

"Yes, I do." He smiled as he saw her startled expression. "I could have led you here the last three times. I have a very good sense of direction and the maze you ran me was nothing compared to the sewers of London. Did I mention I was once a rat catcher?"

Her lips tightened. "So you made a fool of me again."

His smile vanished. "I could never make a fool of you, Jane. You have too much dignity and strength."

For the first time since he had arrived at the bungalow today, she really looked at him. The hardness that was so much a part of his expression was gone, she realized. No, perhaps not entirely gone, but the gentleness with which he was looking at her reminded her of Ian. Impossible, it had to be a trick. He was nothing like his brother. "Sweet words."

"True words." He glanced away from her. "I want to tell you something else." He paused before blurting out, "I'm . . . sorry."

"What?" she said blankly.

"You heard me. Don't ask me to repeat it." He strode on down the path, still not looking at her. "And I won't lie and tell you I wouldn't do the same thing again. I wanted you and I wanted Cinnidar and there's every chance I'd fall from grace."

"Then why apologize? Why this change?"

"You too? Why does everyone insist I've changed? I merely wanted to—"

"Why?" she repeated.

He was silent a moment and then finally said simply, "I think I'm happy. I don't ever remember being happy. I've been content, satisfied, but not happy. It's a very odd feeling."

"And now you're happy because you've got your Cinnidar?"

"It's more than Cinnidar. It's like . . ."

"What?"

"A new life, a chance to start over . . ." He grinned. "Like getting off the train at the last stop and knowing it's where you want to be. Does that make it clearer?"

"Yes." He was describing how she had felt when she left Frenchie's those many years ago, and she felt a sudden sense of kinship with him. "That makes it much clearer."

"Anyway, I wanted to tell you." He paused and then changed the subject. "You really think Li Sung will go to Zabrie?"

She nodded miserably. "He won't listen to me. I wanted him to be happy but—" She had to steady her voice. "He's always helped me and I wanted to help him too. Blast it, I should never have interfered."

"How did he help you?"

"So many ways."

"Tell me one."

"Books. He taught me to read and write and cipher. His father believed knowledge would save Li Sung from staying a common laborer and made him study every book he could get his hands on from the time he was a small child. What Li Sung didn't know, we learned together."

"Kartauk said you've been together a long time."

"He came to Frenchie's, the place I grew up, when he was twelve. His father had been killed and Li Sung's leg crushed in an accident a few months before. He was seventeen when we left with Patrick."

"What kind of accident?"

"His father was a brakeman and was training Li Sung to the trade." Her smile was bitter. "Li Sung was very proud of his father. Chinese were considered good enough to work the rails but not to be an engineer or fire a train, and even brakemen jobs were rare. His father could do all three and taught Li Sung. However, braking the train was his primary duty and one day he and Li Sung were both caught between two railroad cars and crushed."

Ruel's lips pursed in a low whistle.

"Oh, it wasn't an unusual accident. It happened all the time before Westinghouse invented the air brake that could be worked from the cab by the engineer. Before that a link-and-pin coupler fastened one car to another, and to work it a brakeman had to stand between the cars. If he didn't get the pin into the link at the right moment, the cars would come together and crush him." Her lips tightened. "Which may be why the honor of being a brakeman was given to a Chinese. Li Sung's father would probably never have been promoted to engineer."

"And does the maharajah's train have these air brakes?"

She nodded. "I had to cut corners on other things, but I made sure of those brakes." She gave him a sidewise glance. "Why are you asking all these questions about Li Sung?"

"No reason," Ruel said casually. "Just curious."

"You were very strong tonight," Zabrie murmured as she brushed a kiss on Li Sung's shoulder. "Every time you get better and better." She rose from the bed, draped herself in a gossamer-thin shawl that accented rather than hid her nudity. "Wine?"

Li Sung shook his head as he sat up in bed. "I must leave now."

"Not yet. Stay awhile." Zabrie crossed to the table and poured herself a glass of wine. "I have no other customers, and even if I did, I would give them to one of the other women." She turned and smiled at him. "For you."

She was more beautiful than he had ever seen her, Li Sung thought. Or perhaps it was because this was the last time, she appeared more lovely to him.

She moved back toward him. "I should be angry. You have not come to see me in a long time." She sat down beside him on the bed, her middle finger tracing a line across his chest. "Why?"

"I was—" He broke off as her hennaed nail raked his nipple. "I cannot think when you do that, and there is something I must say."

"I don't wish you to think."

His hand covered hers on his chest. "I want to say good-bye."

Her head lifted. "You are leaving Kasanpore? When?"

"Soon."

"That is no answer." She was silent a moment, looking at him. "Take me with you."

His eyes widened. "What?"

"I want to go with you." She set her goblet on the floor beside the bed and leaned over to kiss his chest. "You know I please you and could make you happy. I'm weary of these men who use me and then spit on me because of my birth. You do not treat me this way."

"No." He felt a leap of hope as he gently stroked her shining black hair. The scent of jasmine drifted to him; he loved the way she always smelled of flowers and spices. "I also have known that pain. You truly wish to go with me?"

"Give me a week to settle my affairs here in Kasanpore and I'll—" She caught his expression. "No?"

"Two days."

"It will rush me, but it can be done." She threw aside the shawl and moved over him. "I want you again. We will talk of the details later. Yes?"

"Zabrie . . ." He closed his eyes as her hand closed around him and he began to harden. Did he love her? At times he was sure he loved her. Certainly his body was enslaved by her. "Yes, we will talk later. . . ."

He was a fool, Ruel told himself as he glared at the door of Zabrie's pleasure house through the heavily falling rain. Not only was he a fool but would probably be a drowned fool if he didn't give up this watch and go back to the hotel.

Li Sung walked out of Zabrie's.

Ruel warily straightened away from the wall as he saw Li Sung cross the street and head directly to the alcove where Ruel was standing.

"You appear a little damp," Li Sung said.

"I'm damn near floating away." Ruel grimaced. "You knew I was here?"

"I've grown accustomed to watching behind me in the last weeks. I suppose you had a reason for following me?"

"Maybe I only felt like taking a stroll."

Li Sung smiled derisively as he glanced out at the driving rain. "It is an odd night for a walk. Are you so fond of the rain?"

"I've forgotten it ever did anything else in Kasanpore."

"Are you going to answer me?"

Ruel shrugged. "I thought it wouldn't hurt to make sure you weren't surprised."

"Zabrie would not surprise me."

"It's not wise to trust anyone too far, Li Sung."

"I thank you for your advice."

"But you have no intention of heeding it." Ruel nodded. "I'm not good at taking advice myself. Zabrie asked no questions?"

Li Sung glanced back at the house. "She wishes to go with me."

Ruel went still. "How . . . surprising. And I suppose you told her about our plans to leave in two days."

"I told her."

Ruel said carefully, "May I suggest that wasn't the most clever—"

"Hush." Li Sung's hand closed on Ruel's arm and jerked him farther back into the shadows.

Ruel's gaze followed Li Sung's and his lips pursed in a soundless whistle.

Zabrie had come out of the house and was moving quickly down the street.

"An odd night for a walk." Ruel repeated Li Sung's words.

"Yes." Li Sung's voice was strained. "Come." He started down the street after Zabrie.

Ruel followed him. "Where are we going?"

"I have to see where she is going."

Zabrie's destination became obvious fifteen minutes later when she disappeared through the gates of the Savitsar palace.

"Abdar," Ruel said.

Li Sung stared at the gate through which Zabrie had disappeared.

"No harm done, Li Sung," Ruel said quietly. "We can change our plans now that we know she's betrayed us."

"No harm done," Li Sung repeated dully. He slowly turned and limped down the street. "But we have no need to change our plans. I told Zabrie we were taking a boat from a point down the river to Narinth. I'm quite sure Pachtal and Abdar will be waiting on the dock in Narinth for us two nights from now."

Ruel's gaze narrowed on his face. "You suspected her?"

"I am no fool. At times she made me feel like a giant, but I know I am only a cripple." His lips twisted bitterly. "No, she thought me worse than a cripple, a dupe."

"Well, you're no dupe. You were planning on waiting outside to see if she would go to Abdar?"

"I had to be certain. One can know with one's mind and still not believe." He turned to Ruel. "It is finished and you need no longer stay with me. Neither you nor Jane have reason to feel uneasy any longer."

"Jane has nothing to do with this. You're going back to the temple?"

He nodded.

"It's a long way." Ruel's lids lowered to veil his eyes. "My hotel is only a block from here and Ian keeps a bottle of whiskey in his room."

"I do not drink liquor. It blurs the mind and makes children of wise men."

"Just a thought." Ruel smiled at him. "Sometimes a wee drop helps to keep the damp away. If you change your mind, you're welcome. Good night, Li Sung." He turned the corner and started up the street toward the hotel.

"Wait."

Ruel glanced over his shoulder to see Li Sung limping down the street behind him.

"Perhaps a wee drop."

Chapter 8

The pounding at the bungalow door jerked Jane from sleep. It was the middle of the night. Who could be—

The pounding sounded again, louder.

She hastily threw a robe over her white cotton nightgown, ran to the front door, and flung it open.

Ruel and Li Sung stood on the porch.

"What are you doing here?" Jane whispered. She glanced anxiously over her shoulder, but the knocking had evidently not disturbed Patrick. Her gaze flew back to Li Sung. "What's wrong. Why aren't you at the temple?"

"He wanted to see you." Ruel made a face. "And made his desire known at the top of his voice. It was a question of being thrown out of the hotel or bringing him here."

"What was he doing at the hotel?"

"A wee drop," Li Sung murmured. He swayed and his knees gave way.

Ruel caught him and leaned him against the doorjamb.

"He's drunk," Jane said blankly. "Li Sung never drinks."

"A wee drop . . ." Li Sung's eyes closed.

"*Now* he wants to sleep," Ruel said in disgust. "He was wide awake and noisy as the devil at the hotel."

"You got him drunk," she accused Ruel.

"Aye, it seemed a good idea at the time." Ruel shifted his hold. "Is there a place here he can sleep, or do I have to drag him back to the hotel?"

"The veranda." She stepped aside and watched him half carry, half drag Li Sung across the room toward the french doors. "Why was it a good idea?"

"Do you think I set out to corrupt your virtuous friend?" He dropped him on the couch, snatched up a pillow, and put it under his head. "If I did, you can bet it won't happen again. After the second drink he insisted on shouting Chinese proverbs at the top of his voice."

"Why was it a good idea?" Jane repeated. "And why was he at your hotel and not at the temple?"

"We ran into each other outside Zabrie's, and I invited him back to have a drink."

"Zabrie!" Her gaze went to Li Sung, who was now curled on his side, sleeping peacefully. "And what were you doing outside— You followed him?"

"I was just out for a stroll."

"You followed him."

"He's crippled and I didn't like the idea of Pachtal— Dammit, how do I know why I did it? I seem to be acting on impulse more often than not these days." He picked up a cashmere throw from the chair and tossed it over Li Sung. "You don't have to worry about him going back to Zabrie's. She went straight from Li Sung to Abdar at Savitsar Palace. After which our friend here felt the need of a bit of comforting oblivion."

"I see." She felt the tears sting her eyes as she looked at Li Sung. "I should never have meddled. She hurt him."

"He said she also made him feel like a giant. You have to take the bitter with the sweet."

She swallowed. "Thank you for caring for him. It was very kind."

"I'm *not* kind. I told you, it was an impulse that I—" He stopped and then said gruffly, "I don't like to see you worried and unhappy. It bothered me."

She gazed at him in bewilderment. "How strange."

"I thought so too," he said testily. "And there's something else. I've been doing a bit of thinking since this afternoon—" He stopped and then said in a rush, "Oh, what the hell, there's no other way to say it. I've decided I want to marry you."

She stared at him in shock. She didn't think she had heard him correctly. "I beg your pardon."

"Not right away. It's going to be a few years before I can offer you anything but the chance to watch me slave myself half to death. But when I have the mine working and the money starts rolling in . . ." He grimaced. "God knows when that will be. I may be asking you to wait as long as Ian has for Margaret."

She shook her head dazedly. "I don't understand this."

"Ian says I want a home. He says I need . . ." He shrugged. "Maybe he's right. What's a home without a wife?"

"And that's why you want me?"

"Not altogether. I . . . feel something for you."

"Lust."

"No, something else."

"Guilt."

"No." He suddenly burst out, "Why do you keep asking me questions? I don't want you to leave me. I want to take care of you." His tone became brusque.

"But it wouldn't be a bad proposition for you. I'd make sure you had everything you wanted and wouldn't ask anything except that you occupy my bed and eventually give me a child. Does that sound reasonable?"

"Very reasonable." She felt totally confused. She had never expected this, never even imagined it could happen. Marriage. Ruel. It would be like being wed to a warlock. "More reasonable than the idea of you wanting to marry me."

"Well, what do you say?"

She drew a deep breath and shook her head. "No, thank you."

"Why not?" He said quickly before she could reply, "I know we started out wrong, but I can make it right. I respect you and, though you may not admire me, you respect me too."

"I couldn't trust you."

"You'd learn to trust me. I don't betray my friends, and in time you'd find that out."

"The railroad . . ."

"I'd take care of your Patrick too."

"Patrick doesn't need taking care of," she said quickly. "And even if he did . . . I'd hate the life you've offered me. Can't you see? I'm not the kind of woman you'd want for a wife." She added flatly, "And you're not what I want either."

A flicker of emotion crossed his face, and for a moment she thought she had hurt him. She would have sworn the Ruel she knew could never be hurt by her, but this strange new Ruel was more vulnerable. No, she must have been mistaken, for he was smiling with his usual mockery.

"I beg to disagree. There are portions of my person you still want very much."

She stiffened. "You're wrong."

"I'm not wrong. Do you think I don't feel it too? It's there all the time between us." His awkwardness was abruptly gone and she was suddenly, vibrantly aware of him. And that was what he wanted, she realized with trepidation. In the wink of an eye he had changed into the sensual mandarin of those days before they had come together in the railway car and she could feel the magnetism he was exerting as if it were a tangible entity.

"You'll find I'm always obliging when it comes to giving a lady what she wants." He turned and moved toward the french doors. "And, as I definitely want to stake a claim before we part ways, I can see I'll have to make an attempt to remind you of just what we've both been missing. Expect me for dinner tomorrow night."

"No, I don't want you to—"

"Expect me." He looked back at her, his gaze running over her loose, shabby cotton robe. "I've never seen you in a nightgown before." He frowned. "If you can call that garment a nightgown. Someday I'm going to see you in something more womanly."

He left the veranda and a moment later she heard the front door close behind him.

"Go away, Ruel," she said as soon as she opened the door of the bungalow the next evening. "I told you not to come. I don't want you here."

His brows lifted. "I take it dinner's not ready?" He took off his wet slicker and dropped it on the porch beside the door. He was dressed more formally than she had ever seen him, in a dark brown suit, crisp white shirt, and black cravat at his throat. The light from the porch lantern played on the polished sheen of his black boots and the brilliant tawny streaks in his brown hair. His unexpected elegance caught her off guard and made her awkwardly aware of her own rough clothing.

There was no reason for her to feel defensive, she told herself. He was the intruder here. "Go away."

"Well, if you refuse to feed me, I'll just come in and have a word with Patrick. Is he on the veranda?"

"He's gone to bed."

"Already? It's barely eight-thirty. Didn't he object to you rushing him through dinner and whisking him off to bed?"

"I didn't—" She stopped as she met his knowing

gaze. "What if I did? I didn't want you here and you've made sure Patrick thinks you're his friend. You have no need to talk to him."

"Oh, but I do. I intend to ask for his daughter's hand." He snapped his fingers. "But then, that would confuse him, wouldn't it? He won't admit he has a daughter."

"You're not serious?"

"Of course I'm serious. Since I'm walking the path of virtue, I want to observe all the proper forms. He can't be asleep yet. I'll just go in and—"

"No!" She drew a deep breath. "This is foolishness and I won't have you bothering Patrick."

He suddenly gave in. "Very well."

She started to swing the door shut.

"If you'll come and walk out with me."

"Walk out?"

"At home in Glenclaren it's the custom for an affianced couple to walk out together in the evening. Properly chaperoned, of course."

"I have no desire to 'walk out' with you."

"Then I'll be forced to come in and have my talk with Patrick. I believe he'll give his consent to the match. As you say, he has a liking for me."

He was clearly not to be swayed. "It's raining," she said weakly.

"All right, I'll be satisfied with sitting with you on the veranda." His brows lifted. "Providing Li Sung has vacated the couch."

"He went back to the temple early this morning." She gazed at him in frustration. He was smiling, but she could sense both recklessness and implacable resolution beneath that glittering exterior. She threw open the door and turned on her heel. "Very well, ten minutes."

"Yes, memsahib." He followed her across the room toward the open french doors. "You see how obedient I am? Obeying your every wish, trailing at your heels like your faithful dog, Sam."

"Sam doesn't trail at my heels." She sat down on the

cushioned rattan couch. "Even he has too much sense for that."

"A remark aimed at me?" He sat down beside her. "But I'm not so favored as Sam. I've trespassed and must exhibit the proper show of humility."

"You?"

He chuckled. "I agree the idea is foreign to me, but I'm trying to make an adjustment. Give me your hand."

"Why?"

"I want to hold it. I'm sure even Ian and his Margaret hold hands. It's a proper courting procedure."

"We're not courting."

"Of course we are." He took her hand and threaded his fingers through hers. "I thought I'd made that clear. No, don't jerk away from me. I'm only holding your hand." His tone was soothing. "We'll just sit here and make conversation and listen to the rain."

Her muscles were tensed and she had to force herself to sit still. She was acutely conscious of his shoulder touching hers, their locked hands.

"Relax. I'm no threat to you. Actually, I'm trying to show you how tame I can be."

If she hadn't been so tense, she would have laughed aloud. He was no more tame than the winds preceding a typhoon.

She tried to ignore the heat beginning to spread from the hand he was holding to her wrist and upper arm. "You seem to know a great deal about courting customs in Glenclaren."

"Only from hearsay. I was a wild lad and never had the patience for any of the more proper traditions."

And the mandarin would have no need of patience. He would charm and issue a siren call and everything and everyone would come to him. She moistened her lips. "Is Glenclaren far from—"

"I don't want to talk about Glenclaren. It's a dank, depressing place." He turned and smiled at her. "And didn't suit me at all. It wouldn't suit you either. Once we're wed, we'll live on Cinnidar."

Exasperated, she sought a less personal subject to distract him. "How did you find your Cinnidar?"

"I was on a ship bound from Australia to Africa that put in at Cinnidar to take on food and water. When the ship left, I stayed on."

"Why?"

He shrugged. "I . . . liked it. I felt—" He stopped, searching for words. "It called to me."

"Is it beautiful?"

"I suppose it is." He thought about it. "Yes, Cinnidar is beautiful."

"But that's not why you liked it."

"The moment I saw it I knew it was going to belong to me. I *felt* it." He turned her hand over and idly traced patterns in her palm with his index finger. "And since it was obviously meant to be mine, I couldn't see why fate wouldn't furbish the island with what I loved most."

She chuckled. "Gold."

He nodded. "I had to go and see. There's a trail down the canyon wall, but it was blocked with stones I had to crawl over, and after I reached the canyon floor it took me three weeks to make my way through the jungle and get to the mountain. A few times I didn't think I'd make it. But when I got there . . ." His face lit with eagerness. "Veins, not pockets of gold. Rich wide veins . . . Even the streams were full of nuggets. I could reach down and pick up a nugget as big as a goose egg."

"Did you gather them to take with you?"

He shook his head. "Word of a strike would have gotten out, and Cinnidar had to be legally mine before that happened. So I went back to the port ragged and half starved with nothing but my hands in my pockets and told everyone I'd never made it past the canyon. I shipped out on the next boat that put into port and went to the gold fields in Jaylenburg. It took me three years and two gold fields, but I finally made a big enough strike to provide me with enough money to buy Cinnidar from the maharajah."

Three years of staggering work and deprivation and

all for Cinnidar, she thought. "And now you're going back."

"Yes, I'll send for you as soon as—" He stopped as he saw her expression. "It *will* happen, Jane." He reached out and touched a tendril of hair at her temple. "I've never seen you with your hair loose. I want to see it flowing about your shoulders. I wanted to unbraid it when we were in the railway coach but I was hurting so bad I couldn't wait."

She felt the heat rise to her cheeks, suffusing her throat and breasts.

"I could do it now," Ruel said softly. His index finger rubbed slowly back and forth on her palm, and a tingle ran up her arm. "I could do anything you want me to do. Patrick's asleep and wouldn't bother us. I could close the doors and—"

"No," she whispered. Sweet Mary, her breasts were swelling, pushing against the material of her shirt. Let him not notice. But he probably did know, she realized in despair. He seemed to know how to trigger her every response.

"Do you remember the maharajah's painting? There are so many ways of pleasure, and I want to show you all of them."

She couldn't get her breath and was beginning to tremble as she had that day in the railroad car. She suddenly knew she wanted to kneel down like the woman in the painting, to obey him blindly, to do anything he wanted of her.

She was acutely aware of the faint scent of soap surrounding him, the tiny jolts of sensation as his finger rubbed her palm, the sound of the rain on the thatched roof of the bungalow.

Like the sound of the rain on the maharajah's railway car . . .

"But this is different," he said as if he had read her mind. "I'm not trying to seduce you."

"Aren't you?"

"I want only to show you that you need me as much as I—God, that's not true." He laughed desperately.

"That's how it started, but now I don't give a damn about showing you how tame and respectable I could be."

She should pull away, but she couldn't seem to move. "Let me go," she whispered.

His grasp tightened for a brief instant, and then he slowly released her hand. "You see how good I'm being? I didn't want to let you go." He stood up and strode toward the door. "But I'm keeping my promise. The ten minutes are up and I'm leaving." He paused at the french doors to glance back at her. "But it's not over, and you're not going to get rid of me. I'm staying here in Kasanpore until you and Patrick leave."

"That would be a waste of time. I'm not going to change my mind. And what about your Cinnidar?"

"I've worked and waited years for Cinnidar. I can wait a little longer." He smiled. "You're worth it, Jane Barnaby."

The locomotive was already spouting steam, the head lanterns blazing when Ruel bounded into the cab.

"Kartauk?" Jane asked.

"Safely ensconced at Lanpur Gorge." He grinned. "We rigged a lean-to shelter of sorts for him on the embankment, but he was still swearing because he has to wait in the rain for us. I had to assure him Scotland has no monsoons."

She braced herself against the blast of energy Ruel exuded as he stood smiling at her. After a near sleepless night she had told herself she was ready to withstand that magnetism, but it came as a fresh shock. The rain-wet brown slicker he wore was no more glossy than his tawny-streaked hair, and he glowed with the same brilliant beauty as the lanterns on the front of the locomotive. She had an almost irresistible urge to step forward and touch him.

She glanced quickly away from him. "Ian arrived a quarter of an hour ago. He's in the maharajah's car. He said he planned on napping in splendor while we labored. Why are you late?"

"I paid a visit to the palace and requested an audience with Abdar."

Jane's eyes swung back to him. "What?"

He grinned. "And was told by a servant that His Highness had left this morning to go to Narinth." He turned to Li Sung, who was sitting in the engineer's seat. "It seems your misdirection was successful."

"So it would appear," Li Sung said without expression. "But appearances sometimes lie. Who is to know if Abdar did not guess at the deception and is waiting to ambush us somewhere along the track?"

"Very true." Ruel looked at the engine controls. "Are you sure you know how to drive this monster of a locomotive?"

"My father taught me as a boy and I ran supplies up and down the line in Salisbury." He stiffened. "Of course Patrick never considered a Chinese good enough to engineer a passenger train. Perhaps you agree and would prefer to try yourself?"

"No, thank you. I'll be happy to labor at your command."

"An unusual attitude for a white." Li Sung smiled faintly. "I feel quite giddy with delight. We Chinese are not unaccustomed to being allowed such power over round-eyes."

"It's time we left." Jane told Ruel, "You can stoke the boiler. I'm going to have to be on the lookout for hazards on the track." She signaled to Li Sung, and a moment later the locomotive pulled out of the station. "Patrick said the tracks were clear all the way to Narinth when he inspected them yesterday, but that doesn't mean something might not have happened in the meantime."

They were forced to stop twice before they reached Sikor Gorge, once to clear a fallen tree from the track, the second time to shoo a water buffalo who stood placidly chewing grass half on, half off the rails.

They slowed as they crossed Sikor Gorge, but once

over the raging river Li Sung picked up speed and the locomotive glided smoothly over the tracks.

"Lanpur Gorge is just ahead around the bend," Jane said. "Be on the lookout for Kartauk."

"In this rain he can see the train's lights better than we can see him." Ruel moved over to stand beside her at the window. Through the heavy rain he could catch only glimpses of the yellowish gleam of the Zastu as the train started over Lanpur Bridge. "And you can be sure Kartauk is going to be ready to get out of this rain and jump on board as soon as we slow— What's that?"

Jane heard it too and her heart lurched. "Li Sung!"

"I know." Li Sung's voice was hoarse as he put on more power. "It's only three cars. The thrust may get us across before—"

The locomotive tilted, ground to a halt, jerked sidewise like a snake switching its tail.

"What the hell is happening?" Ruel asked.

"One of the back cars is off the tracks," Jane said. She felt as if the blood were freezing in her veins.

"Abdar!" Ruel swore beneath his breath.

The train jerked again and the cab was suddenly swaying.

"Get her out!" Li Sung snapped to Ruel as he applied the brakes. "The cab's off the track too. I think it's going over."

"Christ!" Ruel picked Jane up and leapt for the side of the track. They hit the bridge with bruising impact and rolled over and over.

The wooden bridge was vibrating beneath them, and between the ties Jane could glimpse the rushing water sixty feet below. This couldn't be happening, she thought frantically. Dear God, why?

"Li Sung!" Jane screamed.

She saw Li Sung at the door of the cab. An instant later he jumped.

Her relief vanished when Li Sung's bad leg folded beneath him as he hit the track. He fell, slipping toward the edge of the bridge.

Ruel muttered something beneath his breath, rolled

over, and grabbed Li Sung's left arm at the moment he slid over the side. "Help me," he grated to Li Sung, the muscles of his upper arms distended with strain as he supported the man's weight. "Give me your other hand too."

"No, let me." Jane was immediately beside him, grabbing the hand Li Sung extended. Together they managed to pull him back on the bridge.

"Run!" Ruel leapt to his feet. "Get to the embankment." He whirled away from them. "I have to go see what—" He broke off as he saw the last car, the maharajah's car, teetering back and forth, its sheer weight causing it to seesaw off the bridge and tip toward the gorge. "Ian!"

Ian was in the maharajah's car, Jane remembered in horror. Why hadn't he jumped? She knew less than a minute had passed since she had jumped from the cab, but it seemed an eternity.

"Get off this damn bridge!" Ruel grabbed Jane's arm and pushed her forward toward the safety of the embankment a few yards away.

The heavy door of the maharajah's car was jerked open. Ian stood in the doorway, a bewildered expression on his face. His forehead was bleeding. "Ruel!"

"Ian! Jump!" Ruel ran along the bridge toward the maharajah's car. The bridge was vibrating, the ties spreading like teeth in a gaping, screaming mouth.

Another sound, even more ominous, a creaking of metal on metal. The bridge jerked, throwing Jane to the ground. Her panicky gaze flew back to the maharajah's car. Ruel had also been thrown to his knees a few yards before he reached the car. As she watched, Ian catapulted back into the car as it fell off the bridge and hung over the abyss suspended only by the coupling link to the two cars still on the track. God, let it hold, she prayed desperately. Let Ian get out!

The coupling link held, but gravity and the weight of the car was too great.

"No!" Ruel struggled to his knees, watching helplessly as all three railway cars tumbled slowly off the bridge toward the muddy water sixty feet below.

"Ian!"

If she lived another hundred years, Jane knew she would never forget Ruel's agonized scream of protest and horror.

The maharajah's private car and passenger car struck the flat rocks lining the bank, crumpling like toys on impact, the wooden sides collapsing as if fashioned of paper. The locomotive sank into the water like a submerging crocodile.

"Dear God . . ." she whispered.

"Watch out for her, Li Sung." Ruel was running past them, skidding down the muddy embankment toward the crumpled car on the rocks below.

"No!" Jane didn't realize she had screamed the word. Ruel was going to be killed! He mustn't die. She couldn't live if Ruel died. She couldn't live . . .

She started after him down the embankment but had gone only a few feet when Li Sung tackled her, knocked her to the ground, and sat astride her.

"Get off me!" She struggled desperately, pounding at Li Sung's chest. "Don't you understand? He's going to die. They're both going to die. I've got to—"

"And you'll die, too, if I let you go," Li Sung said. "Ruel's mad to think he can save his brother. The crash probably killed him."

"How do you know if we don't try?"

"He's right, Jane." Kartauk was suddenly kneeling beside them, a lantern in his hand, his hair plastered about his pale face. "Listen to him."

She closed her eyes, feeling the tears running down her cheeks. Ian was dead and soon Ruel would be dead too. "Did you see it, Kartauk?" she whispered.

"I saw it all," Kartauk said grimly. "And I never want to see anything like it again."

"It fell. It shouldn't have fallen. . . ."

"What?"

"Never mind." She couldn't lie there and give up when Ruel had not. She wasn't certain Ian was dead, and by some miracle perhaps Ruel would manage to get them both out alive. They had to be ready to help if they were needed. Ruel mustn't die. He mustn't die. . . .

"Get off me, Li Sung." She turned to Kartauk. "Rope. Did Ruel include any rope with the supplies he gave you?

The wreckage of the maharajah's car balanced on the rocks percariously, half in the water. Ruel crawled through the only entrance, a gaping opening at the river's edge.

The splendid interior of the car was now a shapeless tangle of girders, trusses, crushed timbers, and smashed and overturned furniture. The porcelain stove was upside down, releasing flames that were now licking hungrily in an attempt to destroy what little was left of the car. The fire would be no problem, Ruel thought, the driving rain was already extinguishing it. He paused just inside the car, his gaze frantically searching the wreckage.

Ian lay on the floor of the train, his body twisted and half buried under the caved-in roof of the car.

Ruel crawled forward and began tearing desperately at the debris covering him.

The car slipped farther into the river; muddy yellow water gushed into the car.

He lifted the divan off Ian.

"No, leave me . . ."

Ruel's gaze flew to Ian's face, and relief rippled through him. His brother's eyes were open, his face contorted with pain, but he was alive.

"The hell I will." Ruel edged the divan to one side.

The car shifted another inch, and water poured over the top of Ruel's boots.

"It's too late," Ian gasped. "Save yourself."

"Shut up." Ruel hands quickly went over Ian's arms and legs. "Nothing seems to be broken. Can you move?"

Ian stirred, then fell back with a low cry.

"No? Then I'll have to drag you." Ruel snatched the ivory-colored cords from the drapes lying on the floor. "I'm going to make a harness. Once I'm in the water, I may not be able to hold on to you." His hands quickly fashioned the harness as he spoke. He slipped on the makeshift harness and then knotted the other end of the cord under Ian's armpits. "Ready? Here we go." He grabbed Ian beneath the armpits and pulled.

Ian screamed.

The cry flayed Ruel. "God, I'm sorry," he muttered as he pulled Ian another foot. "But the car can't stay on these rocks much longer. Once it tumbles into the water, we'll be swept away."

"Not your fault . . . coward . . ."

"You're not a coward." Ruel dragged him another foot. "Only two yards more."

"Stop." Ian groaned. "Can't stand it."

"All right." Ruel stopped pulling and dropped to his knees beside Ian, glaring at him. "Then we'll both stay here and let the goddamn river kill us. Is that what you want? Because I'm not leaving you."

"Ruel, please. Don't . . ." Ian wearily closed his eyes. "All right, pull. . . ."

The next few minutes were excruciating agony for Ian and backbreaking effort for Ruel.

They finally reached the opening, and Ruel stopped to catch his breath. Ian was barely on the verge of consciousness, and how in hell was he to get him out of the car and onto the rocks with the least damage?

The decision was made for him as the car slid forward off the rocks into the water.

The current whipped them away from the railway car as if they were bits of kindling. The next moment Ruel was dashed against the rocks. He instinctively reached out, grabbing for a boulder.

Pain.

Blackness.

He had to hold on. Ian . . . where was Ian? He felt a tug at the harness and turned to see Ian floating a few feet away. He hoisted himself up on the rocks, then turned and started pulling hand over hand on the cord binding him to his brother. The current was fighting him, taking Ian, jerking Ruel back toward the water.

It seemed an eternity before Ian was close enough for Ruel to reach out and drag him up on the rocks.

Ian lay still, no longer conscious. Perhaps not even alive.

"Don't die, damn you. You can't die." Ruel pressed his ear to Ian's breast. Nothing. He shifted his head higher and detected a faint heartbeat. Alive, thank God, but for how long? He adjusted the cords of the harness over his shoulders and began to crawl over the rocks, dragging Ian behind.

One yard. Two yards. Something warm ran down his shoulder. Rain? No, blood from the cords cutting into his shoulders, he realized dimly.

He reached the embankment and started up the steep incline, his boots sinking ankle-deep in the mud.

He dragged Ian five yards. Slipped back two.

Went another three yards. Slipped back five.

He cursed and started up the slope again.

"We'll take him. Take off the harness."

It was Kartauk speaking, on the embankment in front of him, Ruel realized hazily. Kartauk and Jane.

Kartauk swiftly unfastened the cords from Ruel's back. "Lord, you're cut to pieces."

"Ian . . ."

"We'll get him." Jane was replacing the cords around Ian's body with the rope she carried. "Li Sung tied the other end of the rope to a tree at the top of the embankment. As soon as we reach the top, we'll pull him up." She tested the knot. "It's secure. Let's go."

Ruel staggered behind Kartauk and Jane up the embankment. The going was difficult but not impossible without Ian's weight burdening him. It took them ten minutes to reach the top, where Li Sung waited. Together, they pulled Ian up the rest of the slope.

"Is he alive?" Li Sung asked.

"Yes," Ruel said. "Let's get him under Kartauk's lean-to and out of this rain."

A few minutes later they managed to drag Ian underneath the crude tarpaulin-covered shelter. "Take care of him." Ruel turned and staggered away from them toward the bridge.

"Where are you going?" Jane called.

"Kasanpore. Doctor . . ."

"You can barely walk. How can you make it to Kasanpore?"

"No one else. Kartauk can't go," he said jerkily. "Neither can Li Sung . . . crippled."

"What about me?"

"Stop arguing with me." He glanced over his shoulder, his eyes blazing at her. "Just keep Ian alive until I get back."

Jane held her breath as she watched him start across the gorge. The bridge appeared to be still intact, but she couldn't be sure after the punishment it had taken.

Her breath expelled in a rush of relief as Ruel finally reached the bank on the other side. A moment later he was lost to sight around the bend.

Keep Ian alive until I get back.

And how was she going to do that? Jane wondered in despair as she turned to stare down at Ian. He looked as if he was barely clinging to life right now, and it would be hours before Ruel could get back with help. The blanket they had draped over him was already damp and she had no way to keep him dry, no way to build a fire.

And when Ruel returned with help, they would find Kartauk.

She might not be able to keep Ian alive, but there was a chance she could still save Kartauk from Abdar. She turned to Li Sung. "I want you to take Kartauk to Narinth."

"I won't leave you here," Kartauk said.

"Do what I tell you!" She had to pause to steady her voice. "I've lost everything else. I *won't* lose you to Abdar. I'll tell everyone Li Sung was killed in the train wreck. Perhaps Abdar will think you were on the train and killed too. When you get to Narinth, put up at an inn near the waterfront and contact me when you've arrived."

Kartauk frowned. "I don't think—"

"Stop thinking and do what I tell you. I'll be safer here than you will. It may take you days to get to Narinth on foot."

Li Sung grasped Kartauk's arm. "She's right. There's nothing we can do to help her, and your discovery will only endanger her. I will make sure he is kept safe, Jane."

"I know you will," she said dully. "Good luck."

She turned back to stare down at Ian. At this moment it seemed impossible there could be good fortune anywhere in the world. Poor Ian. She doubted if he would ever see Glenclaren or his Margaret again. When she looked up a few minutes later, Li Sung and Kartauk were gone.

She trudged to the edge of the bridge and looked down at the rails crossing the gorge, then beyond them to the wreckage of the train in the river. Her stomach twisted and the bile rose in her throat. She turned and walked back to the lean-to.

Keep him alive.

It seemed an impossible task, but she had to try to do as Ruel had commanded. She had to salvage something from this horror. She had to save Ian for Ruel. She lay down close to Ian on the wet earth, cuddling close to him, trying to share her warmth.

"No!" They were taking him away from her. Didn't they understand he would die if she didn't keep him warm? "No, you can't . . ."

"Shh, it's all right." Ruel's voice. "They're putting him on a stretcher to carry him over the bridge."

She became conscious of voices, lanterns, movement all around her, and struggled to a sitting position. "Is he still alive?"

"Barely." Ruel's tone was clipped as he rose to his

feet and helped her to her feet. "But we have to get him out of this foul weather. Patrick has a wagon waiting on the other side of Sikor Gorge and we'll make better time once we reach there." His gaze searched her face. "You look as pale as Ian. Can you walk across the bridge? There are some ties missing and it's not safe for me to carry you."

"I can walk." She stumbled after the four men carrying Ian, her gaze fixed desperately on the stretcher. "He has to live . . . my fault."

"Don't be ridiculous," Ruel said harshly. "No one's to blame. At first I thought Abdar must have done this, but it seems to me he would have appeared by now, and why would he want to sabotage the train? I'm beginning to think it was only an accident." They reached the other side of the gorge, and he swung her up into his arms. "God, you're shaking yourself to pieces. It's no wonder you're not thinking clearly."

"My fault . . ."

She woke in her bedroom in the bungalow later to find Ruel in a chair beside her bed. He had changed to dry clothes but still looked terrible. Dark circles colored the flesh beneath his eyes, and deep grooves scored either side of his lips.

"Ian?" she whispered.

"Still with us. We were afraid to move him any farther than the bungalow, so Patrick gave up his room and brought a doctor from the fort. Dr. Kendrick's with him now. I suppose he's doing everything he can."

"Of course he is."

He said haltingly, "I want to thank you for helping my brother." He wonderingly repeated the words. "My brother. Do you know I haven't called Ian that since we were boys together? I thought if I could keep him at a distance . . ." He closed his eyes. "I . . . love him, you know."

"Yes, I could see it whenever you were together."

"Could you? Then maybe he could see it too. God

knows I tried hard enough not to admit it. I didn't want to love him. I didn't want to love anyone, but somehow . . ." His eyes opened. "He won't wake up. The doctor says there's not much he can do. Ian might never wake up, just drift away. . . ."

"I'm so sorry, Ruel," she said gently.

His eyes were suddenly glittering fiercely. "There's nothing to be sorry about. Because the doctor's wrong. I'm not going to let Ian die."

"But if there's nothing you can do . . ."

"There's always something you can do." He stood up and strode toward the door. "And I'm going to do it."

The door slammed behind him.

Dear God, she loved him. The knowledge that had exploded inside her when she had seen Ruel running down that embankment was thorn-sharp. Wasn't love supposed to be sweet? She felt no sweetness, only a sense of the inevitable. No matter how she had tried to prevent it, her feelings had grown, deepened until she had been forced to face and acknowledge them. She didn't *want* to feel love for Ruel MacClaren, dammit. He was ruthless, mocking, and self-serving, and the most difficult individual she had ever met.

Ruel is one of the heroes of the world.

Ian had said those words and Ruel had proved him right tonight. If he was sometimes ruthless, he could also be selfless and courageous, giving with no thought for his own safety. As for mockery, it had not been present in the man she had seen a few minutes ago; he had been vulnerable and hurting. An aching sense of helplessness washed over her, and she realized she was feeling Ruel's pain as if it were her own. It was so like him to deny his own helplessness and start moving, struggling to do something, anything.

And she had something to do too.

She lay there steeling herself, sick with dread. Then she threw aside the covers and swung her legs to the floor. She flinched as she stood up, every muscle in her body throbbing with soreness. She ignored the discomfort and moved across the room toward the washstand.

Ten minutes later she shuffled painfully out of the room and went in search of Patrick. She found him on the veranda, lounging in his favorite cushioned rattan chair, the usual glass of whiskey in his hand. God, she hoped he was still sober enough to be coherent.

He didn't change his position as she came out on the veranda. "What are you doing up? You need your rest." He looked down in the depths of his glass. "Go back to bed."

"I need to have a talk with you, Patrick."

"It's a shame about Ruel MacClaren's brother. I don't think he's going to—"

"It shouldn't have happened, Patrick."

"It was an accident. It was that goddamn river." He took a sip of whiskey. "Bad luck. You know accidents happen all the time."

"Not like this one."

His hand tightened on his glass. "Why are you nagging me? Haven't I got enough to worry about? The maharajah is raging mad that we lost his train and swearing he won't pay me."

"I don't care about the maharajah." She tried to steady her voice. "There's a dying man in this house, a good man."

"I couldn't help it," Patrick said defensively. "Who would have thought the river would have enough force to cause the supports to vibrate that much? It should have been all right."

"I saw the rails, Patrick."

He glanced away from her and took a swallow of his whiskey. "I don't know what you're talking about."

"One of the rails broke when we started over the gorge. Those rails were supposed to be of the finest-grade steel, but I went back and took a look at them. They weren't like the rails we'd used on the rest of track. They were iron, not steel. *Iron*, Patrick. You know iron won't support the same kind of stress as steel. Those rails had already been weakened by the constant vibration caused by the river hitting the supports, and when the train started across the bridge, the weight made them—" She stopped, staring at him in astonishment.

Tears were running down Patrick's cheeks. "I didn't want this to happen. I thought it would be all right. It was such a short stretch of track. It should have been fine. I spent too much on the brass for the locomotive and I couldn't get another loan. I didn't *want* anyone to die."

"Oh, Patrick," she whispered. She had hoped he would tell her she was wrong and give her a believable explanation.

"I made a mistake," Patrick said. "But I'm going to pay for it. I'm ruined, Jane. No one will ever hire me again when they hear the maharajah blames me for what happened."

She felt sick. "I can't feel sorry for you, Patrick."

He nodded quickly. "I'll never forgive myself if that man dies."

She wasn't sure she could forgive him even if Ian lived.

"You won't tell anyone about the rails? I told the maharajah it was an unavoidable accident caused by the vibration, that it was the river's fault. . . ." He added quickly, "It was partly true."

"I won't tell anyone," she said wearily. "You may be guilty, but it was my fault too. I thought it strange you wanted to take over the construction after those rails were delivered, but I wanted to believe you were . . ." She trailed off as her own guilt overwhelmed her. If she had followed her instincts, Ian wouldn't be lying in that room on the point of death. She would have seen those rails and known the danger they posed.

"That's my girl," he said, relieved. "And in the meantime, we'll do everything we can to help that poor man."

"I don't want you here," she whispered.

"What?"

"I can't look at you right now." Her tone sounded

hard, she realized, yet she didn't feel hard, only hollow. "Pack your bag and go to the Officers' Club."

Patrick flushed, his eyes widening in astonishment. "But I . . ." He met her gaze and then said lamely, "If you're sure that's what you want."

"That's what I want." She turned and left the veranda.

The darkness was fading and Ian could see a warm, loving light beckoning, welcoming him.

"I know you're awake, Ian. Open your eyes, dammit."

It was Ruel's voice again, demanding, cajoling, talking to him, always talking, taking him away from the light.

"Tired."

"You're not tired. You're giving up. Now open your eyes and look at me."

Ian's lids lifted slowly.

Ruel's face was above him, leaner, cheeks hollowed, blue eyes blazing, compelling.

Tiger burn bright . . .

"Good. Now open your mouth."

Broth, hot, meaty.

"No, don't turn your head away. You're going to eat all of it. You can't fight without strength."

"Pain. Such pain . . ."

"You can stand the pain. Stay with me."

Ruel didn't realize how great the pain was or he wouldn't have asked him to bear it. He must have muttered the words because Ruel was answering.

"I do know. God, I've watched you . . ." His hand covered Ian's on the bed. "But I'm not giving you up to it. You're going to get well and you're going to go home to Glenclaren."

"Glenclaren." Towers, cool hills. "Too . . . far away."

"But I'm right here." Ruel's hand tightened on his. "And you can't leave me. I need you, dammit."

But Ruel never needed anyone. "No."

"I *do* need you. Can't you feel it?"

Ruel's eyes were bright, shimmering, his grip desperately tight. Ian wanted to tell him to release him, to let him go back to the light. Yet Ruel never admitted to needing anyone, so it must be true. Not fair to leave Ruel if he was in need. He supposed he'd have to come back. . . .

"I'll try, lad," Ian said weakly. "I'll try. . . ."

"That's all I ask." Ruel's voice was husky, but Ian was aware of the steely undertone, the implacable will that had pulled him back from the comforting darkness. "I'll do the rest, Ian."

All is well. Kedain's Inn.

Relief flowed through Jane as she folded the note and tore it in small pieces. Li Sung and Kartauk were safe. At least something in the world was going right.

She tossed the pieces of the note in the wastebasket, then whirled around as Ruel walked out of the bedroom. "I've just heard from Li Sung. They've reached Narinth safely."

"Good." Ruel carefully closed the bedroom door behind him. "Ian's sleeping. The doctor's examination this morning nearly drove him insane."

She had heard those cries of agony from the bedroom and felt as tortured as Ruel looked. "At least he's alive and seems to be getting better every day. I think he's put on a pound or two this week."

And as Ian had gained, Ruel had lost. He had put a cot in the sickroom and scarcely left Ian's side during the past three weeks. At least fifteen pounds had slipped away from his lean frame, and yet he didn't appear diminished. Indeed, sometimes when she looked at him he appeared to cast an incandescent glow. The force of will he had expended keeping Ian alive had acted as a flame, burning, sharpening, defining him. "What did the doctor say?"

"Ian's out of danger."

"Thank God."

"That's not what Ian said." Ruel smiled bitterly. "For once he was singularly lacking in piety. He may never walk again."

"Oh, no!"

"Something's wrong with his back," he said jerkily. "He has no feeling in his legs, and he may not even be able to sit up."

"Perhaps it's only temporary. Perhaps the doctor is wrong."

"God, I hope so." Ruel turned away and moved heavily across the room. "I've got to get back to him. I don't want him to wake up and find no one there."

She watched him go back into the bedroom, tears stinging her eyes. In the past weeks, as they had labored to save Ian, she had learned Ruel was much more than the sensual mandarin she had feared. He was also a man who experienced pain and discouragement and could show gentleness as well as strength. She wanted to go after him, comfort him, try to ease the pain she sensed.

"Jane."

She turned to see Patrick standing in the doorway, his face flushed, his manner awkward. "I heard at the club Ian is doing better. I came by to see if there is anything you need."

She shook her head.

"Food? Medicine? We still have a little money left in the cash fund, don't we?"

"Ruel's seeing to everything."

"Oh." He still stood there, turning the brim of his hat in his big hands. "Well, if there's anything . . . Let me know. . . ."

"There's nothing you can do." She paused and then burst out, "Ian may never walk again."

"No," he whispered, stricken.

She nodded jerkily. "It's not fair. You don't know him. He's such a gentle man, such a good man—" Her voice broke.

Patrick was suddenly across the room, gathering her

in his arms. "It's all right." His hand cupped her head, smoothing her hair. "Don't cry, Jane."

It wasn't all right. She wasn't sure anything would be all right again, but Patrick's arms were strong, loving. How many times had she yearned for Patrick to hold her in affection like this?

"That's my girl," he said soothingly. "That's my Jane."

She gave a tremulous sigh and pushed him away. "I'm sorry. I know this kind of thing makes you feel awkward."

"No, I'm the one who is sorry. I've been a terrible fool." Patrick smiled with an effort. "But you've forgiven me, haven't you?"

"It's not my place to forgive—" She broke off and said wearily, "I don't know if I can forgive you or not."

"We've been together too long to harbor bad feelings." He paused and then said in a rush, "I don't like to bring you more bad news, but I'm afraid you're going to have to leave the bungalow by the end of the month. The maharajah has rescinded the lease."

She shook her head. "We can't leave here until Ian is well enough to be moved."

"The maharajah wants us out of Kasanpore, Jane."

"I don't care what he wants," she said fiercely. "I'll not leave while Ruel and Ian need me. If you want to help, find a way to persuade the maharajah to let us stay."

"I'll do my best." Patrick's smile was strained. "Maybe if I go through Colonel Pickering and ask him to intercede . . . he seems to have a liking for Ian MacClaren."

"Do whatever you have to do."

He nodded, still hesitating. "I've been thinking about what we're going to do after we leave here, Jane. Perhaps we should go back to America and start again. It's a long way and maybe no one will hear about—"

"Not now. I don't want to think of anything but Ian right now."

He nodded. "I understand. But you'll see, it may take a while, but everything will be the same as before."

She looked at him in disbelief. "You're wrong."

"Why do you say that?" Anxiety flickered over his face. "You won't leave me? I need you, Jane. We need each other. We're family."

It was the closest he had ever come to saying the words she so desperately wanted to hear. Why did it have to come now? She didn't answer him directly. "You'd better go back to the club and talk to Colonel Pickering."

He opened his mouth to speak and then turned away. "If there's anything else I can do, let me know, darlin'." He hesitated and then reluctantly turned back again to face her. "There's something else you should know. The maharajah asked Colonel Pickering to have one of his engineers conduct an investigation of the train wreck."

Her gaze flew to his face. "Why didn't you tell me?"

"Why should you have to worry about such matters? I don't think Pickering will bother you with questions. I've taken care of everything."

"What did you tell him, Patrick?"

His gaze slid away from her. "It was better that he thought, that they all thought that—"

"Answer me!"

"I told him you ordered the rails." He rushed on quickly, "I had to do it. The maharajah was holding me to blame. Don't you see? They might accuse me of being a fool for trusting a decision like that to a woman but not for negligence or fraud. You can't be hurt by this. I might even be able to save something from this mess for us to—"

"You *lied* about me?"

"Stop looking at me like that. I told you, Pickering's engineer looked at those rails and knew that—"

She couldn't believe it. He had not only done the unthinkable, he was making her shoulder the sole responsibility for that hideous night. "It's not fair." Her voice shook with anger. "You had no right to make me take the entire blame."

"Look, darlin', in a few weeks we'll be away from this place and be able to forget all about it."

"Tell them the truth!"

"It's not the thing to do. Just don't—"

"If you don't tell Colonel Pickering, I will."

"No!" He tried to temper the sharpness of his tone. "Where's your loyalty, girl?"

"Where's your honor, Patrick?"

His tone turned soft, wheedling. "You made me a promise a long time ago. Are you breaking it now?"

She stared at him in disbelief. "What are you saying?"

"I took you out of that place and gave you a respectable life. I gave you a chance to be more than a tent-city whore like your ma. You said you'd always do what I wanted."

"I thought I'd paid that debt."

He flushed but repeated, "You made me a promise."

She felt her eyes sting as she gazed at him. Lost hope, lost faith. If she asked him now, he might even admit he was her father, he might say anything she wanted him to say to save himself.

She would not ask him. "I'll keep my promise, Patrick."

He looked relieved. "You promise you won't tell anyone? No one at all?"

Each word he spoke was like a spike driven into her. "No one. I'll take the sole blame. If anyone asks me, I'll say I ordered the rails."

"It's for the best, darlin'."

"But we're paid in full, Patrick. I owe you no more debts."

"Of course you don't. We can start again, clear and fresh."

"We're not going to start again." Somehow she managed to keep her tone even. "I don't want to see you again, Patrick."

He appeared stricken. "You don't mean that."

"I mean it. I've never meant anything more since

that day I made you take me away from Frenchie's." She turned her back on him and walked away.

She kept the tears from flowing until she closed the door of her room. The dream was over. It had been a foolish dream anyway. She had no need of a father. She had always had Li Sung to help her through the hard times.

But, dear God in heaven, it hurt.

"Come in." Abdar smiled as he beckoned Zabrie to enter. "You must not be frightened."

Zabrie hesitated, glancing warily from Abdar to Pachtal before slowly coming forward into the reception chamber. "You are not angry with me?" She rushed on, the words tumbling out. "It was no fault of mine. Li Sung lied to me. That foul dog deserved his death in that gorge. I had no idea the information I gave you was false."

"I know this. You would not dare to try to fool me." Abdar glanced at Pachtal. "Though my friend Pachtal tried to convince me otherwise. He has a very suspicious nature."

She shot Pachtal a poisonous glance. Ungrateful bastard. She fell to her knees before Abdar. "I did not know. I would never have sent you to Narinth if I had suspected Li Sung had lied to me."

"You were too confident," Pachtal said coldly. "You thought your meager bed skills would overcome his loyalty. I could have told you otherwise."

She flared with anger. "You seemed to find me pleasing enough." Wrong move, she realized instantly, she must be more clever if she was to win through this situation. She forced a smile. "As Your Highness will in the future. I have planned a night to remember to show you how much I regret inconveniencing you."

"Have you indeed?" Abdar's smile widened. "I recall the pleasure you gave me and Pachtal before. I cannot think how you can best that unique episode."

He was intrigued. She lowered her lashes to hide

both her contempt and triumph. Maharajahs or beggars, men were all the same. They would forgive you anything if you could find a way to satisfy their lust. "That was only the beginning. I can make you—"

"Promises." Abdar interrupted. "Words do not interest me." He took a step forward and cupped her cheeks in his hands. "But you do," he said softly. "I find you exceptional. So much life . . . From the first moment I saw you I knew I had to have you."

Satisfaction surged through her. It had been even easier than she thought. "I seek only to give you pleasure," she whispered. "You will permit me?"

"How can I resist you?" His dark eyes were glowing as his fingers trailed down her cheek in a gentle caress. "I believe you're right. This will be a night to remember."

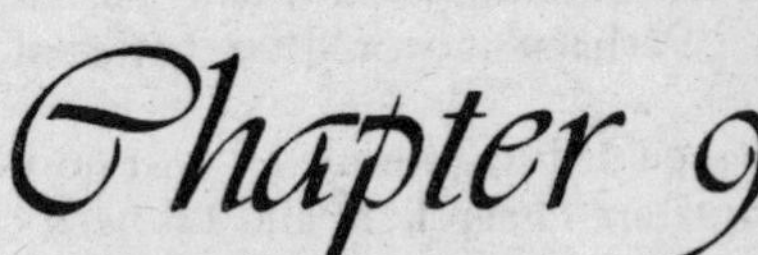

Chapter 9

"You must eat, Ian." Jane looked down with an anxious frown at the untouched tray on the bed beside Ian. "How can you expect to get well if you don't eat?"

"I'm sorry. I'm a great bother, aren't I?" Ian picked up his fork and took a few bites. "There, now I've eaten."

"Not enough."

"That's more than enough for a man flat on his back. It isn't as if I expend a great deal of energy anymore." He shifted from his side to his back and added, "But you mustn't tell Ruel. He worries too much as it is."

"He wants to get you well enough to go back to Glenclaren."

"I've been thinking about that." Ian looked down at his plate. "Perhaps it would be better if I didn't go back."

She looked at him, stunned. "Not go home?"

"Servants are cheap here and I'll need care . . . for a while."

Because he prayed he would soon die and be freed from his bondage. Aching pity flooded through her as she looked at him. His dark hair had grown shaggy and lackluster in the past weeks, his big body distressingly thin, but it was that wistful yearning for release from life that worried her most. "But you love Glenclaren."

His lips thinned with pain. "That's why I'm not going home. I'm no good for Glenclaren anymore."

"Don't be foolish. You'll be a great help to—"

"Margaret?" For the first time she saw bitterness in his expression. "Yes, I'd be a big help to Margaret . . . another invalid for her to nurse. A cripple to lean on her."

"If she's the woman you say she is, she would want you to come home to her."

"There shouldn't have had to be a choice," Ian whispered. "I should have died in that train wreck. God meant me to die that night. Ruel shouldn't have pulled me back."

"You think I have the power to overrule God?" Ruel stood in the doorway, a smile pasted on his pale face. "I'm surprised at you, Ian. That's blasphemy, and besides, you give me too much credit." He strode forward. "I see you haven't eaten your lunch. Why don't you try a little more?"

"Ruel, I can't . . ." He met Ruel's gaze and then sighed, picked up the fork again, and began to eat.

Jane turned and left the room, unable to stand any more. She went to the veranda, her arms crossed over her chest to stop their trembling. Dear God, seeing

Ruel's hurt at that moment was almost as bad as watching Ian's unhappiness and agony.

She heard Ruel come from Ian's room ten minutes later and then the clatter of china as he carried the tray to Sula in the kitchen. Afterward he joined her on the veranda.

"Did you get him to eat?" she asked.

"Oh yes, I always get him to do what I want him to do. Didn't you hear him say how omnipotent I am?"

She didn't look at him. "He didn't really mean to blame you. He doesn't want to die."

"Of course he does," Ruel said harshly. "If I were facing what he is, I'd be cursing him too."

"He isn't cursing you."

"Only because he believes God might really wreak vengeance on my head since I've never been in his good graces."

"You saved Ian's life. There's no greater gift you could give anyone."

"Ian thinks there is."

Death. She shivered and quickly changed the subject. "He wants to stay here in Kasanpore."

"He told me that too." He shook his head. "If I let him stay here, he'll wither away and die. At Glenclaren at least he has a chance of living."

"He seems to be worrying about not being capable of properly running Glenclaren."

"He's right, it's not a job for a cripple. My father was out and about every day overseeing the management of the blasted place."

"Couldn't Ian hire someone?"

"An agent? Yes, but it would be another drain and he'd manage only to keep his head above water. In five years I could have bought him anything he needed. I could have built him a bloody palace in place of that drafty barn. Why the hell wasn't I given those years? You'd think God would take care of his own, wouldn't you?"

"What are you going to do?"

He shook his head wearily. "I've written to Maggie

and taken passage for Ian out of Narinth on the *Bonnie Lady* in three weeks' time."

"Are you going with him?"

He shook his head. "I'm going to Cinnidar after I put him on the ship." He whirled to face her. "Stop looking at me like that. I can do *nothing* for him at Glenclaren right now. If I go to Cinnidar, at least I'll have a chance of giving him what he needs for that damn piece of earth he worships. Money can buy a comfortable life, if not a happy one."

"How could I blame you? You've done more for Ian than anyone could expect you to do."

A bitter smile touched his lips. "More than he wanted me to do anyway." He straightened. "I'm going to the Officers' Club to see Colonel Pickering about arranging transport on one of the troop ships going upriver to Narinth. It will be easier on Ian than traveling overland. Will you watch over him for me until I get back?"

She stiffened, panic surging through her. Ruel had not left Ian's side since the night of the train wreck, and he did not know about the colonel's investigation. What would happen when he—

"What's wrong? Is there a problem?"

Three weeks had gone by since Patrick had told her of the engineers' findings. Perhaps the colonel would assume Ruel knew about it. Perhaps he wouldn't mention it and, if he did, she would have to face it. She smiled with an effort. "No, nothing's wrong. Of course I'll watch over him."

"Of course," he repeated, and for once his smile held no mockery or bitterness, only a rare sweetness. "There's no 'of course' about it. You've put up with Ian's screams and my rantings and worked yourself into a shadow these last weeks without a word of thanks from me."

"I didn't want your thanks. I couldn't have done anything else."

He gazed at her for a long moment. "No, I guess you

couldn't. But I want you to know I'll remember this and find a way to repay you."

For the first time since the train wreck he was really looking at her, and she felt a tiny shock of awareness. She laughed tremulously. "Are you going to build me a palace too?"

"Maybe." He reached out and gently stroked her cheek with his index finger. "I'll have to think about it. You once said you wouldn't be comfortable in a palace."

The gentleness of his touch was poignantly sweet. "I'm surprised you remembered that."

"I have a long memory." His hand dropped away. "For the important things."

She wanted to reach out and touch him, draw close to that flame that always burned within him. Give and accept in spirit as well as flesh. She had thought she had loved him before, but her feelings had increased tenfold in these past days together.

"I'll see you in a few hours." He turned and left the bungalow.

She shivered as fear rippled through her. Perhaps she did not need to worry. Fate could be kind and let her keep this gift. Pickering might not tell him.

"The next troop carrier goes upriver on the twenty-seventh," John Pickering said. "I could ask the officer in charge to give up his quarters for the trip. Will Ian be ready to travel by then?"

"As ready as he'll ever be." Ruel rose to his feet. "You're very kind. Thank you."

"No thanks are necessary. We're all fond of Ian. He's a fine man." The colonel added briskly, "Now, sit back down and I'll order you a drink. You look like you could use one."

Ruel shook his head. "I have to get back to—"

"Sit down," Pickering repeated firmly, "Or I might rethink my kindness."

Ruel dropped back down in his chair. "One drink."

The colonel motioned to a white-clad boy behind

the bar across the room. "If you don't get more rest, you may be the one we have to ship upriver on a stretcher." He waited until the boy had set two whiskeys in front of them before continuing. "I've seen men who look as haggard as you do before, but it's usually after they've been through a battle."

He had been through a battle, Ruel thought. He sipped his whiskey. "I'm fine. Ian's the one who is sick."

"Then why is your hand shaking?"

Pickering was right, Ruel noticed in surprise. His hand holding the glass was trembling. He exerted his will and steadied it before he said, "I've not been getting a great deal of rest. That doesn't mean I'm ill."

"I'm sure Abdar will be sorry to hear that."

He glanced up. "Abdar?"

"Pachtal's been displaying a good deal of curiosity on his behalf. He came to see me last week, asking questions about your purchase of Cinnidar."

"What kind of questions?"

"The most pertinent was why you saw fit to buy it at all. Naturally, since you hadn't seen fit to confide in me, I couldn't oblige him." He shrugged. "But I received the impression his interest was going to continue in the matter. It's for the best you'll be leaving Kasanpore."

"You filed the bill of sale with the magistrates in Calcutta?"

Pickering nodded. "All duly registered. Cinnidar is definitely yours. Abdar can't touch it."

"Legally."

"As long as his father's alive, you won't have to worry about Abdar interfering in the maharajah's affairs."

"We shall see."

"I just thought you should know." He paused. "Pachtal's also been seen wandering around Lanpur Gorge. Can you think of any reason why he should be interested in the investigation?"

Kartauk. The only reason for Pachtal to be at the gorge was if he suspected Kartauk had not been swept away by the river. Then the last word of Pickering's sentence hit home. "Investigation? What investigation?"

Pickering looked at him in surprise. "The investigation of the train wreck. The maharajah asked us to look into the reason for it." He grimaced. "Not a pleasant task. I've always liked Patrick Reilly and hated being responsible for depriving him of his fee."

He went still. "What in hell are you talking about? Patrick told me the force of the waters pouring through the gorge and hitting the supports caused a vibration that weakened the rails."

Pickering regretfully shook his head. "My engineer tells me if those rails hadn't been of inferior quality, they would never have broken."

Ruel felt as if he had been struck in the belly with a knotted fist. He said carefully, "Are you saying that Ian's injury could have been prevented?"

Pickering blinked. "I thought you knew. Patrick must have told Miss Barnaby about the inquiry."

"If he did, she didn't see fit to inform me." He slowly rose to his feet. "I believe I'll go pay a visit to Patrick Reilly. I have a few questions to put to him."

"I'm afraid you won't get any answers from him. He's usually drunk by noon these days." He paused. "Why don't you ask Miss Barnaby those questions? According to Patrick, she was very much aware of what was going on."

Ruel went still. "What are you trying to say?"

Pickering shifted uncomfortably. "Patrick tried to defend her, but several merchants told us she was solely responsible for ordering supplies and he finally admitted she had ordered the rails. It's a damn shame he was fool enough to trust a woman. It's probably destroyed his career."

I had to cut corners.

The door cost us too much.

Jane's words at the gorge came rushing back to him.

It's my fault.

"I have to go," he muttered hoarsely. "I have to leave . . ."

He was barely aware of Pickering's concerned voice calling his name as he turned and stalked out of the club.

Jane's hands clenched nervously on the arms of the chair when she heard Ruel enter the bungalow. She had told herself she wanted this confrontation over, but now she would have done anything to avoid it. Perhaps he would go directly into the bedroom to see Ian and—

"Jane," Ruel called softly.

He didn't sound angry. Perhaps Pickering hadn't told him, she thought hopefully. Dear God, she had prayed Pickering wouldn't say anything. "On the veranda. Was there a problem with Colonel Pickering?"

He appeared in the doorway, silhouetted against the lamplight streaming from the living room.

"Why should there be a problem?" he asked.

She tensed as she realized a strange note underlay the softness of his tone, like a coiled spring stretched taut. "Because you've been gone for hours. It's after ten o'clock."

"Was caring for Ian such a burden for you?"

"No, I just wondered if—" She stopped and then said, "I've already given Ian his dinner and laudanum. He should sleep through the night."

"Even with the laudanum he seldom does that. At first he woke up screaming from the pain, now he only lies there and weeps." His tone harshened. "Do you know what that does to a man? It fills him with shame. I have to pretend I'm asleep or he begs me for pardon for being so weak. God, weak!"

He *did* know. She got up from the chair. "I believe I'll go to bed. Good night, Ruel."

"Not yet. There's something I want to ask you."

It was coming. She braced herself. "What?"

"About the rails."

She had thought she was ready but still went rigid.

"What a violent reaction. Does the thought disturb you?"

"Ruel, I—"

"It disturbed me so much that after I left the Officers' Club I took a long walk." He paused. "To Lanpur Gorge."

She moistened her lips. "Why?"

"I wanted to see the rails for myself. I looked at those shattered rails and I remembered Ian. . . ." He lifted his head and gazed directly into her eyes. She inhaled sharply as she saw the torment and rage burning in him, consuming him, reaching out to consume her as well. "And I decided I'd kill Patrick Reilly."

"No!" The rejection burst instinctively from her lips.

"Why not? No one deserves it more." He paused. "Unless it's you."

She was silent, staring helplessly at him.

"Why don't you say something?" The violence she had sensed was suddenly unleashed. "Goddammit, don't just stand there. Tell me I'm *wrong*. Tell me Pickering is wrong."

"What did he say?"

"He said you were responsible for ordering the supplies. Is that true?"

"Yes," she whispered. "It's true."

He looked as if she had struck him. "Did you mean it when you said the wreck was your fault?"

She flinched. "I meant it."

"Damn you!" He took a step forward, his hands closing on her throat. "And all to make things safe and tidy for your Patrick." His eyes scorched her. "For God's sake, why didn't you *lie* to me. I didn't want to believe it. I would have done anything not to believe it." His grasp tightened on her throat with bruising force. "I don't want to do—"

She struggled desperately to force air into her starved lungs as his hands tightened even more. She was going to die. Her hands flew to her throat, trying to loosen his grip, staring helplessly up into his strained face. "Please . . ." It came out as a croak and she didn't think he heard her. His expression was blind, tortured, twisted.

A shudder racked his body. His hands loosened,

tightened fiercely, then slowly released their grip on her throat. "Why can't I do it?" he muttered. "You deserve it. No one could deserve it more than—" He whirled away from her and strode toward Ian's bedroom. "If you want to live, stay out of my sight." She expected him to slam the door, but the very restraint with which he closed it was chilling.

Her shaking hand went to her bruised throat; it was already starting to ache. She had never been closer to death. Would she have been able to keep her promise and remain silent about Patrick's guilt if Ruel hadn't changed his mind at the last minute?

Clever Patrick. Ruel would not have stopped if his hands had been around Patrick's neck. It could be Patrick had realized whatever punishment Ruel inflicted on her, he would not take her life.

And God knows, she also deserved punishment, she thought wearily. Her willful blindness was as much to blame as Patrick's wicked self-indulgence. Perhaps she deserved to lose any chance for happiness with Ruel.

She turned and moved slowly, heavily, toward her bedroom.

She must stop loving him, she thought dully. Now he would use that weapon or any other to hurt her. She must look on him as the enemy and protect herself. Yes, she must stop loving him.

She didn't expect to sleep but must have dozed, for she woke in the middle of the night to see Ruel standing a few feet from her bed. She went rigid, scrambling back against the headboard.

"Rather like the death scene from *Othello*, isn't it? With one difference, there's nothing innocent about you." The light from the oil lamp he carried cast a halo about him and revealed the bitterness of his smile. "Don't worry, I'm not going to kill you. I've gotten past that point now." He paused. "Perhaps it's better that I find myself incapable of murdering you. Death is too final a revenge. Then you'd be out of this vale of tears while Ian prays every night to follow you."

At that moment she would not have quarreled with death. Life was too painful. Every word he spoke flayed her.

He sat down on the bed and put the lamp on the bedside table. "You're trembling." He leisurely unbuttoned her nightgown. "Are you afraid I'm going to rape you? I could, you know. It doesn't seem to make any difference if I hate you or not. I only have to look at you to turn hard. I'm not sure I'll ever stop wanting you." He pushed aside the cotton fabric and a warm hand cupped her breast.

She inhaled sharply, her breasts lifting and falling under his touch. "Please." She moistened her lips. "You don't want to do this."

"But I do." He took her hand and put it on his arousal. "See?" His thumb moved back and forth across her nipple until it became engorged, pointed, and excruciatingly sensitive. "And you're beginning to want it too. I wouldn't even have to rape you. I could take you on this bed. I could drive in and out of you and make you scream with pleasure."

His eyes were glittering wildly in the lamplight, a reckless smile curving his lips. His beauty burned more brightly than it had that first night she had seen him at Zabrie's. The very room seemed to throb with the emotion he emitted.

Dear God, he was right. She did want him. She wanted to soothe his torment and her own in the only way left open to her. What madness made her not care how tortured and degrading it would be to couple with him? Her body wasn't concerned how he felt about her, it just wanted to assuage the need he was arousing. He might never touch her again after tonight. She *wanted* this time, this touch.

"But I don't want to give you pleasure," he said softly. "Not even to satisfy myself." His hand left her breast and he jerked her nightgown closed. "So I have to find another way."

He had probably never meant to take her. It had just been a way to make her acknowledge her own weakness and his power over her. She swallowed to ease the tightness of her throat. "You have to know how deeply I regret what happened to Ian."

"That's not good enough. I want you to hurt as much as Ian is hurting." His voice suddenly exploded with harshness. "I'm not going to let you walk away free, Jane."

"I didn't expect you to."

He laughed mirthlessly. "The hell you didn't. You thought if you threw open your home to Ian and smiled sweetly at me, that would be enough compensation. Oh no, I'm going to make sure you feel just as much a prisoner as Ian is going to be. I can't be there at Glenclaren with him, but you will. You'll tend to his needs and listen to his cries in the night and know it's your fault he's suffering."

Her eyes widened. "You want me to go with him to Glenclaren?"

"You're going to pay your debt and, if you don't, I'm going to make sure your Patrick suffers more than Ian before I kill him."

"You don't have to threaten me," she said quietly. "I'm perfectly willing to go to Glenclaren. You had only to ask me."

"I have no intention of asking you. I'm telling you what your first payment is going to be."

"First payment?"

"Did you think a few years of servitude was going to be your only punishment? Given the opportunity to consider the possibilities, I'm not so lacking in imagination I won't find a better way to hurt you."

She was tempted to tell him she was already hurting, but she knew he wouldn't believe her. She had never seen such bitterness as she was now confronting. "You'll have to do as you see fit. I'll do everything I can to help Ian." She reached up and rubbed her aching temple. The whole world seemed full of pain tonight. "But Li

Sung and Kartauk must come with me. It's dangerous for them to stay here."

"By all means, take your little covey. Ian will need all the help he can get."

"And Patrick." The words came out of nowhere, startling her. She had thought she was done with Patrick, but the habit of years would not be broken in spite of her disgust and revulsion. She could not leave him to face Ruel's deadly wrath.

His gaze narrowed on her face. "I was thinking of taking dear Patrick with me to Cinnidar to assure your continued support."

"He'd be in your way," she said quickly.

"You think I might kill him." He was silent a moment. "Maybe you're right. If I started thinking about Ian, I couldn't promise not to lose my temper and push the bastard into the canyon. Besides, I don't need a hostage. I'll be in touch with Maggie and I'll know if you're keeping your word."

"I'll keep my word." She added wearily, "And perhaps you'll change your mind in time."

"I won't change my mind." He turned and moved toward the door. "I told you I have a long memory."

The *Bonnie Lady* sailed out of Narinth harbor three weeks later with Jane, Ian, Li Sung, Patrick, and Kartauk on board.

Li Sung glanced back at Ruel standing alone on the dock. "He's staring at you."

"Is he?" She knew very well Ruel was staring at her but did not look back. She had made the mistake of meeting his gaze a moment before as the ship had left the dock and had felt bound, enchained. It was exactly how he meant her to feel. He wanted to remind her this parting was only temporary and that she would never be able to escape him.

"He behaves very strangely with you now. I don't suppose you'd like to tell me why he's—"

"No, I would not." While hiding in the inn in

Narinth, he and Kartauk had not heard of the inquiry and she had no intention of enlightening him. He was already overprotective of her and she knew very well how he would react to her shouldering Patrick's blame.

Why didn't Ruel look away? She could feel his eyes on her. She straightened away from the rail. "Well, I can't stay here any longer. I have to get back to Ian."

Li Sung shook his head. "Kartauk is with him. He seems to be able to amuse him."

She had noticed that herself and had blessed Kartauk during the two days they had spent at the inn prior to their departure. Heaven knows, no one else had been able to raise Ian's spirits. "Where's Patrick?"

"Where he usually is, trying to crawl into his whiskey bottle. He's gotten worse since the wreck."

"Yes."

"I notice you do not try to defend him any longer."

She could not seem to stop protecting Patrick, but she would no longer lie to either herself or anyone else regarding his flaws. "No."

"Why not?"

"He has to shoulder his own burdens. I have enough to worry about."

"Yet you're taking him to Glenclaren."

"He's not going to Glenclaren."

A flicker of surprise crossed Li Sung's face. "He told me he was going with us."

"I'll settle him at a lodging house in Edinburgh. There was a little money left in the cash fund, enough to keep him for a year or so. After that he'll have to find work."

"With no help from you?"

"With no help from me."

He smiled faintly. "Unusual. I wonder what he did to open your eyes?"

Ruel was still looking at her. Why wouldn't he turn and walk away? she wondered desperately. The pain was too great. She had to be free of him.

"You're not going to tell me that either?"

"What?" She would not stand there, pinned by

Ruel's stare like a sacrificial goat for the tiger. She turned and started down the deck. "You should be happy, Li Sung. You were always telling me how foolish I was."

He fell into step with her. "I'm not happy Patrick hurt you. It was what I always feared, but I never wanted it."

"I'll get over it." And she would also break free of Ruel in spite of his determination to make her aware of his power over her. If she had not wanted to go to Glenclaren, no coercion would have forced her to go. It had been her decision to try to right the wrong she had done Ian.

"You're walking too fast. Since you refuse to honor me with your confidence regarding MacClaren and Patrick, may I at least ask where we're running in such a hurry?"

"Sorry." She slowed to accommodate Li Sung's limping gait. She had been running from Ruel, she realized suddenly, away from that implacable will that had jerked Ian back from the gates of death and was now focused on her. "I thought I'd go down to the cargo hold and see how Sam and Bedelia are doing."

"Everyone is going to be so happy to see you." Jane reached out and took Ian's cold hand. "Your Glenclaren is beautiful. I can see why you love it."

Ian didn't take his gaze from the towers in the distance. "Yes, it is beautiful."

She pulled the blanket higher around him. The jarring trip had not been good for him, she thought anxiously. If possible, he looked paler than when they had lifted his stretcher onto the back of this wagon at the docks in Edinburgh two days earlier. "Truly. Everything is going to be fine."

"I can almost believe it," he whispered, still looking at the castle. "Perhaps there really was a reason . . ."

Ten minutes later the wagon rumbled over the wooden drawbridge and into the flagstoned courtyard.

A chipped and stained cistern occupied the center of the courtyard, and scraggly blades of grass grew between the flagstones. Wherever she looked Jane could see signs of age and disrepair.

"It's not always like this," Ian said. "I've been away a long time and places this old need care and nurturing."

"Or tearing down," Kartauk murmured.

Jane gave him a withering glance. "It won't take us long to do a few repairs, Ian." How strange to realize Ruel had grown up in this castle. It was difficult to even connect Ruel with this weathered, ancient place.

"Where is he?" The brass-bracketed front door flew open and a young woman marched down the stairs. "Good God, Ian, have they not got you sitting up yet?"

"Margaret?" Ian said in disbelief. He lifted himself on one elbow to look over the side of the wagon. "What are you doing here?"

"Where else would I be?" She strode toward the wagon. "When I received Ruel's letter I moved Father and myself to Glenclaren. Until you're over this infirmity, it was clearly the most practical thing to do."

Jane felt a ripple of surprise at her first sight of Margaret MacDonald. Soft hands, lace, and a fashionable bustle . . . She could see why Ian had laughed when she had described how she had envisioned his Margaret. She could not see the woman's hands, but her high-collared dark blue gown was faded and shabby with long use, and she moved with a bold economical grace. She was tall and slim, her wheat-colored hair worn in a smooth bun. Her square chin and large, mobile mouth were too strong to be considered beautiful, but she possessed wide-set gray eyes that were startlingly lovely.

Margaret climbed into the wagon and knelt beside Ian. "You look terrible," she told him bluntly. "I can see it's time you came home." She gave him a quick kiss and continued briskly. "But no matter, I'll set everything straight."

"Margaret . . ." Ian's finger reached out and touched her cheek. "Bonnie Margaret."

"Your illness must have affected your eyesight as well

as your limbs," she said tartly. "For bonnie I certainly am not." She turned to Jane and demanded, "Who are you?"

"Jane Barnaby." She gestured to the two men on the front seat of the wagon. "Li Sung and John Kartauk."

"And why are you here?"

"Ruel sent—"

"Never mind, that explains everything," Margaret interrupted. "Ruel was ever cavorting around with the most peculiar people." Her gaze raked appraisingly over Li Sung before dismissing him and fastening on Kartauk. "How strong are you?"

Kartauk blinked. "Strong as a bull. Mighty as Hercules."

"One can usually discount three quarters of what braggarts say, but that may still be sufficient." She turned and called, "Jock!"

A small, burly man with a shock of red hair hurried down the steps.

She ordered Kartauk, "Get down from that seat and help Jock carry Ian up to his chamber." She scooted out of the wagon. "Jock, put him to bed while I go to the scullery and see what I can find for him to eat." She turned to Jane. "Come with me to the scullery and make yourself useful. We have only three servants to run this vast place, and now with four more mouths to feed I don't—"

Jane interjected quickly, "We won't be a burden to you."

"Speak for yourself," Kartauk said as he and Jock carefully eased Ian's stretcher from the wagon. "An artist is always the most precious of burdens, and it is the privilege of all to nurture and care for them."

"You dabble in paints?" Margaret asked.

Kartauk looked pained. "I do not dabble. I create for the ages. I'm a great goldsmith."

"Just so you're a strong goldsmith. I won't have you dropping Ian on the stairs." She turned to Li Sung. "Take the wagon to the stable and unharness those horses. Then come back to the scullery and I'll find something else for you to do."

"You're treating them like servants," Ian protested. "These are our guests, Margaret."

"Glenclaren can afford no guests who will not work for their bread." The gentleness with which she smoothed back his hair belied the harshness of her words. "Now hush, and let me have my way in this. I'll be up as soon as Jock gets you to bed and you've had a short rest." She turned and strode across the courtyard, demanding over her shoulder of Jane, "Coming?"

Jane hurried after her. "Coming."

"Wait." Margaret's gaze fastened on Sam, who was gamboling at Jane's heels. "The dog is yours?"

"Sam will be no trouble."

Margaret's stare shifted to Bedelia, who was following the wagon into the stable. "And the horse?"

"I couldn't leave her in Kasanpore."

"You'll have to get rid of both. We can't afford them," Margaret said flatly.

Jane drew a deep breath and said clearly, "No."

Margaret blinked. "No?"

"They stay. They belong to me and I'll take care of them."

"I see." Grudging respect flickered briefly across Margaret's face before she turned and entered the castle. "See that you do."

The scullery to which Margaret led her was drafty, as crumbling as the courtyard, and could have used a thorough cleaning.

Margaret intercepted Jane's critical glance and said, "I arrived only two days ago and cannot do everything. If it doesn't please you, clean it yourself."

"I didn't mean to—"

"Of course you did. Be honest with me. I have no time for polite mouthings."

Jane found herself smiling. "Then I'll give you none. Since you gave me no quarrel about Sam and Bedelia, I decided to hold my tongue, but the place is a pigsty. Li

Sung and I will set to cleaning it as soon as he gets back from the stable."

"That's better." Margaret indicated a small gray-haired woman seated by a huge open fireplace peeling potatoes. "This is Mary Rhodes. Mary, this is Jane Barnaby. She came with Ian."

"Another mouth to feed," the woman said sourly. "It's not as if you didn't have enough to worry about."

"She'll earn her keep." Margaret strolled across the kitchen toward the fire. "And I'm not worried. It's foolish to worry about things you cannot help. Is the stew done?"

"After I add these potatoes."

"I'll finish here. You go and ready three more chambers."

"Three?"

"Three," Margaret repeated firmly. "And no grumbling. The Lord will provide."

"It's usually you who does the providing," Mary muttered as she handed Margaret her bowl of potatoes and knife and rose to her feet. "I've noticed he leaves you pretty much on your own." She moved toward the door. "Since I'll be nearby, I'll look in on your father too."

"You needn't bother." A sudden smile lit Margaret's face. "But thank you, Mary." Her smile faded as she turned back to Jane. "Dear God, Ian looked ill," she whispered. "Ruel wrote me, but I didn't expect . . ." She sat down in the chair Mary had vacated and quickly started peeling potatoes. "Is there no hope he will walk again?"

"The doctor thought not," Jane said gently.

"A doctor can be as much a fool as any other man. We will ignore him and do our best." She shifted her shoulders as if throwing off a burden, her gaze raking over Jane. "Why do you wear trousers? You look most strange."

Jane stiffened warily. No soft hands or fashionable bustle, but perhaps Margaret was not as different from those other women as Jane had thought. "These are the only clothes I possess. I'm sorry you don't find them appropriate."

Margaret scowled. "A woman should look like a woman. Men think too well of themselves as it is without our flattering them by trying to imitate them."

Jane gazed at her, stunned, then started to laugh. "I had no thought of imitating them. I worked beside men on the railroad and I found it practical to wear these clothes."

"Indeed? Perhaps you do have reason for those outlandish garments, but you should have sought a compromise." Sudden interest flared in Margaret's expression. "Railroad? I approve of women who *do* things. How did you come to work on a rail—" She stopped and shook her head. "You can tell me later. I must concentrate on what is important now. How long do you plan on staying here?"

"I promised Ruel I'd stay as long as Ian needs me."

Margaret's expression clouded. "And God knows how long that will be. He seems to need a great deal of help, and Glenclaren can use all the hands it can muster."

"That's what Ruel said."

"Really? I find that surprising. Glenclaren could crumble into dust for all Ruel cares."

"I understand most people care something for the place where they grew up."

Margaret looked at her in astonishment. "But he didn't grow up here. Annie had a small cottage on the other side of the glen."

"Annie?"

"Annie Cameron, Ruel's mother. Didn't you know Ruel was born on the wrong side of the blanket?"

Jane's eyes widened. "But his name is MacClaren."

"Ruel refused to go by any other name even though his father refused to acknowledge him. He wanted nothing to do with Glenclaren, but he ever loved to stir up trouble and knew it annoyed the laird."

"But Ian always spoke as if . . ." Jane shook her head in confusion. "I don't understand."

"Ian never tells anyone about Annie. I've tried to tell him he bears no guilt for the way the laird treated Ruel, but he won't listen to me. Ruel was his brother and he feels it was partly his fault his father refused to marry the woman and denied Ruel was his son."

"Why did he do that?"

"Glenclaren. The laird already had a son and didn't need another and Annie was not a virtuous woman." She added dryly, "Though that fact didn't seem to make a difference to him until he grew tired of her. At first he was quite mad about her. From what I've heard she was as comely then as Ruel is now. Everyone thought she had cast a spell over the laird."

A mandarin casting spells . . .

"Is she still alive?"

Margaret shook her head. "She went away to Edinburgh when Ruel was about twelve. We heard later that she died of influenza."

"She just left him?"

"He was well able to care for himself." Margaret moved her shoulders impatiently. "Enough about Ruel. The rascal always seems to garner the bulk of attention even when he's not on the same continent." She stood up and carried the potatoes over to the fireplace and poured them into the boiling kettle. "Now, tell me about the Chinese and that arrogant coxcomb who came with you."

Two hours later Margaret swept into Ian's chamber. "Have they made you comfortable?" She glanced at Kartauk sitting beside the bed. "We don't need you here any longer. You may go and find a place to set up your workshop. Jane tells me you may be here awhile and will need a place to putter."

"Putter." He said the word as if it left a bad taste in his mouth. "Dabble. You have no understanding of the importance of my work."

"But I have an excellent understanding of the importance of mine." She gestured toward the door. "Choose anyplace you like, but go."

Kartauk scowled. "What else could I expect in this cold, barbaric country." He left the chamber.

"And good riddance." Margaret crossed to the bed and sat down beside Ian. "I've arranged for the vicar to come to the castle in three days' time and marry us, so you must rest and get your strength back from the journey."

"We're not going to marry."

"Of course we are. Not that I didn't expect this foolishness from you." She gently pushed the hair back from his forehead. "I've watched you trying to save Ruel from himself since the moment he was born, and now you think I need rescuing."

"I won't be another burden to you. Your father—"

"Is fading fast and will soon no longer enter into the situation."

His gaze flew to her face. "You didn't write me."

"Why should I? Would it have helped him?"

"I would have come back to you."

Her expression softened. "Aye, I know."

"I share your sorrow."

She grimaced. "I wish I could feel sorrow, but we both know my father is not a loving man. At times I've thought perhaps God grew weary of his pretense at illness and gave him this true reason for lingering in bed." She smiled with an effort. "Which will probably cause him to send a bolt of lightning to strike me down."

"Never," Ian said softly. "No one could have been kinder and more dutiful than you, Margaret."

"He's my father." She shrugged. "And we both know duty and honor make the only difference between civilization and savagery." She changed the subject. "And speaking of savagery, how is Ruel?"

"The same." Ian paused. "And different."

"Well, that's clear. However, he appears to be displaying a newfound sense of responsibility. I received a draft for two thousand pounds from him yesterday with word he would send more as it became available."

"What!" He immediately shook his head. "That left him only a thousand for his own use. Send it back to him."

"I'll do no such thing. Glenclaren needs it. You need it," Margaret said. "It will be good for Ruel to think of someone else for a change."

"He saved my life at risk of his own."

"Oh, Ruel's very good at those kinds of gestures. It's self-discipline he's lacking."

Ian laughed. "Lord, I've missed you, Margaret." His smile vanished. "But I will not let you wed a cripple. You've wasted enough of your life already."

"Who is to know if you will remain a cripple?" She went on quickly as he opened his lips to protest. "Besides, a strong body is all very well, but a strong heart and mind are more important."

"I cannot give you children. You love children, Margaret."

"Children may still be possible. I will talk to the physician."

He shook his head.

"And many couples are childless. God may have not seen fit to give us a child even if you were hale and hearty."

"No, Margaret."

"Very well, I will wait to wed you . . . until you're able to sit up for the ceremony. By that time you'll be on your way to recovery and won't be so stubborn."

"It can't happen. My back is—"

"It *will* happen. I'll make it happen." She leaned forward and kissed him swiftly on the forehead. "Now, try to rest, the journey must have tired you."

"Everything tires me."

"It will get better." She rose to her feet. "While I fetch a bowl of stew I'll send Jock in to bathe you. I suppose you're too proud to let me perform that task?" She nodded as she saw his expression. "I thought as much." She moved toward the door. "I can think of no reason why God gave the masculine gender such power over females when they're all so lacking in good sense."

Margaret closed the door behind her and immediately closed her eyes tightly as wave after wave of the anger, sorrow, and despair she could not allow anyone to see washed over her. Dear God, poor Ian.

And poor Margaret. Why was she expected to endure this new trial? Sometimes God seemed most unfair.

"You have an interesting face. I may be persuaded to do a head of you."

Her eyes flicked open to see John Kartauk standing a few yards away from her. She flushed as she realized he must have witnessed her moment of weakness. No, perhaps not, for his gaze on her face was appraising but completely dispassionate. She cleared her throat. "I thought I told you to go find yourself a workshop."

"I did." He was still staring at her face. "I've decided to use the scullery."

"The scullery?" she repeated, shocked. "You can't use—"

"Of course I can. I need a furnace, and it will save me the trouble of building one. I can wall up that huge fireplace." He took a step closer and lifted her chin on the curve of his finger. "At first I saw nothing worthwhile in your face, but I believe the jawline is tolerable and the molding of the cheekbones—"

She slapped his hand away. "I will not pose for you."

He looked hurt. "You don't realize the honor I do you, madam. After all, I did refuse Queen Victoria."

Her eyes widened. "The queen asked you to—"

"Well, no, I didn't give her the opportunity. It never pays to insult royalty, but I had already decided to refuse her." He turned and strode down the hall. "When you regain your senses, come and tell me. I must go to the scullery and toss out all those pots and pans."

She hurried after him. "Toss out—you'll do no such thing!"

"Why not? They're in my way."

"Are you mad? We all must eat. You may *not* have the scullery."

"Beauty has more value than food." He frowned. "I

will compromise. I'll permit you to have the scullery in the evening for your cooking."

"You will permit . . ." She drew a deep breath and said through her teeth, "You toss out one cooking pot and I'll use you for tomorrow's stew meat."

He studied her expression over his shoulder. "I believe you would do it." He suddenly chuckled. "You'd find me tough fare, madam. I'm no tender rabbit."

"One pot," she enunciated clearly.

"Oh, very well." He shrugged. "I noticed a space almost as adequate in the stable, but you must help me clear it and tell Jock to find me bricks to build my furnace."

"Jock will be too busy tending Ian to indulge you in your foolishness, and I certainly have no time."

Kartauk sighed. "I've come to a land of uncaring savages who offer me no help and will probably manipulate my talent to suit themselves."

"You accuse *me* of manipulating you because I won't let you—" She broke off as realization dawned. Kartauk was not the one who was being manipulated. "You had no intention of using the scullery," she said flatly.

"No? Then why would I say I intended to do so?"

She did not know the answer. Yet perhaps . . . kindness, an attempt to distract her from her grief without damaging her pride? He had certainly seen her weakness and acted with faultless accuracy to dispel it. No, she must be mistaken. They were strangers, and he could not possibly read her so well.

"I have no idea why you would be so devious," she said tartly. "I've heard men of the East delight in such convoluted maneuvering. No doubt it's an affliction of your heathen blood."

"No doubt," he said blandly. "But I'm sure a God-fearing Scottish lady such as yourself will have no trouble seeing through my heathen trickery."

Before she could answer, he strode ahead of her down the hall and started down the stairs.

• • •

It was after nine o'clock in the evening when Jane and Li Sung finally finished cleaning the scullery and climbed the stone stairs to the front hall.

"Sweet heaven, I'm tired." She arched her back to rid it of stiffness. "And my knees feel as if they're black and blue from scrubbing that blasted floor."

"Go to bed. You will feel better in the morning." Li Sung opened the front door.

"Where are you going?"

"To the stable. Kartauk has found a place for his workshop and quarters. I will live with him."

"But you have a chamber here."

"I'm used to Kartauk."

"But will you be comfortable there?"

"More comfortable than here. The temple had far more potential for comfort than this castle."

"Then we must make the most of what we have. We've done it before."

"Yes." Li Sung paused. "But this is different."

She knew what he meant. Glenclaren seemed foreign to both of them. Neither she nor Li Sung belonged in castles and were far more accustomed to building than maintaining and repairing. "We'll get used to it."

"Because you must help Ian? I would judge Margaret MacDonald is all he needs." He smiled faintly. "More than he needs."

"She cannot do everything. While she helps him regain his strength, I'll do all I can to help his Glenclaren." She added, "But you don't have to stay here if you're not happy."

"What would I do? Search out Patrick in that lodging house in Edinburgh and share his bottle?" he asked bitterly. "I admit there have been times when I've been tempted to choose that escape."

Her eyes widened. "You have?"

"Why do you think I rarely permit myself to drink liquor? It's not easy being a cripple, to limp instead of run."

She reached out and gently touched his arm. "I know, Li Sung."

"No, you do not know." His gaze went to the stairs. "But now Ian knows." He started down the steps. "I will stay here, where there is no temptation."

Jane followed him to the door and watched him limp across the courtyard toward the stable. Did anyone ever really know another person? She had thought she knew Patrick, and he had done that unspeakable thing. She had thought she knew Li Sung, but she was again being proved wrong.

Blue eyes searing, blazing, in a face as beautiful as a fallen angel's.

What had caused the thought of Ruel to pop out of nowhere? She could claim to know him even less than others. Margaret's revelations this afternoon had shocked and disturbed her. She supposed she shouldn't have been so surprised. No one was less predictable and more enigmatic than Ruel.

Yet in those weeks after the wreck she had seen in him a resolution and a will that would never waver.

No, she must not think of Ruel. She had probably only thought she loved him. No, she would not lie to herself. She had loved Ruel, but surely time and distance would make that love fade and wither. She would make sure she kept herself busy enough to block out all thought of him.

In the distance she could see gently rolling hills, the heather a pale blur in the darkness. How different this land was from Kasanpore, as different as the life she must now lead here.

But she must no longer think of that other life. While she could help Ian, her place was here.

Now there was only Glenclaren.

Cinnidar.

Ruel's hands tightened on the rail, his gaze on the island the small fishing boat was approaching. The first time he had seen Cinnidar he had felt this same sense of wonder and excitement, this sense of promise.

Jane had said something like that about her trains, he

remembered suddenly. Her face had been glowing and yet there had been a gravity about—

Dammit, he would *not* think of her.

Instead, he would remember Ian as he had last seen him when he had settled him on the bunk of the *Bonnie Lady*. Pale, wasted . . . in terrible pain.

The ship glided closer to the pier. He was almost home.

He instantly rejected that thought too. Cinnidar was a pot of gold, not home to him. He had no need for a home just as he had no need for Jane Barnaby. What he did need was buried deep in the bowels of that mountain, and he would have to work and sweat to find a way to tear it out. He would have no time to think of anything but the task that lay ahead.

Now there was only Cinnidar.

Chapter 10

October 4, 1879
Glenclaren

Jane hurriedly straightened away from the wall as Margaret came out of Ian's chamber. "How is he?"

"Stubborn." Margaret moved brusquely down the hall toward the staircase. "He won't hear of going to Spain for the winter. I can do nothing with the man."

That statement certainly underscored the seriousness of the situation, Jane thought. Margaret seldom admitted defeat in any area. "You've had the physician speak to him again?"

"This morning," Margaret said tersely. "Ian says Glenclaren needs him now and he will go to Spain in the spring." Her hand momentarily clenched on the banister before she started down the steps. "I told the idiot he will make me a widow before spring if he does not rid himself of that cough, and he cannot do it here. Glenclaren's winters are too harsh."

Jane had witnessed the harshness of those winters for the past three years and felt the same apprehension as Margaret. "Perhaps he will change his mind."

"He hasn't changed it in three months. He keeps talking about Glenclaren and what he has to do this winter. He will *die* here."

"Keep at him," Jane said. "He was so excited about the plans for the new dam."

"A man needs to feel a sense of worth. I knew it was the only way to get him to come alive again." Margaret grimaced. "But after telling him for three years that Glenclaren can't get along without him, how do I convince him he should go off and bask in the sun?"

"Is that why you sent for me? I've already told him the mill is doing well. It's practically running itself now." Jane frowned anxiously. "But I suppose I could talk to him again."

"He won't listen to you either. It's just as well I saw this coming and took measures."

"What measures?"

"Ruel."

Jane stopped in midmotion on the steps.

Margaret cast her a shrewd glance. "You've gone pale as the flour in the bins at your precious mill. Does even the thought of him jar you?"

Jane resumed going down the stairs. "Of course not. If I seem pale, it must be because the hall is dim and the light is fading."

"It's only midafternoon and the light is strong."

"Why should it bother me if you talk of Ruel?"

"For the same reason you haven't mentioned the scamp's name since the first day you arrived here." Margaret wearily shook her head. "It's none of my concern how Ruel has managed to alienate you. I'm aware he has a splendid facility in that direction. If you don't wish to tell me, I can—"

"I do not speak of it because it's not important," Jane interrupted. "It's all in the past."

"The past sometimes has a bearing on the future." Margaret took her blue wool shawl from the clothes tree beside the door and wrapped it around her shoulders. "That's why I thought I should give you warning."

"That you've written to Ruel about Ian?"

Margaret shook her head. "I wrote to Ruel three months ago when Ian first refused to winter in Madrid. I received word this morning from Edinburgh that Ruel should arrive in Glenclaren tomorrow."

Shock took Jane's breath. "He's coming here?"

"I knew I couldn't pry Ian away on my own this time and Ruel's always managed to get his way with him."

Ruel always managed to get his way with everyone, Jane thought. "What about Cinnidar?"

"Ruel's character must have improved considerably since I last saw him. It appears he thinks his brother's life is more important than digging gold." Margaret opened the front door. "So you must put aside any quarrel you may have with Ruel until he manages to persuade Ian he must go to Spain. After that, you may flay him as you see fit."

"Thank you." Jane forced a smile. "But I doubt if I'll see much of him while he's here. Li Sung and I will be too busy at the mill to come to the castle."

"I thought you said the mill was running itself?" Then Margaret shrugged. "Very well, if you wish to hide at the mill, I have no objection."

"I'm not hiding. I'm merely—"

"Avoiding him." Margaret stopped beside the hitching rail where Bedelia was tied. "I doubt he will let you. He inquires very pointedly about your doings in every letter."

Jane's eyes widened. "You never told me."

"There was no need to discuss him if you did not wish it. However, he had a right to ask questions about Glenclaren and its inhabitants, since he was paying the piper." She glanced around the newly paved courtyard and then to the repaired and rebuilt outbuildings. "And he's paid him very well, indeed. The money he's been sending has kept Glenclaren alive and thriving and that means Ian has thrived." She turned back to Jane. "You're going back to the mill now?"

"Unless you wish me to stay."

"Why should you stay? I know you have no liking for the castle. It was no surprise to me when you moved to that cottage near the mill."

"If you'd needed me, I wouldn't have gone."

"I did not need you." Margaret smiled faintly. "But I miss you. Why do you look so surprised? We are friends, are we not?"

"Yes." But Margaret had never said those words before, and it indicated how disturbed she was that she uttered them now. They had formed a strong bond in their efforts to save Ian and Glenclaren, but Margaret guarded her core of privacy as rigidly as Jane did her own and would allow no one too close. Perhaps she should have stayed at the castle and tried to make Margaret's lot easier. Margaret was so strong, Jane sometimes forgot what tremendous problems the other woman had to overcome. It was she, not Ian, who was the guiding force behind everything that happened at Glenclaren, but she never let her husband see it. She had nursed Ian, bullied him, and by sheer force of will gotten him to the point where he could sit up in bed and, infrequently, in his chair. Two years before she had sent for the vicar and insisted the wedding take place. "I'll come back to the castle if you like."

"Don't be foolish. You have your duties and I have mine. We would scarce see each other if you were here." Margaret started across the courtyard.

"Where are you going?"

"Kartauk." Margaret's lips set grimly. "It's not enough I must deal with Ian's stubbornness, now I'm forced to try to curb the rutting of that bull of a goldsmith."

Jane smothered a smile. "Again?"

"You did me no favor when you brought him to Glenclaren. Ellen MacTavish came weeping and wailing to me yesterday morning because Kartauk had taken advantage of her innocence."

"That's a serious charge."

"And a false one. She spreads her legs for every lad in the glen." Margaret frowned. "But that's neither here nor there. It's the third time in two months I've had to deal with his philanderings. Does he think I have nothing better to do than listen to that drivel from his leamans?" She clutched her shawl closer about her. "The dratted man needs to be told a few things." Her stride lengthened as she hurried toward the stable.

Jane's smile faded as Margaret disappeared into Kartauk's workroom. She noticed her hands were trembling on the reins as she mounted Bedelia.

She kicked Bedelia into a trot as she left the courtyard but impulsively turned south instead of north toward the mill as she had originally intended.

A short time later she stood on the hill looking down at the ruin of Annie Cameron's cottage. She had gone there only once before, and that had been during the first month she had come to Glenclaren. At the time she had told herself she had been drawn only by curiosity, but she had known it had been a desperate attempt to exorcise Margaret's haunting words about Ruel and his mother. She had known she had to harden her heart if she was to forget him. She had thought if she saw these ruins she would realize the child who lay alone and abandoned all night in this cottage dying of snakebite was not the Ruel she knew. The hour she had spent here had been both painful and unsuccessful. The memory of that boy still lingered in this glen.

Which was why she had come here today, she realized. There was nothing to fear in that child. He had been vulnerable to pain and had not yet formed the tough determination of the Ruel of Kasanpore. She needed to remember Ruel was very human and could be vanquished. She needed to reassure herself there was nothing to fear.

Not that she was really afraid, she thought quickly. She had merely been shocked by the news Ruel was coming. She could not still love him. She had worked hard to extinguish any lingering embers of that passion she had thought would last forever. Surely her discomposure was a natural reaction when she had not seen Ruel since that last intimidating glimpse at the dock.

How did she know he still felt any bitterness toward her? The separation had made them strangers. He could have changed, softened over the years. He would be eager to get back to his Cinnidar and, if she was fortunate, she might not even see him during his stay at Glenclaren. He might not seek her out.

She closed her eyes and muttered a prayer.

Dear God, let him not seek her out.

"Merciful heavens, this place smells." Margaret wrinkled her nose as she stepped inside the door of Kartauk's workroom. "Dung has a better odor than that foul mixture you use to fire your furnace."

Kartauk grinned at her over his shoulder. "That's because dung is a primary ingredient. It's cheap fuel." He swung open the door of the furnace and slid a tray containing a clay form into the oven. "Which should please your miserly soul, madam."

"Well, this odor does not please me." She strode forward to stand before him. "So I will have my say and be gone."

"Not if you wish me to listen. I must position this tray just right in the furnace." He jerked his head toward the high stool across the room. "Sit down."

"But I have no time to—" She stopped as she realized, as usual, he was paying no attention to her. He never did when absorbed in his blasted work. She sat down on the stool he had indicated and hooked her heels on the rungs. She had been right to come. She was already experiencing an infinitesimal easing of tension as she settled into the familiar pattern they had woven between them. "You have no comfort here. You should spare a day from your dabbles to fashion a chair or two."

"It's good enough for me."

"A blanket on a haystack would be good enough for you. What about Li Sung?"

"He only sleeps here now that the mill is running." He cast her a glance. "You're the only one who complains of lack of comfort. If it offends you, why don't you bring over some of your fine furnishings from the castle?"

"So that you can ruin them with your carelessness?"

"I'm not careless about the things that are important to me."

She could not argue with him on that score. In all the details pertaining to his work he was fanatically scrupulous and painstaking. She had watched him spend two hours positioning one of his figures in the furnace. "It would be better for all of us if something besides those dratted dabbles mattered to you."

He did not glance up. "Have you come to give me a tongue-lashing? What transgression have I committed now?"

"If you'd stop and pay attention for a moment, I would tell you," she said tartly.

"Presently. You may get yourself a cup of coffee if you like."

"And curdle my belly with your vile brew?" She got down from the stool and moved toward the stove. "I suppose I have no choice, if you persist in keeping me waiting."

"No choice at all."

She poured coffee into a cracked but spotlessly clean cup. She had discovered it was one of Kartauk's idiosyncracies that, though shambles might exist around him, everything he touched or used must be gleaming with cleanliness. She stared curiously at the clay bust on the worktable by the furnace; it was in the first stages, the features unrecognizable. "What are you working on this time?"

"Li Sung. I started it this morning."

She strolled back to her stool and sat down again. "I would have thought you'd have done him before this."

"Not while he could see me working on it. There's too much pain in Li Sung. Pain and pride. He believes no one can see his torment and it would disturb him to know that is false." He glanced at her. "Sometimes it is best to hide knowledge when it hurts too much."

She met his gaze and saw wisdom, cynicism . . . and understanding. Too much understanding. She pulled her stare away with an effort. "On occasion you actually display good sound Christian feelings. I wish you'd be as sensitive toward females."

He went still. "You have never asked me for sensitivity before. I didn't think you required it."

"I don't," she said quickly. "I was not speaking of myself."

He relaxed. "Thank God. For a moment I thought I had read you wrong. What a humiliation that would have been."

"Ellen MacTavish."

He smiled. "A lusty maid. She brought me great pleasure."

"More than you brought her. She came running to me wailing you had stolen her virginity."

His smile faded. "Not true. A man has his needs, but I have no traffic with women who lack experience in the joust. Jock assured me she was—"

"Jock? Now you have Ian's servants procuring your harlots?"

"A man has his needs," Kartauk repeated. He sat down on the stool before the worktable. "Is Ellen MacTavish to be the subject of your harping?"

"And Deidre Cameron *and* Martha Belmar."

"Good God, Scottish women are garrulous. They all came to you?"

"I'm the laird's wife. It's the custom for the women of the glen to come to the castle if there's trouble."

"I brought them pleasure, not trouble, and I made no promise of marriage to any woman. Did they say I had?"

"No." Margaret frowned in distaste. "They were mewing like cats in heat because you had not come back to them."

Kartauk's laughter boomed out. "It would not have been fair." He tapped his massive chest with his fist. "To be struck once by the divine lightning is a blessing, more than that would have made them forever dissatisfied with other men."

She closed her eyes. "Sweet Mary, what an arrogant coxcomb you are. I do not know how I can bear to be in the same room with you."

"Because you need me."

"Need?" Her lids flew open. "I don't need anyone. Certainly not an impudent braggart who believes all women are useless if not in bed or posing for one of your infernal statues."

"Not totally useless. I tolerate you who refuse to pose for me and give me neither pleasure nor—"

"*Tolerate* me." She stood up, glaring at him. "It's *I* who tolerate *you*. You occupy this stable, which we now need for horses and livestock, and give neither aid nor—"

"You're right."

"What?"

He smiled gently. "I'm a selfish scoundrel who causes you nothing but grief."

"You certainly are." She gazed at him suspiciously. "Why are you being so agreeable?"

"Perhaps I am lonely and do not wish you to leave. Sit down and finish your coffee."

"You, lonely?" She slowly sat back down on the stool. "You're never lonely."

"How do you know?" He went to the stove and poured himself a cup of coffee. "A man's needs are sometimes not only of the body. Li Sung is not the only one who does not choose to reveal his weaknesses. There are times when we all do things to bring about a desired result without baring our souls." He resumed his seat at the worktable. "Perhaps I struck those women with my lightning because I knew it would bring you to me."

"Nonsense."

He threw back his head and laughed. "You know me too well. You're right, why should a man of my greatness fear to ask for what I want."

"You certainly did not fear to ask what you wanted of Ellen MacTavish," she said tartly.

He shrugged. "Some needs are simpler than others to satisfy. However, I ask myself why you did not feel it necessary to reprove me for my philandering until today when Ellen came to you yesterday morning."

"I was busy yesterday." She looked away from him. "I had no time for trivialities. You surely do not think I made an excuse to see you?"

"Heaven forbid I would so flatter myself." He sipped his coffee. "But I did notice you appear a bit strained today."

"Ellen MacTavish—"

"Would not have caused you to blink an eye. I'm sure you scolded her for her lack of virtue and sent her about her business. What's really wrong?" He met her gaze. "Ian?"

Relief poured through her in a soothing stream. He had guessed, so now she could talk about it. Kartauk always managed to know what she was feeling and would have probed relentlessly until she unburdened herself. This odd bond between them had existed since that afternoon three years earlier when he had come to her sitting room after her father's funeral to express his condolences. She had never understood why she had found herself talking to him when she could confide in no one else. She had revealed feelings toward her father she had not even shown Ian—love, disappointment . . . and bitterness. He had listened impassively and afterward dismissed her confidences as if they had never taken place. He had gone back to his workroom, leaving her blessedly free. "Ian won't go to Spain."

"You knew that three months ago. Ruel will change his mind. When does he come?"

"Tomorrow."

"Then you have nothing to worry about."

"You have greater confidence in Ruel than I do. I'm not sure I was wise in following your advice. Jane was upset when I told her he was coming."

"She must come to terms with Ruel sometime. You need help and he can give it."

"And nothing else matters?"

"I'm very fond of Jane." He looked down into the depths of his cup. "But sometimes it's necessary to make choices."

"And you choose Ian?"

"Ian?" He drank the rest of his coffee in two swallows and set the cup on the table. "But of course. Ian has the greater need. We all must make sacrifices for Ian. He had a bad night?"

"How did you know?"

"You would have not brought up Spain again before Ruel arrived if you'd not been prodded."

"He coughed all night." Her hand tightened on the cup. "And yet when I mentioned Spain he laughed at me. He said Glenclaren needs him. It makes no difference that I need him too."

"Did you tell him that?"

"Are you mad? Isn't he carrying enough burdens without adding guilt?"

"No, you would not want to add to his burden." He smiled. "But I mean nothing to you and have strong shoulders that can shrug off any burden. Tell me, I want to know."

He *did* want to know. His gaze was fixed intently on her face, and she could feel the strength of his will enfolding her.

"Let it go," he said softly. "Give it to me. Start last night when the coughing started."

She drew a deep breath and began.

He listened intently, his clever fingers molding the clay in front of him as the words burst from her in a torrent. She was not conscious of the passing of time, but at one point Kartauk rose to his feet to light the lamp on the wooden support beside the table. Then he sat back down and listened again.

She finally stopped speaking, and silence fell between them. Peace.

Kartauk's powerful hand smashed down on the clay form on the table in front of him!

"What—" Her gaze flew to his face. "Why did you do that? You worked on it all afternoon."

"It was not good enough." He picked up a towel and wiped his hands. "It is better to destroy with one blow than try to make something magnificent out of the commonplace." He grinned. "Not that I could ever be commonplace. For an ordinary man, that effort might have culminated the work of a lifetime."

Her moment of uneasiness vanished, and she smiled back at him. "Arrogance."

"Truth." He stood up and stretched lazily. "And here is another truth. It is time you went back to your Ian. It will be dark soon and he'll begin to worry."

"Yes." She rose to her feet but stood there hesitating. "Are you coming to play chess with Ian after supper tonight?"

"Not tonight." He made a face as he looked down at the mangled clay on the table. "I have work to do here."

She started for the door. "Then I'll no doubt see you when Ruel arrives."

"Possibly." He was frowning with absorption, his hands once more kneading the clay.

He had already forgotten her presence, forgotten her words. Well, that was what she wished, wasn't it? He gave her silence and peace and then closed her away from him. Yet, for some reason, today this isolation bothered her.

She paused at the door as a thought occurred to her. "You've never done one of me, have you?"

"What?"

"You're making a bust of Li Sung without his knowledge. How do I know you haven't modeled one of me as well?"

"You're wondering if I have your likeness secreted

away among my treasures?" He shook his head. "No, madam."

She felt an absurd rush of relief. "I wouldn't put it past you. No one is safe when your art is weighed in the balance."

"True." He lifted his head. "But I've never made a bust of you."

"Why not?" she asked curiously.

"I would not dare."

She started to laugh and then stopped, suddenly breathless and unsure as she met his gaze.

Then he looked down and resumed kneading the clay. He said lightly, "Even I tremble before the laird's lady's righteous wrath."

A tumult of confused emotions streamed through her, relief and disappointment foremost. For a moment she had felt as if she had been about to discover some great and mysterious truth about Kartauk and then been cheated of the knowledge. What did she really know about him? He never spoke of his past, never asked for help except as it pertained to his art, and let no one see beyond that bold, flamboyant exterior. During these years she had taken much from him and given nothing in return. Perhaps he had not been joking when he had said he had needs of the spirit that had to be met. "I did not tell the truth," she said haltingly. "You would be missed if you left Glenclaren."

He stopped in midmotion but did not look at her. "By Ian?"

"Yes." She moistened her lips before she said awkwardly, "And by me. I believe you kinder than you pretend."

"Do you?" He glanced up and a flashing smile lit his face. "But I do not pretend. Don't judge me by your standards. I'm a ruthless heathen, remember?"

She nodded. "How could I forget?"

"And now a heartless womanizer."

The rogue was baiting her. Why the devil was she worrying about the sensitivity of his blasted feelings? "That you most certainly are. From now on when you strike one of those sluts with your divine fire, make sure you stay to put out the blaze yourself."

She heard his roar of laughter as she stalked out of the stable.

Li Sung knocked on the door of Jane's cottage only moments after she arrived back at the mill site.

"What's wrong?" he asked when he saw her face as she opened the door. "Ian?"

Blast it, she had known Li Sung would notice her discomposure and that was the reason she had gone to the cottage instead of directly to the mill. She shook her head. "He's no worse." She saw the envelope in his hand. "For me?"

"It came right after you left. I thought you would want to see it right away." He handed her the envelope. "It's from Lancashire."

Hope leapt as she eagerly tore open the letter. Dear heaven, let the answer be yes. She needed good news today. Bitter disappointment flooded through her as she scanned the brief note.

"Another refusal?" Li Sung's gaze was on her face.

"Yes." She folded the letter and stuffed the letter back in the envelope. "It seems my services aren't needed by the Lancashire railroad."

"That's all they said?"

"Oh no." She smiled crookedly. "Mr. Radkins suggests I occupy myself in more genteel pursuits and forget this foolishness of trying to involve myself in masculine endeavors."

"He is the fool," Li Sung said.

"Well, it appears the world is full of fools. This is the fifth refusal I've received in the last six months." She tossed the envelope on the table. The rejection was a blow she hadn't needed when she was already feeling this sense of panic and uncertainty. "I suppose I should have expected it. The most incompetent of men are perceived as better than a woman."

"We could go back to America," Li Sung suggested. "Perhaps they would be more open than these British."

"That's too far away. I need to be in Scotland or, at least, England, in case Ian needs me."

He shook his head. "I have never understood this guilt you feel for Ian's injury."

She had been tempted during the last three years to tell him the reason, but now she was glad she had not. She did not need to cope with a bristling, defensive Li Sung as well as Ruel.

"Why?" Li Sung asked. "The accident was no one's fault."

How she wished that were true, that she was as free of guilt as Li Sung thought. God in heaven, she was weary of shouldering the knowledge that Ian would be strong and well if she had not blinded herself to what Patrick might do. But she had no choice but to shoulder it when every time she saw Ian her guilt was there before her in all its heart-wrenching tragedy.

"I like Ian. Naturally, I wish to do all I can for him." She abruptly turned away and snatched up her tartan shawl from the chair and moved toward the door. "I feel like a walk. Are you coming with me?"

He shook his head as he limped toward his horse. "My leg has taken enough punishment for one day, and you seem more in the mood for running away than walking. I'm going back to the castle and will see you tomorrow morning." He glanced over his shoulder. "Unless you have further need of me."

She forced a smile. "The day's work is done and the workers have gone home. Why should I have need of you? The letter? I was expecting it."

"And were you expecting the news from the castle that made you look as pale and shaking as you do when you have the fever?"

"I don't look—" She stopped as she met his gaze. "Ruel MacClaren will be arriving at Glenclaren tomorrow."

"I see." He smiled faintly. "No wonder you are disturbed."

"I'm not disturbed. Uneasy, perhaps."

"Why?"

She shrugged. "He . . . unsettles me. He unsettles everybody."

"He has done a great deal for Glenclaren." As she started to protest, he went on. "We may have done the work, but it was his money that made it possible. You can't deny that, Jane."

"I don't deny it." She was silent a moment and then burst out, "I just wish—why couldn't he have stayed away? He doesn't belong here."

"Neither do we," Li Sung said softly. "You know it as well as I, or you would not have sought work away from here. I've seen your restlessness growing for the last year. How long must we stay here?"

"As long as Ian needs us."

Li Sung shook his head. "You and I have given him the Glenclaren he wants, and Margaret provides him with all else."

She watched him awkwardly mount his horse and turn it toward the castle. "Li Sung!"

He glanced back at her.

"Are you truly unhappy here?"

He shook his head. "One place is as good as another to me. Perhaps I, too, am a little restless now that there are no longer any challenges to overcome." He kicked his horse into a trot.

She hugged the green and black tartan shawl closer as she started up the hill. The sun was almost down and the autumn wind cold as it touched her cheeks. She moved quickly, almost running up the rough dirt path. She should really go back to the cottage and fix her evening meal and go to bed but found the prospect unappealing. Though she had been up at dawn and spent the entire day supervising the work at the mill until Margaret's summons had taken her to the castle, she was not tired. Of late she had noticed any weariness she experienced came from sheer monotony. The events of yesterday and today and tomorrow all blended into stultifying sameness.

No, not tomorrow. Tomorrow Ruel would come.

She would not think of Ruel. She would think of the work still to be done at Glenclaren and Li Sung's words. In spite of his denial, she sensed the same discontent in him she had been feeling of late. She had no right to chain Li Sung here because of her own sense of obligation. Yet where could she and Li Sung go if they left Glenclaren? Railroads were the only life they knew, and it had been made bitterly clear no one would hire a cripple and a woman. She would have to consider the possibilities and—

"I see you've taken to wearing the MacClaren tartan."

She froze with shock.

Ruel continued mockingly. "It's too much a contrast with that red mane. It's not what I'd dress you in at all."

She turned slowly to see Ruel walking up the path toward her. He was the same. No trace of the vulnerability for which she had prayed as she had looked down at Annie's cottage. Except for looking tougher, leaner, he had not changed.

God in heaven, what was wrong with her? She felt as if she were going to faint. She couldn't breathe. She felt as chained as she had that day she had left Kasanpore—chained, desperate, sad, and other emotions too chaotic to define. She took a deep breath, trying to steady the rapid pounding of her heart. "You weren't supposed to be here until tomorrow."

"It's never wise to do the expected. It allows one's enemies to prepare themselves."

"You have no enemies here."

"Don't I?" He drew even with her on the path. "Then why has the thought of you tormented me more than any enemy I've ever had?" He smiled at her. "Did you think about me too?"

"No, I didn't think of you at all," she lied. "I've been far too busy."

The wind lifted his hair away from his forehead, revealing the stark beauty of his features. She found herself staring at him with the same fascination she had felt the first time she had seen him.

"So Maggie wrote me." He looked down at the mill in the valley below. "The repairs on the castle, the dairy, the new mill. Ian must be very happy."

"Isn't that what you wanted?"

"Not entirely." His gaze shifted to her face, and she received the shocking impact of those searing blue eyes. "I also wanted you to suffer, and instead you've taken the easy way."

"Easy?" she asked, stung. "I've worked very hard."

"But it's the kind of work that fulfills you, that you'd be unhappy doing without."

"I'm sorry to disappoint you, but Margaret prefers to care for Ian's personal needs."

"I should have expected you to escape, I suppose." He smiled. "But now that I'm here, I can rectify that mistake."

She stared at him incredulously. "You can do nothing to me. I told you it was my choice to come here and it will be my choice if I leave."

"And you've been thinking of leaving Glenclaren, haven't you?" he asked softly. "I've been expecting that for quite a while. Three years is a long time."

"I suppose Margaret mentioned that I've been seeking work with a few of the local railroads."

"No, she spoke only of Glenclaren, but I knew you'd grow restless."

Yes, the mandarin had always known her thoughts, she realized in despair.

He nodded as he read them now. "Aye, I know you. I thought I knew you before, but no one knows you as well as I do now. I didn't want to think about you, but you were *there*." His lips tightened. "I'd lie down to sleep after breaking my back on the mountain and there you were. At first I was angry, but after a while I grew accustomed to you intruding. You became part of my life. You became part of *me*."

She shivered. "You hate me."

"I don't know what I feel for you any longer. I know

only that I have to rid myself of you." He paused. "And I can't do that until I know you've been punished for what you did to Ian."

"Good God, I *have* been punished. Every time I look at him I hurt."

"But you don't look at him. You stay away from the castle in your cozy little cottage by the mill and seldom see his pain."

She refused to justify herself, when he wouldn't believe her anyway. "I'm not going to make excuses. You don't want to hear what I have to say."

"No, it's too late for excuses. Actually, I blame myself for failing to take into account Maggie's zeal. I suppose it doesn't really matter. I'm here now and can shape events to suit myself." He smiled. "I have to get on to the castle. I stopped by only to warn you not to try to run away from me."

"If I chose to leave here, nothing you say could make me stay."

"But I'd find you. Or Li Sung." He paused. "Or Patrick. Did I mention I paid a visit to Patrick at his lodging house in Edinburgh?"

She stiffened warily. "You know you didn't."

"Perhaps because he was less than coherent. Is he always drunk these days?"

"So I understand," she said reservedly.

"I was surprised you'd let him out from under your protective wing. Could it be your fondness for the scalawag is waning?"

She didn't answer.

"But there still seems to be some feeling there. His landlady says your quarterly payments keep him out of the gutter." He nodded. "Yes, I believe I can use Patrick." He reached out and tucked her shawl more closely around her shoulders in a gesture that was oddly possessive. "Go back to the cottage. It's growing cooler and you'll catch a chill."

The gesture caught her off guard and she stared at him in bewilderment. "You wouldn't care if I froze to death."

"That's not true. I'd care very much. I don't want anything or anyone to touch you." He paused. "But me. I want you to realize that I'm the only wind that can blow you either good or ill." The words were spoken softly, casually, but she was aware of an underlying intensity. His fingers reached out and caressingly touched the side of her throat. She experienced a shock of heat that caused her to jerk away from him.

He smiled as he noticed the involuntary response. "I'll be back tomorrow morning to see you. By that time I will have had my talk with Maggie and Ian and be ready to state my proposition."

"You're going to try to persuade Ian to go to Spain?"

"No, I'm taking him home to Cinnidar with me."

Her eyes widened. "He'll never go."

"You're wrong. Ian will come with me." He met her gaze. "And so will you, Jane."

She forgot to breathe. "No," she whispered.

"Don't go to the mill tomorrow morning, or I'll come after you."

"Are you threatening me?"

"Not at the moment. But yes, I am a threat to you. However, sometimes we choose to embrace a threat if we find it to our advantage. And you'll definitely find my proposition to your advantage, Jane." He turned and started down the hill. "By the way, don't wear that shawl tomorrow. It displeases me."

This man who had once asked her to wed him didn't think her worthy to wear the clan tartan. Strange that such a small thing should sting her when she had borne much worse from him. "You may not feel I belong here, but Margaret gave me this shawl and I have every intention of wearing it."

"You believe I'm outraged you're desecrating the honor of the clan by wearing it?" He shook his head. "If I thought you could do that by wearing the blasted thing, I'd dress you in the MacClaren plaid from head to toe. I have no fondness for Glenclaren or its trappings. My father made sure I knew I didn't belong here."

"Then you should not mind me wearing the tartan."

"But then, I'm not always reasonable. The tartan's like a brand of ownership, and I don't like the thought of Glenclaren owning you. Don't wear the shawl again."

The panic she had tried to hide from him raced through her as she watched him walk away. He had only had to appear and she had been immediately plunged into the same emotional turmoil as the moment she had left Kasanpore. Only moments before he had come she had been bewailing the sameness of Glenclaren, but now she desperately wanted that monotony to return.

He could not make her go to Cinnidar, she thought desperately. He could not make her do anything. The time was past when he could play on her emotions and twist her to do his will. She was safe from him now.

She drew a deep, steadying breath, trying to calm herself. Yes, she had still felt the fascination drawing her to him, but that had been only of the flesh. It might be a power he would always have over her, but it was a power she could fight. It wasn't love. She was over that madness now. She had purged herself of that insanity during these years away from him.

It wasn't love.

Chapter 11

"He'll never go," Margaret told Ruel flatly. "If Ian refused to go to Spain, do you think he'll travel halfway across the world to Cinnidar?"

"We have to persuade him to go. Spain is too close to be a solution for him. He would start thinking about Glenclaren and you'd find yourself on the next ship to Scotland."

"You may be right." Margaret frowned. "But I've heard the East is hot and unhealthy."

"Do I look as if it's hurt me?"

Ruel looked tough as a tree trunk, brown as the

acorns that fell from it, and comely as ever, she thought. "But then, the devil takes care of his own."

He burst out laughing. "I believe I've missed you, Maggie. You always did know me better than Ian."

"I once thought so too, but I've been wondering of late. All this outpouring of generosity toward Ian and Glenclaren has led me to question my judgment."

His laughter faded. "I love Ian, Maggie."

"You *have* changed. You would never admit to loving anyone when you left here." She gazed at him challengingly. "If you love him, come to Spain with us and make sure Ian doesn't go back to Glenclaren until he's well."

"I can't, dammit. I have to take the next ship back to Cinnidar. The situation there is . . . delicate."

"Ian's condition is also delicate."

He frowned. "Cinnidar isn't like Kasanpore. It's an island with sea breezes that cool and temper the heat. Do you think I'd risk giving him a setback?"

Margaret studied him. "No," she said finally. "You wouldn't hurt Ian if you could help it."

He bowed his head mockingly. "I suppose I should thank you for having such touching faith in me."

"I don't want thanks, I want assurances."

"Tell me what you need to know. I've told you Cinnidar's climate is good and I can assure you of so many servants, they'll be stumbling over themselves to help and care for Ian."

"Which may be a detriment instead of an asset. I've spent three years fostering Ian's belief in himself. Housing?"

"A palace. The Savitsar family built a palace overlooking the canyon a long time ago. The place has been deserted for decades, but I set workers to repairing and refurbishing it before I left Cinnidar." He smiled faintly. "You can't fault the accommodations, Maggie."

"We shall see." She shook her head impatiently. "Why are we even talking about this? You'll never persuade him to go."

"Not if he lacks confidence Glenclaren will be properly cared for. Do you have anyone who can meet that requirement?"

"He would trust Jane to—"

"Jane will be going with us," Ruel interrupted. "And so will Li Sung. Think of someone else."

"That's no easy task."

"A decision doesn't have to be made tonight. We have a few days."

"Are you going up to see Ian now?"

He shook his head. "Ian's not stupid. He'll know why I'm here the moment he sees me. I'll let him get a good night's sleep before I launch the attack."

"Then I'll tell Mary to show you to a chamber."

He shook his head. "I'll not stay here. My father would rise from his grave at the thought of me resting within these hallowed halls."

"I would have thought that would be reason for you to stay."

"It's not amusing to steal from a dead man." He smiled without mirth. "Though there was a time when I would have offered my soul for a haven here."

"Where will you go?"

He shrugged. "I'll find a place. I'll be back in the morning to talk to Ian."

"Who will say no."

"The first time," Ruel said. "He'll agree in the end, if you can find someone competent to run Glenclaren."

She frowned. "The vicar might know of someone. I'd suggest Kartauk, but Ian would never trust him to run the estate. He'd fear Kartauk would become absorbed in his work and let the castle burn to the ground."

"Kartauk is coming too. I have need of him."

"You may have trouble making use of Kartauk," she said dryly. "He does not have a pliant nature."

"You've found that out?"

"Kartauk has proved . . . helpful." She glanced away from him. "He amuses Ian."

"And does he amuse you too, Maggie?"

Her gaze flew back to him to find his gaze narrowed intently on her. "What do you mean?"

"Nothing." He shrugged. "I've been away a long time, and I'd forgotten how imbued with virtue you are."

"Virtue?" Her eyes widened in shock. "You thought I—"

"It slipped out," he said impatiently. "Forget it."

"I will *not* forget it." Anger poured through her. "I *love* my husband, Ruel. How dare you say—"

"I apologize, dammit. I'll watch my tongue next time."

"You'd do better to watch your foul thoughts." She whirled on her heel and strode toward the door. "And my name is Margaret. I allowed you a certain amount of indulgence when you were a boy, but if you ever call me Maggie again, I shall find a way to punish your impudence."

"Yes, Margaret," he said.

The hint of amusement she detected beneath the meekness in his tone grated abrasively. "I've changed my mind. You've not changed a whit. You're as wild and insufferable as ever."

His amusement instantly vanished. "I need your help to get Ian to Cinnidar. Don't let your anger at me hurt him."

"Do you think I'd do that?" She drew a deep breath and tried to control her temper. "I'll speak to Ian tonight and try to prepare the way for you."

"That's all I ask."

"I doubt if it will do any good." She opened the door. "You'd best be prepared to give up your plan and take Ian to Spain."

"If I don't get back to Cinnidar soon, there may not be a Cinnidar . . . or a Glenclaren." He paused and smiled. "Curious. I wonder why you're so angry with me."

She slammed the door of the study and marched across the foyer toward the staircase.

Ruel had been at Glenclaren only a matter of hours

and he was already throwing her into a turmoil with his wicked tongue and wickeder thoughts. Mother of heaven, she had wanted to slap that comely face and—

Why? Ruel was right, she did not easily lose her temper.

It was perfectly reasonable for her to be angry. He had given her insult.

But he had apologized immediately and she had never let Ruel's impudence disturb her before.

She would dismiss the rascal from her mind, she decided firmly. She had better things to do with her energy than let Ruel upset her like this. She must prepare Ian for Ruel's visit tomorrow.

He had known there was nothing for him here.

Ruel sat his horse on the crest of the hill, his gaze fastened on the thatched cottage a few yards away.

The cottage had been deserted since he had left Glenclaren and was probably overrun with rats and cockroaches. He had known when he left the castle tonight he would not be able to sleep here. He certainly felt no sentiment for the place. He had spent more nights curled up in his blanket in the hills than in this hut. After the laird had lost interest in his mother and rejected her claim that Ruel was his son, she had made it clear Ruel was not welcome when she entertained the men of the glen.

Perhaps he had come here to reinforce how fortunate he was to have escaped this place that had brought him only humiliation and tears. Tears? God in heaven, he had shed no tears since he was a boy of seven. He must be becoming maudlin to be recalling that foolish lad.

Why the devil had he even come here?

Jane.

It had been Jane, gazing at him defiantly, wrapped in that damned MacClaren plaid that had set off the chain of memories and brought him here. He had thought he was prepared, but the moment he had caught sight of her he had felt . . . Dear God, what had he felt? Bitterness, lust . . . and possession. It was the latter emotion that he must strive to vanquish. Revenge would rid him of bitterness, the plan he was about to put in place would eventually slake his lust, but to own was also to be owned. Over the years the thought of her had possessed and now obsessed him.

But this emotional turmoil would end soon. Once he had rid himself of the bitterness and lust, she would no longer be important to him. He would be able to forget her as he had forgotten this cottage, as he had forgotten that boy he had been, as he had forgotten Glenclaren.

"Not overly luxurious but very bright and pleasant." Ruel's gazed over Jane's head at the meager furnishings in the one-room cottage. "May I come in?"

"No," Jane said baldly.

"I thought that would be your response. Then come and walk with me."

Walk out with me.

The words he had spoken that night in Kasanpore came back to her as if they had been spoken yesterday.

"But I'm not courting you this time," he said softly. "We've gone far beyond that madness. I have a proposition to discuss."

Why did the devil always know what she was thinking? she wondered with exasperation. "I have nothing to say to you."

"Oh, I'll probably be the one doing the talking. The only word you need say is yes."

She gazed at him mutinously.

"You can come walk with me or I'll come in. I'm not going away."

She hesitated, and then deliberately picked up her MacClaren shawl from the back of the chair by the door and strode out of the cottage.

"That's better." He closed the door and strolled beside her up the path toward the hill. "Did you tell Li Sung of our talk?"

"No," she said curtly.

"That's all right, you can discuss it later after you have all the details."

"I'm not going to Cinnidar, and you're mad to think Ian will go. Have you talked to him?"

"This morning."

"And?"

"He refused, of course."

She felt a ridiculous rush of relief. Of course Ian had refused. She had been worried for nothing.

"But I'll talk to him again this evening." He paused. "And tomorrow morning, and as many times as it takes until he agrees to go."

Her relief vanished as she recognized the implacable resolution in his tone. She had heard that note a hundred times before during those first days of Ian's illness. Ian had not been able to withstand him then, and she doubted he would now. "I won't go with you."

He smiled as they continued to climb.

"I won't," she said desperately. "You can't make me go. I'd be a fool to let you put me in a position where you could hurt me."

"Unless you saw an advantage to you and your covey that would be worth the risk. I've thought a long time about ways and means of gathering you into my net. I was going to wait until you became a little more desperate, but circumstances have forced me to move a bit faster."

"*Listen* to you. I'm just supposed to walk into this net?"

"No, you'll cautiously edge forward, do everything possible to avoid it, work yourself into exhaustion to escape, and give in only when there's no other choice." He cast her a sideways glance. "Because the carrot I'm going to offer is too delicious for you to refuse."

"What carrot?"

"A railroad."

Her eyes widened in shock. "What?"

"Not only a railroad, but money enough to give you independence and the life you want to lead. Interested?"

"No."

"Yes, you are, but you think I'm trying to trick you. No tricks. My cards are all on the table. You'll know exactly what rewards and penalties to expect."

"This conversation makes no sense."

"Then I'd best hasten to elaborate. I need a railroad to carry gold ore from the mountain across the jungle and then up the canyon wall to the refinery at the harbor. I've managed to carve out a rough path wide enough for pack trains, but that's only a tenth of the load railway cars could carry. I *need* that gold."

"Need or want?"

"Both. I want it because it will make me rich as Midas. And I need it because, if I don't get a large amount of gold processed soon, I won't have the money to support Glenclaren and defend Cinnidar from Abdar."

"Abdar?"

"Did you think the ground had opened up and swallowed him after you left Kasanpore?"

"I haven't thought about him at all." She paused. "Any more than I've thought of you."

He ignored the last remark. "Abdar's very much astir and interested in Cinnidar."

"How do you know?"

"Pachtal showed up on the island over a year ago. I'm sure he took a fascinating report back to Abdar regarding the gold I've been shipping."

"What difference does it make? You own Cinnidar. He can't touch it."

"Not now. But Pickering tells me he'll soon be the ruler of Kasanpore. The maharajah is being treated for a tubercular condition by the British doctors at the fort and Pickering doubts he'll last more than another nine or ten months. That means I must have Cinnidar well fortified by the time Abdar takes power."

"But you *own* it."

"The Savitsars originally annexed Cinnidar by force. If it suits his convenience, there's nothing to stop Abdar from declaring the bill of sale null and void and make a move to take the island back."

"The British would—"

"The British aren't going to interfere with Abdar's actions against an island two hundred and fifty miles off the coast. They know Abdar would like nothing better than to throw the British out of his province and are going to be busy enough trying to keep a firm foothold in Kasanpore. If I'm to keep Cinnidar, I have to be prepared to defend it myself."

"And to do it you need a railroad?"

"And someone to build it." He paused. "You, Jane."

She shook her head.

"It will be a difficult task but not impossible. I've had the terrain surveyed by James Medford, an engineer recommended by Pickering. Have you heard of him?"

"Of course. He's very well respected."

"Medford said the job will have its nightmare aspects but can be built in seven months."

"Then have him do it."

"I gave Medford the job of laying the tracks from the canyon to the refinery at the harbor. I saved the canyon for you."

"Thank you," she said ironically. "I'm surprised you'd trust me with your fine railroad."

"I know you're more than competent." He met her gaze. "And you'd never dare try to substitute shoddy materials with me."

"Wouldn't I?"

He ignored her sarcasm and continued. "Our contract will read that you'll be required to have the line over Elephant Crossing completed eight weeks after work begins, and your track must join with Medford's seven months from the day you start. That's the exact estimated period Medford judged it could be done. If you miss the deadline over Elephant Crossing, you'll forfeit fifty percent of your total fee. If you don't complete the total line in seven months, you forfeit another thirty percent."

"Why are you telling me this? I'm not interested in your terms."

"You will be. Because, if the railroad is completed on

time, I'll give you enough money to start your own company and fund its operation for the first year."

Her eyes widened with shock. "You don't mean it."

"It's all there in the contract. Once the railroad is built, that amount of money will mean nothing to me. But it would mean a great deal to you, wouldn't it, Jane?"

"Yes." It would be a miracle. Freedom to build. Freedom to work. But it was only a deliciously baited trap. She had to stop thinking about it.

"You could give your friend Li Sung a high position in the company. He'd have a place in the community and the respect he deserves. You'd have enough money to properly take care of Patrick."

"Be still," she hissed.

"You want it, Jane," he said softly. "You know you want it."

"Not from you."

"Who else would give it to you? I know a dozen men who would sell their souls for an opportunity like this. Security for the people you care about and the chance to get rich."

Freedom. Li Sung. A railroad.

"I don't want to hear any more."

"Why? When it's so sweet to your ears?"

She whirled on her heel and started down the path. He was beside her in an instant, his hand on her arm.

"Let me go!"

"Not until you've heard me out."

She had already heard an irresistible siren call, and it was tearing her apart. She said jerkily, "You've made your offer. It doesn't tempt me."

"The hell it doesn't," he said grimly. "You wouldn't still be at Glenclaren if you'd been able to get work anywhere else. You *want* this and so do I."

"And it's worth all that money to get me there?"

"Oh yes." He paused. "Because when I have you on Cinnidar, I'm going to find a way to punish you. You won't escape as you did here at Glenclaren."

It was the answer she expected; there was no reason

to feel this jolting hurt. She laughed without mirth. "Good God, then why would I be fool enough to go?"

"I've told you all the reasons." He smiled. "Except one."

She waited.

"Obsession is seldom a singular passion. It demands a response and you're a very responsive woman. You want your railroad, you want safety and happiness for your friends." He paused. "And you want what we had together in Kasanpore."

"No!"

"It's not finished yet. We tasted just enough to tantalize us. We've never had enough. Neither one of us can ever be free of the other until we do." His gaze was almost caressing as it moved over her face. His words were soft, persuasive, weaving a sensual spell around her. "And you want to be free of me, don't you, Jane? Every night I was with you when you lay down in that bed in the cottage, just as you were with me on the mountain. Did you toss and turn and curse me as I did you?"

She moistened her lips. "It wasn't like that. I didn't—" Damn him, he was smiling faintly, knowingly, and she felt suddenly naked, as if he had been there watching her during those nights when she had not been able to close the thought of him out.

She had to get away from him! She whirled and ran down the hill. The cold wind struck her cheeks, but she barely felt it.

She didn't stop until she reached the cottage. She slammed the door, bolted it, ran across the room, and flung herself on the bed.

She was icy cold, shaking uncontrollably.

"Jane."

She tensed, her gaze on the locked door.

"I'll come back tomorrow for your answer," Ruel said. "I'm slipping the contract and Medford's survey report under the door. You'll have plenty of time before tomorrow to examine them both."

"I don't want to see them."

"But you'll still look at them. You'll think of Li Sung

and Patrick. You'll remember how hard it is for a woman to make a place in this world." Two folded documents slithered serpentlike beneath the door. "I'll see you tomorrow, Jane."

She didn't hear the departing footsteps, but she knew he was gone.

She should be relieved, but she was not. It was as if he were in the room with her, looking at her, touching her.

It's not finished yet.

It was true. No matter how she had lied to herself, she had never been able to fight what she felt for Ruel. It had always been there in the background, like a melody with the verse left unsung.

Let it stay unfinished. She didn't want it to start again. She had struggled for three years to banish the love she had felt for Ruel. She could not imagine anything more terrible than caring for a man who wanted only to hurt her. The idea made her so frightened, she felt sick to her stomach.

But she couldn't tear her gaze from the two packets of papers on the floor.

Kartauk sat on the flagstones, his eyes closed, leaning back against the stone wall of the stable.

"You're not working?" Ruel strolled across the courtyard toward Kartauk. "I don't believe I've ever seen you so relaxed."

"I just finished firing a statue in the furnace. It's cooling down." Kartauk opened his eyes. "Margaret tells me I'm to go to Cinnidar. How very kind of you to invite me."

"I was going to get around to it. I've been busy. I need you, Kartauk."

"The entire world needs me."

"They need your work. I need your knowledge of Abdar. There's a good possibility he'll appear on the horizon and I'll need your help."

"I've spent three years avoiding Abdar and you wish

me to place myself in a position where he cannot help but notice me?"

"You're not a retiring gentleman. Wouldn't you like to be permanently free of Abdar?"

"Permanently? Just how do you intend to 'permanently' remove a man in his position?"

"Cinnidar is mine. For all intents and purposes I'm the maharajah of Cinnidar. If Abdar makes an attempt to take it, I'd be within my rights to treat him like any other invader." He smiled grimly. "I have no compunction about making sure he won't get the opportunity to do it twice."

"In which case I can sit here and let you get rid of him for me while I tend to my own concerns."

"True, but his defeat will be swifter and more certain if I have an ally who knows the nature of the beast."

"Beast?" Kartauk savored the word. "He is one, you know. A total monster." He shook his head. "I do not think it wise for me to go."

"Why not?"

"Many reasons."

"You can have your own studio in the palace."

"I've gotten used to my studio here."

"And have you also gotten used to working only in bronze and wood?"

Kartauk's eyes narrowed on Ruel's face. "Are you about to dangle a bribe?"

"An irresistible bribe, a golden bribe. Cash may be a bit slim at present, but there's enough gold to meet even your needs."

"You'll be my patron?"

"Doesn't every ruler need an artist to beautify his palace?"

"Gold . . ."

"And my promise to give you my protection from Abdar."

"As long as you're alive to give it."

Ruel inclined his head. "Point taken. But I fully intend to survive Abdar."

Kartauk studied him for a moment. "It's a gamble."

"Yes."

"All the gold I need?"

Ruel said warily, "Within reason. I can afford a golden door, but I might balk if you decide your artistic soul requires an entire railway car."

"I will be reasonable." Mischief lit Kartauk's face. "Not a passenger car, perhaps only a caboose." He stood up and turned back to the stable. "You've wasted enough of my time. I must go back to work."

"You'll come?"

"How can I resist? Fate has obviously seen fit to tempt me beyond my powers to refuse. Abdar's head and a golden caboose . . ."

"No, Ruel." Ian tried to keep his tone firm. "It's out of the question. I've told you any number of times I'll not leave Glenclaren. Why won't you accept it?"

"Because you're being stupid," Ruel said bluntly. "What difference will six months make? Do you think I'm going to keep you on Cinnidar forever?" His voice lowered persuasively. "Listen to me. Give me six months to heal that cough and I promise I'll send you back to Glenclaren."

Ian shook his head.

Ruel sat back in his chair. "Aren't you being selfish? What about Margaret? Are you going to leave her a widow after all she's done for you?"

Ian's lips twisted. "At times I believe it would be the greatest gift I could give her."

"Then you'd be wrong. Margaret has always loved you and she always will. She wants you alive."

Ian sighed. "I know. Poor lass."

"She doesn't feel sorry for herself."

Ian's tone turned suddenly fierce. "Well, she should. Married to a crock of a man who will probably never be able to give her a child."

"Is that what the doctor said?"

Ian shrugged. "He said there was a possibility of a child. But it's been two years."

"Two years isn't such a long time."

"It's a lifetime," Ian said flatly.

Ruel's lips tightened. "Sorry. I guess it has been for you."

"I didn't mean to sound self-pitying. Sometimes I don't understand—"

"Understand what?"

"Why God meant me to live."

"Are you still searching your soul for answers? I thought you'd decided I was the one who had thrown a rod into the spokes of destiny."

"Did I say that? Forgive me, Ruel."

"For God's sake, there's nothing to forgive."

"There's a great deal for both you and Margaret to forgive. God doesn't make mistakes, so there must be a reason I'm such a burden to you. I just can't see it yet. When I began to get stronger I thought it must have meant I was supposed to give Margaret a child." He smiled bitterly. "But it's becoming clear I can't even do that."

"You were very ill this winter. Once you're strong again, perhaps you—"

"Perhaps," Ian interrupted. "Or perhaps Glenclaren was meant to be my only child." He forced a smile. "So you mustn't try to keep me from caring for my child, Ruel."

"You're making excuses. I doubt if God cares as much for Glenclaren as you do." He paused. "Have you considered the possibility you're using Glenclaren as a way out?"

Ian glanced away. "I don't know what you mean."

"If you stay at Glenclaren this winter, you'll die. It's a mortal sin to take your own life, Ian."

"I wasn't . . ." His stricken gaze shifted to Ruel's face. "Was I?"

"How the hell do I know? You tell me."

"You seem to know too much . . . as usual. Lord, I wish you hadn't come, Ruel."

"I didn't think you'd welcome me."

"It's not that I don't love you. It's just that—"

"I'm the barrier between you and what you want," Ruel finished wearily. "That is what I've been since the moment I pulled you out of the railway car. For God's sake, come to Cinnidar and lie in the sun and get your strength back. Let us try to make things right for you."

"You've already done a great deal for me and Glenclaren. I suppose I'm being very ungrateful."

"I don't want your gratitude. I want you to come to Cinnidar."

Ian didn't answer for a long time. "I'll consider it," he said slowly.

"Good." Ruel stood up and moved toward the door. "Rest now and I'll send Margaret up with your supper."

"No, I don't want—"

The door had already closed behind Ruel, and Ian leaned wearily back against the pillows. Clever Ruel, to have guessed what he had never allowed himself to admit to himself, that he had wanted the light to take him here at Glenclaren, not in a strange land. The light was almost always with him now; sometimes he dreamed about it and woke with a reluctance and wistfulness he was forced to hide from Margaret.

His lovely, strong, caring Margaret. She, too, was drifting away, paling beside the lure of the light.

Yet Ruel was right, he was not being fair. They were all trying so hard to keep him from the light that it must be God's will.

Cinnidar. Even the name sounded exotic and alien from his Glenclaren.

Ruel found Margaret in the study, making entries into an account book. "He's softening. It would do no harm for you to go to him now and add your arguments to mine."

She closed the account book. "I didn't think you'd be able to do it."

"It's not a certain victory yet. Have you arranged for anyone to manage Glenclaren while you're gone?"

"Timothy Drummond, the vicar's son, has recently

returned from the university in Edinburgh. He's a canny, able man who has little imagination but could keep things in order until I return."

"Then tell that to Ian. He appears to regard Glenclaren as an offspring he must nurture and care for." He paused. "He wants very much to give you a child."

"Do you think I don't know that?" she asked fiercely. "He can talk of nothing else. It will not happen."

"Ian said the physician told him—"

"Because I forced him to lie to Ian. He would never have married me if he had known there was no chance."

"No chance at all?"

"Almost none. God sometimes performs miracles, but it's best not to count on Him."

"Too bad."

"Bad? It's worse than bad. Not only does Ian feel guilty for robbing me of a child, but a babe would give him purpose, a reason to live."

"I'm sorry, Magg—Margaret."

"Sorrow won't help Ian. We have to do that." She straightened her shoulders and moved toward the door. "I'll go up and talk to him now."

Li Sung. A railroad.

The words played over and over in Jane's mind. Why was she cowering on this bed, afraid to take up the challenge Ruel had thrown down? He was only a man, like any other man. Well, perhaps not like any other man, but still human and fallible. He had told her he intended to take revenge, but she knew him well enough to realize he would not try to trick her to accomplish it.

A railroad.

Sweet Mary, but she was afraid. She had no doubt Ruel would be completely merciless in any confrontation between them.

A railroad.

Why was she assuming she would not be able to gather the strength to fight Ruel? She had spent the last three years preparing her defenses against him. She was no longer the child he had known in Kasanpore, and who was to say she could not best him?

It was after midnight when Jane slowly got up from the bed and moved across the room to pick up both packets on the floor. She lit the lamp on the table, sat down, and opened the survey report.

"I'll do it," Jane said as soon as she opened the door to Ruel's knock the next morning. She thrust the contract at him. "Here. I've signed the blasted thing. I'll keep the survey report to study and send to the castle tomorrow a list of supplies and equipment I'll need to have immediately on hand when I arrive on Cinnidar. When do I have to be there?"

"As soon as possible. I'll be leaving on the next ship and Ian agreed this morning to follow me within the month. You can travel with Maggie and him." His gaze searched her face. "You look a bit haggard. A sleepless night?"

She ignored the mockery in his question and said brusquely, "I was studying the survey. You said it was accurate?"

"As accurate as Medford could make it, but there are always surprises."

"Those penalties could leave me with almost nothing if anything goes wrong."

He nodded. "Aye, that's true, but there are always penalty clauses in any contract."

"Even the maharajah didn't insist on this heavy a penalty. Lower the first penalty to twenty percent and the second to ten."

He shook his head. "You knew I wouldn't agree to that, or you wouldn't have already signed the contract. Lowering the penalties would lessen the incentive. I want you to work very hard to complete my railroad on time, Jane."

"You want to see me slave at your command and then lose everything."

"That would be one way to punish you, wouldn't it?" He smiled. "Do you wish to tear up the contract?"

She had had little hope of getting him to give her better terms, but she'd had to make the attempt. "It will be done on time."

"Then I believe we have nothing more to discuss." He nodded politely. "I'll see you on Cinnidar."

She watched him walk away, bold, tough, and dauntingly confident.

But she would not be daunted by him, blast it.

She would give him his railroad and grab this chance for an independent life for herself and Li Sung. She would work harder than she ever had in her life and not give herself a chance to think of anything else.

The mandarin would not win this time.

Chapter 12

"It is truly a palace," Li Sung murmured, his gaze on the massive structure on the hill. "But it is not what I'd expect of Ruel."

Jane's grasp involuntarily tightened on Bedelia's reins as she looked at the magnificent palace. Two rows of cypress trees bordered the sides of the road leading up to a courtyard whose center point was a large marble fountain. The central section of the palace was domed, with wings sprawling with faultless symmetry on either side. The long veranda, extending the entire length of the palace, was interspersed with eight arched columns and sported white marble fretted balustrades that shimmered like diamond lace in the late afternoon sunlight. Everything about the structure spoke of exotic beauty . . . and power. Ruel's power. At that moment she did not need such a potent reminder that this was Ruel's kingdom. "Why not? He always said he wanted a palace."

"Words are not actions. Men like him are not truly comfortable surrounded by luxury any more than we are."

"Well, at least Ian will be comfortable." Jane glanced over her shoulder at the large carriage containing Margaret, Kartauk, and Ian lumbering up the hill a few hundred yards behind them. "He stood the trip very well, didn't he? Much better than the trip to Scotland."

"He's stronger now." Li Sung's tone was abstracted as he narrowed his eyes against the glare of the sun setting beyond the palace. "I think I see Ruel on the veranda. Let us hurry."

The man on the veranda was only a blur of white from this distance but she, too, knew it was Ruel. Jane tensed and then forced herself to relax. She had been dreading this moment since they left Scotland and must not reveal any hint of nervousness when she again confronted him. "You go on. I'll stay with the carriage."

Li Sung gave her a shrewd glance. "You cannot avoid him for the next seven months."

"But I don't need to rush to meet him. I'm surprised you're so eager. You certainly didn't display any vast amount of enthusiasm when I told you I'd signed the contract."

"Because you were afraid. I've never seen you afraid before."

"I'm not afraid. It's a splendid opportunity that could mean a great deal to us. Naturally, I wish everything to go well."

"And why should you fear it will not?"

"I don't fear—you read the contract and Medford's report. We can *do* this, Li Sung."

"And the compensation is extraordinarily generous," he said thoughtfully. "Too generous."

"That penalty clause isn't all that generous, but Ruel will comply with the terms of the contract."

"Yes, he will keep his promise. I admit I feel better about the arrangement since we've arrived. Perhaps this Cinnidar is the paradise Ruel believes it."

"He never said it was paradise." She made a face. "And the problems Medford stressed in his report certainly don't indicate any celestial Eden. Jungle, steep mountain grades, marshlands, tigers, elephants."

"We can do this, Jane." Li Sung smiled faintly as he repeated her own words.

"Hoist with my own petard." She felt a sudden lightness of spirit. "Of course we can. Why do you feel better about it now?"

"I do not know. It is a feeling without a reason. I saw the island and it—" He hesitated.

"Called to you?"

"Do not put such nonsensical words in my mouth. Islands do not have voices with which to call."

"Ruel says this one called him."

"He spent years searching for gold. No doubt he saw the mountain and his miner's instinct prompted him to believe this foolishness."

"No doubt." She smothered a smile. Li Sung was, as usual, scoffing at the mystical even while obviously feeling its magnetism. "And to what instinct did you respond?"

"It was most probably the instinct to abandon that ship and get my feet on firm ground again. A man who cannot swim is always uneasy on water." He kicked his horse into a trot. "I will see you at the palace."

Her smile vanished as she watched him disappear around the curve of the road. Strange that both Ruel and Li Sung had felt the same magnetism for this place. Beauty? From that mist-shrouded mountain to the quaint village encircling the harbor, Cinnidar was undoubtedly lovely, but neither Li Sung nor Ruel was susceptible to mere scenery. Perhaps it was because the island possessed an almost magical ambiance. The air seemed lighter, easier to breathe, and yet the *fragrances*

. . . vanilla, sandalwood, jasmine, the cedarlike odor of deodar and a hundred other scents too subtle to distinguish assaulted the senses with every breath.

Dear God, she was reacting as besottedly as Li Sung, she thought impatiently. Cinnidar was just a place like any other, a place she would mold to her needs as Ruel had molded it to his.

"Jane."

She turned to see Margaret's head poking out of the window of the carriage.

"How far? Do you see it yet?"

Jane silently pointed to the palace on the hill.

Margaret's eyes widened as her gaze followed the gesture. "Merciful heavens." She started to laugh. "I believe I'm impressed. The rascal always said he'd do it."

Two white-coated servants rushed to open the door of the carriage the instant it stopped before the entrance of the palace. Four muscular native men appeared a moment later, bearing a huge thronelike chair mounted on four carved poles and shaded with a scarlet-silk tasseled awning. Another boy grabbed Bedelia's reins and led Jane toward the hitching rail, where Ruel stood with Li Sung. Ruel was dressed all in pristine white, his suit and shirt as elegant and impressive as the palace that was now his home.

He nodded politely. "Jane." He stepped forward and lifted her from the mare. "Welcome to Cinnidar."

"Thank you." She could feel the warmth of his hands through the cotton of her shirt and it sent a little shock of sensation through her. She stepped quickly to the side, breaking his grasp. Too quickly. She could see by his suddenly intent expression she had revealed what she had wanted so desperately to conceal. She promptly made it worse by saying hurriedly, "I didn't see any sign of Medford's tracks on the way from the harbor."

His brows lifted. "Do you think I lied to you?"

"I didn't say that."

He nodded to the west. "Medford's camp is a mile

beyond that rain forest. You'll meet him at dinner." He turned and walked toward the carriage.

Kartauk had already stepped down to the ground and was brusquely motioning the servants aside. "I'll help him. He's used to me." He ducked into the carriage and emerged with Ian in his arms. He deftly settled him on the cushioned chair and tucked a silk throw over his knees. "There you are." He grinned. "The last time I saw one of these chairs it was occupied by the maharajah who was being grandly transported around the royal garden. You look much better in it."

"Well, I feel like a bloody fool," Ian said sheepishly. He leaned cautiously back in the chair. "But it's comfortable enough."

"That's all that's important." Ruel's gaze raked Ian's face. "How did you stand the trip?"

"You'd know if you'd bothered to meet us at the harbor," Margaret said as a servant helped her from the carriage. "I'd have thought you'd have had the courtesy to meet us yourself instead of sending that bevy of servants to the harbor. After all, we're here at your insistence."

"I'm properly chastened." Ruel's eyes twinkled. "I realize excuses are unacceptable, but I feel I should explain I arrived here from the mountain only an hour ago. You'd have been even more disapproving if I'd met you in the extremely disheveled and smelly state I was in at that time."

"Then you should have made arrangements to arrive earlier." Margaret cast a glance at the carriage. "However, I must admit the carriage was quite comfortable and your servants eager to please."

"I'm glad my humble efforts weren't wasted." He gestured to a tall, golden-skinned man who had just come out of the palace. "This is Tamar Alkanar. I brought him from his village to watch over Ian."

Like the other servants, Tamar Alkanar wore sandals, a waist-length white coat, and a colorful saronglike length of cloth that draped his narrow hips and ended midcalf. Two broad brass bracelets shone on both wrists.

A gentle smile lit his fine features as he inclined his head in a bow. "I am most happy to greet you." He bowed even lower to Ian. "Be assured I will serve you well and obey your every command."

Margaret nodded graciously at him but turned immediately to Ruel. "We don't need him. Jock stayed at the harbor to supervise the unloading of the luggage, but Ian will prefer he—"

"Jock doesn't speak the local dialect," Ruel interrupted. "You'll need Tamar to help you supervise the other servants."

"And to protect you from the heathen hordes," Kartauk murmured, shooting her a sly smile. "They delight in eating virtuous Scots, you know."

"It wouldn't surprise me. But I've managed to survive three years of your barbarity, so I imagine I'll have no trouble evading them." She started up the steps, motioning to the bearers. "Come along, and mind you, be gentle with him. He's not a sack of rice, you know."

"They will be careful. I will not permit any harm to come to him." Tamar's thick, glossy pigtail bounced as he hurried up the steps to open the tall, carved door for them. A moment later Kartauk, Margaret, and Ian's entourage disappeared within the palace.

Ruel turned to Jane. "Tamar will be back in a few minutes to show you and Li Sung to your quarters. I felt it necessary to get Ian settled first."

"Of course."

"Would you like to go around to the back terrace and get your first good look at the rest of the island? The palace is perched directly over the canyon." He didn't wait for an acquiescence but led them quickly around the palace to a many-leveled terrace tiled in cobalt-blue and emerald-green mosaic. The waters of an ornate fountain tumbled leisurely from terrace to terrace into pools arranged with geometric precision and bordered with white jasmine trees.

Ruel led them through the splendid garden, past a number of reflecting pools, and then up three steps to still another terrace. "The view of the canyon is quite spectacular . . . and intimidating."

"More intimidating than Lanpur Gorge?" Li Sung asked.

Ruel stopped at an ornate stone balustrade. "See for yourself."

They stood on the edge of a sheer cliff that plunged hundreds of feet to the valley below where the jungle spread a dense green carpet as far as the eye could see to the east and west. To the north loomed the mountain, rising with the same stark abruptness as the cliff on which they were standing.

"Medford's survey said it was over a hundred miles from the canyon wall to the mountain. It doesn't look that far from here," Jane said.

"I guarantee it will seem a lot farther when you're trying to hack your way through that jungle," he said dryly.

She had no doubt of that. "Has the mountain no name?"

"Why should it? There's only one." He smiled. "I wouldn't have the temerity to give her a name."

He had said that about his pet fox, she remembered suddenly. He had not given the pet he loved a name for the same reason.

"It might offend her and she's been very good to me." A note of affection threaded his words, and his regard held a warm possessiveness that had not been there when he had strolled through the grandeur of the palace gardens.

He is not a man to be truly comfortable in palaces any more than we are, Li Sung had said.

"The river doesn't have a name either," Ruel added.

"River?" She glanced back at the jungle.

"You can't see it from here because of the trees. It runs south to north before curving east to empty into the sea."

"If your mountain was so good to you, why did it take you three years to scrounge out enough gold to get you even this close to your goal?"

He shrugged. "She offered me opportunity. I couldn't ask more than that. I wouldn't have felt the same sense of accomplishment if she hadn't made me work for it." He grimaced. "Which, I assure you, she did."

She understood exactly what he meant. There was no better feeling in the world than work successfully accomplished against odds. It always gave her a—

She experienced a sudden rush of alarm. She must not allow herself to feel this sense of kinship with Ruel.

She quickly shifted her stare from the mountain to the jungle to the east. "I expected to see the sea. The island must be wider than I thought."

He nodded. "It's only three hundred miles long but it's over six hundred wide." He pointed to the west. "But you can see a faint glimmer of sea there."

"Can we see the road you cut through the jungle from here?" Jane asked.

Ruel shook his head and pointed to the south. "It's beyond those trees. You're planning on laying the tracks on the mule track?"

"If possible. We'll have to do more clearing and widening, but it will still give us a head start. What about my supplies?"

"I've had Medford's crew transport them to the base camp on the mountain. See how helpful I'm being?"

"I'm sure it's greed and not goodwill that's making you so accommodating."

He laughed. "That's true."

"We'll start out for the mountain tomorrow morning. I'll need a map."

"I'll do better than that. I'll go with you and shepherd you all the way to the mountain."

She tensed. "That won't be necessary. I wouldn't wish to inconvenience you."

"It's no inconvenience. I have to go back to the camp anyway. I returned only to make sure Ian is settled." He smiled. "Take advantage of the little help I offer now. Once we reach the mountain, your job officially begins and you can expect nothing else from me."

"I expect nothing now."

"Not even an interpreter to make your needs known to the workers?"

"I'll get Medford to recommend someone."

"Tamar has a cousin who is already at the base camp. Dilam worked as a crew supervisor for Medford, is well liked by the other Cinnidans, and knows elephants."

"I need someone who knows railroads, not elephants."

"You may find it to your advantage to know both. Those jungles have been home to the elephant herds for centuries. They're not fond of intruders in their domain."

She frowned. "Medford's report mentioned elephants but no particular problems. However, I'll accept your Dilam, if I consider him competent."

"Oh, Dilam's exceptionally competent."

"And loyal to you?"

"How suspicious you sound. Dilam won't be a spy in your camp. The Cinnidans are a very independent people. Even I can't buy their loyalty."

"That must be a great disappointment to you."

"No, actually it pleases me." He glanced at Li Sung and raised his voice. "And the Cinnidans have your fondness for pigtails, Li Sung."

"What?" Li Sung turned away from the balustrade, and Jane noticed again that expression of total absorption he had worn ever since he had arrived on Cinnidar. "Oh, yes, I noticed on the way from the village. This proves they must clearly be a very superior people."

"Clearly," Ruel agreed solemnly.

"And they're extremely handsome but they don't look Indian. Their skin is more golden than dusky and they're taller and huskier than most of the Indians I saw in Kasanpore. Are they of mixed blood?"

Ruel shook his head. "Tamar tells me the Cinnidans originally came from one of the Polynesian islands in the South Seas and settled here. Abdar's great-grandfather's 'annexation' was very brutal, and the Cinnidans refused to have anything to do with the Savitsars or their retainers. They moved all their tribes away from the coast to the jungle in the canyon. Since the canyon was nearly inaccessible, they were untroubled by any interference."

"Very clever." Li Sung started to turn back to the balustrade, when his attention was caught by something else. "Who lives there?" He pointed to a charming pagoda-style cottage with a curling slate-blue tiled roof a short distance from the terrace.

"No one. That's the summerhouse. I had it built to use as a retreat when I needed to get away from the palace." He smiled at Jane. "I haven't used it yet, but I'm sure I will soon." Before she could speak he turned away. "Ah, here's Tamar. If you'll excuse me, I'll see you both at dinner."

Jane breathed a sigh of relief as she watched him saunter toward the palace. Except for that brief moment of intimacy when they had first arrived, Ruel had acted with the casual courtesy and good humor of a host welcoming honored guests to his domain. She had no hope his behavior would continue in this vein, but she would gratefully accept any respite until she got her bearings.

"What do you know about elephants?" she asked Li Sung as they followed Tamar into the palace.

"Elephants?"

"Ruel believes they may prove a problem. Didn't you hear anything he was saying?"

"No, I was thinking of something else. The only thing I know about elephants is that I don't like them."

"Why not?"

"They have very big feet." As she continued to frown at him in puzzlement, he went on. "Cripples are extremely cautious of creatures with big feet. It's sometimes not easy for us to get out of the way of them."

She chuckled. "Then we'll have to make sure you don't encounter any at close range."

"That is my most earnest hope."

"If you don't mind my saying so, you're a bloody fool, Ruel," James Medford said bluntly.

Ruel chuckled. "It wouldn't do me any good to mind when you'd say it anyway. You don't have to approve of Miss Barnaby, you have only to make yourself available in case she needs information or advice."

Medford scowled. "Which probably means I'll be building the damn line myself and not getting paid for it."

"Once you meet the lady I believe you'll realize she's not one to take advantage of you." He motioned a servant to refill Medford's glass. "How is your work going?"

"Well enough." Medford was not to be distracted. "Good God, wasn't that mess she made of the line in Kasanpore enough for you?"

Ruel stiffened. "You know about that?"

"Pickering told me."

"You didn't mention it to me."

"Because I couldn't believe you wouldn't change your mind and give me the go-ahead to finish the entire line."

"You're getting greedy." He lifted his whiskey to his lips. "Not that I should complain when I've been accused recently of that fault myself."

"Really? Who was so bold as to dare risk offending the great white rajah of Cinnidar?"

"Jane Barnaby."

"Interesting. At least, I'm now assured she didn't use flattery to cajole you into hiring her."

"She doesn't know the meaning of cajolery."

"Which leaves me with the same puzzle with which I started. Why the devil did you hire her to—" He stopped in midsentence, his gaze on the doorway. "Is that our Miss Barnaby?"

Ruel followed his glance and caught a glimpse of braided red hair shining under the blazing chandeliers. "Yes, that's—" He stiffened in shock as his gaze wandered over Jane.

She wore a simple white gown of some filmy material that bared her arms and shoulders and emphasized the tininess of her waist and the fullness of her breasts. For the first time since he had met her, she looked totally, desirably woman.

"Never mind," Medford murmured.

Ruel jerked his gaze from Jane to see Medford watching him. "What?"

"You don't have to tell me why you gave her the job," Medford said, his glance falling to Ruel's lower body. "It couldn't be more obvious."

Dammit, he had only had to look at the woman to ready like a stallion eager to mount a mare. He said curtly, "I'll bring her over and introduce you."

"Don't hurry, I'm not panting to meet your little . . ."

Ruel didn't hear the rest of the sentence as he moved across the wide salon, his gaze never leaving Jane. Her skin glowed with a soft flush and she was looking warily at him. She should be wary. He wanted to touch that skin, brush his fingertips over her bared shoulders, reach into the gown and cup her breasts. Why not? he thought recklessly. Medford had mockingly referred to him as the rajah of Cinnidar, but that power was very real. He could have her brought to his chamber and do anything he wished to her. He could undo that tight braid and run his fingers through her hair. He could strip off her gown and part her thighs and move—

He stopped before her. "Good evening. I didn't expect such elegance. You look . . . exceptional."

"And that makes you angry?"

"I'm not—" But he was angry, he realized suddenly, angry and frustrated because he wasn't going to take her tonight. Force would not rid him of this damn obsession for her. She had to come to him beaten and defeated. He tried to smile. "I've never seen you in a gown before. You took me off guard."

"Margaret gave it to me." She glanced around the room. "Where is she?"

"She sent a message saying Ian was too tired to come to dinner and they would dine in their suite." His stare went to her bared shoulders. "As always, Maggie's taste is impeccable. How did she convince you to accept such a garment?"

She shrugged. "She always insisted we dress for dinner at the castle and said it was only fair she furnish Li Sung, Kartauk, and me with the appropriate clothing."

When she had lifted her shoulders, the bodice had slipped a trifle, revealing more of the silky flesh of her upper breasts. He felt an aching stirring in his groin. "I'm surprised you obeyed her dictum to wear it."

"Margaret says a gown doesn't make a woman any more than trousers do a man. They're both just trappings that indicate difference, not superiority."

"How compliant you've become. You've changed a great deal since you left Kasanpore."

"It's not compliant to recognize good sense. Of course I've changed. Only fools fail to learn from the years." She added impatiently, "Why all this bother about a gown?"

"I don't like it."

Color flushed her cheeks. "The gown or the fact that I'm no longer the child you knew in Kasanpore?"

"You weren't a child. Even then you were very . . ." His gaze went to her breasts. "Ripe."

The flush burned brighter. "Then what's wrong with my gown?"

It wasn't the gown, he realized suddenly, it was the fact he hadn't been the one to give it to her. It had been Margaret who had persuaded her to give up those mannish togs and he was seething with a jealousy that was as unreasonable as it was fierce. "It's too demure. I gave a great amount of thought to every detail of our coming time together including how I intend to furbish you. Would you like me to tell you about it?"

She inhaled sharply. "No, I'm here to meet Medford. I assume that's him standing by the french doors."

"Yes, that's James. Unfortunately, he's not eager to meet you."

"Why not?"

"He thinks the only reason I hired you was that you're my mistress."

Her lips tightened. "And, of course, you didn't tell him otherwise?"

"Why should I? I'm a truthful man, and that is one of the reasons you're here."

"I'm here to build a railroad."

"But I have every intention of also making you my mistress. A mistress is only a humble vessel meant to please and grovel before her master. You would hate that, wouldn't you?"

He saw the flare of anger in her face, but she said evenly, "I don't have to worry about something that's not going to occur."

"But you knew I meant that role for you before you left Glenclaren. I was very honest with you. I want Cinnidar to defeat you and then I want to do the same thing myself."

"You won't get what you want." Her gaze returned to Medford. "And, blast you, you might have told him I was competent at what I do."

"You'll be even more competent after I have an opportunity to school you."

"I meant . . ." She drew a deep breath and then exhaled slowly. "You know what I meant. Are you going to introduce me to him, or must I do it myself?"

"Aye, I'll introduce you." He turned and led her across the room. "I've made sure Medford will cooperate with you, but don't expect me to be your champion. It's another battle you'll have to fight yourself."

"I'd never make the mistake of believing you'd help me any more than you could possibly avoid."

He had shaken her, but she was trying not to let him see it. She was treating him with a composure and calmness that was thorn-abrasive in his present mood. "Did you know I built the summerhouse for you?" He hadn't meant to tell her that yet, but he had to reach her, touch her. "I wanted a place where I'd have you entirely to myself."

She didn't answer, but he could see the color deepen on her cheeks, the faint acceleration of the lift and fall of her breasts beneath the bodice of her gown.

It was not enough, dammit. "Gold."

She glanced at him, startled. "What?"

"I'm going to dress you in gold silk," he said softly. "A gown that will bare your breasts and limbs. You have lovely limbs."

"Be still," she said hoarsely.

"And I remember how pointed and red your nipples were after I had them in my mouth. How hard they felt on my tongue. Do you remember?"

"No."

"I'll have one of the local seamstresses start on the gown at once. The gold will be quite beautiful with your red hair."

"You'll be wasting your money. It's not going to happen."

"It will happen." His gaze lingered on her breasts. "I'd wager it's starting to happen now. It's only fair really. As James noticed, I'm going to have an extremely uncomfortable evening."

Her gaze went involuntarily to his lower body and then quickly away.

"You see?" he said softly. "It's beginning already and it's not going to end." They had stopped before Medford, and Ruel smiled and asked politely, "James, may I present Miss Jane Barnaby? I'm sure you'll take good care of her while I go and see what's keeping Li Sung and Kartauk."

"You are annoyed," Li Sung observed as they left the salon at the end of the evening. "I was watching you all through dinner while you were talking to Medford. He is a fool?"

"No, I believe he may be a very smart man." She wrinkled her nose. "Though he thinks I'm a little fool, and that will cause difficulties I could do without."

"He will soon learn his mistake. Did he tell you anything we can use?"

She shook her head. "He said all the information he

had gathered was in the survey. He did mention something about the elephants."

"What?"

"He said the Cinnidans revere them and to harm them would cause trouble."

"So we must stand still and let them trample us with their huge feet?"

She shrugged. "We may have nothing to worry about. We'll face that problem when we must. Medford said he had caught only brief glimpses of them while he was doing the survey." She covered a yawn with her hand. "And soon I intend to put everything else out of my mind as well and get a good night's sleep. Are your quarters comfortable?"

"Splendid. I've even been allotted two servants to care for my every wish. This lowly peon is overwhelmed."

"That's probably our host's intention."

"Or perhaps Ruel wishes to pamper us a little before submitting us to the mercy of his mountain of gold." He grimaced. "And those big-footed monsters."

"Perhaps." She was weary of trying to guess Ruel's reasons for doing anything and even more weary of the unbearable tension that enveloped her whenever she was near him. Tonight had been almost unbearable, sitting in that opulent room that shimmered with lacy gilt and breathed of Ruel's power. For the entire evening she had sensed in him a rawness and anger just below the surface. She had no idea what had goaded him into that initial explosion, but she had come out of it feeling bruised and frightened. She could not wait until they reached the mountain and she could be free of him until the job was done. "Medford said the journey to the base camp will take us three days and Ruel usually overnights at Elephant Crossing."

"Elephant Crossing," Li Sung murmured. "That was mentioned in the contract."

She nodded. "The track has to be completed over that crossing in eight weeks."

"Ah, yes, the penalties. We forfeit a high fee if we don't meet the deadline, don't we?"

"Fifty percent."

He gave a low whistle.

"That doesn't matter. We *are* going to make it. We'll take the opportunity tomorrow evening to look over the area." She stopped at her chamber. "Sleep well, Li Sung."

"I will." His tone was abstracted as he moved down the corridor toward his own chamber.

Chapter 13

Ruel got off his mule and started to undo the strap on the backpack. "The sun won't set for another hour. I'll set up camp while you and Li Sung look around."

"There doesn't seem to be much to see." Jane looked around the clearing—an area a good half-mile in diameter denuded of vegetation except for a few thorn trees that lay dead and rotting on the ground. "Why do they call it Elephant Crossing?"

"According to Dilam, the elephants usually stay on the east side of the island but occasionally one or two, sometimes even the entire herd, make a trek to the west and take this route."

"Then why did you cut your road directly through the crossing area?"

"It saved me about a half-mile of clearing." He shrugged. "I've never seen any elephants in all the time I've been running pack trains from the mountain. If I ever did run across a herd, you can bet I'd back away and let them go first."

She frowned. "I can't lay track here if there's a chance of it being damaged by a herd of elephants. I'll have to angle away from the crossing."

Ruel smiled. "It will take more time."

He had known she wouldn't risk building across the clearing, she thought in frustration. "Then I'll cut time somewhere else."

"Why do they go?" Li Sung asked suddenly.

They both turned to look at him.

"The elephants," he said. "You said they only occasionally trek to the west. Why do they go?"

"I have no idea. Dilam says the Cinnidans leave the elephants alone and the herds leave them alone."

"If they're interested enough to know they go west, why don't they know why?"

"Why are you so curious about them?"

"No reason." Li Sung slowly and painfully dismounted and began unsaddling the mule. "It is good to be off this creature. I thought riding a horse was painful until I mounted this beast."

"I would have given you a horse, but a mule is more surefooted on that narrow canyon trail."

"We'll have to send a crew to widen the trail," Jane said.

"It would make no difference. All animals are painful to this limb of mine." Li Sung moved stiffly across the clearing. "I will look over the terrain and see if I can determine another route that will prove adequate."

Ruel looked after him. "He's a brave man. A far more worthy specimen than your Patrick." He shot her a mocking smile. "I'm surprised you didn't bring your father along too."

"He would have been in the way."

"He's always in the way now, isn't he? Yet you still take care of him. Why?"

She unsaddled her mule and dropped the saddle on the ground. "I can't do anything else. When you take care of someone, you become accustomed . . . they belong to you."

"The caretaker."

"What?"

"Nothing, it's just something Kartauk said about you. It's a dangerous weakness."

She recalled Kartauk had once warned her of much the same thing, but only after he had used that 'weakness' to his advantage. "I have no time for this." She started across the clearing. "I'm going after Li Sung."

"Why didn't you tell him to wait for you?"

"He needed the time alone. The trip was hard on him and he doesn't like anyone to see him in pain."

"Not even you?"

"I would feel the same way." She looked at him. "And so would you."

She moved quickly after Li Sung.

Night had fallen when they arrived back at camp, led by the aroma of frying bacon and the beacon of a blazing campfire. Ruel was crouched before the fire, a frying pan in his hand. He glanced up as he ladled the bacon onto three tin plates already heaped with beans and biscuits. "Well, have you charted a new course?"

"There's a possible route to the north." Li Sung took one of the plates and sat down. "But the light faded before we could explore very thoroughly."

"It doesn't matter. There will be plenty of time for that later." Jane sat down and began to eat. "You can take a team back here while I supervise the start on the track down the mountain."

"You don't foresee any lengthy delays?" Ruel asked.

She met his gaze. "None that we can't overcome."

He smiled. "Sometimes delays occur over which we have no control. We'll have to see, won't—"

"What was that?" Li Sung lifted his head, his expression intent. "I heard something."

Jane heard it too this time, faint and far away.

"It's only an elephant trumpeting," Ruel said. "You hear them sometimes."

"I thought they would sound fierce," Jane said. "He sounds . . . sad, lost."

Li Sung gazed at her sternly. "He is neither sad nor lost and there is no need for you to rescue him."

Ruel smiled. "There's no danger of that. He's not nearby."

"Near enough," Li Sung said dryly. "I would prefer to neither see nor hear them."

"Li Sung has a dislike for elephants," Jane explained to Ruel.

"She is kindly trying to disguise my real feelings. I do not dislike them. I fear them." Li Sung paused. "And I envy them."

"Envy? Why?" Ruel asked.

"Power. They possess more strength than any creature on earth. It is always the lot of those who have little power to envy those who do. I have always been considered inferior because of my race and crippled body." He glanced at Ruel. "I also envy you, Ruel. You have power now."

"Power can always be taken away if not guarded well."

"But you know what it feels like to possess it. That is something I will never know."

"Yes, you will." Jane blinked rapidly to hide the tears she must not let fall. "You'll see, Li Sung. Once we have our own railroad, you'll be respected and—"

"It's not the same. It is a power you will have given me, not one I've won myself." He set his plate on the ground. "I believe I'll go to sleep now. You may clean up, Ruel."

Ruel grimaced. "So much for my lauded power. May I point out I've done all the work so far?"

"It is the responsibility of those who hold power to care for those weaker than themselves." Li Sung settled into his bedroll and turned his back on them. "It is only fair, after all."

Ruel turned to look at her, and she could see the reflection of the flames in his eyes. She stiffened as tension gripped her. As long as Li Sung was there, Ruel maintained a civilized facade. But now Li Sung was going to sleep, leaving her to face Ruel alone.

"I agree with Li Sung." She quickly set her own plate down, settled into her bedroll beside Li Sung, and shut her eyes.

She heard Ruel swear softly and then chuckle. "I believe there's something wrong with both your reasoning, but I'll not argue."

No, Ruel never wasted time arguing about the unimportant things, she thought. He would perform the menial tasks with perfect good nature and matchless efficiency and save himself for the bigger battles.

A short time later she heard Ruel crawling into his blankets across the fire. Then there was silence except for the rustling night sounds of the jungle surrounding them, the crackle of the wood in the fire . . . and the occasional trumpeting of an elephant.

Li Sung was probably right about the elephants being neither sad nor lonely, but the sound still filled her with melancholy.

Another elephant trumpeted in the darkness.

She had thought Li Sung asleep but apparently she was mistaken.

His murmur was almost inaudible but still held an element of wistfulness. "Power . . ."

Ruel's mining camp was a tent city as different from his palace as Kasanpore had been from Glenclaren. A hundred or so tents dotted the landscape, a sight not so different from the temporary tent camps of her childhood.

The thought caused Jane's hand to involuntarily clench on the reins.

"Is something wrong?" Ruel's gaze was narrowed on her face. "I know it's not the palace, but I didn't think it was that bad."

She forced a smile. "Nothing's wrong. It just reminded me of—"

"It is not the same," Li Sung interrupted. "See how clean it is here? No rubbish. Perfect order."

She felt an easing of tension as affection surged through her. Trust Li Sung to sense the bitter memories and step in to soothe and comfort her. "No, it's not the same."

"Same as what?" Ruel asked.

She stiffened warily as she saw his arrested expression. "Li Sung and I have seen quite a few tent cities over the years." She added quickly to forestall further questions. "But none this clean. Are you responsible?"

He shook his head. "The Cinnidans are incredibly fastidious. The first thing they demanded when I came to terms with the workers was a communal bathhouse, a *belim* tent, and two hours a day for *belim* and time to police their living quarters."

"Demanded?"

"Did you think I was using slave labor?"

"Let's say I didn't find you so compliant in our negotiations."

"I had no choice with the Cinnidans." He grinned ruefully. "They deigned to work in my mine only on their own terms. If I hadn't acceded to their wishes, they would have stayed happily in their villages and watched me work myself into the grave no matter how much money I offered them."

But he bore them no ill will. Jane noticed the same affectionate possessiveness when he spoke of the Cinnidans as when he had looked at his mountain. "Money has no appeal to them?"

"Money has appeal for everyone, but the Cinnidans don't regard it as necessary to 'felicitous living,' as they call it."

"And what do they think is necessary?" Li Sung asked.

"Children, serene surroundings, time to learn from their teachers, and *belim.*"

"Belim?"

"Games. Cinnidans love games. You can almost always find a game of some sort in progress."

"And we're supposed to get them to work?" Jane asked dryly.

"They're not lazy, but I had a problem with that when I first came here until I realized the secret. You make work a game and put the workers in competition with each other. Every night we declare a winner and award a prize."

"What kind of prize?"

"It changes every day. A day off, a trinket, money . . . The local council gathers to decide the prizes every two weeks."

"And you head the council?" Li Sung asked.

He shook his head. "No one is allowed to sit on a Cinnidar council except the Cinnidans. I've been here three years and never been accorded that honor." He smiled. "But Dilam tells me if I continue to behave in a proper manner, in another year or two I may be permitted to attend, if not participate."

"Is Dilam on the council?"

"Oh yes, Dilam heads the council. A most extraordinary individual." He cast a glance at the setting sun. "I'll take you over to the *belim* tent. Most of the workers gather there for dice and card games before supper. I believe it's time you met our Dilam."

They heard the laughter and excited shouts issuing from the huge tent in the center of the camp from a hundred yards away.

When they entered the tent the noise was deafening. The tent was unfurnished except for colorful rugs covering the bare dirt floor and elaborately carved brass filigree lanterns that illuminated the excited faces of the men and women gathered in several groups. Jane smiled in amusement as she remembered Li Sung's comment about the superiority of the Cinnidans because they wore their hair in pigtails. Well, these Cinnidans certainly had a fondness for the practice; she had never seen so many pigtails in one place. Men and women alike wore their long, dark hair pulled back into thick single braids.

Their entrance received little attention from the crowd, though a few men hailed Ruel with more friendliness than respect. Ruel answered with equal casualness while he looked around the tent. "Ah, dice . . . I thought so. Dilam loves dice. This way." He elbowed his way through the crowd to a circle of men and women kneeling, playing dice in the far corner.

"Dilam, could I speak to you?" Ruel called.

One of the glossy dark-maned heads bent over the dice lifted. "In a moment, Samir Ruel."

Jane stared in shock. Dilam was a woman.

Dilam's glance shifted to Jane. "Ah, they are here? Good."

"I thought you'd approve," Ruel murmured to Jane. "It seems you're not the only woman capable of bossing a railroad crew."

Dilam rolled out the dice. Immediate groans and derisive whoops erupted from the other players. She grinned and said something in Cinnidan before calling to Ruel, "They do not like it because I'm lucky. I told them the gods reward with luck the one who has already been given the gift of cleverness." She began gathering up the stakes. "Wait for me outside. It's too noisy in here for greetings."

Ruel nodded and steered Jane and Li Sung from the tent.

"A woman?" Li Sung asked.

"Medford asked the Cinnidar high council for an intelligent native to supervise his crew, and they sent Dilam. On Cinnidar you don't offend the council by refusing their choice."

"She speaks English very well."

"She learned it in only four weeks. I told you she was extraordinary."

A moment later Dilam strolled out of the tent and came toward them, moving with a springy step and athletic grace. She was of middle height, with broad shoulders and a body that appeared both strong and lithe. She was dressed in a dark green tunic, loose black trousers, and brown sandals that, though worn, appeared spotlessly clean. "You are Jane Barnaby?" She beamed. "I give you greetings. I am Dilam Kankula. You may call me Dilam."

"Thank you." In the dimness of the tent Jane had received only a fleeting impression of sparkling dark eyes and an equally gleaming wide white smile. Now she could see the woman was probably close to her thirtieth year and those fine eyes were set in a square face whose only other claim to beauty was a well-shaped mouth and an expression of intelligence and good humor. "Ruel didn't tell me you were a woman."

"But it is better, yes? We will work in harmony and understanding. I will not have to teach you my value as I did Samir Medford."

"And are there other women on the crew?"

"Oh yes, but not many. Men are better for physical labor. Women have more endurance and reasoning power, but men possess more physical strength. It is best to let the men do what they do best and leave the rest to us."

"I beg your pardon." Li Sung's tone had a distinct edge as he stepped out of the shadows cast by the huge tent.

Dilam's gaze swung to Li Sung and her eyes widened. "*You* are Li Sung? I did not see you there in the shadows behind Jane."

"Even though I'm a mere humble man destined to do only what he does best, I do *not* stand in the shadow of any woman."

"I meant no insult by my words." Her tone was absent, her expression totally absorbed as she gazed at Li Sung. "But it is the truth, you know."

"I do *not* know."

"The Cinnidans have a principally matriarchal society," Ruel said. "Did I forget to mention that?"

The devil knew very well he hadn't mentioned that important fact, Jane thought crossly. Ruel's eyes were shimmering with mischief as he looked from Dilam to a bristling Li Sung.

"I'm sure we'll all get along very well," she said.

"If she does not try to treat me as a mindless beast of burden," Li Sung said caustically.

"Oh no, that is not my intent." Dilam frowned earnestly. "You misunderstand my words. Men are truly splendid creatures."

"Creatures," Li Sung echoed. "Like mules or elephants perchance?"

"They do not deserve to be bunched together. Elephants are much more intelligent than mules."

"And where do men rank in this bestial hierarchy?"

"By the gods, you're prickly," Dilam said, exasperated. "What do you wish me to say?"

"I wish you to explain these acts of splendor of which you deem men capable."

"I think you wish to quarrel with me." Dilam shrugged. "Men are good hunters and warriors. They can also be fine craftsmen."

"But we are not worthy to govern?"

Dilam shook her head. "Their temper is too hot. Before women took over the council, we had many tribal wars."

"And now I suppose peace reigns under your benevolent council."

"Not always." She smiled cheerfully. "But since it takes us nine months to bring a child into the world, we think much more carefully about starting a war that will crush out their lives."

"I'm sure your men have an equal concern for their children," Li Sung said stiffly.

"Then why do they war?" She held up her hand as he started to speak. "We have no real quarrel. I can see you are different." She added, "In some ways."

Jane could see Dilam's words were only exacerbating Li Sung's irritation and interceded hurriedly. "Will you show me to my tent, Dilam? Perhaps we could discuss—"

Dilam was shaking her head. "Samir Ruel will show you where you sleep." She smiled and pointed her index finger at Li Sung. "I take you."

"That is not necessary," Li Sung said coldly.

"It is a pleasure, not a necessity. You are angry with me and I must make things right. I think we *nesling* before supper."

Jane heard a sound that was half gasp, half snort from Ruel.

"*Nesling?*" Li Sung frowned as he cast an inquiring glance at Ruel.

"Copulation," Ruel murmured.

"That's another thing men are good at," Dilam said with another beaming smile. "*Nesling.*"

"How kind that you approve our carnal capability." Li Sung looked at her in outrage. "I think not."

"Oh," she said, disappointed. "I do not please you?"

"You do not please me."

"You please me very much. I find you . . ." She made a face as she read his forbidding expression. "Oh, well, perhaps you will like me better later."

"I doubt it."

"You will not change your mind?" she asked wistfully. "I am truly exceptional at *nesling.*"

"I will not change my mind." Li Sung turned to Ruel. "Where is my tent?"

"I'll show you." Ruel was trying to keep from smiling as he told Dilam, "I'm afraid you'll have to be satisfied with the discussion Jane suggested. Bring her to the *candmar* in an hour."

Dilam watched them as they walked away. "It is not a good beginning." Then she noticed something else. "He limps."

"His leg was crushed when he was a child. It doesn't hinder him. You'll find he works harder than anyone on the crew."

"I know this." She shook her head gloomily. "But the limp explains much. I could have wished for an easier task."

"What do you mean?"

Dilam didn't answer, her gaze still on Li Sung's retreating figure.

"What is a *candmar*?" Jane asked.

"What?" Dilam's glance shifted back to Jane. "Oh, *candmar* means eating place. We all eat together at one campfire in the center of the encampment." She turned and started in the opposite direction. "Come, I will show you where you sleep and then we will come back here. We have time for more dice before supper."

Jane shook her head. "I need to study the map and find what problems there might be on the—"

"We will go play dice," Dilam said adamantly. "Gambling gives zest when one is tired and downhearted. Your head will be clearer when your heart is more content." She studied Jane. "You must learn to enjoy life. You are too solemn."

"I have to build a railroad in seven months. That's a solemn matter."

"Li Sung is also too serious." Dilam jumped on to another subject. "You *nesling* with him?"

"Me?" Jane chuckled. "We're only friends."

"Friends *nesling*. Sometimes that is very pleasant."

Evidently Cinnidar culture was very different from her own, Jane realized. She tried to clarify. "We're like brother and sister."

"Oh, that is good. Then we will also be friends." Dilam smiled broadly. "You *nesling* with Samir Ruel?"

Her smile faded. "No, I don't." She stiffened as a sudden thought occurred to her. "Do you?"

Dilam shook her head, looking at her curiously. "Why does it matter to you?"

"It doesn't matter," she said quickly. "I only wondered."

"You lie," Dilam said flatly. "It matters."

Dilam was right, the raw sharpness of the pain that had torn through her at the thought of Dilam and Ruel together had shocked as well as frightened her. She quickly changed the subject. "Ruel said your people didn't get along with the Savitsar rulers."

"They tried to make slaves of us. We had no weapons to fight them, so we had to run." Dilam's lips tightened. "That time must never come again. One of the reasons the High Council decided to work with Samir Ruel was that we knew it was inevitable that others would again intrude."

"And you preferred the intruder be Ruel?"

"He was an intruder at first but no longer."

"You work well with him?"

Dilam nodded. "Samir Ruel is fair, works as hard as any of us, and knows how to laugh at his mistakes."

"But you still won't allow him on your council."

"In time. He belongs to Cinnidar, but we must season him."

The idea of anyone seasoning Ruel brought a smile to Jane's lips. "I'd like to see that."

"You will." Dilam stopped before a small tent. "This is yours. My tent is two down the way. Refresh yourself and I will come for you in fifteen minutes." She changed her mind. "No, thirty minutes. I have something to do."

Jane's smile lingered as she watched Dilam walk away. She liked the woman. Her bluntness might be a little discomforting, but her good humor and vitality were refreshing. She might also be as valuable as Ruel claimed if she was as energetic in work as she obviously was at play.

Her smile turned to a chuckle as she remembered Li Sung's outraged expression before he had stalked away with Ruel. Yes, Dilam's presence was definitely going to make their task more interesting.

Li Sung was sitting on the ground, fastidiously devouring a piece of roasted rabbit when Ruel arrived at the campfire ninety minutes later, but Jane and Dilam were nowhere to be seen. "Where's Jane?" Ruel asked.

"I have not seen her. I do not know where she is."

Since Dilam was also missing, Ruel had a good idea where they both were. The gambling in the *belim* tent was still going strong, and he had learned Dilam never liked to be disturbed when she was gambling.

A moment later he was elbowing his way through the crowd in the tent. He spotted Dilam almost at once playing *parzak*, a Cinnidan card game, but Jane was not with her. "I thought you'd be here," Ruel told Dilam as he glanced around the tent. "Where's Jane?"

"Over there." Dilam motioned to the dice corner. "But you must not disturb her. She is winning."

The throng was so thick he couldn't see any of the players at the dice circle. "It's time for supper. Food is more important than gambling."

"You never think so when you are the one who is winning." She threw down her cards and stood up. "I will go with you to the *candmar*, but we will let her stay here and have her pleasure,"

"Oh, will we?"

Dilam nodded. "She needs to win. She has no joy." She took Ruel's arm and started to pull him from the tent. "We will send Li Sung for her later."

"I doubt if Li Sung will allow himself to be sent anywhere by you."

"I know," Dilam said glumly. "It is his crippled leg, I think. He is going to cause me much trouble."

Laughter. Jane's laughter—excited, full-bodied, and free, ringing through the tent.

He stopped in his tracks, ignoring Dilam's tugging hand as he turned back. He felt a sense of shock as he realized he could not remember ever hearing Jane laugh like that. Certainly not in Kasanpore or Glenclaren.

She has no joy.

"You will have to be the one to tell him," Dilam said.

"What?"

Jane laughed again. Dammit, he wished the crowd would part so he could see her.

"Li Sung," Dilam said impatiently. "You'll have to be the one to tell him to come back for Jane."

The crowd standing around the dice circle shifted.

Jane knelt with dice in hand, her head thrown back, a soft flush on her cheeks, her face glowing with laughter. She looked young and free and full of joy.

"See? Did I not tell you?" Dilam said softly, "She needs this."

And he wanted her to have it. He wanted her to keep on laughing. He wanted her to look like this for the rest of—

She looked up and saw him watching her.

Her laughter vanished; wariness tightened her lips. It was as if she had drawn a somber cloak around her, closing everything childlike and bright inside her and leaving him outside.

He felt cheated, stung, as if she had robbed him of something. He called sharply to her, "It's time to eat."

"I lost track of time," she said quietly. "I'll come at once."

He nodded curtly and left the tent with Dilam at his heels. Christ, for a moment it had been like those days before the train wreck when he had felt a tenderness for Jane he had never felt for any woman. But the moment was over, he assured himself. He had not brought her to Cinnidar to give her the joyous childhood she had never had but to see that she was punished. She was not a child but the woman who had destroyed his brother's life.

"You did not listen to me," Dilam said. "Why did you not let her—"

"Did it ever occur to you that when I don't listen, it's because I don't wish to hear?"

"I still think you—" She stopped as she saw his expression. "I should not speak?"

"You should not speak," he said emphatically.

Li Sung's temper had definitely not improved, Jane thought. All through supper that evening he had either kept silent or spoken in monosyllables. She supposed she had better bring it out in the open and let him loose his surliness. "Dilam?"

The one word was all it took to bring the explosion.

"She is an abomination," he said between his teeth as he glared at Dilam across the campfire. "Can we not hire someone else?"

"I doubt it. Evidently the Cinnidans would consider it an insult if we didn't accept her. Besides, I like her." She smiled slyly. "And she obviously likes you."

"She regards me as some kind of tame— Do you know she came to my tent after she showed you to yours?"

"No." So that had been the 'something' Dilam had to do.

"She said she forgave me for my blindness in not seeing what awaited me with her and assured me she would be patient."

Jane's lips twitched. "How kind of her."

"Kind? She regards males only as inferior drones to slave for the queen bees."

"I'm sure you're misunderstanding her." Jane's glance followed his. Dilam's face was alight with laughter, her hands gesturing, moving, drawing pictures as she spoke to Ruel. "She's not unattractive, is she?"

"Ugly as sin."

"I don't find her so." But Li Sung clearly was not going to be convinced of anything he chose not to believe, and she was too tired now to continue to try. She got to her feet. "I'm going back to my tent. I still have to study that map of the mountain trail and we need to get an early start tomorrow."

Her answer from Li Sung was a nod and a scowl.

She had scarcely left the campfire when Ruel fell into step with her. "You appeared to be enjoying yourself in the *belim* tent tonight."

The tension that was always present when she was with him caused her to answer tersely, "Yes."

"Did you win much?"

"I don't know. I haven't figured out the Cinnidan currency yet. I don't think so."

"You like the Cinnidans?"

"How could I help it? They're good-natured, intelligent, and I've never seen anyone live with such enjoyment." She looked at him. "You like them yourself. Dilam said you belonged here."

"I do," he said unequivocally.

She was surprised at the admission. "Because of the gold?"

He shook his head. "Cinnidar caught me. I worked the mountain and dealt with the Cinnidans and thought I was slaving only to make myself a rich man. Then one day I stopped working long enough to raise my head and look around and found I'd walked right into the trap."

"Trap?"

"Ian would call it 'home.' I'm not so at ease with the word."

"Why are you telling me this?"

"Why not?" His tone was mocking. "Isn't it time we became reacquainted?"

"No." She stopped at the entrance of her tent. "I don't want to know anything about you."

"How unkind. I want to know everything about you." He met her gaze. "And I have every intention of doing so."

He was not even touching her and her heart was beating harder, her breath coming more shallowly. Panic spurted through her as she recognized the mindless response.

His gaze centered on the pulse leaping in the hollow of her throat. "You see?" he asked softly. "You do want to know me."

He was speaking of knowledge in the biblical sense, and he was right. Her body *did* want to know him. Dear God, it was as if they'd never been parted.

She turned on her heel, entered the tent, and hurriedly closed the flap between them.

"I'll see you tomorrow," Ruel called.

"Probably not." Her voice was uneven, and she forced herself to steady it. "I have to start work tomorrow and I'm sure you'll be busy at the mine."

"Oh, but I have to make sure you're doing a good job. After all, it's my railroad you're building." The words trailed off as he walked away.

She had thought when they reached the mountain she would see less of Ruel, but she was not going to be free of him yet. The knowledge was as frightening as her body's response to him. Perhaps it would not be as bad as she feared. He would probably come to the site only a few times and then go about his business.

He came every day for the next month. Sometimes he would stay five minutes and sometimes an hour.

He would joke with Li Sung and Dilam and the workers or just sit on his horse and watch her as she went about her business.

She woke up in the morning knowing he would come, dreaded his arrival all day, and was acutely, painfully, conscious of his presence every second of his stay. It was like those days in Kasanpore before they came together in the railway car. No, this was worse, she thought. Now she was always aware he not only wanted her body but to hurt her, perhaps even destroy her. The flame to her moth, she thought bitterly.

And, God help her, she was tempted to fly closer to that flame with every passing day.

She was kneeling, measuring track, when a shadow fell across her body. She didn't even have to look up to know it was Ruel. Her senses were so acutely attuned to him, she felt even his shadow as a disturbing presence.

"Why are you still here?" he asked. "Everyone else has stopped for the day."

She didn't look at him as she finished checking the spacing of the rails. "I just wanted to finish this. I'm sure you'll have no objection if I slave a few extra minutes on your behalf."

"No objection at all. I was just wondering if there was something wrong."

"I got a little behind today." She added quickly, "But I'll make it up tomorrow. This is the last quarter-mile on the mountain trail. We start across the canyon floor at dawn."

"I know. Li Sung told me."

"Then he must have also told you there was nothing wrong."

"But then, you don't tell Li Sung everything, do you?"

"Of course I do."

"Did you tell him what we did in the maharajah's railroad car?"

She felt the blood burn her cheeks, but she ignored the question.

"I didn't think so," Ruel said softly. "He might guess there's something between us, but he isn't sure."

"He didn't need to know." She rose jerkily to her feet and moved a few yards farther along on the track, knelt, and began to measure again. "If that's all you wanted, why don't you go away? You can see I'm busy."

"That's not all I wanted." His shadow fell across her again as he moved to stand over her. "I wanted to see you on your knees. It's a sight that gives me extreme pleasure."

Her gaze shifted to stare warily up at him. He stood with legs slightly astride; not only his shadow was dark today. Black leather boots molded his calves, black serge trousers delineated his powerful thighs, a black shirt hugged his torso. Only Ruel's sunstreaked hair and golden, tanned skin lightened the somber elegance of the picture he presented. He looked as beautiful and wicked as the prince of darkness himself.

"Ah, that's even better." He smiled. "I used to dream about you kneeling and staring up at me with just that expression. But it's not quite right. Your hair should be loose and my fingers should be buried in it." He paused. "And we should both be naked."

The picture he had drawn was both sensual and barbaric. Captor and captive. Slave and master. She could almost feel his fingers tugging her hair back to look into her eyes. She felt suddenly helpless, caught, a prisoner. Yet, incredibly, she became aware that beneath the smothering sense of bondage ran a dark ripple of erotic excitement almost as if she wanted to experience that dominance.

No! Fear washed over her at the thought, sweeping away that hot tide of feeling he had ignited.

She rose to her feet and drew herself to her full height. She gazed defiantly in his eyes and said between set teeth, "You bastard, get the hell away from here and let me do my job."

For an instant she didn't think he'd obey, and then he smiled faintly. "If you insist. The mood's broken anyway." He added softly, "But for a moment you could feel it, couldn't you, Jane?"

She didn't answer.

"Aye, you felt it." He stood looking at her, smiling. "Good. I'm not going to be able to visit you quite so frequently now that you've finished this portion of the line. I wanted to leave you with a memory strong enough to linger when I'm not around."

Relief cascaded through her at his words. He would not be here every day from now on. She would be rid of the torment of his presence. "It's about time you began to attend to your own concerns and left me to mine."

"Oh, but I'll be with you in spirit. You won't forget me."

"You're wrong. The moment you're out of my sight I won't remember you're on the same island."

He shook his head before turning away and strolling toward Nugget.

He was so blasted self-assured, it sent a flare of sheer rage through her.

"Wait!" Her voice shook with emotion. "Just who the *hell* do you think you are?"

He turned to face her again. "I beg your pardon?"

"What makes you so sure you have the right to do this to me? Have you lived such a perfect life you can afford to cast the first stone?"

"No, I've done more wicked things in my life than you can even imagine." His expression hardened. "But I've never hurt the innocent without paying the piper.

That's against the rules. We all have to pay for that sin, Jane."

"And I'm supposed to pay you for my transgressions?" she asked scornfully.

"You're damn right you are. When I was a boy I learned I couldn't count on anyone dealing out justice on my behalf. If I wanted justice, I had to be the one to reach out and grab it." His voice turned fierce. "It's not a fair world. I can't count on fate or God to punish you. They might turn their backs and walk away. It has to be *me.*"

She watched him mount Nugget and ride away.

She was trembling. She drew a deep breath and tried to compose herself. She mustn't let him do this to her. She fell to her knees and again began to measure the tracks. She was rid of him and now she must forget him. She must not let him linger in her thoughts as he intended.

She blindly reached out and grasped the rail in front of her. Strong steel, warmed by the sunlight.

Soothing comfort flowed into her. She was not weak. She had the same strength within her as these rails. If she had the will, spirit, and mind to build a railroad, one man could not bend or break her.

The Prince of Darkness!

Jane woke with her heart pounding, her breath coming in gasps.

It was only a dream, she told herself desperately.

The same dream that had come every night since that last afternoon Ruel had visited her. The same dream and the same shameful lingering physical evidence when she awoke. Her nipples were hard and acutely sensitive as they touched the sheet, and there was an aching emptiness between her thighs.

No, it was not quite the same.

She was bathed in sweat.

Strange, it had been cool in the tent when she went to sleep, but she was burning up now.

She got up from her cot, went to the washstand, and splashed cold water on her face. She was still hot, her skin dry and burning to the touch. She had gone through this before, and the symptoms were clear to her.

The fever was back.

The knowledge came almost as a relief. She was ill. She had an excuse for those erotic dreams that had been plaguing her.

It wasn't Ruel, it was the fever.

Chapter 14

"A railroad?" Abdar's nails dug into the satin-padded arms of his chair. "How far along?"

"Medford's branch is near completion, but the line from the mountain was started only seven weeks ago and is in the initial stages. The girl has laid the track from the mining camp down the mountain and into the jungle, but it will—"

"How long?" Abdar snapped.

"My man in Medford's camp says it will be at least four months before the tracks are joined."

"Four months! And in the meantime the Scot is storing gold ore and will be ready to ship as soon as the line is completed. *My* gold." He stood up and moved toward the wall where his latest mask shimmered in the candlelight, powerful, intense, a testimony to his greatness. "I need that gold."

"There is other news." Pachtal paused. "News that will please you. Kartauk is on Cinnidar."

"What?" Abdar whirled to face him. "You are sure? He is not dead?"

"I saw him myself. He is not even in hiding. He lives in the palace and moves freely about the island."

"Because he feels himself safe. He thinks I cannot take him on that cursed island." Abdar scowled. "And he is right. I can do nothing until I am maharajah."

"And when will that be? Has your father's condition worsened since I left on my journey?"

He shook his head. "He may linger on until summer."

"The Scot will be in a much better position to defend himself by that time. The island can be conquered only by an assault on the harbor, and if he has the means to fortify it, we may not—"

"I know. I know," Abdar said impatiently. "Do you think me a dullard? He must not be allowed that time." He turned and moved toward the statue of Kali. "How much love do you have for me?" He could sense Pachtal's sudden tension, and his tone became wheedling. "Will you not help me in this small matter?"

"What do you wish me to do?" Pachtal asked warily.

"He is old and sick. He is going to die anyway."

"He is the maharajah," Pachtal said hoarsely. "You know what the punishment would be if anyone learns I did such a thing. They will burn me alive on his funeral pyre."

"No one would suspect anything if he died a little sooner than expected. Who would have reason to kill a dying man?"

"It is too dangerous."

"I'm not suggesting a dagger. There are other, less obvious methods. Perhaps poison administered over the period of a week or two." He turned to smile at Pachtal.

"You have such a talent for poison. Why else were you given such a gift if not to use it?"

"I don't know if I—"

"I need that gold to serve Kali. If you have love for me, you will do me this service." His index finger caressed the golden dagger of the statue. "You will do Kali this service."

"I will . . . think about it."

"You have never failed me before." He added with soft emphasis, "I have faith you will never do so."

Abdar heard the pad of Pachtal's departing footsteps as he hurriedly left the chamber.

He was frightened, Abdar realized. He had never known Pachtal to rebel against his will, but it might take further efforts to persuade him to do this deed. However, he had no doubt Pachtal eventually would comply with his demand.

Kali always prevailed, and had he not been appointed Kali's guardian on this earthly plane?

"Ruel is here." Li Sung nodded at the tent several hundred yards from the track. "He's come to check on our progress."

"Again?" Jane wiped her perspiring brow on her sleeve. "He'd do better to tend to his own concerns and leave us to get on with ours."

"It's only the fifth time he's come since we left the mountain and started through the jungle," Li Sung pointed out mildly. "It is to his interest to make sure his investment is flourishing."

"Or not flourishing. Well, he'll be disappointed. We're ahead of schedule."

"Why should he be disappointed that we are doing so well?"

She hadn't meant to blurt out that thought, blast it. Her nerves were so raw, Ruel had only to appear to make her tense and defensive. Li Sung knew her too well not to pick up on any careless word, and he was already suspicious. "He loses a good deal of money if we reach Elephant Crossing on time."

"I don't think money is that important to Ruel."

She suddenly exploded. "Are you mad? If you think that, then you don't know him. Why do you think he wanted to own his own kingdom? Of course money is—what are you doing?"

His hand was on her forehead. "Hot. You have the fever again. I thought you looked unwell."

She stepped back. "Not much."

"Enough," he said grimly. "How long?"

She avoided the question. "It doesn't come every day."

"And at night?"

She didn't answer.

"Every night?"

"I take the *quinghao* and it goes away."

"And for how long do you think you can keep it at bay with you working yourself into exhaustion?"

"Until the damned railroad's finished."

He shook his head doubtfully. "Ruel is a fair man. He would allow you more time if you went to him and told him you were not well."

"No!" Good God, all she needed was to have Ruel know she was ill. He was waiting for a weakness in her defenses. "I'll be fine. You're not to tell him. You're not to tell anyone." She started for the tent. "Ask Dilam to check that last quarter-mile track I started to measure."

"No need, I will do it."

She should have known Li Sung would insist on taking over the task and he had already used his leg too much today. "This shouldn't take long. I may be able to do it myself."

His jaw set. "I will do it."

After almost two months of working day and night, she was too bone-weary to argue with him. "Suit yourself."

Ruel glanced up from the survey map he was studying as she came into the tent. "You're making very good time." His finger tapped a circled area on the map on the table. "Four miles from Elephant Crossing."

"We should reach it by day after tomorrow. We're averaging over two miles a day. We'd be doing even better than that if we didn't have to do some additional clearing on each side of the road."

"But you've chosen to angle around the crossing."

"Another three days." She moved toward the table and tapped a spot on the map. "Here. We'll have passed the crossing two days before the deadline specified by the contract."

"Perhaps." He smiled. "And perhaps not. Cinnidar has been kind to you so far, but you mustn't count on your good luck lasting."

"It will last."

"No trouble with the elephants?"

"We haven't seen one elephant since we started through the jungle. Dilam doesn't expect any trouble. She says elephants are creatures of habit and by circumventing the crossing we'll avoid a direct confrontation."

"They're closer than they were three months ago when we passed here. I heard them as I rode into camp."

"We always hear them. It doesn't mean anything. According to Dilam, they're constantly talking to each other."

"I was watching Li Sung and Dilam working together as I came into the encampment. They seem to be getting along much better. No problems there?"

"Li Sung has no problems with Dilam as long as she—"

"Doesn't try *nesling* with him?" Ruel's brow arched inquiringly. "I take it she's given up her aim in that direction?"

She shrugged. "Who knows? She doesn't talk about it, and Li Sung realizes how important this railroad is to both of us. We've all been too busy to worry about anything but getting the work done." She stared directly into his eyes. "Which is what I have to do now."

"You always run away when I come to see you."

"I have work to do. I have no time to talk."

"I also have work to do, but I make time for you." His voice was almost caressing, but the words held a subtle menace. "I'll always make time for you, Jane."

Always. The foreboding word sent a smothering sense of relentless inevitability through her. He would never give up, never leave her until he was satisfied she had suffered enough. God, she was weary of it all. "Are we through here? I have to get back to work."

"Aye, I've found out what I needed to know." He turned away. "I'm going to the refinery in the village and then pay a visit to the palace to see how Ian is faring. I'll be back in five days."

"Don't bother. I won't have time to give you a report. In five days we'll be past the crossing and forging toward the canyon wall."

"Oh, it's no bother." He smiled over his shoulder. "Do you know, part of me actually wants you to meet that deadline. You've done a fine job and I admire good work."

She stared at him, too surprised to speak. Why could he not remain hard and mocking all the time? Just when she had her defenses raised against him he would change, soften, remind her of that other Ruel she had known in Kasanpore. She could feel her defiance draining away as she looked at him. Leave, she prayed silently, go away. He was like her sickness, the fever draining her of strength.

"Since I'm clearly dismissed, I'll do as you so kindly suggest." He turned away. "Good-bye, Jane. Five days."

She stared blindly down at the map after he left. Five days. There was no reason to be nervous. She had fought this fever before and won. The work was going extraordinarily well. The Cinnidans labored quickly and cheerfully and they had not encountered any insurmountable obstacles. What could possibly happen to hinder her from reaching her goal on time?

• • •

Ian leaned back on his pillows, his breath coming in little pants, an expression of unutterable pleasure on his face. "Margaret . . ."

She moved off him and nestled close, her fair hair splaying over his naked shoulder. "I'm surprised you can still speak. I must have not performed well."

"Wonderful . . . You're always wonderful." His hand gently stroked her hair. "Did I give you pleasure?"

"Yes." As usual, the lie stuck in her throat, but Kartauk had told her it was important a man be made to feel powerful and dominant after the act. She kissed his shoulder. "You always please me."

"I don't know how. I lie here like a lump while you do—"

"Haven't you noticed? I'm a very willful woman. I enjoy guiding the course." She raised herself on one elbow to smile teasingly down at him. "Who knows? Considering my nature, you might not have been able to give me half this pleasure if I were forced to only submit meekly."

"You meek?" His finger traced her lips. "Never."

"I certainly hope not." She resumed her former place beside him. "Again?"

He laughed in delight. "Do you think me such a stallion?"

"Of course. Why do you think I made you wed me? I suspected the son of the laird would have the same lustful vigor as his father." She nestled her cheek against his arm. "But I suppose I must let you rest awhile." She could already detect the lethargy signaling exhaustion and knew he'd be asleep in a few minutes. "You're much stronger since you came here. Cinnidar has been good for you."

"Has it?" he asked wistfully. "Then perhaps I can go home soon."

"Not yet." He was not really better. His cough was almost gone, but he was still losing weight and she had the panicky feeling he was drifting away from her.

"Soon? Glenclaren needs me."

"I read you the letter from the vicar. Everything is going splendidly."

She felt the sigh that rippled through his body and knew at once she had said the wrong thing. It was so difficult to strike the balance, she thought in frustration.

"You're right, I'm lying to myself. I'm not needed. Not by you and certainly not by Glenclaren."

"Don't talk foolishness," she said. "We both need you. We'll always need you."

He shook his head.

She could feel the tears sting her eyes, but she must not let them fall. He did not need weakness but strength from her. But, dear heaven, she was weary of fighting this battle. "Do you doubt I love you?"

"No, but love is not need. I give you only pain. If I weren't here, you'd find a strong, whole man who could give you joy . . . and children."

Children. It always came back to that. She made her tone light. "Who knows? You may have given me a babe tonight." He didn't answer and she felt a spurt of panic. Always before she had been able to inject a tiny hope, but even that was fading in him. "It could have happened," she said desperately. What difference did another lie make if it kept him with her? "You're stronger now and you've been—"

"Shh . . ." His lips brushed her temple. "My dear love, my bonnie love. I'm so tired. Won't you let me go?"

Her hand tightened on his arm. Did hearts truly break? She had always thought the phrase foolish, but she felt something breaking, rending inside. "I cannot."

"I believe I would be happier. You want me to be happy."

"So much," she whispered. "You know . . ." She couldn't go on.

"Are you weeping, Margaret? You see, I do hurt you even when I don't mean to."

"I'm not weeping."

"Because you won't let yourself. You will not let me see you weep."

"Why should I wail? I have the man I have loved all my life, who brings me pleasure and who—"

"You never give up, do you? Sweet Margaret . . ."

She was not sweet. Sometimes she thought Ian had no idea of her true nature. At the moment she wanted to scream and kick and shake her fist at the fates that had done this to him. "You mustn't give up either. I need you."

"I dream about it every night now. Do you remember when as children on fine days we would go and sit on the hill among the heather?"

"Aye."

"I think it will be like that, peaceful and full of light and happiness." Ian brushed her hair back from her face. "It's waiting for me."

"Then let it wait another fifty years," she said fiercely. "We will fool it. You will grow stronger every single day and there will be a child for Glenclaren and we will—" He was shaking his head. "It *will* happen. I'll make it happen." She buried her face on his chest, the fear and desperation mounting within her.

"Why, you're trembling, Margaret." His breath feathered the top of her head. "You mustn't upset yourself. All is well. Go to sleep, love."

How could she sleep? He had said all was well, but he had not promised to fight to stay with her and he was wandering farther down that other path with every passing day.

He drifted off to sleep a few minutes later, but she lay staring into the darkness, rigid with fear, holding him.

"You must stop work at once." Margaret swept into Kartauk's workroom and shut the door. "I have to talk to you."

"Oh, must I?" Kartauk asked as he wiped his hands on a towel. "Since you've not deigned to visit me since we've arrived in Cinnidar, I assume it is on a subject of no mean importance."

"Of course it is. I don't waste time on trivial matters." She smoothed the skirt of her gown and sat down on a cushioned fan chair. She glanced around at the gleaming white mosaic floor and walls and multitude of windows whose latticed shutters were thrown wide to let in the sunlight. The furniture was simple but finely crafted, the chamber completely unlike his room at the stable, which she had gradually come to think of as a haven. She forced a smile. "This room is really quite pleasant. I was afraid you'd make a shambles of it as you did your workroom at Glenclaren."

"I've been here only two months. It takes even me an extended period of time to create such glorious disarray."

"Where is your furnace?"

Kartauk nodded to the french doors leading to the veranda. "Ruel had a special cottage built away from the main house. He said he wasn't going to risk me tearing down any of his walls or burning up his palace."

"Very sensible." She straightened the lace on her sleeve. "I suppose you're enjoying dabbling with your precious gold. It seems a hedonistic extravagance when one considers—"

"Why are you here, madam?"

She frowned. "I was getting to it."

"Not with any great speed. I need to finish this frieze before nightfall."

"It's early morning."

"Exactly. Is it Ian?"

"Partly."

"I take it he has not taken a turn for the worse, or you would not be here. Are you satisfied with Tamar's care of him?"

"Tamar? The man is a paragon. Ian has only to lift an eyebrow and Tamar rushes to obey. Jock has nothing to do anymore." She noticed the dog lying slumbering at Kartauk's feet. "What is Sam doing here? I thought he was in the stable."

"Jane asked me to keep him. She has no faith in his

intelligence. She was afraid he would start chasing a squirrel and fall off into the canyon."

"A distinct possibility." She smoothed the hair at her temple. "Are you not going to have the courtesy to ask me to have a cup of that foul liquid you call coffee?"

"No, your hand is trembling so much you would probably drop the cup."

"Nonsense." She quickly clasped her hands together in her lap. "What sort of frieze? Are you going to—"

"You did not come here to discuss my 'dabbles,'" Kartauk interrupted. "Has Ian had a setback?"

"No, he is the same." She looked down at her hands. "But he is—" She stopped and then started again. "I'm going to have a child."

He went still. "You told me the physician said that was not possible for Ian."

"He did." She could feel the heat in her cheeks and knew those annoyingly keen eyes would notice her discomposure as he noticed everything about her. "But it must happen. You must make it happen."

He swore beneath his breath and then said caustically, "And how am I to do that? It is one thing to instruct you on the art of arousing and satisfying a man, but I have no magic incantation I can mumble to make Ian able to impregnate you. Am I supposed to—"

"Be silent," she snapped. "There's no reason for you to be testy. If you will listen, instead of ranting at me, I will tell you what I need of you."

He sat down on his stool and looked at her. "By all means, proceed."

"Ian is . . . I cannot . . ." She drew a deep breath. "If I do not give Ian a reason to live, he will die. He *needs* a child."

Kartauk made no comment, waiting.

"Since God has not seen fit to grant us this boon, I've decided to take matters into my own hands." She looked straight ahead and asked quickly, "Will you mate with me, Kartauk?"

He went still. "What?"

She rushed on. "Only until the babe is conceived. After that, I will not trouble you further."

Silence. Why did he not speak? Though she was not looking at him, she could feel waves of emotion sweeping from him.

He said slowly, each word enunciated precisely, "You are saying I'm to father an infant which you will then pass off as your husband's?"

She nodded jerkily.

"And may I ask why you have chosen me to act as stud to your mare?"

"Don't be crude." She moistened her lips. "You seem to be the reasonable choice. I believe you have a fondness for Ian. You're strong in body and mind and capable of fathering a fine bairn."

"Anything else?"

"It should be no hardship for you. You can't deny you have a lustful nature. Ellen MacTavish and those other women were—"

"Look at me."

"If it wasn't necessary, I wouldn't do this. A child is nec—"

"Look at me, madam."

She reluctantly shifted her gaze to his face. Anger. She had never seen Kartauk in a rage before, but she saw it now.

"You will not use me, madam."

"It's not such a terrible . . . It has to be you. I thought of Ruel, but I—"

"Ruel!"

"He, too, has a lustful nature and he might do it to save Ian, but I could not place that burden on him."

"What burden?"

"Adultery," she whispered. "It's a terrible sin and one I don't expect God to forgive. It is better I suffer his anger alone."

His lips twisted. "And you think me too much of a heathen for God to notice my transgressions?"

"It would be an act of mercy on your part. God would surely understand you're not at fault."

"Dear God, now bedding you is an act of mercy! You're a mad woman."

"When I first realized I might have to do this, I thought perhaps I was mad." She had to stop to steady her voice. "But I've pondered long and hard and there's no other solution. This must be done. Do you think asking you was easy?"

"I've not noticed you asking me. You've only told me what I must do."

"I did not mean to be rude. It is my way to be blunt."

Abruptly his anger vanished and his expression softened. "I know. Blunt, sharp-tongued, and giving. Well, you cannot give Ian his child." He raised his hand to stop her as she opened her lips to protest. "I won't do it, madam."

"Why? Ian will be destroyed if I don't do this."

"And you'll be destroyed if you do. I know you well. You try to bend that straight moral backbone and you'll shatter." He moved toward her. "I'll have no part of it. I have never had a taste for destruction. I ran away from Abdar to avoid it, and I will not help you embrace it."

"I've made my decision, Kartauk."

"Which requires my cooperation." He looked down at her. "No, madam, you'll get no child from me."

He was close enough to her so she could smell the scent of soap, coffee, and clay that clung to him and see the pulse pounding in his strong brown throat and the distended veins in his muscular forearms. She had a sudden sensation of unfamiliarity. She was acutely conscious of his bigness, the wideness of his shoulders, the massive strength of his calves and thighs in the loose trousers, the craggy strength of his features. She felt a sudden flutter of apprehension before she firmly dismissed it as imagination. This was the Kartauk she had known for three years. Her uneasiness must be derived from the prospect of the intimacy she had proposed. "There is another reason I chose you," she said haltingly. "I regard you as my friend. I have had very few friends in my life. I hope I'm not mistaken."

"Mother of God!" His hands hovered over her shoulders as if he'd like to shake her.

"You appear to have an uncommon understanding of me." She blinked rapidly to rid her eyes of tears. "This will be a most difficult undertaking, and it would comfort me to have you with me in this."

His hands clenched and then dropped to his sides. "Go away, madam."

"We haven't finished our discussion. I can't leave until we come to an agreement."

"We are not going to come to an agreement."

"It is necessary we do so. I realize what I propose is neither virtuous nor Christian, but somehow I believe it's right. If there is a child, Ian will live. Can it be so wicked to save a life?"

"Leave me."

"I have no fondness for the act, but Ian seems to think I perform it well. I'll do everything you've instructed me to do and it should not be too unpleasant for you."

He jerked her to her feet and propelled her toward the door.

"I know I'm not bonnie like Ellen MacTavish, but I will endeavor to—"

"My dear madam." He opened the door and pushed her out into the hall. "You're not at all bonnie and as far from the likes of Ellen MacTavish as Cinnidar is from Scotland."

She felt a queer pang even as she drew herself up and stared determinedly at him. "Bonnie or not, it won't hurt you to accommodate me until I'm with child. I shall not insist on any immediate consummation. I, too, must become accustomed to the idea of—" She hesitated.

"Fornicating."

"Conceiving. I'm sure we will both be more comfortable if we make an effort to more fully understand each other. You might make a start by calling me Margaret." She turned and walked down the hall. "I'll pay you another visit tomorrow. Good day, Kartauk."

"Good-bye, madam. Don't return." The door slammed behind her.

Kartauk stared at her coldly. "I told you not to come back. I have no time for your nonsense."

"I will be no bother." Margaret closed the door and moved toward him. "I understand that you have no interest in anything but your work and I've thought of a way to accomplish both our aims."

"I can hardly wait to hear what it is."

"I shall help you." She rolled up the sleeves of her gown. "This is the time of morning Jock gives Ian his bath and after that he takes a nap, so I have three hours free. I will come here every day and aid you in fashioning your dabbles."

He gazed blankly at her. "You're offering yourself as my apprentice?"

"If that is what it's called. We will also talk and become better accustomed to each other's ways. Now, what do I do first?"

"Leave."

"Why do you wear that leather apron? Should I have one on also?"

"I require no apprentice."

"Of course you do. I'm sure every craftsman has an acolyte to do menial tasks. I will sweep and—" She paused, uncertain, before adding vaguely, "Hold things."

"I could have one of Ruel's servants do that."

"But you wouldn't trust them in the same room with one of your precious models," she said triumphantly. "You know I'm not clumsy and would take care not to damage any of your dabbles."

"Madam, I do not . . ." He tried a new direction. "Your plan is without purpose. You have visited me many times during the past three years. I'm sure we have no more to learn about each other."

"You believe you know me, but I have a great deal to

learn about you. I was the one who always talked. You asked questions and I answered."

"Sometimes with much reluctance."

"It is not my nature to confide in all and sundry. It was difficult for me to—but you know that." She added wistfully, "You have been very kind to me in the past. Why can't you be kind to me now?"

"I am being kind to you. More than you know." He gazed at her a long moment. "You're a very obstinate woman. You're not going to give up on this, are you?"

"Certainly not."

He threw up his hands. "Oh, very well."

Her eyes widened. "You mean you'll—"

"Not that, dammit," he said quickly. "I mean I'll take you to apprentice. If I do not keep you busy, you'll only sit and stare and plague me with chatter."

"I do not chatter." She had not realized he had regarded her confidences as chatter and the knowledge gave her a hurtful pang. She said stiltedly, "Though I can see how you would think me verbose. I should not have afflicted my ramblings on you. Please forgive me."

"You did not force them on me, I took them," he said curtly. "And, by God, you needed me to take them. I was your priest in the confessional. I gave you haven and absolution. Have you considered if I did what you asked of me that I would no longer fulfill that need? Your haven would be gone."

She felt a surge of loneliness at the thought. "Ian's need is greater than mine."

"You're a foolish woman. You gave years of service to a selfish father only because he seeded the woman who bore you and now you wish to sacrifice yourself for Ian." He paused and then added deliberately, "And all because you feel guilt that you do not love them enough."

She gazed at him, shocked. "I did love them."

He shook his head. "Love must be nurtured and your father gave you nothing in return."

She could not deny that truth. "But Ian is—"

"You loved Ian as a playmate and a friend. In time it might have changed, but because of the accident he also became your child. That's what he is now, a beloved child who must be protected."

"You lie," she said fiercely. "He is my husband and I love him with my whole heart."

"Not with your whole heart, that's why guilt is making you willing to destroy yourself to make amends to him."

"It's not true," she whispered. "You should not say such things."

"Why not?" He smiled recklessly. "I've always known however honest you are with others you've never been honest with yourself."

"Then why did you not state your views before?"

"You're a rare and splendid woman, and I had no desire to hurt you." He met her gaze directly. "But, if you continue on this course you've set, I will never let you hide again. Build a wall and I'll tear it down. Tell me a half-truth and I'll probe and rip until the entire truth is laid bare. No more comfort. No more haven."

She had never felt more vulnerable or frightened. She smiled with great effort. "Life should be faced head-on. I'm a woman grown and need no havens. You're wrong about me, Kartauk."

"And you're willing to risk learning I'm right?"

"Since it's not true, there is no risk." She took a step closer to the table and looked down at the frieze. "Now tell me what the markings on this dabble are supposed to represent."

He did not immediately answer, and she looked up to see him watching her, smiling faintly. "You will no longer refer to my work as 'dabbles,' madam."

"Margaret," she corrected him. "And I will speak my mind as I see fit."

"No, from this day forward you will speak only the truth. You have a great appreciation for my work, for all beauty. Perhaps a greater appreciation than anyone I have ever known."

"Why do you say that?" she asked warily.

"I have seen you look at a sunset." He added softly, "And I have seen you look at my 'dabbles.' "

She felt a tiny flicker of alarm. She had realized how insightful he could be, but he had never indicated he had seen this deeply. "Why should I pretend not to admire something when I do?"

"Perhaps because beauty can hurt as well as please. Perhaps because you consider such a love of beauty a softness that would get in the way of your revered duty."

"That is not—" She stopped, feeling more helpless and unsure than she had since she was a small child.

"No haven, madam." He added softly, "And no mercy."

"I have asked for neither." She glanced away from him. "You did not answer me. Will I need one of those leather aprons you wear?"

"By all means." His smile contained an element of sadness as he reached in the cabinet beneath his table, drew out an apron, and handed it to her. "We must not have you soiling yourself. You clearly have an impulsive nature that leads to such disasters."

Screams . . . thunder . . .

Jarred from sleep, Jane jerked upright on her cot.

The scream came again and was followed immediately by the thunder.

"Come!" Li Sung burst into her tent. "Hurry. The tracks."

Li Sung, who was never armed, was carrying a rifle. She threw the covers aside and quickly thrust her feet into her boots. "What's happening? What is it?"

"Elephant."

The scream came again, wild, angry, demonic. "That couldn't be an elephant. It doesn't sound like anything we've heard before." She jumped to her feet and ran toward the tent opening.

"Dilam says it's a rogue."

She caught sight of Dilam running down the rows of sleeping workers, torch in hand, rousing them. "Forget that," she called. "Come with us. We may need you."

Dilam nodded, and the next moment she was beside

her. They ran down the tracks in the direction from which the screaming was coming with Li Sung limping as quickly as he could behind.

"What the devil is a rogue?" she asked tersely.

"An elephant that has been cast out from the herd," Dilam said. "Sometimes he goes mad with loneliness. Very dangerous."

The scream came again. Closer.

Then a grinding metallic noise frightened her more than the enraged trumpeting. "Dammit, he's tearing up my tracks!"

They rounded a corner and Jane caught her first sight of the elephant.

He was a huge gray-brown monster with one tattered ear. He stood with a section of a rail in his trunk, and as she watched he hurled it away from him as if it were a toothpick and reached for another. "Stop him!"

The elephant's head lifted and he glared at them with small bloodshot eyes. He trumpeted with rage and whirled to face them.

Jane could feel the blood stop in her veins. He was like a demonic creature from the nightmare depths of hell.

Li Sung muttered a curse as he moved to the side of the track and lifted the rifle.

"No!" Dilam shouted. She reached out and knocked down the barrel of the rifle. "It's Danor."

Li Sung said, "I don't care what—"

The elephant charged toward Li Sung, deadly tusks lowered.

Dilam dove out of the way. Jane pushed Li Sung to the side with such force, they both fell to the ground and rolled out of the way just as the rogue reached them.

The elephant thundered past them.

Dilam grabbed the rifle from the ground where Li Sung had dropped it. "Stay down."

"And let him step on me with those monstrous feet?" Li Sung asked. "I think not. Give me the rifle."

Dilam ignored him, lifted the rifle, and fired over the elephant's head.

The elephant stopped, his trunk weaving back and forth.

Dilam fired two more shots.

"What are you doing?" Jane asked impatiently. "Warning shots won't help. An elephant can't know a bullet will hurt him. You'll have to shoot him."

"No!" Dilam fired three more shots over the elephant's head.

The elephant shifted from foot to foot and lifted his trunk again. Then, abruptly, he turned and lumbered off into the jungle.

Jane let her breath out in a little rush, trying to steady her heartbeat. "Will he come back?"

"Not tonight," Dilam said. She handed the rifle back to Li Sung and bowed politely. "I regret being so rude as to take your weapon, but it was Danor. I could not let you hurt him. He is a very special elephant."

"You said he was a rogue."

Dilam's jaw set stubbornly. "I did not know it was Danor. It is possible he has not gone rogue and, even if he has, he is still very special. I cannot let you kill him."

"He almost killed us," Jane said.

"Me," Li Sung corrected her grimly as he rose to his feet. "He charged me. He evidently thought this lowly cripple was the weakest link. I have a desire to show him his error. I'm going after him."

"Don't be ridiculous, Li Sung. The elephant is just plain crazy. How could he know you were crippled? We don't have time right now to go after him," Jane said curtly as she turned to examine the tracks. "And Lord knows what he did to the—my God!"

She gazed with horror at the devastation before her. Rails were uprooted, ties broken as far as she could see. She grabbed the torch from Dilam and began to walk down the track. She was scarcely aware of Dilam and Li Sung following her as she encountered disaster after disaster.

Chaos everywhere.

"Very bad," Dilam murmured after they had traveled for some distance along the track.

It was worse than bad, Jane thought grimly. Over two miles of damage to be repaired and that meant losing a full day.

"It can't happen again," she said. "I don't care how special your elephant is. I won't lose any more time cleaning up after him."

Dilam offered tentatively, "Perhaps he'll decide not to do it again."

"Decide? How does a rogue elephant decide anything? You said yourself he was insane."

"That was before I knew it was Danor. Danor has superior understanding."

"He damn well understands how to destroy my railroad." She ran her fingers through her hair. "How did one elephant manage to do this much damage so quickly? We didn't even hear him until fifteen minutes ago."

"Because he didn't want us to hear him."

"What do you mean?"

"He started trumpeting only the last quarter-mile or we would not have heard him. He must have had some reason for wishing to attract our attention."

Jane gazed at her in astonishment. "You're saying he planned this?"

"I do not know, but he is not as other elephants."

"I don't care if he's not like other elephants. I want to know if this will happen again."

She hesitated, troubled. "It is possible. He obviously did not like being interrupted."

Jane had a fleeting memory of deadly tusks lowered to charge. "I noticed that."

"But I will put guards on the track tomorrow night," Dilam assured her.

"You can't put guards along the entire line," Li Sung said. "It is best we hunt him down and shoot him."

Dilam's expression became shuttered. "I will not help you do this."

"Did you see what he did? Those tracks are—" Jane stopped, trying to control her temper. "I wouldn't kill any animal needlessly, but this elephant is vicious. Why won't you help us?"

"He saved the life of my child. It would be dishonor if I destroyed his savior."

"Then find someone else to lead us to him."

"I cannot do that," Dilam said stubbornly. "It would be the same thing. I will place guards on the track."

"I could try to find him by myself," Li Sung offered.

"You'd get lost," Jane said curtly. "You don't know anything about jungles."

"And less about elephants," Li Sung conceded. "But I know I don't like this one, and even I could hit a target that size."

"If you shoot him in the right spot. I'm not even sure a bullet would pierce that skin. It's too dangerous. He almost killed you tonight."

"I told you he did not like me." His lips tightened. "I assure you the aversion is mutual. I will go after him."

She shook her head.

Li Sung gave her a cold glance. "You think the task too much for a cripple?"

"I didn't say . . . Li Sung, don't *do* this to me right now." She turned to Dilam. "This must not happen again. I want those guards armed. Do you understand?"

"I understand."

But she hadn't promised she would tell the guards to shoot the elephant, Jane thought in frustration. She turned on her heel and headed back toward the camp.

Li Sung walked beside her. "You are worried about the deadline?"

"Of course I'm worried."

"We still have one day's grace."

"If that blasted elephant doesn't do any more damage."

"If he does, I will go after him."

He meant it. For some idiotic reason Li Sung was taking this elephant attack on an intensely personal level. Now she would not only have to worry about meeting the deadline but about Li Sung storming around in the jungle, trying to find that rogue. She suppressed a sudden surge of panic and desperation. She still had two days. She would just have to work harder to make sure two days was enough to repair the damage and clear the crossing.

And pray that demented elephant didn't take it into his head to wreck any more of her track.

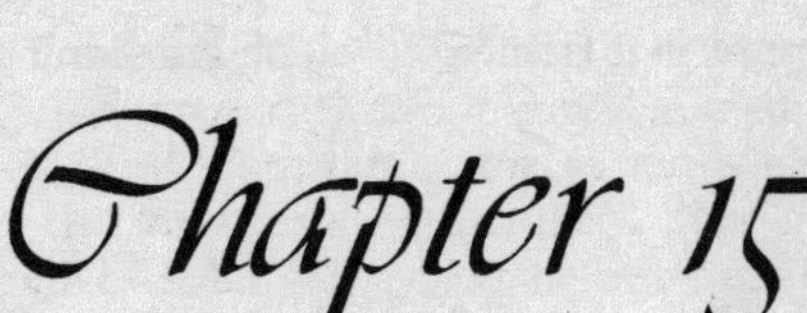

Chapter 15

Li Sung knelt beside Dilam's blanket and shook her shoulder. "Wake up."

Dilam drowsily opened her eyes. "You wish to *nesling?*

"No, I certainly do not."

Dilam yawned, rolled over, and closed her eyes. "Then I need to sleep. I just got back into my blankets and must be up again in three hours. We will talk tomorrow."

"Why should you sleep when I cannot? You're the only one who can give me the answers."

"What answers?"

"Tell me about elephants."

Dilam opened her eyes and raised herself on one elbow. "What do you wish to know?"

"Everything."

"Because you wish to go after Danor?"

"Perhaps."

"What other reason could there be?"

"Very well, I want to go after him."

"Why are you so angry with him?" Dilam asked curiously.

Why was he angry, Li Sung wondered in frustration. He was aware his emotion was entirely out of proportion. All he knew was that when he had looked at that tattered-eared monster he had felt something explode inside him. "He tried to kill me. Isn't that reason enough?"

"Yes." Dilam studied his face. "But I don't believe you are . . . I think you heard the *makhol*."

"*Makhol?*"

"The summons. My father told me that sometimes an elephant will lay its will upon a man and for the rest of their lives elephant and man are one. Only rarely does this happen even with a *mahout*, an elephant handler." She frowned thoughtfully. "Very curious. I've never heard of anyone but a very young child hearing the *makhol*."

Li Sung said sarcastically, "I assure you, I heard no summons and have no desire to be one with any elephant, much less that brute."

"So you wish to know about elephants only so you can kill Danor if he comes again?"

Li Sung nodded jerkily. "And now I suppose you won't talk to me."

"I did not say that."

"What about protecting this noble savior of your child?"

"I do not fear for Danor."

"You should," Li Sung said grimly.

"I do not think so." Dilam smiled as she sat up and wrapped her blanket around her. "Very well, I will tell you all I know of elephants. They are very like us, you know. They live very long lives, sometimes over sixty years and do not reach adulthood until they are in their teens. They travel in family herds of eight or ten and often join together with larger herds. I have counted over a hundred in Danor's herd. Usually the leader is the largest cow elephant of the herd."

"Another matriarch," Li Sung said sourly. "No wonder you like elephants."

Dilam smiled slyly. "I told you they were intelligent. The herd bull has to be very clever and strong to maintain his position. If another male elephant challenges and wins, the defeated bull leaves the herd and goes off alone. Often despair makes him turn violent and he turns rogue."

"Like Danor?"

"Perhaps." She shrugged. "I know Danor's mate is leader of the herd. I have seen them together. An elephant sometimes eats over a thousand pounds of food a day and his favorite fare is the top branches of low trees. They are very tender, and if he cannot reach those branches he will push the tree over to get at them. That is why you see all those fallen trees as an elephant moves through the jungle. They must eat all the time or grow weak."

"I am not interested in Danor's menu."

"No, you would rather know how to kill him. I will tell you this also, but you asked for everything and that is what you will receive. Only the males have tusks and they can do much damage with them."

"I noticed."

"I am not sure Danor meant to trample or gore you. They can be very surefooted and he could have swerved when you jumped aside."

"He meant to kill me."

"You will clearly not believe anything else." She made a face and went on. "Elephants like water and are very at ease in it. I have seen an entire herd swimming underneath the water to get to the opposite bank, only occasionally lifting their trunks above the surface to breathe air. It is like watching—"

"That is not important to me. Since I do not swim, I have no intention of confronting him anywhere but on dry land."

"Do not interrupt. I will say what I wish to say."

Li Sung opened his lips to argue and then closed them with the words unspoken. He had learned in the past months Dilam could be very stubborn and it would do him no harm to hear her out.

She nodded with satisfaction and again began to speak. Another twenty minutes passed before she finally fell silent.

"You have given me a great deal of information I cannot use," Li Sung said. "I will have to filter the gold from the dross."

"It is all gold," Dilam said. "You merely have to fashion it to your needs." She yawned. "Now, if that is all you wish to know, I will go back to sleep."

He should go back to his own blankets, Li Sung thought. He'd learned all he needed to know. Yet, there was something else bothering him.

"Well?" she prompted.

"You never mentioned you had children before this," he said slowly.

"You were not ready to be interested in that knowledge. I have two children, both fine boys. Medor is nine and Kalmar is four. They are being cared for by the women of the High Council while I am on this mission."

"Males?" He scowled. "How unfortunate for you. No females to carry on your tradition of domination and glory."

She sighed. "You do not understand. We do not dominate, it's merely . . . If a male wishes to sit on the High Council, he may do so. He must just prove himself worthy." A grin lit her face. "But the tests are hard and the men of our tribe usually prefer to enjoy life and leave the decision-making to us."

"And does your husband also prefer to let you make the decisions?"

Her smile vanished. "My husband is dead, but no, he never wanted to govern. Senat was a hunter and took joy in it. He took joy in everything he did."

"Which of your children did Danor save?"

"Medor. He was only five then. You wish to hear about it?"

He nodded.

She hesitated and then shifted her shoulders as if bracing herself. "My husband Senat, Medor, and I often went down to the banks of the river near our village in the evening to watch the elephants. Medor loved to see them play and spray one another. One evening while we were there a tiger came to drink. There was no warning. One moment we were laughing together on the bank and the next the tiger was charging toward us. Senat pushed me aside and stepped in front of the tiger." She had to stop a moment before continuing in a whisper. "There was blood, so much blood. Senat was on the ground and I yelled at Medor to run back to the village for help. I grabbed Senat's lance and rushed toward the tiger, hoping to distract his attention from mauling my husband. Medor did not obey me. He rushed toward me, screaming. The tiger ignored me, left my husband, and raced toward Medor.

"An elephant charged out of the herd and down the bank. Danor. He picked Medor up in his trunk just as the tiger sprang. The tiger's teeth caught Danor's ear and ripped it."

Dilam had turned pale and her lips had tightened with pain. Li Sung had never dreamed when he had asked her to tell him the tale that it would be so fraught with tragedy.

"I intrude," Li Sung said gruffly. "You do not have to tell me more."

"It is almost over. Danor reared and trampled the tiger." She shivered and pulled the blanket around her shoulders. "I lived. Medor lived. Senat died. Life held no joy for me for a long time. Then I found I was with child again and the joy returned. It was as if I had been given a gift by Senat to comfort me in my grief and tell me life was still good. Was that not a wondrous thing?"

"Yes, very wondrous." She, too, appeared a little wondrous to him in this moment, simple and earthy and almost beautiful in her strength. He said quietly, "This does not change anything. In my mind your Danor is still a monster."

"I know." She grimaced. "You will not let yourself think clearly because you are fighting the *makhol.* Such lack of reason is common to males. It will not matter." She lay back down and closed her eyes. "Now go away and let me sleep."

"How bad is the damage?" Ruel asked, his gaze on Li Sung, who was supervising the workers clearing the chaos of rails and timbers that had once been the track.

Jane didn't look at him. "You'll be disappointed to know it's not as bad as it looks. I'll still make my deadline."

"One elephant did all this?"

"Dilam says he's a very special elephant." She smiled bitterly. "I tend to agree with her." She straightened her shoulders. "But it will make no difference. We know to watch out for him now. It won't happen again."

"No?"

"No." She strode away from him toward Li Sung. "I have no more time for you. I have work to do. Go back to your mine and dig another ton of gold or something."

"I don't think so," Ruel murmured. "I believe I'll stay the night and see what happens. It seems I have an unexpected ally."

Dear God, she was hot.

She bent over the washbasin and splashed water into her face. Cool . . . that was better. She dabbed her face with a towel and wandered over to the tent opening to let the breeze dry it more thoroughly, her gaze going to the campfire several yards away.

Ruel must be telling stories, Jane thought with an odd feeling of wistfulness.

She always went to her tent immediately after supper when he was present, but she knew he often amused Dilam, Li Sung, and the other Cinnidans with one of his outlandish tales when he came to visit. This story must be particularly fascinating, for everyone was gazing at Ruel as if mesmerized.

Ruel's own face was alive, blue eyes shimmering in the firelight and, though she couldn't hear the words, she knew how well he could build pictures with words to charm and persuade. At that moment she could almost see the aura of spellbinding power he was casting.

Mandarin.

No, that was the fever distorting her thinking again.

She turned away from the entrance and moved heavily toward her knapsack resting on the ground beside the cot. She would take a few drops of the *quinghao* and go to sleep and the fever would leave her.

After she took the medicine she lay down on her cot and breathed evenly, deeply, trying to relax. She must rest. Lately she had felt as if the weariness and tension of the past months had crystallized within her and would shatter at the slightest blow. That must not happen. It *would* not happen. Think of the railroad. Think of the life of freedom that would soon open to her. See, she was easing already. Her knotted muscles were beginning to unlock. In a few minutes the fever would lessen and she would be fine. Then sleep would take her and she would forget the mandarin. . . .

Jane knew as soon as she saw Li Sung's expression in the dim light streaming through the tent entrance behind him. She sat up on her cot. "The elephant?" she asked unsteadily.

Li Sung nodded. "Last night. Dilam just received word from one of the outlying guards."

She threw aside her blanket. "I'll be right with you."

"There's no hurry, he's gone now. The damage is up line. I'll saddle the horses and wake up Ruel."

Ruel. She had forgotten Ruel was here. Panic and anger washed over her. It wasn't fair. Why should all her hard work and hopes be destroyed by this force she couldn't control? But maybe it wasn't too bad this time. It was almost sunrise and they hadn't heard the elephant at all during the night.

There was no use worrying what might be; she had to go see for herself. She swung her feet to the ground and stood up. A wave of dizziness washed over her, and she reached out blindly for the tent pole to steady herself. Damn this fever; she had no *time* for it.

Five minutes later she came out of the tent to see Li Sung, Dilam, and Ruel already mounted. She didn't speak to any of them as she swung onto Bedelia and turned the mare toward the track.

It couldn't happen, Jane thought numbly as she gazed at the ruin before her.

"What's the extent of the damage?" Li Sung asked Dilam.

"Five miles of track gone."

"And where were your fine guards?" Li Sung asked bitterly as he moved off the track toward the path Danor had carved through the jungle.

Dilam shrugged. "We did not expect him to strike this far from the base camp. It's nearly fifteen miles from where he did damage the last time."

"Five miles," Jane muttered. There was no way she could repair the damage by the end of the day. She could feel Ruel's gaze on her face and she knew she should try to hide her shock and panic. This was what he wanted her to feel and she mustn't give him that satisfaction. She kept her gaze fixed straight ahead on the terrible damage inflicted by Danor so that she wouldn't have to see his gloating satisfaction. "It can't go on. We've got to stop this, Dilam."

Dilam did not look at her as she turned and walked

toward her horse. "I will go back to the crossing and fetch workers to clear the damage."

She was ignoring her words, Jane realized with frustration. The damn elephant could wreck her entire line and Dilam would do nothing to stop him.

"Jane," Ruel said.

She suddenly could take no more. Something inside her shattered, and despair turned to wild, reckless anger. "I suppose you're happy now. You've won."

"Aye, I've won."

The odd note in his voice made her whirl on him. His expression reflected no mockery, none of the gloating satisfaction she had thought would be there. She could not fathom what he was thinking. She didn't *care* what he was thinking. The rage exploding through her was a hot tide blurring everything in its wake. "But it's not enough for you, is it? You still want more. You want to see me on my knees. Isn't that what you said? You still want to punish me." Her eyes blazed at him. "Well, I'm going to give you your chance."

He stiffened. "Indeed?"

"It's never going to end." Her words came fast, feverish. "I can see that now. Not until you think you've hurt me enough. Well, I can take anything you want to deal out to me. Go back to your damn summerhouse and wait for me."

"What?"

"You heard me. I'll come to the summerhouse and let you do whatever you want to me. That's what you want, isn't it?" The words tumbled out fiercely, feverishly. "You want to punish me. That's what you've always wanted. That's why I'm here."

"I've never denied that."

"Oh no, you were always honest with me," she said bitterly. "Come to Cinnidar and I'll give you the world."

"I didn't say I'd give it to you. I said I'd give you the chance to win it."

"And I lost the first battle. Well, I'm not going to lose again. I'm going to finish the line on time."

"What's that got to do with you coming to the—"

"I don't *want* you here. You get in my way. I want you out of my life. I don't want to see or hear or think of you again. I want you to stay away from me until my work is done." Her voice was rising, but she made no attempt to control it. "And you won't do that until you've had your fill of revenge. Well, I'm giving you the opportunity to take it."

"I think you're too upset to know what you're saying," he said slowly.

"I know I'm sick to death of having you hover over me like a vulture. I know I want it *over.*"

He stared at her flushed face and glittering eyes for a long time. "By God, so do I!" He turned his horse with a jerky motion. "Be at the summerhouse by sundown tomorrow night. Leave your horse at the palace stable and come on foot. I don't want anyone to know you're there." He kicked his horse into a trot, heading south.

"What are we going to do?"

She turned to see Li Sung limping toward her. She drew a deep breath, trying to hide her discomposure.

"Are we to let this elephant continue with his destruction?" he asked.

"You know we can't do that. We'll have to do something about him," she said curtly. "But first we have to repair this damage."

"Again."

"Yes, again," she said, exasperated. "What other choice do we have?"

"I could go after the elephant."

"No!" She tempered the sharpness of her tone. "I'll need you here to supervise the workers and send me word if there's any other problem with the elephant. Tomorrow morning I have to go to the palace to discuss the contract penalties with Ruel."

"Dilam can do that as well as I."

"I want you here. Dilam would probably stand by and let that elephant tear up every rail from here to the mountain."

"The elephant appears to have great determination." Li Sung's gaze wandered once again to the torn and broken trees that marked the elephant's passage back into the jungle. "He went west again. I wonder why."

At least she didn't have to worry about Li Sung's interference, she thought wearily as she watched him limp toward his horse. This strange obsession he had with the elephant was obscuring everything else in its wake.

She wished she could block out Ruel and what awaited her tomorrow night with a similar single-mindedness. Her rage was beginning to fade, apprehension taking its place. Yet, though provoked by desperation and despair, the instinct had been sound. She could not continue with these shredded nerves and emotional upheavals Ruel brought. It had to end.

But she *would* block him out for now. There was work to do and time enough to face the ordeal when she must. She would not allow him to make her suffer more through anticipation.

She turned her horse and followed Li Sung back to Elephant Crossing.

"It's an elephant." Margaret gazed down at the exquisitely carved design on the small black stone on the worktable. The elephant, its trunk lifted in the act of trumpeting, was amazingly lifelike with every muscle skillfully delineated. The elaborate circle of leaves embossing the rim of the round stone was equally lovely.

"It relieves me to know you at least recognize the species in my humble effort," Kartauk said.

Margaret snorted. "Humble? You don't know the meaning of the word." She drew closer to the table. "But I admit this is very fine work. It wasn't here yesterday when I left. When did you do it?"

"Last night. I couldn't sleep, so I decided to make this seal for Ruel."

"Seal? No one uses seals anymore."

Kartauk grinned. "Exactly. Only heads of state on official documents." He pointed to a tiny monogram at the bottom of the stone. "Don't you think the conceit will amuse our Ruel?"

"With all this pampering he gets when he returns to the palace, he needs no more exaggeration of his consequence."

"Nevertheless, as a court artist I must please my patron."

"I think you did it more to please yourself," she said shrewdly. "Have you ever done a seal before?"

He threw back his head and laughed. "No, and I've always wanted to explore Cellini's methods in the art. I think you're beginning to know me too well. A man needs his little self-deceptions."

"Nothing pertaining to you is little." She looked quickly down at the stone again. "Why the elephant?"

"Since the second part of the elephant game won him the island from the maharajah, I thought it only appropriate." He delved into one of the small clay pots on the table beside him and drew out a generous scoop of slightly hardened black wax.

She watched in fascination as he fashioned a relief on the design on the stone. His big square hands were astonishingly deft and skillful, and she never tired of seeing him perform this magic of creating beauty from nothing but the materials provided by nature. There was something sensual, almost loving, about the way his hands moved on wax and stone.

"Besides, I like elephants," he said. "The maharajah permitted me to make dozens of statues of the beasts when I was at the palace."

"Did you not become bored?"

"After a while, but the end was worth the labor. I made sure there was an elephant in every room of the palace." He smiled slyly. "And Abdar hated every one. He detests the breed."

"Why?"

"His father told me he fell from the back of one when he was a child and the elephant stepped on his arm and broke it. Unfortunately, a servant snatched him from beneath the elephant's feet before he could finish the job." He took a fine paintbrush, dipped it into the olive oil, and moistened the wax relief. "I've had a fondness for the creatures ever since I heard the tale."

"That is an unkind thought."

"Abdar is an unkind man. Like to like." He dipped his fingers into another pot and fashioned a little wall of clean clay all around the seal. "Pray God you never find out how unkind."

"You said Ruel expects him to come here."

"Yes."

"Then why did you agree to come to Cinnidar?"

"Many reasons."

"Such as?"

He stood up and strolled to the stove across the room, where a small pot of liquid was boiling. "I have no time for questions. Fetch me that long-haired brush from the cabinet, apprentice."

She moved toward the cabinet. "You pose enough questions of your own when it suits you."

"But you have no dark secrets to hide. Everything about you is as clear as a mountain stream."

"You make me sound very shallow."

He carefully poured the boiling plaster of Paris over the wax, painstakingly guiding it into the interstices of the wax with the brush she handed him. "Not shallow. Just clear and unpolluted. I doubt if your depths have ever been plumbed."

She made a face. "You've done your share of plumbing."

He raised his head and looked at her. "I've tested the waters," he said softly. "I've not even begun to go beyond the surface. I assure you that you would know it if I had. I'm very good at . . . plumbing."

She felt a strange heat, a breathlessness like the one she had first experienced in the stable at Glenclaren. She hurriedly looked down at the relief. "What do you . . ." Her voice was trembling and she paused to steady it. "What's the next step?"

He didn't answer, and she forced herself to raise her gaze to his face and saw power, strength, intensity, and something else she couldn't identify. "To which step are you referring?" he asked.

She frowned. "Don't play your word games with me. You know I'm talking about the seal."

"Ah yes, the seal." He sat down on his stool. "After the plaster is set I will remove it from the wax, clean out the matrix with a knife, and polish it up."

"Then you're ready to cast it?"

"Yes, I'll give it twelve hours to set and start the furnace heating tonight." He raised his brow. "Your interest warms my heart. Tell me, apprentice, do you fancy making your own seal?"

"Of course not," she said curtly. "I have no such pretensions of grandeur."

"We all have our pretensions and self-deceptions. It just makes the 'plumbing' more interesting."

She quickly changed the subject. "To whom did you apprentice as a boy?"

"My father. He was a fine artist, the best goldsmith in all Istanbul. He did much work for the members of the court and the sultan himself. He taught me well. But when I was thirteen he told me to leave his home and his shop."

"Why?"

"Jealousy. Even as a lad I was showing great promise and a piece of my work had caught the eye of the sultan."

"And he cast you off for so little reason?" she asked, shocked.

"It was not little to him." He shrugged. "I knew it would happen sometime. He was a fine craftsman, but I had the spark."

"Spark?"

"Genius," he said simply. "Michelangelo had it and so did Cellini in lesser measure. I knew almost at once that it was mine also. I did not blame my father. It is not easy to live with such a gift if you do not have it yourself. It would have been torture for me under the same circumstances."

"But you would not have cast him off."

He smiled. "How do you know?"

"I know." She found, to her astonishment, that it was true. She had learned more of Kartauk than she had realized in these past weeks. Though, heaven knows, he was arrogant, he was not vain. He possessed an enormous confidence in his artistic abilities, but his mocking glorification of his other gifts was mere flamboyance. He had been amazingly patient with her clumsy presence in his domain and far kinder than she had thought he would be. She felt a sudden anger at his father, who had administered that first hurt that had caused him to hide his kindness beneath that veil of mockery. "He was wrong to treat you so badly."

"I told you I did not blame him."

But he had been hurt by the rejection. "What of your mother?"

He shrugged. "She was beautiful and vain and loved the trinkets my father created for her. She would not endanger her position by arguing with him about such a small matter as a discarded son." He studied her expression. "Why are you upset? It did not matter. I got on very well. I went to the sultan and persuaded him to give me a studio in the palace."

"You were only a young boy. Didn't you miss them?"

He did not answer directly. "You can forget anything if you work hard enough."

"Can you?"

"Why do you ask? You know it's true. No one works harder than you, madam. Are you not weary enough to forget everything when you finally go to your rest?"

"I have no need of forgetting. I'm well satisfied with my lot."

He gazed at her without speaking.

"Why should I not be?" she asked defiantly. "I have a good life, better than most. I have no material wants and a husband I love." She took off the leather apron and tossed it on the worktable. "It's time I went back to Ian. I have no time for such nonsensical—" She broke off as she met his gaze and was suddenly breathless again. "Stop looking at me."

"I enjoy looking at you." He obediently lowered his gaze to the work in front of him. "You're right, it is wise of you to leave. It would be wiser of you to not come back."

She strode toward the door. "Are you starting that folderol again? I thought you'd come to accept my presence here. Of course I'll return. Thank God, you're not always in such a strange mood. I'm sure you'll be quite yourself tomorrow."

"I'm myself right now. That's why I'm warning you."

"We're getting along very well. Of late, I've even noticed a certain affinity."

"For God's sake, don't you know that that's where the danger lies?" The sudden violence in his voice sent a flicker of apprehension through her.

"What do you mean?" she whispered.

"Think about it." He looked down at the mold. "And don't come back, Margaret."

Margaret. It was the first time he had used her given name. Such a little thing, and yet she experienced an odd shock of intimacy.

"Kartauk." She moistened her lips. He, too, had a given name and she wanted to use it, feel its cadence on her lips. "John . . ."

He stiffened at the table, but his head did not lift. She felt another surge of panic as she realized she wanted him to raise his head, to look at her as he had a moment before. She instantly rejected the thought, her emotions swinging wildly in the opposite direction. She wanted him to close her out, to free her as he had a hundred times before. He did neither. He sat at the worktable, staring down at the seal she knew he did not see, holding her, chaining her.

Then he started to lift his head and she felt her heart lurch. "No!"

The next instant she was jerking open the door, running down the long, gleaming corridors toward her own chamber, running toward Ian.

Lust.

Dear God, she *wanted* him, desired him in that animal way she only pretended with Ian. She had given Kartauk the response she owed only to her husband.

Betrayal.

The flames curled around the platform, at last consuming the silk-wrapped body of the maharajah. The fragrance of burning sandalwood lay heavy on the air as the funeral pyre set his father's soul free by returning his body to air, fire, water, and earth.

It was almost over, Abdar thought. The sorrowful wailing of the spectators rose, drowning out both the crackling of the flames and the screams of the bound concubines chosen to join his father in death on the pyre.

Pachtal was a trifle pale, he thought as he gazed appraisingly at him through the thick haze of black smoke. Oh, well, it was of no consequence. No one would question such an appropriate physical response at this time of bereavement.

He dared not smile, but he nodded slowly at Pachtal and then turned back to the flames. All was going well. He must just be patient.

Kasanpore custom decreed three months of mourning before he could mount the throne.

Three more months before he could turn his attention to Cinnidar.

Perhaps.

But was it not the right of Kali's true son to destroy custom and create his own laws?

"You're very quiet tonight," Ian said as he lifted his cup of tea to his lips. "Tired, Margaret?"

"Perhaps a little." She forced herself to smile as she settled herself more comfortably on the stool by his big chair. "But it will pass."

"What's Kartauk creating these days. Another statue?"

"No, a seal for his majesty, King Ruel of Cinnidar." She pulled the plaid blanket higher over his legs. "I told him it was a mistake to pamper the rascal's self-love to such an extent, but he won't listen to me."

Ian chuckled. "I don't agree. It will amuse Ruel, and he needs something to lighten his humor. He's been working like a galley slave lately."

"He enjoys it." She looked away from him into the fire. "But it could be you're right about me being overtired. As a matter of fact, I've decided to end this foolishness of working with Kartauk. It takes too much of my time."

"No," Ian said quietly. "I won't have it."

She lifted her head, startled. "What?"

"If you're doing too much, spend less time with me. I won't have you cheated of your pleasure."

"Pleasure? When Kartauk isn't having me fetch and carry, he sets me to making unimportant trinkets or ignores me entirely. What pleasure could I derive from that?"

"Enough to make your step lighter and your smile brighter when you come back to me."

"Truly?" If what Ian said was fact, then her decision to abandon her plan was wiser than she had thought. How blind she had been not to realize the subtle changes that had taken place within her in the past weeks.

"You need such distractions." Ian smiled wearily. "God knows, I give you nothing to lift your spirits."

"You lift my spirit just by being with you."

"You lie." Ian smiled. "But it's a kind lie. I give you nothing but worry and hardship."

"Oh no." She lifted his hand to her cheek. It was thinner now, almost transparent in the firelight. "Worry yes, when you won't help me fight. But not hardship. Love doesn't recognize hardship."

His hand gently stroked her hair. "Well, I recognize it and I won't have you cheated any more than you are already. You'll go back to Kartauk's studio tomorrow morning and fashion me a seal like the one he's making for Ruel. It will make me feel quite grand to affix a seal to my letters to Glenclaren."

"No, I don't want—"

"I don't need you," he interrupted gently. "Don't you see that, Margaret?"

She could see it and the knowledge filled her with fear. He was growing further away from her every day. "If you love me, you will—" She stopped. She would not burden him with guilt when he carried so many other burdens. Besides, appeals would do no good at this point. He needed a motivation stronger than she could furnish him.

The child.

Was she giving herself excuses for the sin of adultery? she wondered desperately. At first she'd had no doubts as to the purity of her motives, but now she could not be sure. It could have been lust guiding her toward Kartauk all along. "I don't want to go back," she whispered.

"Of course you do. If you won't do it for yourself, go to please me." He smiled teasingly. "I need that seal for Glenclaren."

And he needed a child for Glenclaren, a child to keep him alive. Even if being with Kartauk gave her a lustful pleasure, wouldn't she be forgiven if she could save Ian? Oh, she did not *know*.

"Margaret?"

"Very well." She buried her face in the soft cashmere of the throw across his lap. "You'll have your seal."

Dear God, but what would she have when this was over?

Margaret hesitated outside the door of the studio, then quickly opened it and sailed into the room. "Good morning, Kartauk. How are you today? I know I'm a little late, but I had to—"

He was coming toward her, and his expression . . .

She didn't want to acknowledge what was revealed in that expression. She lowered her eyes to the gleaming white mosaic floor. He had stopped before her and she could see his broad, strong feet encased in brown leather sandals, smell the familiar scent of wax, wood, and plaster of Paris. She moistened her lips. "I suppose you're going to lecture me on coming back here. It will do you no good. I thought long and hard about it. Ian is going on about my needing distraction, and I decided there was no reason why I shouldn't when he—"

"Hush." His voice was thick, almost guttural. "I don't want to hear his name." His hands tangled in her hair and he jerked her head back to look into her eyes. "You should not have come back."

"I told you, I wasn't going to, but . . ." She couldn't take her gaze from his face. He was staring at her with the same consuming intensity she had seen on his face when he looked at one of his statues. "But Ian wanted—" She swallowed to ease the tightness of her throat. "A seal."

"The hell he did."

Then his lips were on hers, hard, warm, brutal with need. He was pulling the pins from her hair, muttering words in a language she didn't understand as his lips moved from her mouth to her cheeks to her throat in hot, bruising caresses. She could feel the soft, silky texture of his beard as it brushed her flesh, and his big hands were now on her shoulders, kneading, learning, then on her throat, the swell of her breasts . . . She was wrong, they were not caresses. It was like being devoured, absorbed. He pulled her into the hollow of his hips, and she felt the shocking hardness of his arousal against her softness. Shocking and yet right. Mother of heaven, there must be something evil in her heart for this to feel so right.

Her hair was tumbling about her shoulders in wild disarray; his fingers were combing through it. He lifted his head. "You want me." His words came fiercely. "*Me.*"

"Aye." Nothing seemed more clear at the moment. "Aye, Kartauk."

His arms crushed her back to him, robbed her of

breath. Desire. Lust. Safety. How could she feel so safe while tottering on this precipice? It was going to happen. She had thought she was prepared, but now she was trembling, frightened as a child taking its first step. "What do I do?" she gasped. "Help me. Do you want me to do the things you told me to do with Ian?"

He stiffened against her, his hands halting in midmotion in the thickness of her hair. "I told you not to—" A shudder ran through him. "Christ, I wish you hadn't said that." He pushed her away from him.

She immediately tried to move closer.

"No." He grated through set teeth as he kept her at bay. "No, Margaret."

"Why not?" She could not believe he was rejecting her. "I thought—"

"So did I." He drew a deep breath as his hands slowly unclasped her shoulders and dropped away from her. He took a step back. "I thought about it all night. I've been thinking about it since you started this lunacy weeks ago." He turned and moved jerkily back to the worktable. "Sit down."

She stood there, staring at him, feeling more uncertain then ever before in her life. "Why? You find me pleasing. I know I'm no Ellen MacTavish, but you're not unmoved by me."

"Unmoved? God in heaven, that's true enough." His voice was hoarse as he sat down at the worktable. "Yes, you could say that you move me."

She started toward him. "Then it seems unreasonable not to—"

"Stop right there," he said sharply. "Don't come near me."

She halted and smiled tremulously, "If you don't find me distasteful, then why do you not strike me with your divine lightning?"

"Because you're not like other women."

"I believe I have the required limbs, eyes, and breasts."

"You also have a tender heart, a priest's conscience, and the softness of a feather mattress beneath that cool exterior." He shook his head. "I cannot hurt you. I *will* not hurt you."

"But you want me."

"I love you."

Her eyes widened in shock.

"You're surprised?" His smile was bittersweet. "Oh yes, I knew from that first moment you walked out of the castle into the courtyard and started ordering me about."

"You could not." Her voice was barely audible even to herself. "I'm no Helen of Troy to so bedazzle men."

"You bedazzled me. You shone like purest gold in the sunlight, all strength, courage, and loving heart. You still shine with it. At times, when you're weary or discouraged, it's only a dull glow, but at other times you sparkle and shimmer as if—"

"Fine words," she said shakily.

"Words you don't want to hear. Do you think I don't know that?" His big hand clenched slowly into a fist on the table. "I'm allowed lust, but not love. I regret you cannot have one without the other. That's what I tried to tell you yesterday. We've come too close." He met her gaze. "Have the honesty to admit it."

His words were probing through the barriers she had raised, battering her. "I . . . do not deny I lust after you."

"No, lust is safe. Not good, but safe. I knew when you walked in here this morning you'd come to terms with it. But love is a betrayal of Ian. You won't face that, will you?"

"What are you saying? I love Ian." The pain was growing too great. She closed her eyes to shut it out, shut him out. "I do love him."

"Yes, I know you do." He paused. "But you love me too."

Her lids flew open. "No!"

A flicker of anger crossed his face. "Dammit, admit it. Give me that much at least."

"A woman cannot love two men."

"Because all the poets and troubadours babble that

there is only one great love in every life? Bah, there are many kinds of love, and we could have the very best kind." His brown eyes glittered in his taut face. "We could have lust and humor and understanding. We're the same kind of people, two halves of a whole."

She shook her head. "We're nothing alike."

"The only difference between us is the conscience that chains you to—"

"I don't want to hear this."

"Because you don't want to believe it. I told you there would be no mercy." He smiled bitterly. "But I've extended you more mercy than I thought possible. I've given you three long years of keeping the flame turned low so it would not burn you. I could have taken you a moment ago, and I promise I would have made sure you knew what you felt was more than lust."

"Then why didn't you?"

"Because I didn't want to see the look in your eyes when you realized you had just committed adultery with the man you love. You're a strong woman, but I don't think you could have survived that blow."

"I don't love you. I *won't* love you," she said desperately.

"You do, but we will talk no more about it at present." He shifted his massive shoulders as if shrugging off a burden. "You say Ian wants a seal of his own? Then let's set about it. We'll have to do—"

"What are you talking about?" she asked blankly. "A seal?"

He nodded brusquely. "I've decided we'll continue as we have been. You've proved surprisingly valuable as an apprentice, a little too talkative, but I can tolerate that fault."

He was pretending what had gone before had not happened. "I can't just ignore—"

"Of course you can. Ian wants you to be amused. I believe I can guarantee to distract you. As for the other" —he met her gaze—"I'll wait until you make the first move."

"I'll never make it."

"But how can you not when you need a child for Ian?" He smiled sadly. "Poor Margaret, what a quandary."

"It's different now. I could not . . ." She lifted a trembling hand to her temple. "I cannot think."

"I do not ask you to think. I would far prefer you to only feel. Someday, if I'm fortunate, you'll oblige me by shutting down that pesky conscience and letting yourself take what we both need."

She shook her head.

He shrugged. "Then I'm no worse off than before, am I? Nothing has really changed."

How could he say that? Everything had changed. Each nerve and muscle in her body seemed tuned to his every response, every gesture. "You're right, I shouldn't have come here," she said shakily.

"Have I, at last, convinced you of that?" He smiled. "Too late, Margaret. My grand period of self-sacrifice is over. Now I'll take what I can get. If you don't come to me, I'll go to Ian every evening and spend a charming few hours with the two of you."

"You wouldn't do that."

"Why not? I'm very fond of Ian, and he's been complaining I haven't visited him enough of late. You can come here in the mornings or you can sit there beside Ian and have me watch you and know every moment what I'm thinking, what I'm wanting to do with you."

She wouldn't be able to bear it, and Kartauk was aware of that as he was aware of everything else about her. "I was thinking just yesterday that you were kind, but that's not true. You're very cruel."

"I'm neither kind nor cruel. I'm only a hungry man who *will* be fed. Even if it must be hard crusts instead of hearty fare." He turned and walked toward the door leading to the veranda. "You look a bit distraught, and it takes a steady hand for the carving of a seal. I think we'll wait until tomorrow to start to fashion it. And after we finish the seal, I think it's time I did a statue of you. . . ."

Chapter 16

Ruel gazed blindly at the sun starting its descent behind the mountain.

Jane should be here within the hour.

He should be satisfied. He *was* satisfied, dammit.

The forfeiting of the penalty money had hurt her, not only because of the loss itself but because the defeat had been to him. She had been made to feel helpless and defeated.

She needs to win.

Dilam's words in the *belim* tent came back to him. Well, she hadn't won this time. He would never forget her expression of numb horror as she had looked at the damage wrought by the elephant. He had felt something twist inside him and he wanted to reach out and—

Comfort? The instinct meant nothing, he assured himself. It was entirely natural to admire a foe who had fought a valiant fight, but that did not mean he was softening toward her. He could not soften.

He turned heavily away from the window and moved across the room to the chair by the fireplace. Soon it would be over. The loss at Elephant Crossing had been only the beginning. By the time she left this summerhouse, he would have the satisfaction of knowing she had been punished as she deserved. That's what he wanted, wasn't it?

Christ, of course it was what he wanted. This rawness fraying his nerves was only impatience now that he was so close to his aim.

Impatience . . . and lust.

The dark blue curled tile roof of the summerhouse shimmered gray in the moonlight. Light streamed from the arched windows, casting fan-shaped shadows on the grass.

He was waiting for her.

Naturally, he was waiting for her, Jane thought impatiently. He had been waiting for her for over three years.

She braced herself and then walked quickly down the terrace steps and the path leading to the summerhouse.

She could get through this. He was only Ruel, not the mandarin she had let her fears exaggerate to giant proportions. He could not harm her if she did not allow it. She drew a deep breath as she reached the door and then flung it open. She said flatly, "I'm here."

"I see you are." Ruel was sitting in a superbly crafted Louis XV chair before a marble-tiled fireplace. He wore all white, as he had the day they had arrived at the palace, and his golden tan and sun-streaked hair shimmered in the firelight in sharp contrast to the elegant garb. He appeared perfectly at ease in this tastefully furnished room with its air of restrained European luxury. But then, Ruel always appeared confident and at ease wherever he was, she thought bitterly, be it pounding spikes in a torrent of rain, presiding at the dinner table at the palace, or cooking bacon over a campfire in the middle of the jungle.

He rose to his feet and wrinkled his nose. "And, unfortunately, I not only see you, I also smell you."

"I could hardly ride twenty-five miles in heat and dust and not smell of horse." She closed the door. "If you don't like it, I can leave."

"Oh no, I was never one to forgo a meal because I had to prepare it myself. It makes the feast only more satisfying to know it's been created to one's exact specifications." He stood up and moved across the room toward the lavender- and cream-colored brocade curtain that divided the room. "In fact, I anticipated this little problem. I had boiling hot water brought from the palace ten minutes ago." He pulled aside the curtain to reveal a small area that appeared much larger due to the mirrors that graced all three walls. A royal-blue and white Chinese carpet gave only occasional glimpses of the polished oak floor and, across the room, a white satin spread covered a wide bed draped in diaphanous mosquito netting. He smiled faintly as he followed her gaze and then gestured to a hip bath filled with steaming water occupying the corner immediately to the left of the brocade curtain. "It's fortunate you were on time, or the water would have turned cold."

"It wouldn't have mattered," she said quietly. "I assume you're going to watch me?"

Some indefinable emotion flickered across his face. "Most certainly."

She sat down on a wide white satin-tufted chaise longue a few feet from the tub and took off her boots and wool socks. "I thought you would."

"Why?"

"You want me to feel . . . exposed, humiliated."

She stood up and started unbuttoning her shirt. "It's all a part of it."

"How perceptive of you to realize that. Actually, I had in mind something else as well." He paused. "A mistress is handled with a little too much delicacy. I thought I'd let you sample the joys of being treated as your mother was treated."

She felt as if she had been kicked in the stomach. Her fingers clenched on the second button. "You did?"

"Can you think of a more fitting revenge? You surely didn't think I'd beat you with a whip or strap you in an iron maiden? Remember when we discussed my aversion to snakes and I said everyone was afraid of something?" His gaze narrowed on her face. "Isn't this what you fear most? To be a whore like your mother?"

"Yes," she whispered. Slavery, submission, captivity. God, she should have known Ruel would have the instinct to strike her the cruelest blow possible.

"Well, aren't you going to run away?"

For a moment she was wildly tempted, but that would be another defeat. "No."

For an instant she thought she saw a flicker of disappointment in his expression, but she must have been mistaken, for he was now smiling mockingly. "Then, by all means, proceed. Your water is cooling."

"Not yet." She met his gaze. "I want your promise."

"My promise?"

"When I leave here, we're quits. I want your promise you'll avoid coming to the site except when absolutely necessary."

"I thought we'd already agreed on that."

"I want your promise."

He was silent a moment before he said curtly, "You have it."

"Good." She was acutely conscious of his eyes on her as she quickly stripped off the rest of her clothes and turned toward the tub.

"Wait. Turn around."

She went rigid and then slowly turned to face him.

He was leaning against the wall, his gaze moving

slowly over her. "You're thinner than you were at Glenclaren. I couldn't tell in those clothes."

"I always lose weight when I work hard."

His lips tightened. "I suppose that comment was made to make me feel guilty for forcing you to—"

"You didn't force me. It was my choice." She stared challengingly into his eyes. "And I almost beat you."

He smiled faintly. "Yes, you did. But almost isn't good enough." His gaze moved down to the curls surrounding her womanhood. "Turn in a circle. Slowly."

She felt heat suffuse her body but somehow managed to keep her expression blank as she obeyed him.

"Even though you're thinner, your breasts are fuller than they were three years ago."

"May I get in the tub now?" she asked jerkily.

"Not yet. Turn your back to me."

Her teeth sank into her lower lip as she turned around and stood still, spine rigid.

"Marvelous buttocks." His voice thickened. "Tight and firm . . . Do you remember the painting in the maharajah's car?"

She felt like a slave on an auction block, like one of the whores in Frenchie's tent. Slavery. Block it out, she told herself. She was giving him what he wanted; he was making her feel what he wished her to feel. "No, I don't remember. Are you finished?"

"Yes," he said hoarsely. "Get into the tub."

She quickly covered the few steps to the hip bath and the next moment thankfully sank into the soapy water. Don't look at him. Just get it over with. The heady scent of jasmine and lemon drifted up to her from the water as she grabbed the sponge floating on the surface and began briskly rubbing her shoulders.

"Not so rough," he said mockingly. "I don't want you damaged."

She stared blindly down at the water in the tub. "It's not going to work. You're going to be disappointed."

"Am I?" His voice came from behind her. "Why do you think so?"

"I'm not going—" she paused as she felt his hands on

her hair, quickly unloosening her braid—"to let you hurt me."

"No?" His fingers moved through her braid from scalp to the ends of her hair, gently tugging and separating until it was in wild disarray around her shoulders.

Clever Ruel. The soft, silky hair brushing her flesh increased tenfold her feeling of vulnerability and womanliness. She moistened her lips. "I had time to think while I was riding here. I can stand anything for a few days."

"Can you?" She could hear him moving behind her. "How do you know it will be for only a few days?"

"A few days," she repeated firmly. "You'll grow tired of it and go back to doing what's important to you."

"This is important to me."

"Not like Cinnidar."

"At times I'm not sure of that."

"You'll be certain when boredom sets in." She rushed on. "And then I'll go back and I'll finish that railroad on schedule."

"And what if your disobliging elephant pays you another visit?"

She had been trying not to think of that possibility. "Li Sung will see that Dilam guards against that happening. It was all I could do to keep him from rushing into the jungle after Danor."

"I've noticed he appears a bit obsessed with getting rid of him." He moved from behind her and seated himself on the chaise longue a few feet from the tub. "I sympathize. I understand obsession."

He was naked, his thighs slightly parted to reveal bold arousal.

Her lungs constricted and she found herself unable to look away from his lower body. Soon that part of him would be joined to her, he would be moving in and out, and she would feel that helpless bonding she had first known in the maharajah's railway car. This time he would not be careful of her and she should be frightened. She *was* frightened, but there also existed that dark fascination he always held for her.

"I assume Li Sung will send a message if there's any further trouble?"

"What?" She managed to pull her gaze away from him and looked down at the water again. "I don't expect any more problems."

"Danor seems to do the unexpected. Lift your breasts. I want to see the water glisten on them."

Her hand tightened on the sponge.

"Anything I want, I believe you said," he reminded her softly. "I'm perfectly willing to guide you in this, but you do have a promise to keep."

She closed her eyes tightly and dropped the sponge. Her hands reached up to cup the undersides of her breasts.

"That's right." His voice was closer, beside her now. "Higher. Now offer them to me. Good . . ."

His lips closed on her nipple.

She gasped and her eyes flew open. His mouth was enveloping her breast, but his light eyes were fastened on hers, watching her expression as he slowly sucked and bit at the sensitive tip. The muscles of her stomach clenched in instinctive response as sensation after sensation rippled through her. "Now keep quite still and I'll give you a reward for obedience." His hands were beneath the water, probing, finding. She gasped as his thumb began to press and rotate on the tiny nub. Hot, explosive splinters of sensation rippled through her with every motion. His other hand moved still farther down as he murmured, "Don't tighten up."

She couldn't help it. One finger. Two. Three. She arched back against the tub, her hands gripping the porcelain sides as his fingers plunged deep, out, in, fast, slow, in a rhythm that caused her to bite her lips to keep from crying out. He finally sat back on his heels. "Very good." His chest was lifting and falling with the harshness of his breathing. "Perhaps a little too good. I'm growing impatient. I believe we'll put an end to this first lesson. We'll have plenty of time for others." He stood up and reached for the large towel on the chaise longue. "Stand up."

She didn't know if she could stand. Her knees were shaking, her entire body was shaking with the effort not to reveal her response to him.

"Up." Ruel didn't wait for her to obey but jerked her out of the tub and into the folds of the towel. He cast a quick glance at the bed. "Too far." He dropped back down on the chaise longue. "I can't—wait."

His fingers were searching, adjusting, drawing her limbs on either side of his hips. His hands cupped her buttocks and jerked her forward, impaling her to the quick.

She cried out as she felt the warm, hard length in the depths of her. Heat. Tightness. Hunger. No, not hunger, let it not be hunger.

He was moving, bucking, keeping her sealed tight but making her feel every inch, every sensation. Her nipples were hardening against his chest, she realized in despair. "Hold me tighter," he muttered, punctuating every word with a thrust. "Give—me—more."

She didn't want to give anything but found her legs instinctively tightening around him. That spiraling tension she had known in the railway car had returned and was growing with every second. How could her body betray her when it meant victory for him?

He moved, turned, and somehow she was on her back, lying sidewise on the chaise. There was room only for her torso on the tufted cushion and her head arched over the edge, her hair brushing the floor with Ruel's every thrust. She could feel a scream building in her throat, building in her entire body, waiting to be released.

"Stop holding back," Ruel muttered as he rotated, drew out slowly, and then plunged deep. "Give it to me."

She could fight him no longer. The primal scream broke free, her body convulsed, climaxed, and she heard his low cry of satisfaction above her. She was barely aware of the short flurry of thrusts that brought him his own release. He had won, she thought wearily. He had manipulated her body and taken what he wanted, and she had not been able to keep even that final victory from him.

He was carrying her toward the bed, the towel still draped loosely about her.

Her breath was coming in gasps as she looked up at him.

"You didn't expect it, did you?" he asked as he deposited her on the bed. "Our bodies don't care if we hate or love. It's going to happen every time. I'll make it happen whether you want it or not."

"No!"

"Yes, I've never had a taste for compliance even in my whores."

She flinched at the unexpected thrust. "You took me by surprise," she said haltingly. "It won't happen again."

"It will and very soon. I find I'm fairly insatiable where you're concerned, and I assure you that's just the first surprise. I've had three years to plan many, many more." He reached over to the bedside table, and the next moment he was holding something before her. "Do you remember that night at Zabrie's?"

A mask, an extravagant sable and turquoise feather mask.

A picture flooded back to her of Ruel standing in the center of the room, mocking blue eyes glittering as he gazed at her through the slits in a mask very like this one.

"I recall very little of that night. It's not a memory I treasure."

"Nor I." He brushed the feathered mask over her nipple. "But that's because I was undergoing a great deal of frustration at the time."

Her breasts were swelling, her nipples becoming more acutely sensitive with every lazy stroke of the feathers. "Is that necessary? I wish . . . you would stop it," she said haltingly.

"Presently." He moved the mask down and brushed it lightly back and forth over her lower abdomen.

She felt a hot tingling begin between her thighs. Not

again, she told herself despairingly. Lie still. Don't give him any more response than he can take from you.

"Zabrie was very clever. She knew that in a house of pleasure a man doesn't care who a woman is as long as she gives him what he wants," he murmured. "There's nothing more anonymous than a mask, is there, Jane?"

She didn't answer.

He moved over her, parted her thighs, and entered her again, sliding slowly to the hilt. "Ah, you're ready for me. I thought you would be. You're proving very accommodating." He placed the feathered mask on her face and leisurely tied the velvet cords behind her head before arranging her hair to fan around her on the pillow. He sat quite still, gazing at her. "You look quite splendidly erotic." His tone was mocking, but his voice had thickened, hoarsened.

Sweet heaven, she was clenching around him.

"And evidently that's also how you feel." He smiled faintly. "I approve. That's how a woman of pleasure should feel and behave. You're learning fast, Jane. When we've taken the edge off this, I'll give you another lesson." He began to move with excruciating, teasing slowness. He whispered, "There are many other purposes and places for feathers than the obvious."

"You didn't do it right," Jane murmured as she gazed at the window through which the first gray light of dawn was beginning to stream.

"Really?" Ruel gathered her closer, his fingers idly toying with her red hair spread across his shoulder. "I would never have known it by your response."

"Oh, you made me feel . . ." She trailed off. He already knew how he had made her feel during these last hours. Possessed, completely in his power, bent to his will like a twig in a windstorm. Her body ached with that possession, and yet she knew he could arouse her again if he chose to do so. Yet, gradually, she had begun to realize something that had filled her with infinite relief. "But I'm not afraid of you anymore."

"I didn't know you ever were."

"I think you did. I'm not very clever about hiding my feelings." She gazed unseeingly at the patterns of pale sunlight on the royal-blue and cream carpet. "But you didn't know why."

"Are you going to tell me?"

She whispered, "I was afraid you'd make me love you again."

He stiffened. "Love?"

"I did love you . . . a long time ago. I was afraid it would come back."

"I'm sure that possibility no longer exists."

"No, it's gone now. I feel hollow inside, as if I had been filled with sand and it had all poured out of me."

"A great relief, no doubt."

"Yes, it would have been terrible. I thought for a while back in Kasanpore that you could be—"

"I could be what?"

"It doesn't matter." Nothing seemed to matter. She felt as if she were floating. Fever? she wondered. She would have to remember to take her *quinghao* tomorrow morning. . . .

"On the contrary, I find this confession of devotion fascinating."

"You were so different from me, different from anyone I'd ever known. I used to think of you as one of those Chinese mandarins."

"What the hell is a mandarin?"

"Li Sung says they're men of power in China. In ancient days some of them gained their influence with the emperors through magic."

"I'm hardly a magician."

"No one else had ever made me feel like you did. But you also made me feel . . . helpless." She whispered, "I was afraid you'd turn me into her."

"Your mother?"

"Yes, I guess I've always been afraid that I really belonged in one of those places and fate was only waiting to find a way to pull me back." She smiled sadly. "What better tool could fate use than a mandarin? But now I know you can't do that. It's only my body, not my mind. You can't really change what I am. When I leave here I'll be the same person I was when I came. I've cheated you, Ruel."

"Don't be too sure. I've only just begun."

"But it's too late now. You might have succeeded if you'd done it right, if you'd made me remember the old days." Her gaze shifted to the crumpled mask on the bedside table. "Silk curtains and scented rooms . . . exotic feather masks. That's not what I remember, that's not what I've been afraid of all these years."

"It seems I've been remiss in my preparations. Would you care to tell me a few of those fond memories?"

"Sheets that smell of dirt and sweat and urine, the red glass bowl of the opium pipe my mother smoked, watching Frenchie counting the money . . ." She closed her eyes. "I'm very tired. May I go to sleep now?"

"Aren't you afraid I'll try to duplicate those charming surroundings now that you've confided in me?"

"No."

"Why not?"

"I don't know. You're not—" She was so tired, she could barely think, much less talk. "You're not Frenchie."

"Thank God." He didn't speak for a moment and then said lightly, "As it happens, I'm much too fond of my own comforts these days to want to undergo that ordeal. I'll have to find another way of accomplishing my ends."

"It's too late. I'm not afraid anymore. You can't hurt me if I don't feel anything for you. I'm free of you, Ruel."

He ran his hands through her hair. "Are you?"

"Yes, I know what I am now. . . ."

She was asleep.

Ruel's hands ran slowly through her hair again.

You didn't do it right.

He had to ignore the picture she had drawn for him with those few sentences. He would not let pity turn him from his purpose. The punishment he had chosen for her was trifling in comparison to what she had let happen to Ian.

He had hurt her as he had told her he would; he had made her feel used, without dignity or pride, a mindless object of lust and pleasure.

No, she had not been without dignity even at the end. She had just kept her word and given whatever he asked of her. He hadn't expected anything else. She had never broken faith since the day he had met her.

Except when she had built the bridge over Lanpur Gorge. She had traded in iron instead of steel and Ian had been the one to suffer for it. If she had to falter, why the hell couldn't it have been at some other time, some other place. He could have forgiven anything but what had happened to—

Forgiven? It was too late for forgiveness between them. He had taken his revenge and would take it again until it was time for her to leave. What he had done was just. It was not right for Ian to suffer and no one else.

I know myself now, she had said.

But did he know himself? Did he know how much of what had happened tonight was revenge and how much the fever of lust? The more he had of her, the more starved he became.

Starved and enchained. At times he had felt more enslaved than Jane during these past hours.

He would get over it. The first wild burst of passion was always the strongest. By the time she left the summerhouse, he would surely slake himself of both lust and revenge.

I don't love you anymore.

I'm free of you.

He pulled her closer with a movement unconsciously possessive. She murmured something inaudible into his shoulder and was asleep again.

He did not sleep for another two hours. He was too filled with anger and frustration and— It was *not* pity.

You didn't do it right. . . .

Li Sung frowned. "None of your guards sighted the elephant anywhere?"

Dilam shook her head. "A peaceful night."

"You're sure?"

"You appear disappointed."

"Foolishness," Li Sung said curtly. "After his rampage I merely thought it odd he had left us in peace for two nights in a row. Why would I want the elephant to come and destroy what we have built?"

"Why indeed?"

He knew what Dilam was thinking. *Makhol.* More foolishness. "There's work to do." Li Sung turned away with a jerky movement and walked toward the track, carefully keeping his gaze from wandering toward the west. Dilam was wrong. It was not some mystical bond that was attracting him to the elephant. It was anger . . . and fear.

Margaret threw open the door of the studio and announced belligerently, "I have no intention of continuing to come here. I'm here today only because I couldn't think of a way to—"

"Keep me from getting what I want," Kartauk finished impatiently. "I know, I know. Now, come over and put on your apron. We have work to do."

She felt a surge of relief as she realized there was no hint of intimacy in his tone. So much for the worrying and soul-searching she had undergone all night. He had closed the door and it was as if yesterday had never happened. She moved across the studio toward the worktable. "And I shall not pose for you."

"Not now," he said absently as he measured moist sand into a small box. "I have to cast Ruel's seal. I'll think about the statue another day."

"It will do you no good to ponder the matter. I will not pose." She reached under the table for her apron and put it on, her gaze upon the mold they had started two days ago. "What do we do first?"

"We powder the plaster model with fine charcoal dust." He did so and then pressed the model into one of the two caster boxes on the worktable before him. Wonderful hands; skilled, graceful, sure. Yet they had not been this sure when he had touched her yesterday, but trembling with need. "Then we dry the portion of the model where the figures come. Are you listening?"

"Of course." She guiltily looked away from his hands. "What next?"

"*Pasta di pane crudo.*"

"What?"

"Dough." He scooped up doughy paste from one of his bowls, shaped it like a cake the same size and thickness the seal was to be, and carefully placed it over the design formed by the plaster. "The dough is to make the shape of the body of the seal. Take the other caster sand box and fill it full of sand."

She scooped the moist sand into the box. "And then?"

"We let that sand dry and then set that box over the first box. Two halves of a whole."

That's what he had said about what they could have together. Two halves of a whole.

"Pack the moist sand very tightly. You've spilled some. . . ."

It was no wonder. Her hands were trembling as much as his had been the day before. He had closed the door. Why couldn't she do the same?

"After a time we'll separate the boxes, take out the dough cake, and cut a mouth and two vent holes in the mold. When both are dry, we'll smoke the mold over with a little candle smoke and let it cool. It's always best to pour hot gold into cold interstices."

"Is that all I'm supposed to remember?"

His thick brows lifted. "Is that not enough? Should I have given you a greater challenge, apprentice?"

"This is quite enough."

"I hope you paid careful attention. You'll do Ian's seal by yourself."

Her eyes widened. "What? The entire seal?"

"I'll prepare the materials, you'll do the work."

"But I'm not ready to do something like this. What if I make a mistake?"

He smiled. "Hope that you do. You learn most from your mistakes."

She grimaced. "And you would stand by and let me waste hours of work on nothing?"

"I told you to listen. If you ruin your seal, I will explain once more and only once before you do it again."

She tried frantically to remember the order of the steps he had taken in the process. "What comes next?"

"We melt the gold, but I think you have enough to remember. We won't go into that now."

"Thank you," she said sarcastically. "I suppose I'm required to memorize that process as well. Have you no other words of wisdom to impart?"

He did not look at her as he stood up and took off his leather apron. "Yes, concentrate only on the work at hand."

"I could scarcely do anything else."

"And remember to keep the flame turned low."

"I thought we were not going to go into melting the—"

I kept the flame turned low for three long years.

Kartauk had been aware of what she had been feeling but had ignored it, putting her at ease, giving her something to cling to in this unknown sea of emotions. She experienced a glowing warmth deep within her that had an element of despair. How could she guard against him when he showed such kindness and empathy?

"I understand," she said in a low voice.

"Of course you do. You're a very intelligent woman, apprentice." He moved toward the veranda door. "Tidy up this mess while I go to the furnace room and select a sheet of gold for the melting."

Chapter 17

The clouds hovered gray and heavy over the mountain. Just the sight of them made Jane feel as if they were pressing down, smothering her in a sluggish languor. No, it wasn't the weather. The day had only just turned threatening and yet she had been experiencing this heaviness since she had opened her eyes that morning.

"I'd like to ride over and see James Medford later this afternoon," she said over her shoulder to Ruel. "I need to talk to him about the schedule for joining the rails."

"Restless already?" Ruel's lips tightened. "It's

been only two days. I'll have to apply myself to keep you more interested."

He was angry. Jane had been aware of Ruel's growing edginess for the entire day. He had been prowling around the summerhouse like a caged lion for the past few hours. "You're restless yourself. Neither of us is accustomed to being cooped up with no work to do."

"This is your work for the time being."

She whirled away from the window, holding tight to the sheet she had draped around herself. "Good heavens, we cannot fornicate every hour of the day. It's only making you bad-tempered."

"I'm *not* bad-tempered."

"You most certainly are."

He scowled. "Then it's your job to distract and soothe me."

"You shouldn't need soothing. I told you that you'd be disappointed."

"I'm *not* disappointed. I've done exactly what I said I'd do." His smile was a mere baring of teeth. "And enjoyed every minute of it."

"No, you haven't." She frowned, trying to put together the pieces of his behavior. "For some reason . . . oh, I think you've enjoyed my body but not the other."

"What other?"

"You didn't like hurting me."

He stiffened. "I've not noticed any bruises."

She did have a few bruises on her body but not by his intent. It would have been impossible not to have gone through the orgy of sexual indulgences of the past forty-eight hours without showing any signs. "You know the kind of wounds you inflicted. It gave you no satisfaction."

"I regret you're reading me wrong. I'm very satisfied with every aspect of our time together and, if you'd admit to it, I believe you received an equal satisfaction."

"Because you gave me pleasure?" She shook her head. "Every time you gave me that pleasure it hurt me. It stripped my pride and made me feel less than myself, just as you intended it to do."

"I'm surprised you're telling me this."

"I wouldn't have admitted it when I came here." She shrugged. "It's different now. I don't mind giving you small victories. You need them more than I do. It must be terrible to live with such a passion for revenge."

"How condescending of you." His lips thinned. "You might consider how you would feel if it were Li Sung instead of Ian who was going through torment before blaming me for wanting to settle accounts."

She shook her head wearily. "I don't know how I would feel. It's too horrible to imagine." She met his gaze. "And I've never blamed you. I don't blame you now. I'm just glad it's over."

A multitude of expressions crossed his face, but she could single out only shock, frustration, anger, and desire. "Oh, it's not over yet." He smiled recklessly. "And I believe you'd best prepare to give me another victory." His gaze wandered over her. "If you must cover yourself, it won't be with that sheet. I believe it's time for you to don more appropriate apparel. Put on the cloth-of-gold gown in the armoire."

At first she didn't understand, but her eyes widened as she recalled his words that first night she had arrived on Cinnidar. "You actually had it made?"

"Of course. I always keep my promises. Put it on."

"Don't you think this promise could be—" She broke off as she saw his face. His eyes were shimmering recklessly and she could sense the core of violence and frustration just below the surface ready to explode. She shrugged. "If you insist. It's not worth arguing about." She walked toward the armoire across the room.

A few moments later the three mirrors on the wall reflected her image gowned in a loose garment that was still blatantly sexual. It draped only one shoulder in the Greek fashion and then dipped across her body to bare one breast. The skirt was slit to the waist to show her limbs with every movement. She could feel the color sting her cheeks as she looked at herself. She felt more naked in this gown than she had totally nude.

"Lovely." Ruel's arms slid around her from behind, one hand cupping her breast. "Just as I imagined you."

She met his gaze in the mirror. "As a whore?"

"What else?" he asked mockingly, his thumb and forefinger pulling at her nipple.

A hot shiver went through her. The muscles of her stomach contracted. "This gown doesn't make me a whore any more than your treating me like one."

"But it bothers you."

"Yes, it bothers me. Does that please you?"

"Of course it pleases me. Why shouldn't it—" He stopped and again his expression reflected that mixture of frustration and discontent. "Kneel down on the carpet, dammit."

"The bed is only a few feet away."

"The floor."

She shrugged and fell to her knees.

"Now get up on your hands and knees."

It was beginning again—dark excitement, domination, and . . . anticipation. She moistened her lips. "Why?"

"I believe it's time we tried something new." He lifted her gown above her waist and the next moment she felt his warm palms caressing her buttocks. "The painting in the maharajah's railroad car . . ."

He plunged deep, taking her breath. He stopped, his hardness sealed within her while his hands went around to cup and fondle her breasts. "We have to faithfully reproduce the painting, don't we?" He began to move slowly, making her feel every inch. She involuntarily tightened around him as a spasm of heat tore through her. "Ah, that's what I want. Now look back at me. I want to see your expression."

She turned her head to stare at him. She knew what he was seeing—heat, lust, anger at herself for not being able to resist the passion he ignited so easily. His own face was flushed, his lips heavy with sensuality, set in an expression of painful pleasure, and yet once more she discerned that odd torment. "It's not the same," she gasped. "Don't you see? It . . . can never be the same no matter what you see in my face. It's your expression that's wrong. I told you the painting was false. Men aren't gentle. Never gentle . . ."

He went still. "Damn you," he said hoarsely. "*Damn* you." He exploded, plunging in a fury of movement.

Her fingers dug into the carpet as the storm rose, each stroke whipping her into a mindless frenzy. She wasn't sure how long it lasted until she felt the burst of wild sensation that signaled both their release.

She collapsed on the floor and a moment later felt him leave her. She was completely enervated, unable to move. She became vaguely aware he was picking her up, depositing her on the bed.

"Are you all right?" he asked stiltedly.

The heaviness she had felt all day seemed to be pressing down on her, crushing the breath from her body. "Tired . . ."

He pulled the covers up to her chin and then lay down beside her. He gazed straight ahead, not touching her. "I lost my temper."

She didn't answer.

"All right, you don't have to wear the damn gown again," he burst out.

"It doesn't matter."

"Take it off."

"I'm too tired."

He muttered a curse beneath his breath. The next moment he was pulling the gown down her body and throwing it into a glittering golden heap on the floor. He pulled the covers up around her again. "Satisfied?"

It was not like Ruel to be so defensive, she thought dimly, but it was no more unusual than his other behavior today. "It doesn't matter," she repeated, and closed her eyes. "Not important . . ."

"Take me with you, Patrick," Jane muttered. Her voice rose. "Take me with you!"

"What the hell—" Ruel roused from sleep to see Jane tossing wildly on the bed next to him. Her eyes were closed. She was only dreaming, he realized with relief.

He reached over to shake her shoulder. "Wake up, it's only—" Her flesh was burning hot under his hand. "Jane?"

"I don't want to be like her." Her breath was coming in pants. "I won't be any bother. Take me with you, Patrick."

"Jesus, what the hell's wrong? Wake up." He sat up in bed and lit the lamp on the bedside table before reaching over and shaking her again. "Open your eyes, dammit."

Her eyes opened but stared without seeing. "The train. He's leaving on the train." She panicked. "Don't leave me, Patrick."

"No one's leaving you." His arms closed around her. God, she was hot. His heart was pounding as hard as hers as he tried to make her lie still against him. "It's all right. No one is going to leave you."

"Yes, he will. Unless I make him take me."

"Christ, stop thrashing around."

"Patrick!"

What could he do? She wasn't in her right senses and he was afraid to leave her alone even to fetch help. Tamar wouldn't return until he brought breakfast.

"Please, I don't want to be like her," she whispered.

His arms tightened around her. He knew who she was talking about and the memory she was reliving. While awake she may have conquered her demons, but now she was a child again with all the fears and torments of the mind let loose.

The torments he had deliberately brought her here to set free.

Who could be hammering at the door at this time of night? Margaret wondered drowsily.

Then, as she came fully awake, she glanced quickly at Ian. Thank goodness he had not been disturbed. She struggled into her robe, thrust her feet into slippers, and marched across the room to throw open the door. Ruel. She should have known who would be so lacking in consideration.

"Merciful saints, must you come pounding in the middle of the night? Ian needs his sleep, and it's a wonder you didn't wake him. Why could it not—" She broke off as she saw his strained face and glittering eyes. "What's wrong?"

"I need you," he said hoarsely. "Can you come?"

"Come where?" She cast a glance over her shoulder. Ian was still sleeping soundly. The pain had been bad last night and she had been forced to give him extra laudanum. She stepped into the hall and quietly closed the door behind her.

"The summerhouse." He took her elbow and strode down the hall, half leading, half dragging her. "I need you."

"That's the first time I've ever heard you say that," she said dryly. "I can hardly wait to hear in what manner."

"You know about sickness," he said jerkily. "You took care of your father and Ian."

"You're ill?"

"Jane."

"Jane's here?" she asked, startled.

"Would I be coming after you if she were not? Stop asking questions and hurry. I've left her alone too long already."

Her pace quickened. "What's wrong?"

"If I knew that, I wouldn't have called you. Fever. Chills. She's out of her head. She doesn't know me."

"Have you sent for the physician?"

"Of course I have, but it may be hours before Tamar gets back with him. She needs someone now."

"What is she doing at the summerhouse?"

He looked straight ahead. "That's not your concern."

"What have you been up to, Ruel?"

He didn't answer.

It was clear he was not going to confide in her the

exact nature of this particular deviltry. "I may not be able to help."

"You can try." He opened the french doors leading to the terrace. He added haltingly, "Please."

Good God, Ruel must be frantic if he was desperate enough to plead. "I'll try."

Margaret came out of the summerhouse and closed the door behind her. "She's better."

A muscle jerked in Ruel's cheek. "Thank God."

"The fever's down and she woke up long enough to answer some of the doctor's questions. He said the fever should leave her entirely in a few hours."

"What the hell's wrong with her?"

"Malaria. She contracted it in Kasanpore and the fever recurs periodically."

"She never told me."

"Nor me," Margaret said. "And I've known her for three years. She's not a woman who confides her weaknesses." She wearily rubbed the back of her neck. "I must go back in case Ian needs me. I'll come and see her this afternoon."

"No, I'll take care of her from now on."

"You don't appear to have done much in that nature as yet."

He flinched. "I said I'd do it. She might find facing you awkward."

"You're trying to save her shame? How unusual. Your tardy gallantry is unnecessary. Jane and I understand each other. She knows I wouldn't blame her for your sins." She met his gaze. "And I'm not sure it's not my duty to take her back to the palace with me."

"She wouldn't go."

"I think she would. She wouldn't admit it, but she's always been afraid of you."

"Not anymore," he said with a crooked smile. "Not when she's not burning up with fever. And even if she were, she wouldn't go. We have an arrangement."

She snorted. "She has more intelligence than to

make a pact with a conscienceless rogue like you. Why is she here?"

"You wouldn't want to know."

"You may be right." She was suddenly overcome with weariness. She did not need this additional burden weighing on her when she was so bewildered and strained herself. Who was she to call Ruel down for his iniquities when she had lately found herself falling into the same temptation? "Can I trust you not to—"

"Oh, for God's sake, do you think I'm going to jump into bed with her while she can barely lift her hand?" he asked explosively.

Whatever had happened here, Jane's illness had shaken Ruel. She had never seen him so pale and distraught as when he had appeared at her door. She could not be sure it would last, but Jane was safe with him for the time being. "If you need anything of me, let me know."

She started back up the path toward the palace.

Ruel looked like a death head, Jane thought hazily. Something had to be done. She would tell him she would take the watch over Ian tonight. Not that she had much hope of success when Ruel was so afraid Ian would slip away if he wasn't there to pull him back. "Have to . . . rest."

Ruel's gaze flew to her face. "What?"

"You should rest more. You look . . ." She trailed off as she came fully awake. This was not the bungalow in Kasanpore in those days they had worked together to keep Ian alive. This was the summerhouse . . .

"You're the one who needs rest." Ruel leaned forward and put a glass of water to her lips. "Drink."

She swallowed the water. "I've been ill?"

"Fever. For the past two days. The doctor said it was a comparatively mild attack." His lips tightened. "It didn't seem mild to me."

She vaguely recalled the doctor staring down at her,

asking her questions, talking to someone else across the bed. "Margaret . . . was here too?"

"Yes. Why didn't you tell me you'd had malaria?"

"Why should I?" She frowned. "Two days. I have to get back to work."

"I sent word to Li Sung to tell him you'd be delayed."

"You told him I was sick? You shouldn't have done that. He'll only worry."

"I told him you were out of danger." He scowled. "And it's about time someone worried about you. Li Sung should have seen you were working yourself toward something like this."

"My fault . . . I forgot to take the *quinghao* after I got here."

"*Quinghao?*"

"It's an ancient Chinese herbal medicine. Li Sung gave it to me when I first fell sick with the disease in Kasanpore."

"Do you take it all the time?"

"Not all the time. Only when I think I may be coming down with—"

"And just how long have you been taking it since you came to Cinnidar?" he asked with measured precision.

She didn't answer.

"How long?" Ruel persisted.

"Four weeks."

"My God."

"It wasn't bad. Just night fever."

"That sapped you of strength during the day." His right hand grabbed the arm of the chair. "You had it the night you came here, didn't you? Dammit, you probably would never have even come if you'd been in your right senses."

Looking back at that hazy, disoriented period, she wasn't sure if he was right or wrong. "I don't know. It seemed the only thing to do at the time." She added quickly, "What's important is that I'm over it now and I'll be on my feet in no time. I had an attack last year while I was at Glenclaren and I was back at the mill the next day."

"An attack as bad as this?"

She shook her head. "But that doesn't mean I—" She stopped and asked wearily, "Why should it matter to you?"

"Because I—" He glanced away from her as he set the glass on the nightstand. "Because I need that railroad built."

He had been about to say something else, something completely different. She frowned in puzzlement. "We're only a few days behind schedule and this illness won't hold us up. Li Sung is very competent. I'll go back to the crossing tomorrow."

"The hell you will." His glance shifted swiftly back to her face, blue eyes blazing. "So you can collapse again the next day or the day after that? You'll stay here and rest for another week."

"The hell I will." She repeated his words. "You need that railroad built, and so do I. I can be sick some other time."

"And you will. That's what I'm saying, dammit. Rest now and you might—" He stopped as he saw her face. "All right, four days."

She shook her head.

"Four days and I'll bring Medford over here tomorrow afternoon to discuss the joining of the rails so that you won't feel the time's completely wasted."

She really did need to see Medford. She studied Ruel's determined expression and decided if she didn't compromise she would only have to spend the strength she needed for convalescence arguing with him. "Three days."

"Done." Ruel smiled.

She stared at him, startled. It was a real smile that lit his face with warmth and humor, the kind of smile she had received from him rarely even in those days before the train wreck. "Why are you—there's something different."

His lids immediately hooded his eyes. "Different?"

The impression of warmth was gone and Ruel was once more an enigma. Yet she was sure for a moment there had been something very odd in his demeanor.

"Go back to sleep." He stood up. "I'll go to the palace and send Tamar with a message for Medford. Satisfied?"

She was too bewildered and weak to be satisfied about anything. "I suppose I am."

He lingered, looking down at her. "It's going to be all right, you know," he said haltingly. "I'm not—" He stopped again and then made an impatient motion with his hand. "Oh, what the hell!" He whirled on his heel and strode out of the summerhouse.

She gazed blankly after him.

Something had definitely changed.

The covers shifted and a draft of cool air roused her from sleep. Warm flesh, the scent of leather and spice. Ruel was beside her.

"Ruel . . ."

"Shh." He drew her close, her back to him spoon-fashion. "Go back to sleep."

"Medford?"

"Four o'clock tomorrow." He stroked the hair tumbling over his arm. "How do you feel?"

She felt drained of strength but oddly content and safe in his arms. "Better."

His next words came with a strange awkwardness. "I thought about letting you sleep alone, but I want to be here if you dream again. It can't be good for you to toss and turn like that."

"Dream?"

"You don't remember?"

"No, how did you know I was dreaming?"

"I could hardly not be aware of it when you were screaming at the top of your lungs."

She felt a flicker of uneasiness at the knowledge that she had unknowingly exposed herself. "Screaming about what?"

He didn't answer for a moment. "I couldn't make out the words. None of it made sense."

Relief flooded her and she relaxed against him. "Naturally, nightmares never do."

"Go to sleep. You won't have any nightmares tonight."

She had an idea that he was right. Her eyes closed and she let the veils of sleep fall around her. She did not have to worry about anything. Ruel would keep the dragons of the night away. . . .

"That wraps it up." Medford rolled the maps and stood up. "If there are any changes, send someone to let me know. When do you think you'll reach the canyon wall?"

"On schedule." Jane made a face. "We're having trouble with a rogue elephant damaging the track, but we'll find a way to overcome the difficulty."

He smiled. "I believe you will. You've done a fine job."

She looked at him, surprised. "You think so?"

"It's early days yet," he qualified quickly. "But I've been impressed with the way you've proceeded so far. It's not what I expected of you."

"I was aware of that," she said dryly.

"But you've not let your liaison with Ruel affect your work. I was afraid after—" He stopped, grimacing. "I wasn't supposed to mention that."

"What?"

"Ruel said he'd tear out my tongue if I didn't keep our talk on a strictly business basis." He shrugged. "He should have known better. I'm not a man who hides what he thinks."

"I've noticed," she said, her mind on what he had said. Why had Ruel tried to protect her when he had not done so before?

"Time for you to go, Medford." Ruel stood in the doorway. "She has to rest now."

"I was just leaving." He nodded to Jane as he moved

hastily toward the door. "I hope you recover quickly, Miss Barnaby."

"Good day, Mr. Medford."

"He stayed too long." Ruel scowled as he closed the door behind the engineer. "I told him one hour. Did he tire you?"

"No," she said slowly. "But I'm confused."

"Fever?" He swore beneath his breath as he moved across the room. "That damn doctor said it shouldn't come back right away." He touched her forehead. "You don't feel hot."

"I don't have a fever." She turned her head to avoid his touch. "And I don't have to be ill to be bewildered about how you're treating me. Why are you being so kind to me?"

"No wonder you're confused. You haven't received an overabundance of the commodity from me, have you?" He smiled mockingly. "Pure self-interest. I need you well to build my railroad."

"I . . . don't think so."

He dropped down into the Louis XV chair in front of the window. "What other reason could there be?"

She wished she could see his face. He sat there, his legs indolently stretched before him, the sunlight forming an areola about his hair, his face in shadow. "I'm not sure, but I think it's because I became ill."

"Are you saying I pity you?"

"No." She was silent, trying to fit the pieces together. "I believe it's because you took care of me. Kartauk says some people are natural caretakers and the more they guard and protect, the stronger the obligation to keep on doing it."

"Oh, yes, he told me you were one of the caretakers of the world. I assure you I'm not so giving by nature."

"You gave to Ian."

"Ian is the exception."

"Is he?"

"I believe I've proved that during the last few days." He got to his feet. "I'm growing bored with all this searching of souls. Do you play poker?"

She nodded. "But I'm not as good as Li Sung."

"I didn't think you would be. Bluffing wouldn't come easily to you." He opened the drawer of the table next to him. "While I'm truly superb in the art."

"Then why should I play with you?"

"To pass the time." He sat down at the table and started to shuffle the deck. "And to give me a victory. I'm feeling in dire need of one."

"Then what satisfaction would I receive?"

He smiled. "I'm a running patterer, remember? I might be persuaded to give you the benefit of my skill to compensate. Sit down and I'll tell you how I found my first gold mine."

"Is it an interesting story?"

"At the time it was harrowing rather than interesting. I was nineteen and still had a few lessons to learn." He began to deal the cards. "But I'll make it entertaining for you."

She was sure he would do that. He would amuse and intrigue, cloaking the grimness of the tale in glittering eloquence, but perhaps she might catch glimpses of that younger, more vulnerable Ruel.

"Well?" Ruel picked up his cards.

She had never felt more confident or sure of her own strength of will than she had these past days. He could no longer hurt her, so why shouldn't she satisfy her curiosity about him?

"Why not?" She moved across the room toward him. "As you say, it will pass the time."

"Jane is with Ruel at the summerhouse," Margaret said as she watched Kartauk pack the sand around the mold of Ian's seal.

"Oh?" He raised a shaggy brow. "And is that troubling your stern Scottish morality?"

"No, though I suppose it should. I'm afraid he's going to hurt her."

"Leave them alone, Margaret. You can't save the world."

"Only a heathen does not try to change bad to good." She wearily shook her head. "But sometimes the lines become blurred, don't they?"

"Good God, I believe I detect a softening in that rigid backbone. Jane's not nearly so vulnerable as she used to be, and she and Ruel must play out what's between them in their own way and time. Neither of them would thank you for interfering."

"Ruel is—"

"Many things," Kartauk interrupted. "And will be many more before he is fully formed. It will be interesting to watch."

"You don't think he's wicked?"

"Ruel?" He shook his head. "I don't doubt he believes he is, but he doesn't know the meaning of wickedness."

"And you do?"

"Oh, yes, I studied under a master."

"Abdar?"

He nodded. "A true and complete monster."

It was the first time he had made more than a passing mention of Abdar. She asked curiously, "Then why did you stay so long with him?"

"My work was principally done for his father, the maharajah, and I had little to do with Abdar until the year before I left the palace. Then the maharajah became interested in his railroad and Abdar received permission to have my services put at his disposal." He shrugged. "After six months I decided I could stomach no more and departed."

"What work did you do for him?"

"I did a statue of his favorite goddess, Kali. It was quite a splendid effort."

"Kali?"

"The goddess of destruction. Abdar regards himself as her true son, sent to earth to do her work." His lips set grimly. "But he also believes that his power must be constantly fed. That's why he needed me."

"To create statues?"

"No." He paused. "Masks."

"Masks?"

"Masks of gold." He turned to look at her. "Are you sure you wish to hear this? It's not a pretty tale."

"Yes, go on."

"Abdar believes his power is strengthened by the emotion of those around him, and the stronger the soul, the more powerful emotion to feed on. But emotions are fleeting and Abdar grew more and more irritated. He decided he needed to stabilize the emotion, freeze it so that he could draw on it at any time." He lifted a brow. "And what better method to freeze an emotion than death?"

Her eyes widened in shock.

"You wanted to hear it. Abdar believed if he could capture that last tremendous burst of emotion and energy, he could draw it into himself."

"Death masks," she whispered. "He had you create death masks?"

"I did three for him. The first was of one of his concubines, a young woman named Mirad. Her body was brought to me early one morning by Pachtal, and I was told the woman had died during the night of a seizure and Abdar wished a mask in gold to remember her by. It had to be of gold because it was the purest and most immortal of metals. I made the mask. Actually, it turned out very well. The woman was beautiful and her expression sad but serene.

A week later Pachtal brought me another dead woman with the same story. This mask was much harder to do. The muscles of her face were twisted, frozen in an expression of pain and terror."

"Another death so soon?"

"I found it odd as well, but I didn't allow myself the indulgence of questioning him. The third body that was brought to me was that of a young boy no more than eleven or twelve, and his face—" His lips thinned. "I could lie to myself no longer. No sane man could want that face preserved for eternity. I refused to do the mask.

"An hour later Abdar paid me a visit and told me that I would make his masks and ask no questions or he would cut off my hands. I was to be the divine tool of Kali and create him masks with which to surround himself so that he could look on them and draw their energy into himself."

"He murdered them?" she whispered.

"Oh yes, with Pachtal's help. Pachtal experimented with various poisons to get the exact effect Abdar wanted. Abdar told me he had decided that pain gave the greatest explosion of energy, so he had Pachtal accommodate him with a poison that induced the required result."

She felt sick. "You're right. They are monsters. And Ruel believes Abdar will come here?"

He nodded. "That's why he's working so hard to be prepared for him. He wants to bring a final end to Abdar."

Her gaze searched his face. "That *is* why you came to Cinnidar, isn't it? You want Abdar killed too."

"I admit I think the world would be a brighter place without him. I'm tired of hiding my glorious light under a basket." He met her gaze. "But that's not why I came."

"Then why did—" She inhaled sharply. Another precipice. These days it seemed every word and gesture could become fraught with danger in the space of a heartbeat. It was a moment before she could look back down at the mold in the box. "When do we pour the gold?"

"Soon." He said slowly. "It's unwise to lack patience in these matters even when it's difficult to wait."

Ruel's gaze narrowed on Jane's face. "You're bluffing." He spread out his hand. "Two kings. Call."

Jane threw down her cards in disgust. "How did you know? I thought I was getting better."

"You are." He gathered up the cards. "No outward signs. If I hadn't known you, I might have been fooled."

"Then how did you know, blast it."

"Instinct. With some people you can sense their tension. It's nothing you can put your finger on."

Well, he could certainly sense her emotions, she thought ruefully. She had won only four games out of the many they had played in the past day and a half. It should have been an exasperating experience, and yet for some reason she had not found it so. "Instinct? You can't be that good. I probably twitched an eyebrow or something. I'll watch it next time. Deal."

He set the cards on the table. "Later. Time for your nap."

"I'm not tired. Deal."

"Later," he repeated. "Right now you rest."

"I'm well again," she protested. "I'm going back to work tomorrow."

"I've been thinking about that. You should have another week."

"Tomorrow," she repeated flatly. "And I'm not going to rest any—"

She stopped, startled, as a knock sounded on the door. No one came to the summerhouse except Tamar, who delivered their meals, and it was only midafternoon.

Ruel threw open the door to reveal Dilam standing on the doorstep.

Jane's heart lurched and she jumped to her feet. "What's wrong?" She moved quickly across the room. "Is Li Sung well?"

"Li Sung is in good health," Dilam said. "It is the elephant."

Jane muttered an imprecation. "How bad?"

"All went well. We finished the repairs and extended the tracks to a mile beyond the crossing. All that time Danor did not come."

"How *bad*?"

"We thought he had given it up. Then last night." She shrugged. "Three miles of track ruined. Li Sung was not pleased."

"Neither am I," Jane said grimly.

"Li Sung went after him."

She should have known Li Sung would react like this. Why the devil did he have such an obsession with the beast? "Alone?"

"It will come to that," Dilam said. "I sent him to the mine to see if any of the workers there would go with him, but I knew they would not."

"Then why send him there?"

"I needed time to get to you and tell you what he planned." Dilam frowned worriedly. "I do not think Danor will hurt him, but I do not—you will go after him, yes?"

"Yes. How much time do I have?"

"Li Sung will probably start after the elephant tonight or early tomorrow morning. He should have very little head start on you if you come at once."

"And just how does he think he's going to find this elephant," Ruel asked.

Dilam looked at him in surprise. "It is not difficult to track an elephant. They hardly creep unnoticed through the jungle."

That was true enough, Jane thought as she remembered the broken branches and uprooted trees that had marked Danor's path. "Go saddle my horse, Dilam. I'll meet you at the stable in fifteen minutes." She shut the door and moved across the room to the armoire. "Don't worry, this won't hold us up," she told Ruel. "Dilam will supervise the workers while Li Sung and I get rid of the elephant."

"If you don't have a relapse trying to track down Li Sung in that jungle," Ruel said grimly.

"I'm going after him."

"I'm not arguing with you. I didn't think you'd do anything else." Ruel strode toward the door. "Heaven forbid you take care of your own health when Li Sung wants to kill an elephant."

"May I point out that elephant is destroying your track?"

"He could also destroy—" Ruel stopped in midsentence as he opened the door. "I'll meet you at the stable. I have some affairs to tidy up here before I can leave."

"You're going back to the mountain?"

"Hell no, I'm going elephant hunting." The door slammed behind him.

"I'll make camp." Ruel lifted her off her horse and turned away. "Sit down somewhere before you fall down."

"I can help."

"Of course you can. You're white as a sheet and you've been reeling in the saddle for the last two miles," Ruel said sarcastically. "But you're fit as a fiddle."

She was too tired to argue with him. He had been moody and bad-tempered since they had left the palace the day before, and her nerves were as raw as his appeared to be. She collapsed on a fallen log beside the clearing and watched as he unsaddled the horses and began to gather wood for a fire.

Neither of them spoke until after they had eaten and Ruel was scraping the remains of the food on the plates into the fire. "You didn't eat much," he said curtly. "How do you expect to gain any strength if you starve yourself?"

"I had enough." She changed the subject. "I thought we'd have caught up with Li Sung by now."

"I thought so too. We traveled at a pretty good clip, so he has to be close. We're bound to catch up with him in the morning." He spread out their bedrolls on either side of the fire. "If he's not gone completely berserk and tries blundering through the jungle in the dark."

"Li Sung's not gone berserk."

"We're all mad. Why else are we in the middle of the jungle chasing a damn elephant?"

"You didn't have to come with me."

"Didn't I?"

"I would have been fine."

"I'm not doing it for you," he said jerkily. "I need that line finished before Abdar decides to pay us a visit."

"It will be finished."

"And the first shipment to the dock will probably be your corpse."

She had suddenly had enough. "Why should you care?" she flared at him. "Then you'll be free of me."

"Dammit, I'll *never* be free of you." He whirled and jerked her to her feet, his eyes glittering wildly in his set face. "God help me, I don't want to be free of you. I want you alive. I want you . . . Jesus, I want you with me for the rest of my life."

She stared at him, stunned.

"Stop looking at me like that. Do you think I like it, that I haven't been fighting it? But it's here, dammit, and I can't do anything about it."

She laughed shakily. "What a tender declaration. Don't worry, I'm sure it's only a temporary affliction and will soon go away."

"It's not gone away in three years. I think I knew in Kasanpore there was no escape, and now we've come full circle." His hands kneaded her shoulders with an odd yearning movement. "And sometimes there is . . . tenderness."

"Pity, you mean." She stepped back from him. "Caretaking."

"Caretaking? Those are your words. You scared the hell out of me. I thought I was going to lose you." His grip tightened. "I'm not going to lose you, Jane. Not ever."

She felt the panic rising. Everything had seemed so clear. She had been so sure of her ability to fight him and yet now she was experiencing a strange weakness and uncertainty. She must not let him sway her. "Lose me? You've never had me. You're never going to have me. I'm not such a fool that I'd let you come close to me after all that's gone between us."

"We're already close. We're so close we're almost a part of each other. You feel it and so do I. We're so close that we never really left each other even though you were oceans away."

The intensity of his emotion was reaching out to her, surrounding her, smothering her.

"No," she whispered.

"Yes." His finger reached out and gently touched the

plane of her cheek. "Oh yes, we have to have each other. We have to be together."

"Ian."

He went still. "I can work it out."

"Forgive? Forget?" She smiled sadly. "Not you, Ruel."

"I'll work it out," he repeated. "I have no choice."

"But I do have a choice." She turned away from him and moved toward her bedroll. "And I have no intention of letting myself be hurt by you again. Ever since we met you've manipulated me, pulled me to and fro to suit yourself, but it's finished now. When this is over I'm going to be free to live my life as I wish and you'll not be a part of it." She forced herself to glance at him over her shoulder. "I can't believe you'd think I'd want anything else."

"Then I'll have to change your mind, won't I?" One corner of his lips lifted in a sardonic smile. "Oh, I know it's not going to be easy after what I've done to you. I'll do what I can to smooth the way for both of us, but you'll have to work through it too."

Dear God, she had seen how determined and irresistible Ruel could be when he was focusing his attention on a goal. Now he wanted to focus that will on her for a lifetime instead of a few days of revenge. The mere idea terrified her. She wanted peace to live her own life as she saw fit. She settled down in her blankets and turned her back to him, trying to shut out his words, trying to shut him out.

"We could share one bedroll, you know," he said softly. "We'd probably both sleep better. We're used to each other now."

The truth of his words frightened her even more. They were used to each other's bodies, used to all the textures and scents and flavors, used to the rhythms of passion. They knew each other in the most erotic and seductive of intimacies. Yet there had been other moments in the past few days when their togetherness had taken on a gentler, even comfortable quality. He was no longer a dark secret to her, and that knowledge in itself was alluring. He was a battle she had fought and lost . . . and won.

"For God's sake, I'd only hold you. I'm not fool enough to think you're well enough to—" He broke off. "It would be a start."

She couldn't let it start. "No." She could feel his gaze on her back. She had been so relieved when she had thought herself free of him. Let him not say anything more. Let him not touch her.

With relief she heard him move toward his own bedroll and settle into the blankets. The silence was unbroken for several moments. Then he said in a low voice, "Think about it, Jane. If you're honest with yourself, you'll admit you don't have any choice either."

Her eyes were suddenly stinging with unshed tears. He had mentioned need and lust but not love. Not that she wanted him to love her, she told herself quickly. She knew that was as impossible for him as it was for her now. She was tired and not completely over her illness or she would not feel this sense of desolate loneliness and isolation. She would get over it. She mustn't answer him or let him come any closer.

She hoped he was wrong about her not having a choice. Of course he was wrong. He had to be wrong.

Chapter 18

They did not overtake Li Sung until late afternoon of the next day.

"Li Sung!"

Li Sung stiffened at Ruel's hail and then turned to confront them. The relief Jane felt immediately turned to concern. Li Sung's usually golden skin was parchment-pale, his mouth set in lines of strain, and his expression distinctly forbidding.

"You should not be here," he said.

"Neither should you," she said. "Are you ill? You look terrible."

"So do you." Li Sung smiled faintly. "And you are

the one who has been ill. I have merely been enduring the usual agonies inflicted when riding on this equine beast for too long."

Even a half-day's ride was painful to Li Sung, and he had been driving himself unmercifully for three days. She hid the pity the thought brought and said lightly, "It serves you right for going after the elephant without me."

He grimaced. "I did not trust you not to soften when I caught up with him. Your heart is too tender. I want to shoot him, not adopt him."

"You shouldn't have worried. He's not a dog or a cat, and he destroyed my tracks," Jane said. "Do you have any idea how far ahead he is?"

"Not far."

"How do you know?" Ruel asked. "Have you heard him?"

"No."

"Then how do you know?" Ruel persisted. "He could be angling back toward the crossing by another route."

"He is not." He gestured impatiently as Ruel opened his lips. "And I do not know why I am sure, but I am. I tell you, he is just ahead."

"I'm not arguing. I have a firm belief in instinct," Ruel said quietly. "If he's just ahead, then you won't mind stopping for the night. This clearing seems to be as good a place as any. We can fetch water from that pond we passed a quarter of a mile back."

Li Sung frowned. "It is still early. If I keep on the trail, I might be able to overtake him."

"And you might not." Ruel got off his horse. "And even if we do catch up with him, we might be too tired to be any threat."

Li Sung stiffened. "I am weary, not helpless."

"I wasn't talking about you." Ruel reached up and plucked Jane from the saddle. "Jane's been ill, remember?" He met her gaze warningly as she started to protest. "You may be able to drive yourself without collapsing, but you might think of someone else besides yourself."

"She should not have come."

"We're here," Ruel said flatly. "Deal with it."

Li Sung hesitated before nodding reluctantly. "Very well." He got off his horse and then had to grab the pommel of the saddle to steady himself as his stiffened legs threatened to give way.

Jane hastily averted her eyes from this betraying sign of weakness. "I'll gather the wood."

"I'll do it." Li Sung released the saddle. "Danor has left more than enough torn up trees in his wake to accommodate our needs." He limped toward the path left by the elephant.

"It was clever of you not to let Li Sung know it was him you were concerned about," she said in a low voice.

"Hell, I can't claim any great degree of cleverness. I only told the truth. I am worried about you." He turned away before she could speak. "I'll set up camp. You go after Li Sung and see if you can persuade him to stay here while I go after the elephant."

"Alone?" she asked, startled. "Don't tell me you were a hunter too at one time?"

He shook his head. "The only animals I ever hunted were the rats in the London sewers."

She vaguely remembered him telling her he had been a rat catcher that night at Zabrie's. "A rat is hardly in the same class as an elephant."

"The principle is the same. At least, I'm more qualified than you or Li Sung." He unfastened the girth of his saddle. "Go to him."

She stood there, watching him. The mere thought of him stalking that mad elephant alone sent panic racing through her.

"Go on," he repeated.

She hurriedly turned and followed Li Sung.

"This was very foolish of you," she said quietly as she fell into step with him. "I told you we'd find another solution."

He didn't answer her.

"You can't claim you're here to stop him from doing more damage. That's just an excuse. You just have some insane desire to destroy the elephant."

He didn't reply.

She had to say something to break through that wall of silence. "Ruel wants us to stay here while he goes after Danor."

"No!" Li Sung whirled to face her, his eyes blazing. "He's *mine*!"

Shock rippled through her. She had never seen Li Sung display such passion about anything. "I didn't say I'd let him do it. I just said he—"

"This is not your concern. Go back to the crossing."

"You're my concern. Just as I'd be your concern if I were the one running after that crazy elephant."

The emotion faded from his face, and he looked away from her. "You are right. I would feel the same."

"Then we go after him together."

He nodded reluctantly. "Very well."

They walked in silence for a moment.

"But you are wrong." His gaze went compulsively to the path Danor had made through the trees. "I am not running after Danor anymore."

She looked at him inquiringly.

"He is waiting."

"What?"

He whispered, "He is waiting for me."

"And what will you do when you catch up with him?" Ruel asked as he stirred the wood of the fire.

"Shoot him," Li Sung said.

"There can't be many vulnerable spots on an elephant."

"I'll aim for the eyes." Li Sung stared into the flames. "Dilam said that's the only way to assure a quick kill."

"You're not a wonderful shot," Jane pointed out. "And you may not get a second chance."

"I'll think about that when I find him."

"You're not thinking at all. You're just feeling."

"Perhaps." Li Sung's gaze lifted from his coffee. "But it is useless to try to dissuade me."

Jane had suspected this but she had to make the attempt. "I don't understand it. Why?"

"He tried to kill me."

"You're acting as if he set out to do it deliberately. He's an elephant, for God's sake."

Li Sung shrugged and didn't answer.

"That's it, isn't it?" Ruel asked suddenly. "It's because he *is* an elephant."

Li Sung stared at him impassively.

"Power," Ruel said softly, his gaze narrowed on Li Sung's face. "Tell me, are you going to eat his heart too?"

"What?"

"In Brazil I heard about the men of a tribe who ate the hearts of captured enemy warriors because they thought that by doing so they would absorb their foe's strength and courage."

"And you think I'm privy to such superstition?"

"Are you?"

"I am no fool. I realize that the only thing I'll win from killing Danor is revenge. Sometimes that is enough."

"And sometimes it isn't," Ruel said wearily.

"You surprise me." Li Sung smiled faintly. "I would have thought you would understand my feeling in this."

"Oh, I understand." Ruel glanced at Jane. "No one could understand revenge better than I do. Isn't that right, Jane?"

She sensed beneath the self-mockery in his voice an underlying pain that hurt her. She wanted to reach out and touch him, soothe him. She spoke hastily to Li Sung. "We'd better get some sleep if you intend to start out at first light. Why don't we—"

An elephant trumpeted in the darkness.

Li Sung sat upright, his gaze flying to the path leading west. "Close."

He was right, Jane thought, Danor must be very

close, but there had been a puzzling difference in the elephant's cry from the angry trumpeting she had heard that night at the track. It was as if—

Li Sung was on his feet, grabbing his rifle.

"Li Sung, wait until daylight," she said, alarmed. "If he's that close, a few more hours aren't going to make any difference."

"Now!" Li Sung slung a cartridge belt over his shoulder and limped from the campfire. "You wait until daylight. I don't need you."

"The hell we will." Ruel was already extinguishing the fire. "Can't you at least wait until we saddle up?"

"No need." Li Sung's words trailed behind him as the jungle closed around him. "He's close. . . ."

Jane jumped to her feet and ran after Li Sung.

She heard Ruel call her name but she paid no attention.

The elephant trumpeted again. Beckoning. Calling.

Calling Li Sung toward destruction.

"Blast it, Li Sung, wait for me!" Jane called to the shadowy figure stalking ahead.

"Save your breath." Ruel pulled aside a thorny shrub to let her pass. "There's no stopping him. Just try to keep up."

How could Li Sung travel so fast with his crippled leg? He was moving through the jungle at almost a run.

The elephant trumpeted again, closer.

Alarm, uneasiness, and bewilderment tumbled through her. There was something in that cry that bothered her. Of course it bothered her, she thought impatiently. The blasted elephant was drawing Li Sung into danger. "Li Sung!"

Li Sung must have decided to heed her plea to wait, she saw with relief. He had stopped a few hundred yards ahead of them. Then, as they drew closer, she saw he was staring straight ahead, his body peculiarly rigid.

"Is it the elephant? Be care—" She stopped as she

and Ruel came abreast of him and she saw what had startled him.

Skeletons.

Gleaming white bones everywhere, covering the vast clearing before them in a macabre blanket. The moon had gone behind a cloud, but the skeletons seemed to give off a chilling shimmer of their own in the darkness.

"What is it?" she whispered.

"An elephant graveyard," Li Sung said. "That must be why they make the trek west."

"I don't understand."

"Dilam said that when an elephant senses he is going to die, sometimes he travels many miles to a place of death." Li Sung's gaze traveled over the bone-littered landscape. "This appears to be such a place."

Jane shivered. "It certainly does."

"But why did Danor come here?" Ruel asked thoughtfully.

Li Sung moved his shoulders as if shaking off the oppressiveness of the sight before him. "How do I know?" He smiled grimly. "Perhaps he senses I'm going to kill him."

The trumpeting sounded again and Jane's gaze flew across the graveyard. At the edge of the trees she could barely discern the massive figure of the elephant, his trunk lifted.

Li Sung made a low sound of satisfaction and started across the bone-strewn clearing.

Jane and Ruel followed quickly, but Li Sung had already reached the middle of the graveyard by the time they caught up with him.

The elephant stood watching them approach.

"Why isn't he charging?" Jane murmured, remembering the elephant's bloodshot eyes and thundering attack at sight of them at the crossing.

"I'd just as soon he refrained," Ruel said dryly.

Li Sung had come within range of the elephant. He lifted the rifle and sighted down the barrel.

The elephant did not move.

The moon came from behind the clouds and lit both the clearing and Danor's face with pale clarity.

"Wait!" Jane grabbed Li Sung's arm. "There's something—"

"Let me go." Li Sung tried to shake her off.

"No, not yet. I see something . . ." She ran ahead of him toward the elephant.

"Jane!" Ruel called.

"He's not going to hurt me. Can't you see . . ." She stopped only a dozen yards from the elephant, making sure she was in Li Sung's line of fire. "Don't shoot him, Li Sung."

"Get out of my way, Jane."

"Come here," Jane called, her stare never leaving Danor. She had been right, the moonlight revealed something damp and shimmering on the elephant's face.

"So he can try to trample me again?"

Ruel reached her side. "Dammit, Jane, do you want to get killed? Why the hell do you—"

"Shh!" She pointed to a shadowy bulk on the ground to the left of Danor. "I think he's . . . isn't that . . ."

"Another elephant." Ruel moved cautiously forward, keeping a wary eye on Danor. "Stay behind me. I'll take a look."

Danor lifted his trunk and trumpeted again, this time in warning.

Ruel stopped in his tracks. "I don't believe I'll go any farther. He doesn't appear to like me."

"He doesn't like anyone in this world." Li Sung limped toward them, the rifle cradled in readiness in the crook of his arm. "And if you'll step out of the way, I'll send him out of it."

"He's not going to hurt anyone," Jane said. "I think he's only protecting— Can't you see? He's *weeping*, Li Sung."

"Nonsense."

"You're not even looking at him. I tell you, he's mourning." Jane pointed to the fallen elephant. "We've got to see if there's anything we can do to help."

"After I kill Danor, we'll look at the other elephant."

"Stop it!" Jane said in exasperation. "You don't have to kill him now."

"Necessity doesn't always coincide with desire." He lifted the rifle.

Jane started toward the elephant. "I said no."

Danor shifted back and forth, turning on her threateningly.

Ruel reached out and grabbed her arm. "He doesn't like you either. How ungrateful when you're the only one determined to save him."

An explosive sound came from Li Sung as he moved ahead of them toward the elephant. "I knew I should not have let you come with me. Must you be shown how vicious he is?" He strode toward the elephant, the rifle in readiness. "Come after me now, elephant."

Danor stood unmoving, his stare on Li Sung. Another tear rolled down his leathery face before he slowly lowered his trunk to the head of the fallen elephant and began tugging as if trying to lift the beast to its feet.

Li Sung stopped in back of the fallen elephant, staring in frustration and challenge at Danor across the animal's body.

"Is the elephant dead?" Jane called.

Li Sung glanced down at the elephant. "I don't know." He reached out and touched the leathery hide. "Warm. Perhaps not."

"Then why was Danor trumpeting?" Jane edged closer. "Is it a female?"

"Yes."

"Then she must be his mate."

"Possibly." Li Sung scowled. "And now I suppose you're feeling so soft-hearted toward him you're going to let him tear up the rest of the railroad to assuage his grief."

"I didn't say that. But we have to help her if we can. We can't let—" She stopped as Danor's head lifted and he fixed his gaze on her. "You'll have to see if there's anything we can do. He's not going to let anyone but you near him."

"Which shows how stupid he is. He does not know

an enemy when he sees one." Li Sung moved around the fallen elephant. "The female is dead. Her eyes are open and—" He stopped in midsentence.

"What is it?" Jane called.

"A baby."

"What?"

"You heard me." Li Sung took another step closer, his gaze on something obscured by the female's bulk. "It's a baby elephant."

"Alive?" Ruel asked.

Li Sung nodded. "He's trying to nurse."

"How old?"

"How do I know?" Li Sung asked testily. "A few days, I suppose."

"I want to see him," Jane said.

"Of course you do. Another helpless creature for you to cosset," Li Sung said caustically. "This is not a stray puppy, Jane."

"I want to see him," Jane repeated. "Danor seems to accept you. Come back and take Ruel's and my hands and lead us to the female."

"Then I could not hold the rifle."

"You won't need the rifle," Jane said in exasperation. "Look at him. It's enough to break your heart."

"I'll carry the rifle," Ruel said. "You'd better do as she says, Li Sung. She's going to go over there anyway."

Li Sung moved toward them. "I know." He surrendered the rifle to Ruel, clasped both of their hands, and led them toward the elephants. "Now he'll probably trample all of us into the rest of these bones."

"Hush, Li Sung." Jane tensed as Danor lifted his head and stared at the three of them. No anger, she saw only overwhelming sadness, resignation . . . and acceptance.

Then the elephant lowered his head and resumed poking and prodding his fallen mate, urging her to rise to her feet.

"I think it's going to be all right." Jane moved around the female's body.

The baby elephant was lying with his legs outspread, nuzzling his mother's teat.

Jane felt the tears sting her eyes. "Poor baby."

"No!" Li Sung said sharply. "No, Jane."

"We can't let him die."

"We can't save him. He needs milk to survive and his mother is dead. Who is going to nurse him?" Li Sung's gaze went to the bones of the graveyard. "One of those?"

"If we can get him back to the herd, maybe one of the females will adopt him."

"The herd could be a hundred miles to the east."

"Then we'd better start right away."

"And how are we going to find the herd?"

Jane gestured to Danor.

"You think he's going to lead us to the herd like a horse going back to his stable?"

"Dilam said he had superior intelligence." Her brows knitted thoughtfully. "It could be that's why he tore up the tracks."

"He tore up the tracks because it pleased him to do so."

She shook her head. "Maybe he wanted us to follow him. Perhaps he knew he couldn't save his mate but he wanted to give the baby a chance. We've got to give him that chance."

"No," Li Sung said flatly.

"Yes," Ruel said.

Li Sung swung to face him. "You agree with this madness?"

"She wants it done." Ruel shrugged. "So we do it."

Jane looked at him in surprise.

He smiled as he studied her face. "I told you I'd work on it," he said softly. "I have to start somewhere."

She tore her gaze away from him. "Li Sung, you'll have to get the baby away from the mother. I'm not sure Danor would let us do it." She started back across the graveyard. "I'll go back to camp and pack up. Ruel, you stay with Li Sung. He may need help."

"Yes, ma'am," Ruel said meekly.

• • •

An hour later Li Sung and Ruel appeared at camp, driving before them the tiny elephant. The baby was only three feet high, tottering and weaving uncertainly with every step. He was big-eyed, clumsy, and totally endearing.

"Did you have any trouble?" she asked Ruel.

"Not with Danor. He let Li Sung do whatever he wished with the baby." He made a face and nodded toward the elephant. "But we had trouble convincing this little fellow to leave his mother, and it's not easy to shift a hundred-and-fifty-pound infant anywhere he doesn't want to go."

"Where's Danor?"

"Still trying to wake her," Ruel said. "We may have to find the herd on our own."

"He's so sweet." Jane reached out and gently caressed the baby's trunk. "We'll have to give him a name."

"Why?" Li Sung asked. "So you'll have a name to mourn him by when he dies?"

"He's not going to die." The elephant curled his trunk about her wrist. "I've always liked the name Caleb. We'll call him Caleb."

Li Sung made a noise somewhere between a grunt and a snort.

The elephant released her wrist and started to totter toward her.

Jane's brow knitted worriedly. "He doesn't seem too steady on his feet."

"He's weak." Ruel said. "There's no telling how much milk the mother was able to give him before she died."

"What can we feed him, Li Sung?"

Li Sung looked at her without speaking.

"Li Sung?" she prompted.

"He will die anyway."

"We don't know that. Tell me what to feed him."

"Water or milk," Li Sung said reluctantly. "He's probably too young for anything else."

Caleb's legs gave out, and he fell in a heap to the ground. Jane felt a melting tenderness as she looked at the helpless baby.

In spite of his disapproval, Li Sung appeared to be similarly affected. "He needs milk, but perhaps water will help ease his hunger. I will go to the pond and get some." He snatched a canteen from the saddle and stalked off down the path.

"It isn't like Li Sung to be so hard," Jane murmured as she stared after him. "I don't understand him."

"I do," Ruel said. "He feels cheated. He was braced for a warrior's battle and now he finds himself acting as nursemaid to his foe's offspring. It's not easy for him to accept."

"Danor doesn't think of him as a foe."

"He can't accept that either." He started down the path. "Stay by the fire and don't let Caleb wander off. I'll be right back."

"What are you going to do?"

"He's not going to be able to walk long. I'm going to find some branches to use as poles and fashion a stretcher I can fasten to my saddle and drag him behind."

"Ruel."

He glanced over his shoulder.

She reached out and gently touched the baby elephant's trunk. "He *is* going to live, isn't he?"

"You want him to live, he'll live," Ruel stated unequivocally. He strode out of view into the shrubbery.

It was absurd to feel this rush of relief at his words. Yet the mandarin had spoken, and if he had been capable of jerking Ian back from the gates of death, why not this big, clumsy baby?

Nugget made no protest when Ruel attached the two poles to the saddle but went into a bucking fit when Caleb was placed on the stretcher close to his hindquarters. Li Sung's horse and Bedelia had a similar reaction when Ruel tried to attach the stretcher to their saddles.

Ruel swore beneath his breath. "Dammit, I didn't need this."

"What do you expect when you try to put an elephant and a horse in tandem?" Li Sung asked.

Jane frowned worriedly. "What can we do?" Caleb would never be able to make the trip on foot, when he could stand on his feet for only short periods before collapsing.

"We don't seem to have any choice," Ruel said grimly. He unfastened the poles from Bedelia's saddle and began forming a harness with a rope. "You'll have to lead Nugget and I'll be the beast of burden."

"Much as I approve the benefit to your character of such a humbling experience, may I remind you he weighs over a hundred and fifty pounds?" Li Sung said.

"And I'm sure I'll feel every pound before we stop for the night." Ruel slipped the harness over his shoulders. "Let's go."

"Wait." Jane took two shirts from her saddlebag and crossed to Ruel to tuck them under the harness to protect his shoulders from the ropes. "I'm afraid they won't help much, dragging that kind of weight."

He smiled. "Thank you."

"I'm not the one dragging Caleb through the jungle." She got back on Bedelia. "Tell us when you need to stop and rest."

"Don't worry." He made a face as he lurched forward. "I assure you I will."

They stopped to rest twice during the night but did not make camp until just before dawn. Jane reined in at a small clearing near a stream and got down off her horse.

"Li Sung, grab two canteens and get some more water for Caleb while I make a fire."

"I live only to serve," Li Sung said sarcastically as he took the canteens and moved stiffly toward the stream. "Now I am water bearer for an elephant."

"And what task am I assigned, memsahib?" Ruel asked.

"Li Sung and I can do anything that needs doing," she said as she began gathering wood from the side of the path. "Sit down and rest."

"Am I being pampered? How unusual."

"It's hardly pampering to let you rest after you spent the last six hours dragging an elephant behind you."

"I won't argue." He unfastened his harness and sat down on the ground beside Caleb's stretcher. "Pamper me."

Weariness layered the usual mockery in his tone. She turned to look at him, but it was too dark to see his expression. He was only a shadow figure hunched beside Caleb's stretcher. "Did the pads help to cushion the ropes?"

"Well enough." He changed the subject. "We'll have to replace this blanket I stretched over these poles before long. It's wearing thin."

"I'll give you one of mine before we start again." She knelt beside the pile of wood and kindling and lit the fire before glancing over her shoulder. "It's a wonder it lasted this long, pulled over that rough ground with Caleb on—"

There was blood on Ruel's shirt.

She jumped to her feet and hurried to his side. His face was pale in the firelight, his lips set with strain. "I thought you said the pads helped. You lied to me."

He shrugged. "They did as good a job as could be expected."

She fell to her knees beside him and started to unbutton his shirt. "We'll have to double them tomorrow." She unbuttoned his shirt. "And I can help. I can take one pole and help pull."

"You're still weak from that damn fever. I'll manage alone."

"Don't be foolish. I'm getting stronger every day, and there's no reason why I can't—" She broke off as she pulled the shirt off his shoulders and saw the ugly chafing caused by the ropes. His right shoulder was crisscrossed with angry red marks, the flesh cut and bleeding across the collarbone. She whispered, "Good God, this must have been terribly painful."

"It wasn't pleasant."

"You should have told me."

"So that you could weep over me as you did over Caleb?" He smiled. "Doesn't it touch your heart that I've shed my blood for your sake?"

"Don't joke," she said huskily. She fetched a canteen and handkerchief from her saddlebag, knelt again beside him, and began to wash the lacerated flesh. "Why do you always have to joke?"

"To show what a brave and stalwart specimen I am. I understand it's considered the thing to do."

Her hand was shaking and she had to steady it before starting to wrap the cloth around his shoulder. "We'll have to think of another way to help Caleb. You can't go on like this."

"Yes, I can. I can do anything I have to do."

"It was my decision to bring Caleb. I can't let you suffer because—"

"I'm going to do it, Jane."

"Why?"

"Because then you'll know that every drop of blood I shed is for your sake." He held her gaze. "And every time you care for my wounds, it will bind you closer to me."

"What are you talking about?"

"You said it yourself, Jane. You're a caretaker." He looked down at her hands binding the bandage at his shoulder. "And when you take care of someone, they belong to you. I want to belong to you."

She stared at him in disbelief.

A sudden smile lit his face as he glanced at Caleb. "Besides, I like this little fellow. I'd do it even if I weren't courting you."

"Courting?" That word brought a rush of memories of that night on the veranda in Kasanpore. "We can't go back," she said stiltedly.

"I don't want to go back. I want a new start."

"We can't do that either." She finished tying the bandage and glanced at his left shoulder. The halter hadn't damaged it as much as the other, but he should have stopped long before this. His shoulders were rope-burned almost as badly as they had been after he had come up the slope from Lanpur Gorge dragging Ian behind him. No, that wasn't true, she recalled. His flesh had been in bloody rags then and she had—

"What's the matter?" Ruel's gaze was on her face. "What the hell is wrong now?"

"The halter," she whispered. "I just remembered Lanpur Gorge."

For a minute his expression hardened before he forced a smile. "You can't go back," he repeated her words. "So stop thinking about it."

She shook her head. "It's not possible."

"Everything is possible." He glanced at Caleb. "What were his chances of living two days ago?"

"Not much better than now." Li Sung came toward them, carrying the canteens. "I see he marked you. Truly his father's child." In spite of his harsh words, both his hands and expression were gentle as he knelt beside the baby and gently poured water into Caleb's mouth. "No doubt he will also grow into a killer rogue."

Jane was too weary and shaken to argue with Li Sung. And if she was weary, what must Ruel feel like? "Go to sleep," she told both of them as she went to her own blankets by the fire.

"I believe I'll do that." Ruel stretched out next to Caleb on the blanket and closed his eyes.

Jane frowned. "You can't sleep there."

"Watch me." He closed his eyes. "Too tired to move . . ."

"I'll make up your blankets for you."

"I'm fine . . ." He turned on his side. "Four hours. No more. We can't afford the time. We have to get Caleb to . . ." He trailed off, and Jane realized he had fallen into an exhausted sleep.

Li Sung soon followed him in slumber, but she lay there unable to sleep in spite of her weariness. Ruel's words and actions had thrown her into a turmoil of emotion—worry, tenderness, admiration, and a multitude of other fragmented feelings too dangerous to examine closely. Just when she had thought herself free of the mandarin, he had changed and become a man, a vulnerable man whom she was beginning to find . . . lovable.

Dear God, what was she doing searching her soul when she should be sleeping? she thought impatiently. She huddled down in her blankets and closed her eyes. The heat from the fire felt warm and soothing, the crackling of the logs a cozy song in the darkness.

But an early morning chill lingered in the air.

Ruel was several yards distant from the fire.

She got to her feet, grabbed one of her blankets, and marched over to where Ruel and Caleb were lying. Ruel was sleeping soundly, but Caleb opened his glowing eyes as she tucked the blanket over Ruel. The baby elephant's trunk lifted to touch her cheek. "Shh." She patted his head, got to her feet, and went back to her blanket by the fire.

Caretaker.

Well, what if she was? There was nothing wrong with sharing a blanket with someone who had sacrificed so much for her sake. Nothing wrong at all.

The crashing of shrubbery woke Jane, Ruel, and Li Sung from sleep on the second night of their trek back to the crossing. Jane opened her eyes to see Danor standing, looking at them from the edge of the trees. His eyes glittered in the campfire, and she had an uneasy memory of that moment on the tracks when she had thought the elephant a mad rogue.

Fear vanished as she saw Danor come slowly forward to stand over the stretcher by the fire where the baby elephant lay. His trunk curled around Caleb's neck and then began probing gently, inquiringly, at his body as he had at that of his dead mate's.

The baby was too weak now to do more than raise

his head, his trunk seeking and then locking with Danor's.

The sight was inexpressibly touching, and Jane felt the tears burn her lids.

Then Danor disentangled his trunk, backed away, and lumbered past the fire and into the jungle.

Li Sung said sourly, "He disturbs our sleep and then leaves it to us to care for his child. We will probably not see him again."

"He went in the direction of the crossing," Ruel pointed out.

"So he's rejoining the herd. That does not mean we will see him again." Li Sung lay down again and closed his eyes. "Which will be the most fortuitous circumstance occurring since we arrived in Cinnidar."

Jane shook her head in resignation as she pulled her blanket around her shoulders. She had never seen Li Sung as stubborn as he was being about the bull elephant. He was wrong. She knew Danor had been concerned about the baby.

He was not the only one concerned. Her gaze went to the baby elephant. He was growing weaker. They had been feeding him water to assuage his hunger, but how long could he live without nourishment?

"He'll live."

She turned to see Ruel's gaze on her face.

"Will he?" she whispered. "Even if we reach the herd in time to save him, we might not find a nursing cow who will accept him."

"Then I'll ride up to the Cinnidar village and bring back some goats for milking."

In spite of her concern, she had to chuckle at the unlikely thought of Ruel as shepherd. "It would take an entire herd to feed him."

"Then I'll bring a herd."

Her laughter faded as she met his gaze. She had no doubt he would do it. His patience and determination in caring for Caleb had been a great comfort to her in the past two days. "You may have to."

"Will you please cease your chatter?" Li Sung asked.

"It is enough that Danor has burdened us with his offspring, you do not have to talk about him all night."

"Do you like it?" Margaret's eager gaze searched Ian's face. "I couldn't manage the Glenclaren coat of arms, so I just settled for your initials and a stalk of heather."

"It's very fine." Ian gently touched the gold seal with his index finger. "And just what I wanted. A coat of arms would have been much too grand for me."

"Nothing's too grand for you." She sat down on the stool beside his chair. "Are you not the laird? I had to do it twice. I ruined the first one. Naturally, that heathen Kartauk didn't have the courtesy to tell me I was erring and made me do the entire process over. He said you always learn better from your mistakes."

"That sounds like Kartauk. He always believes in drinking deep of every experience regardless of later regrets."

"Not every experience."

A note in Margaret's voice caused Ian to lift his gaze to her face and found to his surprise that a flush had risen to her cheeks.

"I mean, he's not as heedless as you might think," she said quickly.

"No?"

"His work—" She stopped and then rushed on. "He's very careful. . . ." She jumped to her feet. "It's time for your supper. I'll go tell Tamar."

"I'm not hungry yet."

"You will be. You must eat."

"Margaret."

She stopped at the door, her spine rigid. "Yes."

"Ask Kartauk to join us for supper."

She did not turn around. "Why?"

Fear. She was afraid. His Margaret, who feared nothing and no one, was afraid.

"I need to sharpen my chess game, and he has not supped with us for a long time. I miss his company."

He could see the muscles of her back ease. "He's been busy."

"He can spare one evening." He kept his voice carefully light. "I wish to thank him for helping you fashion my fine seal."

"I will tell him but I cannot promise he will come."

"Shall I write him a note?"

"No!" She turned to face him. "You really wish to see him?"

"One always wishes to see a good friend," he said quietly. "And it's been too long, Margaret."

"Very well, I'll see that he joins us." She turned on her heel and left the chamber.

His smile faded and he leaned back, closed his eyes, and let the pain wash over him.

God in heaven, why could you not have been merciful? Margaret did not need this additional cross to bear.

Perhaps he was wrong. Perhaps it was not true.

He would know when he saw them together.

"Tamar, will you fetch another bottle of wine?" Ian made a face before glancing down at the chess board again. "This vintage doesn't please me."

"Certainly, Samir Ian." Tamar instantly moved toward the door. "I regret I failed you in this. Perhaps whiskey instead? I know you like that better."

"You know he can't have whiskey, Tamar," Margaret said. "The doctor said he was to drink nothing stronger than wine."

"He should not have forbidden him whiskey, if that is what he likes," Tamar said with a frown. "Whiskey, Samir Ian?"

"This wine tastes fine to me," Kartauk said.

"If Samir Ian says the wine is bad, it is bad," Tamar said with a touch of belligerence.

"Just another bottle of wine, Tamar," Ian said quickly.

Kartauk chuckled as the door closed behind the servant. "Good God, I see what you mean, Margaret. Is he always this obliging, Ian?"

"Always." Ian smiled faintly. "The Cinnidans are so robust themselves, they have a horror of ill health. Tamar would have drowned himself in the sea before he would have become the crock I am. He sees no reason to deny me any pleasure just to prolong my life."

Margaret frowned. "You're not a crock and he should not have offered you—"

"He meant only to make me happy," Ian interrupted. He changed the subject. "Margaret has been raving about your workmanship on Ruel's seal, but I cannot believe it finer than mine, Kartauk." Ian moved his knight on the board. "An elephant is all very well, but it lacks a certain dignity."

"Are you saying the apprentice is more talented than the master?" Kartauk looked up from the chess board with a grin. "Blasphemy."

"I'm saying I should judge for myself. Let me see Ruel's wondrous seal."

"Now?"

Ian nodded. "I'm tormented by curiosity. I must see it."

"Then I'll go fetch it from the studio." Kartauk started to get up from his chair. "It will take only a minute."

"No, not you." Ian turned to Margaret. "Would you go and fetch it, love? I plan on checkmating this rascal within the next few moves."

"If you wish." She moved immediately toward the door. "Though you'll be disappointed. My work is a mere dabble compared to Kartauk's."

"You never disappoint me, Margaret."

The chamber was silent for a time after the door closed behind her.

"Well, you've gotten rid of both of them," Kartauk commented as he moved his queen. "Why did you want Margaret gone?"

He should have known Kartauk would realize the seal was only a ploy, Ian thought with relief. Thank God

Kartauk's bluntness was equaled by his perceptiveness. "She was uneasy. It was an uncomfortable evening for her, poor lass."

"Was it?"

"You know it was." He kept his gaze on the chess board, but he could sense Kartauk's wariness. "Which is why I will not ask you to come here again."

"Why did you ask me tonight?"

"I had to know. I had to be certain."

Kartauk's sudden tension was so well masked as to have been imperceptible if Ian had not been watching for it. "Certain about what?"

Ian hesitated, searching for words. "I don't mind for myself, you know. Oh, at first there was a sting. I've loved her all my life and gotten used to thinking of her as mine. I remember walking up that hill beyond the castle with her when she was only a lass of ten and thinking, all of our life is going to be like this. All of our life we'll be together. Such happy times . . ." He trailed off and then smiled with an effort. "But those times are over, aren't they? And I'd be a true dog in the manger to blame anyone but fate and myself for their passing. Margaret didn't leave me; I've been the one leaving her these last years."

Kartauk was silent for a moment. "I suppose I should deny it."

"No lies," Ian said. "Please, no lies. We have no time for them."

"No lies." Kartauk was silent again before he said haltingly, "I did not want to love her, but I do not regret it."

"You should not," Ian said gently. "Love is rare and beautiful. It enriches life."

"Margaret has never been unfaithful to you." Kartauk shrugged. "I am not like you. I do not think any pleasure is a sin. There was a time . . . but it never happened."

"I know, and it never will." Ian raised his gaze from the board. "It's only fair you realize that truth. She may love you but she will never leave me until the day I die."

He grimaced. "And I can't even promise to do that with any great dispatch. I cannot bring myself to commit a mortal sin by taking my own life, or I would have been out of the way long ago."

"No one wants you out of the way," Kartauk said gruffly.

"No one but me." Ian smiled sadly. "I pray for it every night but I'm never taken." He went on brusquely. "But that is neither here nor there. The important thing is to keep Margaret as content as possible."

"You wish me to leave Cinnidar?"

"Of course not. I would not deprive Margaret of your company. You will continue to keep her amused and busy, to protect her and love her as you are doing right now. However, I must deprive myself. She is so guilt-ridden, it's clearly a torment for her to see us in the same room." He met Kartauk's gaze. "And she must never know we've had this talk. You agree?"

"I agree." Kartauk nodded slowly. He blinked rapidly and looked down at the chess board. "You're a fine man, Ian MacClaren, and stronger than I would be in the same situation."

"Strong? I don't feel strong." He leaned wearily back on his pillows. "I'm just trying to do what needs to be done to help us all survive. I can't let Margaret suffer any more than she—" His gaze flew to the door. "She's coming." He quickly moved his bishop and then looked up with a smile as Margaret walked into the room. "You've been very quick. I still haven't defeated him. Come here and let me see the seal."

She handed him Ruel's gold seal and stood beside him as he examined it. "I told you it was much better."

"It's quite splendid." Ian put it beside his own seal on the bed. He lifted her hand and pressed his lips to her palm. "But I prefer the one you made for me. Ruel may have his elephants. My stalk of heather reminds me of Glenclaren."

Chapter 19

Dilam came to meet them when they were only two miles from the encampment at the crossing. Jane was immediately alarmed. "What's wrong?"

Dilam smiled. "Nothing. The work goes well."

"Then why are you here?"

"Curiosity. I wondered . . ." Her gaze went to the baby elephant on the stretcher. "Ah, I see. Danor's?"

"Yes. The mother is dead. The baby will be, too, if we don't find a way to feed him."

"I think you will find such a way." She looked at

Li Sung. "It was wise of you to send Danor on ahead."

"I sent that fiend nowhere," Li Sung said curtly.

"Ahead?" Jane asked, puzzled.

"You will see." Dilam turned her horse and led them toward the encampment. Fifteen minutes later they emerged from the jungle at the crossing.

"What the—" Jane reined in Bedelia, her eyes widening in shock.

Elephants! Hundreds of elephants—bulls, cows, babies—milling around the glade.

"Good heavens," she murmured weakly.

"They came at dawn," Dilam said. "We were startled."

"I can imagine."

Ruel's gaze searched the herd. "I don't see Danor."

"He is there." Li Sung pointed impatiently. "How can you miss him? With that tattered ear he stands out like Satan in a crowd of angels."

Dilam's brows lifted in surprise. "You are still fighting the *makhol?* You are even more stubborn than I thought."

"*Makhol?*" Jane asked.

"It's only foolishness," Li Sung said quickly. "The herd is here. Now, how are we going to rid ourselves of this baby and get on with our work?"

"Danor seems to have the situation under control so far. Why don't we see what he can do?" Ruel got down from his horse and unfastened the branches that formed the support for the stretcher. "Come on, Li Sung, let's pull the stretcher out into the middle of the herd and see what happens."

"What will happen is that we'll both be trampled by the beasts." Li Sung got off his horse. "At least, I will be trampled. You can run faster than me."

"I'll do it," Jane offered.

"No!" Li Sung said sharply. "It is my—" He stopped and shook his head. "Madness."

Jane wasn't sure he wasn't right as she watched Ruel and Li Sung each take one of the poles and drag the baby elephant into the center of the herd. The two men appeared pitifully small and weak surrounded by the huge beasts, and the elephants clearly didn't appreciate the intrusion.

The elephants were closing around them!

Her hands grasped nervously at her reins as the two men were suddenly lost to view.

"Be at ease," Dilam said softly. "Look, Danor."

Danor was edging forward, shouldering aside the other elephants until a narrow path was formed which allowed Li Sung and Ruel to slip through the herd.

Jane breathed a sigh of relief when the two men finally made it to the edge of the glade. "Caleb?"

"I don't know," Ruel said. "We'll have to see what happens. I saw at least four nursing cows among the herd, but they didn't seem very interested in adopting an orphan. Even if they'd stand still for it, I don't think the baby has the strength to get on his feet to nurse." He grimaced ruefully. "I may still have to go after the goats."

"I wish they'd move so I could see." Jane had a sudden horrible thought. "What if they step on him? He can't get up. They'll kill him!"

"Elephants usually take care of their own," Dilam said soothingly. "And Danor is there."

Jane's worried gaze searched the milling elephants. She couldn't see either Danor or the baby. "There are so many of them and . . ." Then a large bull blocking her vision wandered off toward the trees and she caught a glimpse of a small familiar figure in the center of the herd.

The baby was nursing!

Caleb was standing, suckling hungrily at the teat of a small gray-brown female. His legs were obviously wobbly, but he was supported by the trunks of Danor and another female elephant.

"It's going to be all right." Her face was alight with joy as she turned to Ruel. "He's going to live."

He smiled, his gaze lingering on her face. "And I don't have to turn goat tender after all. What a relief.

I'm sure it would have been disastrous to my consequence."

"If we're through acting nursemaid to this elephant, maybe we can get back to work," Li Sung said. "We have track to lay while there's still light."

Dilam nodded. "We can complete another quarter of a mile before dusk." She turned to Ruel. "Tamar is at the encampment. He came with a message from James Medford."

Ruel frowned. "Why didn't you tell me?"

"You were busy. And this appeared of more importance."

"Elephants are always more important to her than humans," Li Sung said caustically.

"I'll go with you," Jane told Ruel. She turned to Li Sung. "I'll be with you as soon as we see what Medford has to say."

"I do not have to be guarded and nurtured like your precious elephant." He tore his gaze from Danor and the baby and got back on his horse. "I will see you back at camp at supper. If fortune is with us, all those elephants will have moved back where they came from by then."

"Something's wrong," Jane said as she saw Ruel's expression when he came toward her after speaking to Tamar. "Is it the railroad? Does Medford have a problem?"

"No, but we may have more problems than we can handle. Medford just got a message from Pickering. The maharajah is dead."

"No! So soon?"

"Pickering suspects Abdar may have hastened his demise, but it's not wise to suggest that possibility with Abdar in power."

"He'll start for here immediately?"

Ruel shook his head. "There's a three-month period of mourning before Abdar ascends the throne. Until that time he has no more power than he had before. We may even have a month or two grace after that before he turns his attention in our direction, but we can't count on it."

"Three months," Jane muttered. "I can't possibly complete the line in that time."

"It's got to be done in two," Ruel said flatly. "I'll need the extra month for shipping the gold and fortifying the harbor."

"Impossible."

"It's got to be done. Medford's almost finished his portion of the line. I'll set him to laying the track down the canyon trail." He frowned in concentration. "And I'll close down the mine and transfer the workers to the railroad and supervise that crew myself. Will that make it possible?"

"Possible but not probable. The jungle is much denser ahead. It will need extensive clearing along the track."

"I'll recruit more help from the Cinnidar village."

"It still may not be enough."

"I *need* this done, Jane. I could lose everything I've worked for all these years." He gazed directly into her eyes. "I need your help. Will you give it to me?"

She had never thought he would ask her for anything. He had always demanded, not asked, but he wasn't demanding now. Nor was he trying to use that mesmerizing charm that was his most potent weapon. He had stated his need simply and honestly. He loved this island. It was home to him. She felt an odd surge of fierce protectiveness as she looked at him. Dammit, she would not let Abdar either hurt him or take his home. "I'll see to it." She turned and moved toward the tent. "Come with me. We'll need to look at the map. There's a stretch of marshland just ahead that I was planning to go around. It's a nightmare finding firm ground to lay the track and working in all that mud, but we can cut seven miles off the final stretch if I go through it instead of around. That will help, won't it?"

"Seven miles will help a hell of a lot."

"Then you can take your crew and start laying the

track beyond the marsh while Li Sung, Dilam, and I work our way through it. If we can—"

"Jane."

She looked at him. "Yes?"

He smiled, that rare beautiful smile. "Thank you."

The words were beautiful too, and filled her with a perilous happiness. She lifted the flap of the tent. "You're quite welcome." She made a face. "At the moment. I'm not sure I'll feel quite so magnanimous when we begin going through that marsh."

"Why do they not go away?" Li Sung said as he gazed in exasperation over his shoulder at the elephants standing in the trees. "It has been over a week now and they still try to follow behind us like tame dogs."

She smothered a smile. "Dilam says Danor likes you. *Makhol.*"

He scowled. "She told you that foolishness?"

"Or perhaps he misses his mate."

"Then let him go court another one and leave me alone."

"I believe Dilam is right. Why else would Danor keep the herd nearby? And he watches you all the time."

"Maybe he is looking for an opportunity to smash me into the marsh." He grimaced. "Though I could not be much worse off. I've been mud from head to toe for the last three days."

"So have we all." Jane wearily wiped her brow as she gazed at the workers trying to keep their balance in the slippery mud beside the track. "Another mile and we'll be out of it." Her gaze wistfully shifted to the river a half-mile distant. "It will be good to wash the muck off this evening."

"That's five hours away." Li Sung turned and moved cautiously along the side of the rails, measuring the width of the track. "Let's hope we are out of this marsh by—what the—"

He lost his footing, his feet slid out from under him, and he fell to the ground. The next moment he was sliding helplessly down the slippery incline to splash into a mud-filled ditch.

He came to the surface, floundering, spitting a mixture of Chinese and English curses, completely encased in grainy yellow mud from head to toe.

"Are you hurt?" Jane called. The ground was soft, and she doubted if he had come to any harm. Dear heaven, she mustn't laugh. Li Sung would kill her if she laughed.

She couldn't help it. Heavens, he looked funny.

"Stop that snickering." Li Sung glared at her, his black eyes shining from his mud-coated face. He gazed at the Cinnidan laborers who had stopped working to grin at his dilemma. "And you too. It is not—no! Get him away from me!"

Danor had suddenly appeared and was lumbering down the slippery incline toward Li Sung.

Jane's amusement vanished. "Good God, what on earth is he doing?"

Danor wrapped his trunk around Li Sung and heaved him out of the ditch.

"Let me go, you armor-plated baboon," Li Sung spat out, struggling futilely in the elephant's grasp. He shouted. "Dilam!"

"I am here." Dilam beamed at him as she trotted down the track toward them.

"But you're not *doing* anything. You're supposed to know about elephants. Make him—"

"He will not hurt you." She frowned. "I do not think."

Danor turned and trotted up the embankment and off across the flat marsh, moving so quickly his heavy bulk did not have a chance to sink into the soft muddy ground.

"Jane!" Li Sung shouted. "Are you going to shoot this beast or not?"

Jane found herself laughing helplessly again. "He's not hurting you, is he? Surely you wouldn't want me to kill him for stinging your pride?"

"The hell I wouldn't." The words drifted back to her as Danor picked up speed. "Put me down!"

Jane could see where Danor was headed now, and she started after them at a run, her boots sinking into the muddy earth with every step. "Don't worry. I think he'll drop you soon."

"And then step on my head."

She was breathless with laughter as well as running. "No, I don't believe you'll have to worry about that."

Danor stopped at the bank of the river—and tossed Li Sung into the water.

Li Sung came up sputtering and cursing. Danor lumbered into the water, filled his trunk, and sprayed Li Sung in the face.

"He is trying to drown me."

"No." Jane gasped, tears pouring down her face. "I think he's trying to give you a bath."

"Stupid beast!" Li Sung hit the water with his hand, sending a spray at the elephant.

Danor promptly squirted him again.

"This is . . ." Li Sung looked at Jane and then at the elephant and suddenly his anger ebbed and his lips began to twitch. "Completely unfair." The smile became a chuckle. "I do not have a monstrous nose with which to gather water."

Danor's trunk wound around Li Sung's shoulders, moving gently up and down his body. It was almost a loving caress, Jane thought, like the way the elephant had touched his baby that night in the jungle.

Li Sung's expression became oddly arrested. He stood quite still, his head tilted as if listening to something. "All right, I forgive you," Li Sung said grudgingly. "But only because I needed the bath." He grimaced ruefully. "And the laughter. I feel better now." He turned and waded back to shore.

"So do I." Jane reached out a hand to help him up the bank. "It doesn't seem nearly so long until sundown now."

Li Sung looked back at the elephant, but Danor was now ignoring them, siphoning and spraying water on himself. "Selfish beast. Look at him enjoy himself. He does not have to labor from sunrise to sundown."

In spite of the content of the words, Jane noticed a lack of antagonism that was usually present in Li Sung's tone when he spoke of Danor. It was as if that moment in the lake had washed away more than the mud encasing her friend.

Li Sung frowned when he looked at Jane. "What are you smiling about now?"

She started across the marsh toward the track where Dilam stood waiting, a broad grin on her face. "Was I smiling?"

Danor was there again, standing in the shadows of the trees across the clearing.

Li Sung turned over on his side and pulled his blankets up to his neck, deliberately ignoring the elephant.

The stupid beast could stay there all night, as he had for the past three nights. He would pay no attention to him. He needed his sleep.

The elephant was still watching him.

Li Sung muttered a curse and tossed aside his blanket. He moved past the sleeping workers as he stalked toward Danor. "Go *away.*"

The elephant took a step closer to Li Sung.

"Have you nothing better to do than torment me? Go take care of your baby or something."

The elephant made a soft, rumbling sound deep in his throat.

"I do not want you. What use do I have for an elephant?"

Danor's trunk reached out and gently, tentatively, touched his cheek.

"Stop it!" Li Sung stepped back.

Danor stepped forward, his trunk moving caressingly down Li Sung's body.

Togetherness. Affection. Serenity. Li Sung closed his eyes as the same emotions he had experienced that moment in the river surged through him.

"I do not want—" He stopped with a sigh of resignation. "But you do not care what I want, do you? Perhaps you do not want it either. Maybe you do miss your mate. We will have to see if we can't find you another." He touched Danor's trunk. It was rough and leathery, yet oddly comforting, like touching the bark of a tree grown in a beloved childhood garden. "All right, we will try to be friends. It is not impossible we may find a common—no!"

He was lifted high and the next moment deposited on the elephant's back. "This is too much. I did not want you to—"

Togetherness, bonding, and something else . . .

Power.

He had never felt so strong or so complete.

Danor began to walk slowly across the glade toward the herd, his gait smooth, almost rolling. He felt no pain as he did when mounted on a horse or mule, Li Sung realized with amazement. His bad leg was lifted and held at an angle that was without strain. He felt whole again, as he had as a boy before he had become a cripple.

A wild sense of exhilaration flowed through him. He lifted his face and felt the wind touch his cheeks and something else touch his soul. *Makhol?* It did not seem such a bizarre idea now. He didn't know what bond there was between them, but he knew he had never been more content or alive than at that moment.

"Jane! Wake up!

Li Sung's voice, Jane realized sleepily, but there was something strange . . .

"Jane!"

She came fully awake and the next moment she was off her cot and at the tent entrance. "What's wrong? Is there—"

Li Sung sat on Danor's back just a few yards from her tent. "Li Sung!" she whispered.

"I wanted to share it with you," he said simply.

She didn't have to ask what he had chosen to share.

It was all there in his expression—joy, exhilaration, exultation.

"How did it happen?"

"Danor." He patted the elephant's head. "He has great determination."

"I noticed that. You look very comfortable up there."

"It's like nothing . . ." He trailed off. "I can't explain."

"You don't have to." She smiled. "*Makhol.*"

A brilliant smile lit his face, and he suddenly looked younger than the boy who had come to Frenchie's that day so long ago. "*Makhol.*" He touched Danor's left ear, and the elephant turned away from Jane's tent. "We are learning to accommodate each other, but I may have to stay up here all night." He made a face. "I still have not figured out how to tell him I want down. . . ."

His words trailed off as Danor moved back across the clearing toward the herd.

Jane gazed after him for a long time before she let the tent flap fall and turned back to her cot. Tomorrow would be another exhausting day, and she must get some sleep. She was happy for Li Sung. How could she not be happy when he had found something that made him look like that? Nothing had really changed. He had come to share his happiness with her as a good friend would.

She was foolish to feel this aching sense of something lost forever.

"You cannot do it," Pachtal said positively.

"But of course I can." Abdar smiled. "I'm the maharajah."

"You have not been crowned yet. It will be another month before you're free to go to Cinnidar."

"I cannot wait. Your informant said the line is close to completion. Am I to wait until MacClaren has the means to fortify against me?" Abdar turned and gazed at the masks mounted on his wall and murmured, "I must tell Benares to pack up those masks."

"You're taking them with you?" Pachtal asked. "All of them?"

"Of course, and Benares must also come in case I find anyone worthy of Kali on Cinnidar. I will need power to defeat MacClaren."

"You will need an army."

Abdar frowned. "Do you question Kali's power?"

"I do not question," Pachtal said quickly. "I only suggest that Kali might triumph sooner with assistance."

"I agree." Abdar's frown disappeared. "We shall have an army."

"Not until you ascend the throne."

"Why do you argue with me? Do you think I'm not aware of the difficulties? I have thought of a way to solve the problem." Abdar smiled. "Can you not see I am devastated by grief over my father's death? My physician has become so concerned that he insists I must leave the city and seek a change of scene."

Pachtal waited.

"We will announce to my father's mourning subjects that I'm going to Narinth to the summer palace to recover my health."

"And the army?"

"I'll need a large escort to protect me on my journey. Everyone knows that the British colonel would like nothing better than to find a way to oust me from power. If we catch MacClaren by surprise, I will not need more than a few troops. You will arrange to have a ship ready downriver."

"But will these troops follow your orders when they learn you are breaking the mourning and going to Cinnidar instead of Narinth?"

"Oh, I believe they will. Once you point out that when we return from Cinnidar, a month will have passed and I will be eligible to ascend the throne." He paused. "And punish all who displease me."

"It could succeed," Pachtal said slowly.

"It will succeed. The plan was given to me by the divine Kali and she cannot fail."

"And what if Pickering suspects your plan? He is no fool."

"I cannot attend to everything. I will have to rely on Kali to take care of Pickering." He smiled at Pachtal. "Kali . . . and my friend, Pachtal."

"You are joking," he said, startled. "I cannot kill an Englishman."

"Not death. Merely a temporary stomach disorder that will make him too ill to care what I am doing for a few weeks. Is that not possible?"

Pachtal smiled. "Entirely possible."

"Why so quiet?" Ruel filled Jane's coffee cup and his own before sitting down beside her before the fire.

"I don't have anything to say." She sipped the coffee, gazing down into the flames. She was aware of the usual friendly hum of talk around the *candmar* but felt oddly remote from it. "Do I have to talk all the time?"

"Not all the time. Just when something's wrong. I hate like hell knowing there's something bothering you and not knowing how to fix it. Is it me?"

"I don't know what you're talking about."

"The hell you don't," he said roughly. "What did I do?"

"Nothing."

He reached out and covered her hand with his own. The warm, hard touch of his flesh against her own made her gaze fly to his face.

"That's better," he said curtly. "You're looking at me. Now talk to me. You've been working yourself into the ground for my sake trying to get this damn track laid and yet for the past three days you've never even smiled at me."

"I didn't realize smiling was required."

"It's not required. I just miss it." He turned her hand over and began tracing patterns on her palm with his index finger. "It . . . warms me."

She looked at him, startled. "Ruel . . ."

"I thought it was getting better. Do I have to go out

and find another baby elephant to pull around just to get you to smile at me?"

The motion of his finger on her palm was causing little ripples of sensation to tingle up her wrist and arm. He had touched her like this when he had sat beside her on the veranda in Kasanpore, she remembered. He had stroked her palm and talked of Cinnidar . . . and the painting in the maharajah's car.

She felt a flush heat her cheeks. Like the woman in the painting, she had knelt for him in the summerhouse. She had felt him inside her, his hands caressing her while he rode her as if they were two mating animals unable to get enough of each other. The erotic memory was suddenly there like another presence beside them in the firelight. She could almost feel his hands cupping her breasts as he plunged—

She tried to pull her hand away, but his hand closed on her own.

"No." He met her gaze. "Let me touch you. I have to get near you some way."

He was getting too near, she thought breathlessly. For the past days he had been companion and ally, damping down any hint of physical sexuality, but now the sensuality that was so much a part of him was there before her.

"I wouldn't do this if there were any other way," he said thickly. "It's not what I want for us." He laughed desperately. "Correction. I want it like hell. It's just not all I want and I'm afraid I'll scare you off if I reach out and grab." His fingers moved up and stroked the thin skin of her wrist.

A hot shiver went through her. "Let me go, Ruel."

"Why?" He glanced at the crowd of laborers around the campfire as his fingers continued to feather the sensitive skin at her wrist. "No one is paying any attention. The Cinnidans are always touching each other in affection."

She knew that was true and Ruel's caress was probably not even visible to most of them, half hidden as it was between their bodies. The knowledge did nothing to rid her of this feeling of excruciating intimacy.

"Besides, you like it. You want it. Let me come to your tent tonight," he murmured. "I'll make you—"

Li Sung sat down next to them. "I have something to talk to you about."

Jane drew a quivering breath of relief as Ruel's hand dropped away from her wrist.

Ruel shot her a look that was composed equally of frustration and ruefulness. He picked up his coffee cup and turned his gaze to Li Sung. "Talk."

Li Sung said, "I believe I know a way to make the construction go faster."

"How?"

"By using the elephants," Li Sung said. "Our slow-down right now is because of the clearing problem. In Kasanpore, elephants were sometimes used for clearing."

"Wild elephants?"

"No, elephants that had been trained for years by their handlers, their *mahouts*. But I have talked to Dilam about this and, if I can get Danor to clear the trees I want him to clear, she thinks the other elephants will follow him. Since they have to consume such vast quantities of leaves anyway, we might as well guide them in the way that's most useful to us."

Ruel turned to Jane. "Do you think it will work?"

"I'll have to think about it. This is as much a surprise to me as it is to you. Li Sung didn't mention the plan to me."

"I forgot," Li Sung said absently, and then went on. "If you and Jane combine crews, Dilam and I will be freed to take the elephants and go on ahead to clear the terrain along the track route from here to the canyon wall."

"Just the two of you?"

"I'll need three Cinnidan elephant handlers to help me besides Dilam. It would be dangerous to have too many people in the area with that many uncontrolled elephants milling around."

Ruel turned to Jane. "Well?"

"We could try it," she said slowly. "If we can get the Cinnidan High Council to provide these *mahouts*."

"They will." Li Sung smiled confidently. "I visited Dilam's village last night and spoke to them. The handlers will be here tomorrow."

"I'm surprised they gave in so easily," Ruel said. "They're very careful of the safety of their people."

Li Sung smiled. "I took the precaution of making a splendid entrance into the village on Danor's back. They were very impressed."

"Well, you seem to have everything under control." Jane smiled with an effort. "It's a fine idea. We'll have to see if it works."

"It will work." Li Sung stood up. "I'll go tell Dilam you approve."

"Yes, do that." Ruel smiled as he watched Li Sung walk away. He added in a lower voice to Jane, "Not that it matters. I have an idea he would have gone ahead and done it anyway. Our Li Sung is changing. You won't find him in your shadow these days."

"He was never in my shadow," she protested.

"Wasn't he?"

"I never meant—" She stopped, appalled. "Did I make him feel that?"

Ruel shook his head. "No, he stayed there because he had no reason to step out . . . until now."

Jane watched Li Sung move across the clearing to where Dilam was sitting with a group of Cinnidans. Ruel was right, Li Sung had changed enormously in the past two weeks. Even the way he moved was different. Though he still limped, his gait was quick and purposeful and, when he stopped beside Dilam and began speaking, his expression was intent, alert, and held more humor and determination than she had ever seen in him. This Li Sung would never be content in anyone's shadow.

She looked down at the coffee in her cup. "The Cinnidans think he's some kind of magician when they see him riding Danor."

"Power." Ruel's gaze was still on Li Sung. "I think the elephant shared his power with him, but now Li Sung knows he doesn't need it."

"What do you mean?"

"He's found it in himself." Ruel suddenly chuckled. "God, how smugly profound I sound. But it's true. At this rate, he may be invited to sit on their council before I do."

"Perhaps." Jane threw the remainder of her coffee into the flames and abruptly stood up. "I'm going to my tent."

Ruel's smile faded. "You don't have to run away from me. I'm too much an opportunist not to realize I can't do anything more tonight. I would never have even started it if I hadn't wanted to find out why you were upset with me."

"I'm not upset with you," she burst out. "Everything in my world doesn't revolve around you. There are other things that—" She turned on her heel. "Good night."

"Other things? What other—" He stopped, paused and then said, "Good night."

She could feel his thoughtful gaze on her back until she entered the shadows beyond the firelight.

Shadows. The word reminded her of Ruel's words about Li Sung. She had never wanted to keep Li Sung in her shadow. She had always wanted sunlight and happiness for him, to give him everything he wanted and needed.

But he did not need anything from her any more and what he wanted he could win for himself.

She would just have to become accustomed to this new Li Sung.

"It's hard to believe," Ruel murmured as he watched Danor press his forehead against the bole of a young tree and push against it. "I've never seen this before. Amazing . . ."

Danor pushed again and the tree moved, the roots tore from the earth, and the tree toppled to the ground.

Jane nodded. "Li Sung seems to be able to do anything with that elephant. I think we're going to be able to give you your railroad in those two months. We're up to almost five miles a day." She smiled with an effort. "I'm very grateful, of course."

"Are you?"

She turned to see Ruel's gaze fixed on her face. "Do you doubt it?"

"Yes." He held up his hand. "Oh, I'm sure you're happy about the increase in production, but there's something wrong."

"What could be wrong?"

"Li Sung," Ruel said softly. "He doesn't need you anymore."

Pain twisted within her. "He never needed me. Li Sung was always completely independent."

"Not this independent. He relied on you for understanding and affection."

"We're still friends and friends always need each other."

"He's mad about that elephant and he's become accepted by the Cinnidans as he's never been accepted by any people."

"I know." She could hear the huskiness in her voice and swallowed. "And I'm happy for him."

"He's not going to want to leave the elephant or these people. If you leave Cinnidar, you'll have to go alone."

"And I suppose that pleases you."

"Yes, it does," Ruel admitted. "Because with Li Sung here, it gives you another reason to stay after the railroad is finished."

"I can't stay."

"You can do whatever you wish to do." He smiled. "I simply hope to make sure your wishes coincide with mine. And I think I'm getting closer to doing that every day."

He was getting closer. Since that evening by the fire he had never again touched her, but they worked together, ate together, strove toward a common goal. He was always there, helping her, encouraging her, sharing her problems and triumphs. Sometimes she felt so close to him that it was as if they were one person. She tried to change the subject. "Have you had a report from Medford lately?"

"This morning. He's almost reached the canyon floor. Another two days should do it." His gaze searched her face. "You look tired. How much rest have you been getting?"

"Enough."

He muttered a curse. "You said yourself you're ahead of schedule. Let me and Dilam and Li Sung shoulder the load for a while."

"Abdar will be—"

"And let me worry about Abdar."

She shook her head.

He stared at her in exasperation. "*Damn*, you're stubborn!"

He turned Nugget and kicked him into a gallop, leaving her in a cloud of dust as he headed back to the site.

He came riding back late that afternoon, leading Bedelia. "Come on," he said curtly. "I have something to show you."

"Can't it wait?" She wiped away the perspiration from her forehead on her sleeve. "We still have a few hours before dark."

"It won't wait," he said. "I've told Dilam to come back and supervise the crew until it's time to pack up for the day."

"But Li Sung needs Dilam with the elephants."

"Come on." His tone was inflexible and so was his expression. "Now."

It was clear he was not going to be dissuaded. She mounted Bedelia. "What's the problem? Where are we going?"

"You'll see." He spurred ahead, heading south. "Follow me."

At first she thought he was taking her to the clearing area where they'd been that morning, but before they got to it he veered to the east and took a trail through the jungle. Twenty minutes later they came out of the jungle on the bank of a lake.

"Here we are." He reined in Nugget in the feathery shade of a casuarina tree and slipped out of the saddle. "Get down."

"Where are we?" she asked blankly as she gazed around at the color and beauty shimmering wherever she looked. Scarlet poppies carpeted the banks, and across the lake flame-of-the-forest trees bloomed brilliant orange, casting fiery reflections in the cool, serene blue of the water. Farther down the opposite bank twenty or thirty elephants lazily cavorted in the shallows. "I don't understand. What am I supposed to see?"

He came around and lifted her off the horse. "Flowers, water, birds, elephants." He took a blanket off Nugget and spread it on the moss. "Me."

"You brought me here to look at scenery?"

"I brought you here to rest. Now do it."

"I don't want to rest."

"Do it anyway." He met her gaze. "You don't have to be wary of me. I was desperate the other evening. I thought I'd made a mistake somewhere along the way and I was trying to regain ground any way I could. I knew even then it wasn't the best way." Before she could answer he turned and pointed at the elephants across the lake. "Recognize anyone familiar?"

Her impatient glance followed his gesture. "I see elephants every day. I don't need to come here to—" Her eyes widened as she saw what he wanted her to see. "Caleb?"

"Caleb," he confirmed.

"I haven't seen him since we first arrived."

"Dilam told me that the cows often keep separate from the bulls, and Caleb would have had to stay with his adopted mother. I tracked him down last week."

"Why?"

"I was caught in my own trap. I took care of him."

He smiled faintly. "Now he belongs to me. You should understand that."

"He's bigger," she said softly. Then she laughed as she saw him squirt another elephant with water. "And not nearly as docile."

"Don't you want to watch him for a while?" he asked coaxingly. "What's a few hours?"

She should go back. She glanced at Caleb again. "Well, maybe for a little while." She sat down on the blanket and linked her arms around her knees. "He's funny, isn't he?"

He sat down beside her, close, not touching her. "Very amusing."

Minutes passed and the tension gradually ebbed out of her. Three blue-breasted wild peacocks took heavy flight as the elephants moved farther down the shore, but the birds soon settled back to ground. No threat. No hurry. Just beauty and gentleness and affection. The soft breeze touched her cheeks, and the scent of flowers was all around her, pervading her senses.

"I can be amusing too," Ruel said, his gaze on Caleb. "If I put my mind to it."

"Running patterer . . ." she murmured.

"Aye, I can entertain you. I can take care of you. I can please your body." He added grimly, "And I'll never leave you for a damn elephant."

She was jarred from the euphoria by his words. "What are you saying?"

"I'm saying I want to be Li Sung and Patrick and Caleb to you." He smiled crookedly. "More. I want to mean more to you than your blessed railroad. I'm saying I want to be the one to make you laugh and to give you children."

She gazed at him, startled.

"I'm saying that I—" He stopped and then said in an awkward rush—"love you." His breath expelled. "There, it's out, and damned difficult too. I hope you're satisfied."

Satisfied? At one time she would have given almost

anything to hear him say those words, and even now they filled her with a bittersweet joy. "It's too late."

He frowned. "I know I didn't say it right, but it's true and we've got to live with it." He reached out and touched her cheek with great gentleness. "It's been growing and getting bigger every day until I feel . . . it's not only lust." He grimaced. "Though God knows there's not been many nights I haven't gone to sleep hard as hell. I want to care for you. I want to make you happy. Do you believe me?"

She wanted to believe him. She did not dare. "No."

He went still and for an instant she knew she had hurt him. "I guess I deserved that." He suddenly erupted with explosive intensity. "But, by God, you *will* believe me. You'll believe me and you'll trust me and you'll learn to love me again. You already care something for me now, but you won't admit it. Maybe you don't feel what I feel for you, but you do feel something." He drew a deep breath and then attempted a casual shrug. "Oh well, I didn't expect it to be easy. I'll just have to be patient."

"It won't do you any good." she said huskily.

"The hell it won't," he said. "It's just that you don't trust me. You think I'll hurt you again. It won't happen. I love you."

"Until you see Ian and me in the same room. Then how much would you love me?"

He did not flinch. "I love Ian, but it doesn't even compare with what I feel for you. Try me."

She shook her head. "I'm not that courageous." She made a motion to get up. "I've got to get back to the site."

"Sit back down. We'll go back after sundown. There's no need for you to run away. The declaration is over." He lay back on the blanket and closed his eyes.

She did not want to lie there and think about what he had just told her; the words were too seductively sweet. She looked at him in the sunlight, his hair ablaze, his body graceful and sinuous, his lashes curving on his cheeks. He was mandarin and hero and running patterer.

He was determination, sensual delight, and wicked mischief. He was everything that was pleasing to the eye and tempting to the senses. Everything she wanted. Everything she could not have.

She loved him.

The knowledge came softly, sadly, absolutely. Why had she thought she could ever stop loving him? Because she was afraid, she realized. The scars were too deep. The risk was too great.

"Lie down," he said again without opening his eyes.

She could not have him, but she could have this moment of peace and sweetness. She hesitated and then slowly lay down beside him. She would have only memories after she left Cinnidar, and she would seize and hold this one. "Maybe for just a little longer," she said as she closed her eyes. She could hear the sound of the birds and the soft, steady sound of his breathing next to her. . . .

"Jane."

She opened her eyes to see Ruel bending over her. The sun streaming through the trees was now behind him, lighting his hair and leaving his face in shadow.

"Ruel . . ." she murmured drowsily.

"It's time to go. You've been sleeping for over an hour. The sun will go down pretty soon."

"Will it?" She reached out and touched his hair. So soft . . . Her hand trailed down to brush his cheek, testing the textures of him.

He stiffened. "Wake up, Jane."

"I am awake."

"The hell you are." He frowned anxiously as a thought occurred to him. "Do you have the fever again?"

She did feel warm and hazy, but she knew it was not from a recurrence of the fever. "No."

She took his hand and put it on her breast. The ripple of shock that went through him was equaled by her own surprise. She had acted without thought, on instinct alone. Yet she did not regret it. Another memory . . .

"Don't do this to me," he said hoarsely. "I didn't bring you here for this, dammit."

Her breast was swelling beneath his hand, the nipple hardening. She said breathlessly, "I don't feel like resting anymore."

"I can tell." His palm slowly closed on her breast and heat tore through her body. "You're sure?"

She was starting to tremble. "Yes."

He drew a deep, ragged breath. "God, I'm glad."

He began to unbutton her shirt.

It was not like any time before. At first the rhythm was as slow and sweet as a lullaby, but later it was neither of those things. It was frantic and hot and mindless, capturing them both in a tempest of feeling. Yet she realized that storm had none of the darkness of domination. He was leading, not conquering.

The climax left her limp and gasping, her arms clutching him tightly to her.

His chest was heaving, his face buried in her shoulder. His voice was low and muffled. "Why, Jane?"

Without thinking, she told him the truth. "I wanted something to remember after I leave Cinnidar."

He flinched as if she had struck him. "I hope I made the experience properly memorable."

She had hurt him again with her careless words. "I mean, I woke up and you were there and I—"

"You don't have to explain." He lifted his head and looked down at her. "I've been used by women before. It's just never mattered to me." He swung off her, stood up, and lifted her up in his arms. "I have no intention of becoming only a memory, but I'm not above snatching a few pleasant ones of my own."

He started walking toward the lake.

"What are you doing?" she asked, startled. "Ruel, this is—"

He stepped off the bank and into the lake.

The shock of the cold water made her gasp. "You call this pleasant?"

He grinned as he set her on her feet. "You'll get used to it." His hands moved around in back of her head to loosen her braid. "I want to see your hair." He threaded his fingers through its thickness. "Silky . . . I've always loved your hair." His fingers grabbed the soft mass, holding her head back as he looked into her eyes. "I love you."

She stood there, staring up at him. She couldn't tell him how she felt. She couldn't put herself in his power again.

"But of course you don't believe me." He smiled with an effort. "Are you still cold?"

"No," she whispered.

His hands fell away from her and he stepped back. He deliberately hit the water, splashing her in the face. "How about now?" he asked with a wicked grin.

She sputtered. "Are you trying to drown me?"

"Just following Caleb's example. You seemed to find him amusing." He splashed her again.

"Ruel, that was—" His face was alive with such boyish deviltry that she broke into helpless laughter. He had changed from sober intensity to wicked mischief in the space of a heartbeat, and she welcomed the transformation with relief. "Let's swim."

He shook his head. "I'd rather splash you. You looked like an indignant ten-year-old," Ruel said. "I'd like to have seen you that young."

In the hour that followed she felt as if he had given her back the childhood she had never had as they played and swam in the water. She felt young and joyous and without a care. She was disappointed when at sundown Ruel waded back to shore and began to dress.

She followed him with reluctance. The air was still warm, but she shivered as the breeze touched her damp body. She hurriedly dried herself on the blanket and started to pull on her clothes.

He picked up her shirt from the ground and held it for her.

She slipped her arms into the sleeves. "I'm capable of dressing myself."

He began to button her shirt. "I want to do this. Kneel down," he murmured. "There's something else I want to do."

The maharajah's painting. Her gaze flew to his face as a sudden memory of that day in the summerhouse came back to her.

His lips tightened as he realized what she was thinking. "No, though I'd like to try that again someday. I think I'd get it right this time. You wouldn't find fault with the way I look at you now, would you?"

She remembered the tenderness in his expression as he had looked at her while they were standing in the lake. "No." She slowly sank to her knees on the blanket.

He knelt behind her, his fingers braiding her hair. "I've wanted to do this since that first day you took me to the temple to see Kartauk. I watched Li Sung care for you and I was jealous as hell. I should have known then . . ."

His fingers were not as practiced as Li Sung's, and it took him a long time to complete the thick braid. She didn't care, she thought dreamily. She felt cosseted and infinitely treasured.

"There. It's done." He stood up and pulled her to her feet. "And now I have to get you back to camp before you take a chill."

He lifted her onto Bedelia, but his hand closed over hers as she reached for the reins.

His voice was suddenly harsh with feeling as he blurted out, "When will you realize I'm not going to ever cause you pain again? When the hell are you going to believe me?"

She wanted to believe him, to take the chance. The temptation was so strong, it was nearly irresistible, but she was afraid. She looked at him helplessly. "I can't. I told you, there's too much—" Her voice was uneven as she struggled with tears. "I *can't!*"

The next moment she was galloping wildly through the jungle back to the encampment.

Chapter 20

"There's something you have to see," Kartauk said. He grabbed Margaret's wrist and pulled her down the hall toward the front entrance.

"Let me go." She struggled to release herself. "I have to get back to Ian. It's almost time for his lunch."

"He's going to miss it."

"Why should he have to—" She fell silent as she saw the frightening grimness of Kartauk's expression.

He pulled her out on the front veranda and pointed down the hill toward the seaport. "Look."

Fire.

The dock and warehouses bordering the sea below blazed in an inferno of destruction, sending black curls of smoke to darken the heavens.

"What is it?" Margaret whispered.

"I have an idea, but I've sent Tamar to find out for sure." Kartauk strode quickly back to the door. "You go to the servants' quarters and fetch the bearers and Ian's chair. I'll get Ian ready to travel."

"What's happening?" Margaret followed him. "You know how hard it is for Ian to travel."

"It will be harder on him to stay," Kartauk said. "If it's Abdar knocking at the gate."

"Abdar! But Ruel said we should have another two months."

"It seems Abdar has decided not to honor tradition." He moved down the hall. "I've told Jock to saddle your horse and bring it around for you. Be sure to tell the bearers to put extra cushions on Ian's chair. It's going to be a rough journey for him down that incline to the canyon."

"Terrible. Couldn't we hide somewhere in the rain forest near the palace?"

Kartauk shook his head. "They'd find us. We have to get to Ruel."

"But will the bearers be quick enough?"

"We have no choice. We can't get a coach down that narrow canyon trail. It's barely wide enough for the tracks that Medford laid." He snapped over his shoulder. "Move!"

She nodded and flew down the corridor toward the servants' quarters.

Kartauk threw open the door to Ian's chamber and found him in his chair by the window, staring down at black smoke rising from the seaport.

"We're leaving," he said curtly.

Ian shifted his gaze from the fire to Kartauk's face. "Abdar?"

Kartauk nodded. "More than likely. I sent Tamar to

determine how much time we have." He went to the armoire and pulled out Ian's cloak. "You may need this." As he withdrew a large carpet bag he glanced at the collection of medicine vials on the table beside Ian's chair. "We'll need a valise to put those in."

"There's a small leather box in the bottom of the armoire that Margaret packed them in when we came from Glenclaren." He sat up straighter in the chair. "Bring it here. I'll pack them while you pack Margaret's things. Where is she?"

"Fetching your bearers."

"Ah yes, even in the direst emergency I must travel in suitable pomp and glory." He took the leather valise Kartauk handed him and began to place the vials carefully in the case. "Be sure to pack Margaret's blue shawl. It's warm and she looks so lovely in it."

Kartauk grabbed the shawl and tossed it in the carpet bag. "You're being very calm."

"Why not? When I have you and Margaret to care for my well-being." Ian smiled. "What is scum like Abdar when one is surrounded by one's friends?"

"A threat."

Tamar burst through the door, his usual calm demeanor vanished. "Abdar! We must depart!"

"You're sure it's Abdar?" Kartauk asked.

Tamar nodded. "His soldiers wear blue and white livery as you told me."

Kartauk swore. "How many?"

"Perhaps two hundred. But they carry English rifles."

Kartauk frowned. "Two hundred. Why not more?"

"It seems quite enough to me," Ian said mildly.

Kartauk nodded and turned back to Tamar. "How much time do we have?"

"Not long. The soldiers fired the docks as they set out for the palace. I ran into Abdar's forces outside of town and turned around and came back."

"Then he's right behind you," Ian said. "And we have no time for my foolish bearers." He met Kartauk's gaze. "Margaret."

Ian was right. It would take a miracle for the bearers to avoid Abdar's pursuit down that canyon trail, and if Margaret accompanied them she would not desert Ian even if it meant being captured herself. He nodded. "I'll see to it. Finish his packing and get him into his chair, Tamar. He's leaving immediately."

He had to step around the four Cinnidan bearers as they entered Ian's chamber. He grasped Margaret's arm as she would have followed them. "No." He half pulled, half pushed her down the corridor. "I'll tend to him. You go on ahead."

"Are you mad? I won't leave without Ian."

"Someone has to warn Medford and Ruel to be ready for Abdar. Medford's camp is directly at the bottom of the canyon wall. Give him the warning and then ride on to Ruel's camp. The last time I heard from him he was located about fifteen miles from Medford. Tell him Abdar has a force of only two hundred and that, though they're well armed, I don't think he will have any reinforcements to draw on. There's a good chance he's overstepped his power with this move."

"*You* go warn Ruel. My place is with Ian."

It was what he expected of her, strong as gold and brave as a lion. "Are you strong enough to protect him in battle?" He pushed her down the veranda steps toward Jock, who was holding her horse. "You have a great heart, but I am mighty as Goliath."

"Whom David defeated without batting an eyelash."

"He struck a lucky blow." Kartauk grinned. "Goliath should have won." He said to Jock. "Don't let her stop until she reaches Ruel."

Jock nodded. "Aye."

"I'm not going until—"

"Do you trust me?" Kartauk asked. "Do you truly trust me, Margaret?"

"Aye, but I still—"

"This is the right thing to do for all of us. It may be the only way to save the day. I promise Ian will be right behind you." He smiled and suddenly his face was illuminated with love. "Go, Margaret, trust me."

He lifted her to the saddle and swatted the horse's rear, sending it into a gallop toward the canyon.

He turned immediately and climbed the veranda steps. He wished he could have watched her leave, to see the slender straightness of her back, the way she held her head in that proud manner he loved so well. It did not seem much for a man to ask.

But there was no time.

Margaret and Jock were almost halfway down the canyon trail before she had time to realize the exact portent of Kartauk's words.

"My God," she murmured as panic swept through her.

He had promised Ian would be on her heels.

He had said nothing about himself.

Ian was still sitting in the chair by the window when Kartauk entered his chamber. He turned to Tamar, who stood against the far wall beside the Cinnidan bearers. "Why isn't he in his traveling chair? I told you to get him ready."

Tamar shook his head. "And he told me not to move him. It is he I must obey."

"She's gone?" Ian asked.

Kartauk nodded. "Not without protest. We have to send you on your way to be sure she doesn't turn back. I promised you'd be right behind her." He crossed to Ian's chair. "Brace yourself. I'm going to lift you."

"Not yet." Ian grimaced as he nodded at the glass of wine on the table beside him. "After I finish the wine. I've just taken my laudanum and I must wait until it takes effect. The trip down that canyon will prove excruciating. I'll only be a moment."

"We don't have many moments."

Ian picked up his wineglass. "You don't intend to go with me, do you?"

Kartauk went still. "Why do you say that?"

"You said *send*, not *bring*, and such an action would be reasonable considering your character."

"Considering my character, you should expect me to do just the opposite. No one has more self-concern than me."

"Not where Margaret is involved." He sipped his wine. "I take it you think it's necessary to stay and delay Abdar from following us."

Kartauk nodded. "Abdar would enjoy having Ruel's brother to toy with."

"But not you?"

He shrugged. "I've dealt with Abdar for years. I know him."

"But there is still danger for you."

"Finish your wine. You have to leave."

Ian nodded and obediently swallowed the rest of the wine. "I know I mustn't keep you, but since I've been sitting here I've suddenly realized something. Something that's been troubling me since that night at Lanpur Gorge."

"We haven't time for this." Kartauk took an impatient step forward.

"God always has a purpose, but I couldn't see His hand in saving me that night. It's all coming clearer now."

"I'm going to lift you." Kartauk bent to gather him into his arms.

"I really wouldn't do that," Ian murmured as he nodded at Tamar over Kartauk's shoulder. "You appear so concerned about me, and if I fell it would cause me great pain."

"I won't drop you."

"I'm afraid you would have no choice."

"Nonsense, I'm strong as an—"

He broke off as the vase Tamar wielded shattered on his head. He grunted, his eyes glazing over. He slumped to the floor.

"You see?" Ian asked as he gazed down at Kartauk. "I really could not allow you to cheat me, my friend." He lifted his gaze to Tamar. "Very good. Get him on a horse. Quickly."

Tamar hesitated. "I do not think—"

"You said you would always obey my every command." He smiled gently. "Don't worry, this is a good thing I've done, Tamar."

"No." Tamar met his gaze with understanding. "It is a great thing." He nodded to one of the bearers, who helped him lift Kartauk's massive bulk.

"Wait!" Ian said. "Tell the bearers to take the chair down the mountain. Tie Kartauk's horse's reins to the back of the chair and let them lead him down."

Tamar frowned, puzzled. "Take the chair without you?"

"Margaret will be on the lookout for the chair. If she doesn't see it, she'll return instead of going on to Ruel."

Tamar nodded and issued quick orders to the bearers. "I will be back as soon as I get them under way."

"No, I want you to hide on the grounds. When the soldiers find you, don't fight them. Ruel may need a man here at the palace."

"I would rather come back here."

Ian shook his head.

Tamar hesitated and then said softly, "It will be as you wish."

In moments Ian was left alone in the chamber. Contentment flowed over him. It was done. Well, not entirely done, but soon it would be over. He should have had more faith. He should have known that God would have more compassion than to let him suffer with no reason. He had been given a role of splendor and heroism to play out the end of his humdrum life.

He settled back in his chair to wait for Abdar.

"There." Jock pointed up the trail. "I see them!"

Them? Hope leapt in Margaret as she shaded her eyes against the sun. From this distance she could barely make out the chair about a quarter of the way down the trail, but wasn't there also a horseman just behind the chair's ornate fringed awning?

"Come," Jock urged. "Medford's camp is right ahead."

"Aye." Margaret spurred ahead. It could be both of them. Kartauk could have come with Ian. Let it be both of them, she prayed. Be merciful and let them both be saved.

He was afraid, Ian realized. He hadn't expected fear, and yet here it was, ugly and twisted and dark. He mustn't think of darkness. He must think only of the light.

They were coming.

He heard shouts from outside the palace and then the sounds of boots on the fine wood floors and doors being thrown open up and down the long corridor.

They were closer, right outside his own closed door.

He tensed as the door was thrown open and Abdar stamped into the chamber.

"Ah, at last! I feared there was no one here." Abdar came toward him, his usually blank face twisted with annoyance. "I know you. You are the brother, the crippled one."

Ian inclined his head. "I recall our first meeting in great detail, Your Highness."

"Where are the others?"

"Others?"

"Where is Kartauk?"

Ian vaguely looked around the chamber. "He was here a moment ago." He leaned back in his chair. "You must forgive me, Your Highness. I've just taken my laudanum and I cannot think clearly. I think he is in his furnace room . . . across the veranda. Or perhaps the summerhouse. He was quite disturbed you were coming."

"He had a right to be disturbed." Abdar turned to a handsome young man behind him. "Go search for him, Pachtal. Bring him here."

Pachtal quickly left the room.

Abdar turned back to Ian. "I had word that your wife had accompanied you to Cinnidar. Where is she?"

"She became frightened and fled. I believe she's hiding somewhere on the grounds."

"Leaving you alone?"

"She had no choice. Was she to give up her life to save that of a helpless cripple?"

Ian could see he had struck a note of reason in Abdar with that answer. Abdar slowly nodded and turned to an officer. "Search also for the woman."

After the officer had left, Abdar moved across the room toward Ian. "You should not have come back. Your brother has offended Kali by attempting to steal her treasure."

"Her treasure or your treasure?" Ian asked.

"It is all the same."

"Is it?" Ian closed his eyes. "Forgive me, Your Highness. I cannot fight the laudanum any longer."

Moments passed, and he could hear Abdar restlessly prowling back and forth about the chamber. Finally Abdar exploded. "I do not think you drugged. You seek to ignore me."

"The laudanum . . ."

"I will triumph, you know."

"Will you?"

"He has no army, no arms. I have fine rifles furnished from the armory of your Colonel Pickering."

"How pleasant for you."

"You do not believe me?"

"I believe you think you will triumph." He smiled faintly. "However, as my Margaret was wont to say, Ruel was never one to be accommodating."

"He will have no—"

"Kartauk is not here." Pachtal hurried back into the chamber. "We have searched the palace and the grounds. We found only one Cinnidan servant. The rest have fled."

Abdar swore as he whirled back to Ian. "Where is he?"

Ian's lids lifted. "May I suggest you ask Kali?"

"You defy me?" Patches of color flared in Abdar's cheeks. "You miserable cripple. You have the temerity to express contempt for *me?*"

"I do appear to have that temerity. I'm a bit surprised myself. For a while I was afraid I wouldn't be able to do this well. Ruel is much better at this sort of thing than I am." He met Abdar's gaze. "Yes, I do have contempt for you, Abdar. Both for you and your heathen goddess of destruction."

"Kali will show you her power. She will strike down all who—"

"Kali does not exist," Ian interrupted softly. "There is no real destruction. What is destroyed merely becomes something else."

"You lie." Abdar's eyes blazed at him. "She does exist. I will show you, she exists." He turned to Pachtal. "Where is Benares?"

"Still at the ship."

"What is he doing there?" Abdar screamed shrilly. "Send for him. What good is he, if he is not where I want him?"

"You said you might not need him," Pachtal said soothingly. "You thought if Kartauk was here, he might be persuaded to—"

"But Kartauk is not here. He ran away to the protection of that Scottish dog. I must make do with Benares. Tell him to come and bring the masks."

"All of them?"

"Of course, all of them. I must meditate and surround myself with power before I launch my attack on the Scot."

"Would it not be better to go now and surprise him?"

"We have no surprise now that Kartauk has carried word to him of our arrival. I will crush him at my leisure." His plump, childlike face lit with a smile as he stared at Ian. "You are too weak and drug-ridden to be worthy of a place in my collection, but I believe I can use you to strike fear into your brother's heart." He turned to Pachtal. "Do it. We will use that Cinnidan servant to take the mask to the Scot. It must be done well, you understand. Very well."

"I have never failed you in this, have I?" Pachtal asked.

"No, and you must not fail me now." Abdar left the room.

Pachtal smiled at Ian. "You have displeased His Highness. I fear you will suffer for it." He came toward him. "But first we'll wait a few hours for Benares to arrive and the laudanum wears off. I must strive to get the appropriate response."

Eagerness surged through Ian. It would soon be here. When the moment came, he must struggle, he must fight it as decreed by holy law, but it was coming nearer.

He could almost see the light.

"It was not my fault." Benares's voice cracked with panic. "I'm only a craftsman. You are the one responsible. It was your mistake."

"I made no mistake," Pachtal said harshly. How could it have happened? he wondered. It was incredible. "I will not take the blame."

"You *must* take it." Benares's eyes were glittering, his hands shaking. The goldsmith had never before dared to speak to Pachtal in this manner, but his fear of Pachtal was clearly submerged by his terror of Abdar.

He was not without fear himself, Pachtal realized. Abdar had been growing stranger and darker ever since his father's death, and he did not know what effect this blunder would have on his temper. Abdar's rage might fall on him as well as on Benares, and he had no wish to join the collection gracing Abdar's walls.

"I will not ask you to take the blame." He turned away. "Pack it in a box and send for that Cinnidan servant, Tamar. Tell him to take the box and deliver it to Medford's camp to send on to the Scot. Abdar will never see it. I will tell Abdar I misunderstood his orders and thought he meant to send it directly to MacClaren."

"He will be very angry," Benares said doubtfully.

"Not as angry as if he had seen this . . . this monstrosity." He nodded at the gold mask. "You keep your counsel and I'll keep mine, and we will both survive."

"My God, it's Margaret!" Ruel jumped to his feet and moved toward the rider approaching the campfire.

Jane followed him, her heart pounding with fear. Margaret's very presence here heralded disaster, and she was riding astride, her white gown dirty and torn, her fair hair streaming down her back.

Ruel grabbed the reins as her mare skidded to a stop. "Ian?" he asked curtly.

"Behind me," Margaret gasped. "I told Medford to keep him at his camp until I could come for him. Kartauk said you had to know at once."

"Know what?"

"Abdar. Two hundred men . . . the dock was burning . . ."

Ruel swore. "Dammit, I didn't expect this so soon! How far behind?"

She shook her head. "I don't know. There was no sign of pursuit as I came down the canyon. Medford said he'd start to strike camp and put a watch on the trail."

"Let her get down," Jane said as she moved closer. "Can't you see she's exhausted?"

"Sorry." Ruel's voice was abstracted as he lifted Margaret down from the mare. "Kartauk?"

"I'm not sure." Margaret leaned against the saddle and closed her eyes. "He may have been following Ian's chair. I saw a horse . . ."

"Come and sit down." Jane slid her arm around Margaret's waist and led her toward her blanket near the campfire. "Get her coffee, Ruel."

Ruel turned and walked toward the pot hanging above the embers.

Margaret collapsed on the blanket. "I think Kartauk . . ." She wrapped her arms around herself to still her trembling. "I believe he meant . . . to stay."

"Why would he do that?" Jane asked.

"Because he's a foolish man who thinks only he knows the proper thing to do." In spite of the tart words, tears were running down her cheeks. "He should have given me the choice to—" She stopped and wiped her damp cheeks with the back of her hand. "But no, he'd rather stay and be killed by that fiend. He was always too obstinate for his—" Her voice broke and she was forced to stop.

"Even if he did stay, that doesn't mean he's dead." Ruel thrust the metal cup into her hand. "Kartauk's a clever man and Abdar wanted him alive."

"For how long?" Margaret asked fiercely. "He told me about that monster. Kartauk won't give Abdar what he wants, and when he refuses, he'll die."

"You said he might have followed Ian," Jane reminded her gently. "You don't know that he stayed."

"That's right." Margaret took a deep breath. "There's still hope, isn't there? I'm behaving very foolishly." She sat up straighter. "Kartauk said to tell you that Abdar's force were foot soldiers, armed with English rifles, and he did not believe there would be reinforcements."

"With two hundred armed men they probably think he won't need them," Ruel said grimly. "Since I have no army at all." He jumped to his feet. "But he's wrong, damn him."

"What do we do?" Jane asked.

"You and Margaret move this camp across the river. It will be a better defensive position. If anything happens and I don't return or send you word, cut the hanging bridge and head for the Cinnidan village." He moved toward his horse. "I'm going to Medford's camp and make sure Ian and Kartauk made it safely."

"And if they didn't?" Margaret asked unevenly.

Ruel glanced at her. "Then I go after them."

"Even if it's only Kartauk?"

He frowned. "Of course. Kartauk's here because I brought him to Cinnidar. Did you expect me to say anything else?"

"I suppose not," she said, relieved.

"What about Dilam and Li Sung?" Jane asked suddenly. "Did you stop at their camp, Margaret?"

She shook her head. "I passed it, of course, but I didn't stop." She wearily rubbed her temple. "Elephants . . . I never saw so many elephants."

Jane turned to Ruel. "Surely Dilam could help."

"And risk killing her people? Not likely."

"I think you may be wrong. She said something the first night I met her . . . I'll go to their camp and talk to her."

"I want you across the river," Ruel said.

"After I talk to Dilam." She got to her feet. "You stay here and rest, Margaret."

"I'm going with Ruel," Margaret said. "I'll need another horse, the mare is exhausted."

"Not only the horse," Jane said, gazing at Margaret's white, strained face. She did not attempt to dissuade her. Ian might still be in jeopardy, and she knew she would not be able to rest either if she thought Ruel was in danger. Then the absurdity of that thought hit home to her.

Dear God, Ruel *was* in danger. He might be riding right toward Abdar's forces. She wanted to scream, to tell him to stay, to tell him they could run away, lose themselves in the jungle until the danger passed. "Ruel!"

He turned to look at her.

She couldn't stop him. Cinnidar was his home. These were now his people.

"Be careful," she whispered.

He smiled at her. "And you."

The smile was brilliant, loving, its light banishing the grimness from his expression. She felt warmed, comforted, suddenly flooded with confidence. Together they could get through this. She stood up. "Finish your coffee, Margaret. I'll go saddle Bedelia and a fresh horse for you."

• • •

"It is bad," Dilam said soberly after Jane had stopped talking. Then, more firmly, "It must not happen." She turned to Li Sung. "We must stop them. I will not have the Savitsars back on my island."

"I'm surprised you include me." Li Sung lifted his brows. "Can you women not do without the help of lowly males in this endeavor?"

Dilam grinned. "I told you men were fine warriors. It is now time for you to prove yourself."

"I do not have to prove myself to you."

Dilam's smile faded. "No, you do not. I know what you are."

Jane looked from one to the other. The exchange between them held no sharpness, only a gentle raillery and amused understanding. It was clear that the elephant was not the only one who had won over Li Sung since this clearing operation had started.

"We need your help but we don't want to endanger your people, Dilam." She added, "Abdar's men have rifles."

"You told me." Dilam frowned. "But we know the island. That is also a weapon. Li Sung tells me this Abdar is even worse than the Savitsar who came before. I will not have such horrors visited upon our people again."

"It will not happen." Li Sung smiled into her eyes. "Did you know that in my language there are two characters for the word *crisis?* One means danger, the other means opportunity. We need only to heed the danger and seize the opportunity." He turned to Jane. "You say Ruel wants the camp moved across the river?"

She nodded.

"Then we will do it." He said to Dilam, "Perhaps you will have the kindness to go to your village and obtain several more worthless males to fight your battles?"

"I might be able to find a few capable of performing the task," Dilam said as she rose to her feet. "What of the elephants?"

Jane had forgotten about the elephants. There were

so many things to think about, so many dangers to face. "Abdar hates elephants. To keep them safe, you'll have to drive them east across the river and back into the jungle."

Li Sung nodded. "It can be done. Dilam and I will start them across the river before she goes to the village."

Jane stood up. "Then let's get to it."

Chapter 21

Ruel arrived at the new encampment across the river near noon the next day. As soon as he stepped out of the canoe, Jane knew the news was bad. His face was drained of color and held the same strain and emptiness it had reflected when he had looked down at the ruins of the train tracks at Lanpur Gorge.

"What is it?" she whispered.

"He's dead," he said jerkily.

"Who? Kartauk?"

"Ian." He gazed straight ahead. "Kartauk was brought into Medford's camp unconscious. Tamar struck him on the head on orders from Ian. He knew someone had to delay Abdar or they'd all be caught. Ian decided it should be him."

"Oh no!" Overpowering sadness swept through her. It wasn't fair. Ian—gentle, sweet Ian, who had been robbed of so much. "You're sure?"

"Abdar was kind enough to send proof. Ian's death mask."

"His what?"

"Kartauk says he collects the damn things. Abdar sent Tamar with Ian's mask." He added jerkily, "With a warning to me not to resist him."

"You saw it?" she asked, sick.

He shook his head. "Margaret wouldn't let us open the box. She gave it to Medford to keep. Kartauk had told her what the masks looked like." His lips thinned into a pinched line. "Abdar never chose an easy death for any of his victims."

"If you didn't actually see the mask, then maybe it's a trick. Maybe Ian is still alive."

"Goddammit, he's *not* alive!" Ruel exploded harshly. "Tamar saw the mask as it was put in the box." He added, "And he saw Ian's body in the same room."

Her last hope fled and she drew a deep, shaky breath. "How is Margaret?"

"Sick, numb, angry."

Her eyes lifted to his face. "And how are you?"

"Sick, but I'm not numb." His gaze shifted to her face. "I'm going to butcher the son of a bitch."

She shivered as she saw the cold savagery in his expression. Then she thought of Ian and felt a surge of the same cold anger. "How?"

"I have a few ideas. Where's Li Sung?"

She nodded across the clearing, where Li Sung was talking to a Cinnidan. "He sent Dilam to her village to bring back their warriors. They should be here soon."

"Good. We're going to need them. Medford has broken camp but he's waiting until he sees Abdar's forces start down the canyon trail before he retreats. His men don't have more than twenty rifles among them."

"And we have twelve." Jane shrugged. "But the Cinnidans wouldn't know how to use them if we had them."

"After we have both Dilam's and Medford's people on this side of the river, we'll burn the hanging bridge."

She nodded. "It will take time for Abdar to build rafts for that size force, and we may need that time. How long do we have, do you think?"

"I have no idea. I don't even know why Abdar didn't follow Margaret and Kartauk immediately. Kartauk told me once he wasn't sane. We'll have to take advantage of his lunacy in any way we can."

"Li Sung and I have been constructing brush barriers all along the shore. We're out of range of their rifles from across the river, but we'll need protection so they can't pick us off once they start across."

"Good idea." His voice was abstracted as he started across the clearing toward Li Sung. He walked stiffly, carefully, as if he were made of glass and was afraid he would shatter and fly apart.

She wanted to be with him, to comfort him, to ease the aching rawness of the pain she sensed. She started to follow him and then stopped. She could feel the tears brimming and knew she would be no help to him now. They would both be better off keeping busy at their own tasks. She turned back and walked toward the barriers.

"I don't like it," Li Sung said. "It is too dangerous."

"It's the only way." Ruel looked him in the eye. "You're worried about losing what you've found here. Well, it could all be gone in a month if Abdar takes Cinnidar. He's not going to have any mercy on either the Cinnidans or those elephants you love so much."

"I know this," Li Sung said. "But I do not like . . ." He shook his head. "And it is not only my own loss I worry about. There is Jane and you."

"Me?" Ruel smiled in mirth. "I'm touched by your concern."

"I am concerned." Li Sung smiled gently. "Jane has

great dreams that could be toppled. And you are in pain."

Ruel flinched. "I assure you the pain will go away when I've killed Abdar."

"Will it?"

"Try me and see. Help me."

"I will think on it." Li Sung wrinkled his nose. "It is true my natural aversion might be influencing my judgment in this instance."

"My judgment isn't impaired. This will work if we do it right." Ruel turned away. "And we'll do it right."

"Dilam's crossing the river." Jane had come to stand beside them. "I counted about seventy warriors with her."

"Then you'll have to make a decision soon," Ruel told Li Sung. "Abdar's not going to give us much more time."

"When Dilam comes we will discuss it." Li Sung held up his hand as Ruel opened his lips to protest. "I will need her help if I decide your plan is wise."

Darkness fell and Medford still had not come. When he failed to arrive by midnight, guards were posted and they went to their blankets to rest.

To rest but not to sleep, Jane thought wearily. She felt too worried and afraid to let go of awareness. She turned on her side to look at Ruel across the campfire. He was not sleeping either. He lay on his back, every muscle rigid, staring into the darkness, and she was again reminded of brittle crystal, ready to explode . . . or be shattered. He had barely spoken a word to any of them all evening, withdrawing into himself, withdrawing into his anger and sorrow. She should let him have his solitude. If he had wanted her help, he would have asked for it.

What was she thinking? Ruel had difficulty admitting he needed anything or anyone.

She threw aside the blanket, jumped to her feet, and moved around the fire.

She knelt beside Ruel and lifted his blanket. "Move over."

He didn't look at her. "No."

She lay down beside him.

"Go away. I don't want you here."

"Too bad. I'm staying." She drew the blanket around her. She lay there, not touching him, sensing his stiffness and resistance.

"I knew you'd come," he said harshly. "It was bound to happen. You have to have something to mother. Well, I'm not a young boy with a crushed leg or a damn baby elephant. I don't need you. I don't need anyone."

"I didn't say you did." She slid her arms around his taut, strained body. "I'm the one who needs you. I'm frightened of tomorrow, and I feel as if I have this wound inside that won't stop bleeding."

He was silent a moment. "You do?"

She nodded. "It would help if you would hold me. I don't think I'd feel so alone."

He didn't respond for a moment, and then his arms slowly slid around her. "You're not alone."

"Neither are you," she whispered. "If you want me, I'll always be here."

He stiffened even more. "Pity?"

"Love."

"I find it strange you find it necessary to make this declaration now."

"You once said you knew I loved you."

"I also know you have a nature soft as mush."

"Very well, there's pity too."

He swore beneath his breath.

"There's nothing wrong with pity, Ruel."

"The hell there isn't."

"Blast it, I won't say I'm sorry for giving you pity. When I was ill, didn't you pity me? When Zabrie hurt Li Sung, didn't you want to help him?" Her arms tightened around him. "Now shut up and go to sleep."

"I'm not tired."

"Then talk to me." She paused. "Talk to me about Ian."

She could feel the ripple of shock that went through him. "There's nothing to say. He's dead."

"Then we're just going to forget him?"

"Of course I'm not going to forget him." He spoke through his teeth. "I'm going to kill Abdar."

"And me? Are you going to kill me too? It would never have happened if Ian hadn't been crippled. He would have been able to escape."

"Be quiet," he said hoarsely. "It wasn't your fault."

"A month ago you would have blamed me."

"I don't want to talk about this."

"And I won't be silent about it. Say it. It's my fault."

"It's not your fault." He suddenly exploded. "It's mine."

She looked at him, startled. "What?"

"It's always been my fault. I blamed you, but I guess I always knew I was the one responsible. Ian would never have been in Kasanpore if it hadn't been for me."

"But he followed you from Scotland. You didn't even want him there."

It was as if he hadn't heard her. "And I should have been more careful getting him out of the wreck."

"You saved his life."

"I crippled him," Ruel said fiercely. "I ruined his life and then I brought him here to die."

She had never dreamed he could harbor this agony of guilt. Yet she should have known. Ruel never did anything in half measures. His emotions and reactions were always stronger, deeper, and more intense than anyone else's. And she was partially responsible for his guilt, she suddenly realized. He loved her and wanted to exonerate her, to shoulder her guilt himself. She had to do something. That was an easy decision, but what was she to do? Arguing would only make him more stubborn.

"All right, it is your fault." She went on, feeling her way. "But it's my fault too, and you forgave me. You have to forgive yourself."

He shook his head.

"Listen to me. Ian loved you. He wanted you to be happy."

He didn't answer.

"He died to help you and Margaret and Kartauk have the good life he wanted for you all. Are you going to let him die for nothing?"

She thought she felt a slight easing in those painfully knotted muscles, but she couldn't be sure.

"How can you be so stubborn? He wanted—" She stopped as she felt something warm and damp on her temple. "Ruel?"

"I love you," he said unevenly. His arms tightened around her. "God, I love you."

Now she could let her own tears come. Her last resistance to him flowed away with them. Life was too short to be afraid, love too precious not to risk everything to hold it. "I believe you."

"You do? It's about time," he said huskily. He was silent for a long time. "It . . . hurts, Jane."

"I know." She brushed her lips along the line of his cheek. She knew his moment of weakness would not last, but she felt a surge of fierce maternal protectiveness. She wanted to shelter and keep him from all harm. For the first time she realized the true power Ian had wielded over Margaret. A man who needed you was the greatest mandarin of all. "But we'll share it and soon it will get better for us. It has to get better."

"Aye." His arms tightened around her. "It will get better, love."

Margaret, Kartauk, James Medford, and his people arrived at midafternoon the next day.

"Where's Ruel?" Medford asked Jane as soon as he stepped off the bridge.

Jane nodded to the south. "Downriver with Li Sung and Dilam. Abdar?"

"We sighted him starting down the canyon trail before we left," Medford said as he set off in the direction she had indicated. "Six hours."

As usual, Medford's conversation was blunt and sparing, Jane thought as she turned back to watch Margaret, closely followed by Kartauk, cross the final few yards to the bank. She had thought Margaret looked bad the night she had arrived at their camp, but now she was shocked at the tragic difference she saw. Strong, vibrant Margaret appeared almost fragile, her face pinched and pallid, great dark circles imprinted beneath her eyes.

"Hello, Jane."

"You know how sorry I am," Jane said gently. "Is there anything I can do?"

Margaret shook her head. "There's nothing anyone can do."

Jane gestured to the campfire in the middle of the encampment. "You must be tired. Why don't you go sit down by the fire and get some rest?"

"If you like," Margaret said dully.

Jane gazed worriedly after her as the other woman moved toward the campfire. Ruel had said Margaret was numb, but she had never dreamed to see her this lacking in vitality.

"Do not comfort her."

She turned to see Kartauk gazing after Margaret.

"Don't be ridiculous," she snapped. "She's suffered a great loss. Of course I'm going to comfort her."

"She does not need time to dwell on it. Give her work to do. You have to make her come alive again."

"I can't perform miracles," Jane said wearily. "If you know how to accomplish it, perhaps you should make the attempt."

"She has said scarcely two sentences to me since I woke with a raging headache at Medford's camp." He smiled crookedly. "She cannot even look at me. I betrayed her."

Her eyes widened. "How?"

"I told her to trust me and then I had the bad judgment to underestimate Ian. It's not a mistake easily forgiven when it means a man's life."

"Margaret told me you meant to stay in his place."

"But I didn't." He shrugged. "Which makes the situation complicated."

"She would never have wanted you to sacrifice your life, Kartauk."

"I know. But she has more conscience than is good for her and she's not an easy woman." His gaze lingered on Margaret for a moment longer before he looked away. "I cannot help her this time," he said gruffly. "You will have to do it. Help her to heal. Keep her busy. Make her work so hard, she doesn't have time to think."

Why, he loved her, Jane realized suddenly. She remembered Margaret's frantic anxiety about Kartauk's safety. Love there too? How could they possibly sort out the guilt and love and sorrow. A complicated situation indeed, she thought sadly. Why could nothing in this world come easily?

"I'll keep her busy," she promised. "We need all the hands we can get to help form the barriers." She changed the subject. "Ruel is downriver and wishes to speak to you right away. He has a plan and needs your help."

"He has it." Kartauk smiled crookedly as he started off along the riverbank. "God knows, I need to keep busy too."

The last of the canoes and rafts were brought across the river to the new encampment, and Jane supervised the destruction of the hanging bridge. The brush barriers were completed by sundown and there was nothing further for them all to do but wait.

Near eight o'clock they saw the flare of torches of Abdar's soldiers coming down the trail from the direction of the canyon wall.

"Well?" Ruel asked Li Sung. "Time's run out. For God's sake, give me an answer."

"You have prepared the instruments?" Li Sung asked.

"Aye."

"Dilam believes there is worth to your idea, but there will have to be a distraction."

"Abdar will be distracted," Ruel promised grimly. "I'll take care of that."

Li Sung smiled. "That is all I ask."

"Ready?" Kartauk asked Ruel, his gaze on Abdar's encampment across the river. During the past three hours a sprawling military camp had mushroomed with a multitude of tents dotting the bank. Torches on tall iron stands lined the shore, casting fiery reflections in the dark waters.

Ruel nodded as he walked around the brush barrier and strode to the edge of the riverbank. He sent his voice echoing over the expanse of water. "Abdar!"

No answer.

He shouted louder. "Abdar!"

It was Pachtal who appeared on the bank, illuminated by the pool of light formed by the torches.

"Give it up, MacClaren," Pachtal called. "Cannot you see you are defeated?"

"I want to talk to Abdar."

"He's in the tent, meditating."

"Get him."

"Why should I disturb him when I can accept your surrender?"

"I am here, Scot." Abdar suddenly appeared at Pachtal's side.

Hatred rushed through Ruel as he stared at Abdar's smooth, bland face. Control it, he told himself. Think. Don't feel. "We have things to talk about. Will you honor a flag of truce if I come over to your encampment?"

"Why should I do that? In a day or two we will be able to launch rafts and crush you."

"I'm not a fool, Abdar. It's clear you've won the game, but I can make it hard or easy for you. Let Kartauk and me come over and we'll—"

"Kartauk?" Abdar interrupted, interest flaring. "Kartauk will come?"

"Kartauk has an excellent instinct for survival, and he's aware that we need to negotiate."

"He should have negotiated three years ago if he wished me to be merciful." Abdar's pleased laugh rang out. "But come ahead, Scot, I will listen to your pleas."

"This is a mistake," Pachtal protested. "It could be a trick. We have no need to—"

"Do not question my wisdom," Abdar snapped. "It is you who have become prone to mistakes. Call me when they arrive." He whirled and vanished from the pool of light.

"Success," Kartauk murmured when Ruel once more stepped beyond the barriers. "The first step."

Ruel nodded grimly. "I hope it's not going to be our last. Let's get over there before he changes his mind."

"No one told me you would be going too." They both turned to see Margaret standing a few feet away, staring incredulously at Kartauk. "Why? There is no need for both of you to go."

Kartauk shrugged. "Abdar enjoys my company, and Ruel is only a puling Scot. He needs my help."

"Don't joke about this. It's not enough you tried to kill yourself before. Now you must complete the task." She drew her shawl closer around her shaking body. Then suddenly her eyes were blazing at him. "Well, go! I don't care. It is nothing to me if that monster draws and quarters you. I hope he does. It would serve you well for being so foolish as to—" Her voice broke, and she was running away from them.

Kartauk gazed after her with a curious expression on his face.

"She didn't know what she was saying," Ruel said quietly.

"Margaret always knows what she's saying."

Kartauk was now smiling faintly, Ruel noticed. "You don't appear upset."

"I'm not upset. She's coming alive again." Kartauk turned away. "Let's go."

• • •

Jane was waiting at the canoe when Kartauk and Ruel approached it five minutes later. "I'm going with you."

"No," Ruel said. "We don't need you."

"You *do* need me. You need every distraction you can muster. Abdar regards you only as an annoyance, but he has a personal animosity toward me for depriving him of Kartauk."

"But he will have me," Kartauk said. "Such a prize should be enough. Stay here, Jane."

Jane ignored him as her gaze met Ruel's. "I either get into that canoe with you or I swim across. Take your choice."

Ruel stared at her in frustration. "Dammit, what are you trying to do to me?" he said hoarsely. "I can't lose you too."

"Do I swim?"

"*Damn* you." He grasped her waist and lifted her into the boat. "But you'll leave Abdar to me and obey instructions. Do you hear me?"

"I hear you."

"You notice she doesn't say she will obey," Kartauk said. "I consider that a significant omission."

Ruel didn't answer as he picked up the paddle and dipped it into the water.

Pachtal, Abdar, and a guard of ten soldiers stood waiting on the bank when the canoe reached the opposite shore.

"Ah, what an extraordinary pleasure," Abdar said as he saw Jane in the canoe. "I was not expecting you. Kali has given me good fortune."

"Why all three?" Pachtal asked slowly. "I have no liking for this, Your Highness. Why should all of them be so willing to risk their lives?"

"They could not help themselves. I told you, if I drew power from my masks, all would come to me." Abdar smiled. "And so you did, Miss Barnaby. You may think you came to help your friends persuade me to spare you, but it's not true. Kali called you."

"Kali does not exist," Jane said.

"Be quiet," Ruel said harshly. "Do you want to make things worse for us?"

Abdar's attention shifted to Ruel. "You were always the clever one, Scot. Under other circumstances Kali could have used your services. You are far more sensible than your brother."

Ruel shrugged. "He was always a fool."

"Yet we have heard that you have cared for that crippled fool for three years," Pachtal said.

"Our God promises paradise for such acts. It cost me little and I thought it worth the chance." He met Abdar's gaze. "You should understand that."

Abdar laughed. "Oh, I do. Gods may be manipulated as well as manipulate."

"May we get out of this boat?" Kartauk asked. "Or are we to conduct this entire conversation in these uncomfortable circumstances."

"Arrogance." Abdar's smile faded. "You've learned little, Kartauk."

"I've learned I like life." Kartauk paused. "And I've learned that sometimes I have to make certain concessions to keep it."

A flare of interest touched Abdar's face. "Indeed? Then by all means we must talk. Come to my tent." He turned and walked toward a large tent several yards from the bank. "Search them for weapons and bring them, Pachtal."

"Yes, Your Highness." Pachtal's gaze was on the opposite bank. "I do not like this. It is most strange . . ."

"That we come to bargain for our lives?" Ruel asked as he got out of the canoe and lifted Jane onto the bank. "Not against these kinds of odds."

"Perhaps." Pachtal's comely face lit in a vicious smile. "But I doubt if your bargaining will do you any good. His Highness has every intention of having you join his collection. He believes you will add great power." He turned to Jane. "And you will join him there after you have provided us diversion."

"I promise I will be very diverting," Jane said. "Perhaps too diverting for your taste."

"Oh, you intend to fight? That is always very exhilarating." Pachtal quickly searched them before turning to an officer. "Watch for other canoes being launched from across the river. This is too easy."

"Do you see any canoes?" Ruel asked. "Unfortunately, you caught us off guard."

"I suppose it is possible." Pachtal gestured toward the large tent. "His Highness will grow impatient."

"We wouldn't want that," Ruel murmured. He took Jane's hand and moved toward the tent. His touch felt warm and comforting, dispersing some of the chill creeping through her.

Even that warmth was banished when they entered the tent.

White candles in tall golden stands lit the dim interior, their light falling on Abdar, who sat with legs crossed on an enormous white satin cushion, and shimmering on the multitude of gold masks on the ground surrounding him in an obscene circle.

Jane gasped, her stomach clenching as the impact of the horror and pain of those masks struck her.

"Steady," Ruel said in an undertone, his grip tightening on her hand.

She swallowed and pulled her gaze from the masks. Dear God, she had never been aware of Abdar's full malevolence until this moment.

"Power," Abdar said softly, and she became aware of his gaze on her face. "You feel it, don't you?"

If evil was power, then she did feel it here. "No."

His lips curled peevishly. "You lie. You must feel it." He threw out his hand to the ground before him. "Sit."

When they sat down, the masks were only inches from her knees, gleaming gold and tortured in the candlelight. She tried not to look at them.

"Benares's work is not nearly as fine as yours, Kartauk." Abdar picked up one of the masks. "You would have done great things with this subject. She had great life force."

Zabrie.

Jane had thought her horror complete, but it was

even more terrible to recognize someone she knew among those tortured spirits.

"He was always too impatient in the final stages," Kartauk said without expression. "It is a common mistake."

"One you never made."

"But then, I am superb."

"True." Abdar put the mask down. "But can I trust you not to run away again? That is the question. I do not like to be disappointed."

"Can we dispense with this talk of masks and discuss terms?" Ruel asked.

"You appear a trifle irritated." Abdar smiled slyly. "Were you not pleased with the mask I sent you? Pachtal assures me it was one of Benares's best efforts. I was very disappointed I did not get to see it myself. Perhaps you will return it to me for my collection?"

Ruel's face remained without expression. "I think not."

"Why did you not see it?" Kartauk asked suddenly. Jane noticed his gaze was fixed on Pachtal, and for the first time she became aware of the curious tension of Pachtal's demeanor.

"I misunderstood His Highness's orders and sent the mask without letting him view it," Pachtal said stiffly. "He was right to be angry with me."

"Terms," Ruel prompted Abdar.

"I will choose the time for such discussion," Abdar said haughtily. "You have nothing with which to bargain, or you would not be here."

"That's not totally true. You need gold and I have the trust of the Cinnidans. For a percentage of the profits I could run the mine and deal with the Cinnidans for you."

"I do not need the Cinnidans. I understand my grandfather found them surly and uncooperative. I will bring my own people from Kasanpore."

"But that would mean a delay you don't want. Together we could—"

"What was that?" Pachtal asked, his head tilted, listening.

Abdar frowned. "I heard nothing."

"There was . . . something. A sort of whoosh . . . like water or . . ." Pachtal strode out of the tent. "I'll return shortly. I'm sure I heard—"

Unearthly screams filled the air.

Abdar jumped to his feet and ran toward the tent entrance. "Pachtal! What is it?"

"Stay here." Ruel told Jane as he followed Abdar. "Keep her here in the tent where she's safe, Kartauk."

She ignored him and ran out of the tent. She had known what to expect, but the sight that met her eyes was still astounding. All along the shore, elephants were surfacing from the river, leathery coats gleaming wetly, like nightmare creatures from the deep. The riders on their backs were almost naked, carrying only spears and the reed pipes they had used to breathe underwater as the elephants had swum beneath the surface from downriver.

The herd of elephants was already running through the encampment, the vanguard led by Li Sung on Danor. The soldiers, caught completely off guard, were fleeing before the elephants thundering toward them, over them.

Chaos broke out everywhere—soldiers running, shouting, guns exploding.

"Out of the way!" Dilam leaned down from the female elephant she was riding and grabbed one of the standing torches bordering the shore. She fired Abdar's tent and then turned the elephant and followed Li Sung, lighting tents and shrubbery along the way.

"So much for keeping you safe inside," Kartauk murmured as he grabbed Jane's arm and drew her away from the burning tent.

"Where's Ruel?" Her gaze frantically searched the melee of elephants and soldiers. "I don't see him."

"That's not surprising." He pulled her toward the trees lining the banks. "With all this smoke and confusion, it would be odd if you did."

She shook off his grip. "Let me alone. I'm not going anywhere without Ruel." The entire encampment was now ablaze, and she could barely discern figures in the thick smoke. She could hear Abdar screaming, shouting orders, and moved toward the sound. She knew Ruel would be wherever Abdar could be found. Her eyes stung from the smoke, and her lungs felt scorched. She dodged to the side as an elephant thundered out of the thick black haze.

She could no longer hear Abdar for the screaming of the soldiers and the trumpeting of the elephants. "Ruel!"

"Harlot!" Pachtal emerged from the haze, his face twisted with rage. He lifted his hand and she saw a glimpse of steel gleaming—a dagger!

"Down!" Kartauk knocked her to her knees as Pachtal's knife tore toward her breast.

Pachtal lunged forward, off balance. Kartauk stepped behind him, his massive arm encircling Pachtal's throat.

Pachtal was cursing, his eyes popping from a face no longer beautiful. Kartauk's arm jerked backward and Jane heard a sickening crack as Pachtal's neck broke.

He looked so surprised, Jane thought dazedly. Not pained, just . . . surprised.

Kartauk released him and Pachtal slumped to the ground.

"And good riddance," Kartauk said as he bent down and retrieved Pachtal's dagger. "I could only wish it were Abdar, but Ruel will be attending to him."

"How do you know?" Jane asked frantically. "He can't even see in this smoke. Abdar could slip up behind him."

"There he is." Kartauk was looking at something beyond her shoulder.

She whirled to see Ruel only a few yards away.

Abdar lay on the ground, his leg bent at an awkward angle, his lip cut and bleeding. Ruel stood over him, his hair, loosened from its queue by the struggle, falling wild and full about his face.

Dear God, his expression . . .

Tiger burn bright.

Ian's words came back to her. Ruel was burning now with a terrible beauty, flaming with hatred and vengeance.

Abdar screeched something inaudible at him as he tried to scramble to his knees.

"Ruel!" Kartauk called.

When Ruel looked up, Kartauk tossed him the knife he had taken from Pachtal.

Ruel let the knife fall to the ground. "No. Too quick." He picked Abdar up and carried him thrashing and struggling deeper into the smoke near the blazing tent. "You and Jane get over into the trees."

"Kali will punish you," Abdar sobbed. "You will see. Kali will strike you down."

"You can talk it over with her soon," Ruel said as he carried Abdar past the tent and dropped him on the riverbank. "Li Sung!"

"Here!" Li Sung called out of the veil of smoke across the clearing.

Ruel walked over to the protection of the trees, where Jane and Kartauk now stood. "The elephants have done their part," he shouted. "Take them back across the river!"

"Gladly," Li Sung said. "They have no liking for all this fire and smoke."

"No!" Abdar screamed as he realized what the order meant.

Too quick, Ruel had said about the dagger. This might also be quick, but Abdar would die in an agony of terror, the death he feared the most.

"No, do not—" Abdar broke off as he saw the elephants thundering toward him out of the smoke. "This is not Kali's will! This is not—"

Jane doubted if the elephants even saw Abdar on the bank in their eagerness to get away from the fire and smoke surrounding them.

This was justice. She would not have lifted a hand to save him, but she could not watch it. She closed her eyes but could not shut out Abdar's screams as the elephants crushed him beneath their feet.

She opened her eyes when the screams stopped but avoided looking at Abdar.

Ruel had not closed his eyes. He was staring at Abdar's broken remains with savage satisfaction.

Tiger burn bright.

"You go ahead." Kartauk told Jane and Ruel as they got into the canoe to return to the encampment. "I have something to do here."

"What?" Ruel asked.

"The masks." Kartauk looked back toward the ragged, blackened ruins of Abdar's tent. "The tent was only partially destroyed. They're still there."

Jane shivered. "Then let them stay there. You can't possibly want them."

"I cannot leave them," Kartauk said simply. "Gold is forever. Throw those masks into the river and in a thousand years from now the river will be gone but those masks will still exist. Do you like the thought of that?"

"No." Jane knew the memory of those hideous masks would haunt her for the rest of her life. "How can you destroy them?"

"I cannot destroy them. I told you, gold is immortal." He smiled faintly. "But I can change them. I can melt down the gold and make something beautiful from that ugliness."

"Ian's too?"

"I'm not sure." His brow wrinkled thoughtfully. "There was something odd about the way Pachtal behaved when it was mentioned." He stepped back away from the canoe. "I will come back to the encampment as soon as I find all the masks."

Chapter 22

When Jane and Ruel arrived, the encampment had the air of a circus fairground with Cinnadans milling around, laughing and gesturing, reliving their victory.

Jane's spirits could not help but be lifted in response. Her gaze searched the throng. "I don't see Li Sung."

Ruel nodded across the clearing. "There he is."

Li Sung was coming toward them but was forced to stop every few steps to speak to one of the jubilant warriors. His face reflected the same euphoria when he finally reached them. "Were we not magnificent?"

"Magnificent. What's the damage?" Ruel asked.

"No deaths. Seven wounded." He nodded at a hastily erected lean-to across the encampment. "Margaret and Tamar are tending them."

"And the elephants?"

"One was shot. Dilam is cleansing the wound now. She believes it is not bad."

"Good," Jane said, relieved. "I was afraid it would be worse. There was so much shooting."

"The soldiers were so frightened, they couldn't even hit a target as big as an elephant. They will probably not stop running until they get back to their ship." Li Sung grinned. "It was truly an exhilarating experience."

A smile tugged at Jane's lips. "Even crossing that river underwater?"

Li Sung made a face. "You can be sure I made certain those reeds you and Ruel crafted had no blockages. Water will never be my favorite element."

"But you did well with it," Ruel said. "You couldn't have done better, Li Sung."

"You are correct," Li Sung agreed. "I was splendid. Even Dilam grants I was adequate." He turned. "I will see you later. I must go help Dilam with the wounded elephant."

Jane stared after him as he limped away through the throng. He was still dressed in the loincloth he had worn to cross the river, his limbs bare.

"What's wrong?" Ruel asked as he saw her startled expression.

"His bad leg . . . he's always kept it covered, even from me."

"It doesn't seem to bother him now. Perhaps he's decided he has nothing to hide," Ruel said. "We all seem to have let ourselves come out in the open."

She looked at him with amused surprise. He actually thought what he said was true. She doubted if Ruel would ever be completely open even with her. He would always be the mysterious mandarin who had dominated her thoughts and emotions these last three years. Yet he would also be the man who had torn his flesh to shreds dragging Caleb through the jungle and the brittle, tortured man she had held in her arms two nights ago. "Well, what do we do now?"

"Tomorrow we go back to the palace to assess the damage and start repairs." His face clouded. "And there are arrangements to be made."

Ian.

She nodded and took a step closer to him. "Hadn't we better go find Margaret and tell her about Abdar?"

He took her hand. "Aye, it will be good to give her some good news for a change."

Kartauk did not return to the encampment for another four hours. Margaret was waiting when his canoe finally approached the shore.

"Well, did you manage to stir up enough trouble to suit you?" she asked as he stepped out of the canoe. "Jane and Ruel came back immediately, but you had to stay and rake among the ashes like a ghoul in a cemetery."

"Such tender sentiment." He pulled the canoe up the bank. "Did you wait here to call me a ghoul or only out of curiosity?"

"Curiosity?"

He nodded at the sack in the bottom of the canoe. "They told you about the masks, didn't they?"

"You're making it sound as if you believe I'd stay to see that horror. I should have known you'd lack the delicacy of feeling to understand."

"Then why wait on this damp riverbank for my unworthy self?"

"You know why I'm here."

"But this time you must put it into words."

She stared at him belligerently and then reluctantly said, "I regret what I said before you left. My words were hasty. I did not mean . . . I have no desire to see you die."

"I'm greatly relieved."

"You are no such thing," she said sharply. "You know

me too well not to read my true feelings, and it is most unkind of you to make me explain myself."

"Most unkind," he agreed. "Now build a fire while I go to Medford's tent and fetch Ian's mask."

She flinched, her gaze going to the sack. "Jane told me you were going to melt down the masks."

"*We* are going to melt them down, apprentice."

"I don't think I can—"

"It needs doing," he interrupted. "And you can do anything if you put your mind to it."

"Tonight?"

"Tonight." He strode away from her. "Make the fire here on the bank. It will take most of the night, and we don't want to disturb the others."

The fire was blazing briskly when he returned carrying the wooden box she recognized as the object Tamar had brought to Medford's camp. She avoided looking at it as she stirred the logs beneath a huge black kettle. "I've already put the other masks in the kettle. I tried not to look at them, but I couldn't help it. You're right, Abdar was a monster."

"You could have waited," he said gently. "I would have spared you that."

She repeated his words. "It needed doing." She smiled shakily. "But I believe I'll let you add Ian's to that perverse collection."

"No."

She felt as if he had struck her. "You would spare me these other monstrosities, but not the deepest cut? It's just like your heathen whimsy."

He held out the box. "Open it."

"No!" She sat down by the fire and drew up her knees. "I will not look at it."

He opened the box himself. "Do I have to take it out and hold it up before your face?"

"Why are you doing this?" She kept her gaze fixed on the fire. "I do not deserve this from you."

"You do not deserve to scourge yourself with memory for the rest of your life either." His voice softened.

"Have I lost your trust entirely? This is not another betrayal, Margaret."

She looked at him in bewilderment. "What are you talking about? I never thought you betrayed me."

"Not even in your heart?" He held out the box. "Prove it. Show me you trust me."

She swallowed. "Do not make—" She stopped as she met his gaze. She whispered, "No mercy, Kartauk?"

He smiled. "No mercy, madam."

Her glance slowly, reluctantly, lowered to the mask in the box.

She inhaled sharply as shock rippled through her. "Dear God in heaven." She reached out and tentatively touched the golden lips of the mask. "He looks . . ."

"Joy," Kartauk said softly. "He didn't let Pachtal and Abdar win. He beat them."

"But you said the poison was excruciating."

"I'm sure it was. But I don't think he felt it. He looks as though he had just beheld a miracle."

"The light . . ." She felt the hard core of grief begin to melt within her. "I forgot about the light."

"Never forget it again." He paused. "Even if you have to keep this mask to remind you."

She stared at the mask, and then slowly shook her head. "I don't need anything Abdar sanctioned to remind me of Ian." She got to her feet and dropped the mask into the kettle with the others. Her eyes were shimmering with tears as she turned to him with a tremulous smile. "Make something beautiful, Kartauk. Make something so beautiful it will shake the heavens and light the heart of everyone who sees it."

"A great challenge." He smiled back at her. "It's fortunate you've chosen an artist great enough to meet it." He picked up the lid and placed it over the mouth of the kettle. "We'll have to keep the fire burning hotly all night to maintain a melting temperature." He sat back down. "Naturally, as a lowly apprentice it will be your duty to fetch sufficient wood for the task."

"While you sit on your backside and supervise?"

"But of course."

She sat back down beside him. "It does not surprise me. Heathen laziness."

"Exactly."

They tended the fire all night, most of the time sitting in comfortable silence. It was near dawn when she said haltingly, "I have something to say."

"I thought you would."

"Even though Ian is dead, I can never—" She stopped and then said, "I cannot feel for you as I did."

"I know."

"Everything is different. Changed."

"Everything always changes. Seasons pass, children are born, men die." He nodded to the kettle. "Those masks are no more. Another change."

"I mean I cannot—"

"Hush." He met her gaze. "I know what you are trying to say. I always know." He reached down and stirred the fire. "I believe we need more wood, apprentice."

"That big crate goes down to the ship, Tamar," Jane said as she briskly walked down the palace corridor. She pointed to a large alabaster vase in the corner of the foyer by the front door. "And pack that too. It's always been a particular favorite of—"

"You are going somewhere?" Li Sung stood in the doorway, his gaze wandering over the three servants trailing behind Jane, carrying boxes and articles of furniture.

"Of course not," Jane said. "Margaret is taking Ian back to Glenclaren for burial. She's sailing two days from now and I thought she'd like to have a few pieces of furniture to brighten up that huge barn of a castle."

"They will not be suitable," Li Sung said. "Glenclaren is not Cinnidar."

"Beauty is always suitable." She gestured toward the servants to go ahead and led Li Sung out to the terrace. "How is the work on the docks coming?"

"Not too bad. There was much damage to the warehouses and Medford is going to have to replace five miles of his track. We were lucky that Abdar was in too big a hurry to get to Ruel to do equal damage to the canyon tracks."

"Very lucky," she agreed. "I judge once we've finished with the repairs here it should take us only another month to complete the line."

He shook his head. "Two months."

She frowned. "Why? I don't perceive any problems."

"You have a very great problem. You're going to lack my remarkable self at the helm as second in command."

"What?"

"I'm going away. Ruel can wait for his railroad."

"Away? Where are you going?"

"Dilam says this is a splendid time for me to visit the High Council."

"Why would you want to do that?"

He grinned. "I believe it's time this matriarchal society was forced to admit a few male leaders."

"Can't it wait?"

He shook his head. "The battle against Abdar gave me much respect. I must strike while the iron is hot." He added, "Besides, I must meet Dilam's children. It is time."

She smiled faintly. "*Nesling?*"

"Much more than *nesling*," he said softly.

"She's a fine woman. Good fortune, Li Sung." The happiness she felt for him was free of the wistfulness she had known before. How foolish she had been not to realize that though they were going different ways, the bond between them would always be there, too strong to break. "So you came to tell me I must complete the railroad without you?"

His smile disappeared. "No, I came to see Ruel."

"Why?"

"To tell him he is a fool."

She stiffened warily. "A fool?"

"A blind fool. He believes you ordered the rails that caused the wreck at Lanpur Gorge, doesn't he?"

She stared at him in bewildered horror. After all this time, how could he have learned—

Medford. She should have realized this would happen with Li Sung and Medford working so closely together during these last weeks. "Medford told you?"

"You should have been the one to tell me. Are we not friends?"

"I didn't want—"

"I know why you did not tell me." He met her gaze. "But why did you not tell Ruel? Why did you not tell the rest of the world?"

"I didn't have the choice," she said wearily.

He studied her for a moment and then nodded slowly. "Patrick. I thought as much. A promise?"

"And a debt paid."

"Well, I made no promise. I will tell Ruel."

"No!"

Li Sung stared at her incredulously. "You wish him to continue to think badly of you?"

"That's all in the past."

"He should know you were innocent."

"I was not totally innocent. I deliberately blinded myself to—" She saw his jaw set stubbornly and hurried on. "Ruel now feels more guilt than I do about Ian. I won't let him be alone in this."

He nodded slowly. "I should have known it was something of that nature. But carrying this burden is beyond the realm of caretaking, Jane."

"It's no burden." Jane smiled, eager to make him understand. "Don't you see? I want to do it. Ruel loves me in spite of what he thinks I did. It takes a great deal of love to overcome an obstacle like that. He's given me a great and wonderful gift."

"You will never tell him?"

She shook her head. "And you must not either."

"You cannot keep such a thing a secret forever. He could not live with you and not come to realize you could never do this."

"Promise me you won't tell Ruel."

"Won't tell me what?" Ruel was coming up the

steps. "More bad news, Li Sung? I thought the construction was going well."

Jane tensed, her gaze flying pleadingly to Li Sung's face.

"It is." Li Sung hesitated and then said, "Jane wanted to break the news to you herself."

"What news?"

"I'm going away for a while. You may have to wait to see your railroad completed."

Jane's breath expelled in a sigh of relief.

"I must go." Li Sung started down the terrace steps. "She will tell you the rest."

Ruel watched him enter the palace before turning back to Jane. "What's the problem?"

"No problem." She linked her arm in his. "But as Li Sung said, we're going to have a delay. He and Dilam are planning a strategy to make him a member of the High Council."

"A delay is a big problem."

"We can make use of it. I've decided Li Sung is right. You can wait for your railroad."

He smiled at her and teased. "You'll be in breach of your contract." His curious gaze went back to the arched doorway through which Li Sung had disappeared. "That's not all, is it? What's this all ab—"

She had to distract him. "We'll renegotiate." She paused. "After the wedding."

He went still. "Wedding?"

"A wedding usually follows a courtship. You did say you were courting me."

"You didn't mention—"

"Are you trying to say you don't wish to marry me? I warn you, I'm not a woman to take such an insult lightly."

"Of course I wish to marry you," he said impatiently. "It's you who have avoided the issue. You told me once that you had no liking for the life I offered you."

"Is the offer the same?"

"You would still have to live on Cinnidar." His lips twisted ruefully. "Though I suppose I could raze this place to the ground if you hate the idea of living in a palace as much as you claimed."

"Li Sung thinks Cinnidar is paradise. Paradise isn't such a bad place to live." She smiled as she glanced around her at the splendid many-leveled terrace. "And a palace is what you make it. I suppose I could make an adjustment."

"And your railroad?"

Her smile faded. "I need work to do. Useful work. I can't give it up."

"We have a railroad here, dammit."

"Suppose I'm not satisfied with just running your railroad? Suppose I want to build my own?"

"You can build it here. You can build all over the damn island."

She looked at him, troubled. "There's room for only one railroad on Cinnidar."

He threw up his hands. "All right, I promised you a railroad if you completed the contract on time. You'll get your railroad. You can have mine. I'll sign it and the right of way over to you." He smiled ruefully. "That's a hell of a lot of power I'm giving you over me. If you decide to cut off my gold shipments, I'm stranded. Does that satisfy you?"

She smiled happily. "Yes, it satisfies me. I believe it will be good for you to have to worry a bit."

"I'd worry more if you left me." He reached out and grasped her shoulders. "I've been thinking about it. Do you remember when you told me your entire world didn't revolve around me?"

She had only a vague memory of that night when she had felt so abandoned by Li Sung. "I think so."

"Well, my world does revolve around you."

She laughed. "I'm honored. It's not every woman who has a kingdom like Cinnidar revolving around her."

"I'm not joking." He drew her close. "I don't ever want to go back to the way it was before." His next words were muffled in her hair. "I was . . . lonely."

She felt the tears sting her eyes. This rare admission

from Ruel was very difficult for him and only emphasized his trust in her. "So was I."

"Not like me. You reach out and gather people to you. I can beckon them near but I can't trust anyone enough to be close to them."

She slid her arms around him. "Some people you can't shut away. They don't let you."

"I had to be close to you," he said hoarsely. "I needed to be close to you. If you left me now, I don't think I could stand it. I'd want to shout and roar and break the world into a million pieces."

Tiger burn bright.

She fought back tears as she said lightly, "We wouldn't want that to happen. I guess I'd better not leave you."

"Promise me."

He was oddly rigid against her, and she instinctively reached up to soothingly stroke the tight tendons of his nape. "Why should I leave you?"

"Promise me."

His mother had walked away and left him. Ian, the only other person he had loved, had also left him. Death had not really taken his brother; he had walked joyously toward it. "You have my word," she said softly. "I will never, never leave you."

The tension left him and he stood there holding her while the pink haze of sunset lazily crept over the terrace and blushed the mirrored waters of the geometric pools with a rosy glow. "I will make you happy, you know," he said. "I promise I'll make you forget how we started."

"No, you won't." She looked up at him. "I don't want to forget one minute of it. The bad times and good are so blended together, I can't give up one and keep the other, and, by God, I won't give up one second of the good times."

"I'm glad you think the good was worth the bad. But it will get better." He gave her a quick kiss, stepped back and slipped his arm around her waist, and led her to the balustrade overlooking the canyon. "I'll be such a damn good husband, even Maggie will approve of me."

The descending sun bathed the mountain in scarlet glory.

Beauty. Splendor. Paradise.

Ruel didn't appear to appreciate the view. His expression had suddenly become abstracted. "I'll have to send the crews back to work the mine tomorrow," he said absently. "I've had them working down at the docks helping Li Sung." He was silent a moment and then suddenly turned and asked her, "How would you like to go to Johannesburg?"

Her eyes widened with shock. "Johannesburg!"

"Not for long," he said quickly. "I thought maybe— Since there's going to be a delay anyway, we might—"

"Why would you want to go to Johannesburg?"

"Well, today a freighter landed at the dock and the captain said there are reports of another big gold strike just north of the city there."

She stared at him in bewilderment. "You have a whole mountain of gold just waiting for you to mine here."

He made a face. "I guess you're right. Life in those camps can be pretty rough, and you'd probably hate it. I know I don't need any more gold. I'm being completely unreasonable."

He was not being reasonable, but he was being entirely Ruel MacClaren, Jane realized suddenly.

He's not a man who is comfortable living in palaces, Li Sung had said.

Cinnidar might be home for Ruel, but there would always be part of him that craved the adventure of the search. After a lifetime of challenging himself and the rest of the world, he would never be able to tamely accept living in this palace and the luxurious life Cinnidar offered.

Any more than she would be able to accept it.

Her spirits lifted at the thought, and relief poured through her with dizzying force. She had been willing to live here because this was Ruel's home and she loved him and wished him to be happy, but she had not really been content with the idea. Paradise was a fine place to come back to when you were ready, but there was still a world out there to build and conquer.

"Do you suppose those miners would need a railroad to take their gold to the city?" she asked.

A brilliant smile lit his face. "It wouldn't surprise me."

"Well, then I think we really should go to Johannesburg." Her eyes twinkled. "After all, your mine might play out in a hundred years or so, and then our great-grandchildren would be left destitute."

"There's always that possibility." He threw back his head and laughed joyously before picking her up and swinging her in a circle. "You really wouldn't mind going? You're not just telling me that?"

She shook her head. "I'd like to get off the train there and look around and see the sights. Cinnidar will be the last stop on the line, but I'm not ready for it yet."

He hugged her close. "I promise it will be for only a short while."

Their stay in Johannesburg might be for only a little while, but there would probably be other places, other times when Ruel grew restless and would want a change. Who knows? She might be the one to grow restless. They would have to learn to accommodate each other's needs in the years ahead. That was what love meant, and God knows she did love Ruel MacClaren with her whole heart. "We'll have to see."

"Now that we have our next move planned . . ." His hand tenderly stroked her hair back from her face as he whispered, "What didn't you really want Li Sung to tell me?"

Ruel was being as tenacious as always. She should have known he wouldn't be distracted, she thought resignedly. "Nothing important."

"A secret? Secrets are always tantalizing." He kissed her lightly on the mouth. "I'll find out sooner or later, you know."

He probably would find out the truth, but perhaps it would be at a time when the pain was not so fresh. In the meantime she would make sure they both had something to think about besides the past. She changed the subject. "I'll want to be back on Cinnidar by this time next year."

He frowned. "We'll try."

"No, it's important. We have to be here."

"What's so urgent? We can put Li Sung and Dilam in charge of the railway and the mine."

She shook her head. "While we're in Johannesburg I believe we should put our efforts to work on another project."

"What project?"

"One to which every ruler of a kingdom should give serious attention."

"What the hell are you talking about?"

"A child." She nestled closer and whispered, "I want to have a child, Ruel. I want our child to be born here on Cinnidar next year."

Margaret boarded the *Golden Hare* two days later to set out for Scotland.

"We'll come back to Glenclaren for a visit next year," Jane said. "But if there's anything we can do to help, you must write us immediately."

"I'm not so helpless that I cannot tend to matters myself," Margaret said impatiently. "Though I'll admit I'll be glad of your company." She gave Jane a brusque hug before turning to Ruel. "Treat her well or you'll answer to me."

"I tremble in terror at the thought." Ruel brushed her cheek with his lips. "Good journey, Maggie."

"Marg—" She broke off. It was a small impudence and not worth bothering about. Ruel would never reform, but he was coming along much better than she had dreamed possible. "Of course I will have a good journey."

"She will not have it any other way. No storm would dare to touch her."

Kartauk. She tensed as she turned to see him striding up the gangplank. She had seen him only in passing since that night at the encampment, and she had told herself she hoped he would not come to bid her good-bye. Yet now joy was mixed with the sadness surging through her.

He stopped before her. "Even the supreme deity must bow before Margaret's will."

"Heathen blasphemy," Margaret said. "Just what I would expect of you."

Jane glanced from one to the other and then gave Margaret a final quick embrace. "Good-bye, Margaret." She took Ruel's arm and tugged peremptorily. "Come on, Ruel."

He smiled with amusement and mockingly inclined his head. "As you command. I live only to make you happy."

Margaret snorted as she watched them walk down the gangplank. "Not likely."

"I disagree," Kartauk said. "There is a certain amount of truth in his words. I'm surprised you cannot see it yourself." He turned to look at her. "But then, your judgment is clouded at present."

She hurriedly glanced away from him. "It is kind of you to come bid me farewell. I did not expect it." She held out her gloved hand. "Good-bye, Kartauk."

He took her hand. "You would have expected it if you didn't have your head buried in the sand." He frowned. "I do not like this glove." He stripped off her black glove and she felt the warm shock of flesh on flesh as both his big palms enclosed her own. "That's better. Now I can get on with it. I will give you a year of mourning before I come to you. I would allow you more, but that would probably be a disaster. I would find you in a nunnery or married to some dried-up cleric who would give you only duty and no joy."

She stared at him in astonishment. "I told you there could be nothing for us."

"Because you're confused and filled with false guilt. You're not usually so muddle-headed. Given time, I'm sure you will realize Ian would want you to take your happiness where you find it." He smiled. "With me."

She shook her head. "I would always remember—"

"Yes, you will," he interrupted. "But I will see that the memories are not bitter."

She stared at him dazedly. She heard the departure bell ring and welcomed it with relief. She must banish him and also this hope springing within her. "You must go."

He lifted her palm to his lips. "One year, Margaret." He dropped her hand and turned away. "Expect me."

She watched him start down the gangplank, her heart pounding, her emotions in chaos. She rushed to the rail. "No, don't come. You won't be welcome."

"I'll be welcome."

"What of your work for Ruel?"

"We may come back here."

"My place is at Glenclaren."

"We will discuss it after we're wed."

"We will not wed."

He stepped onto the dock. "Of course we will. You're not a woman to live in sin."

"I mean, we will not—"

"Of course, if you really wish to stay in that cold land, I suppose I could reconsider my decision not to give your Queen Victoria the benefit of my genius." He frowned. "But I will not do a head of her. Those double chins . . ."

The gangplank had been taken up and the ship was moving away from the shore. He stood there on the dock with his powerful legs astride and the breeze lifting his glossy brown hair.

"It will do you no good to come," she called desperately. "Stay here, Kartauk."

He shook his head. "How can I? I've discovered I cannot bear the thought of any other apprentice. You know I cannot allow my work to suffer."

"I will only say no."

"At first. But not last, my Margaret." He smiled and his expression lit with such loving confidence, she had to believe him. "In the end you will say, 'Aye, Kartauk.' "

ABOUT THE AUTHOR

IRIS JOHANSEN, who has more than twenty-seven million copies of her books in print, has won many awards for her achievements in writing. The best-selling author of *Stalemate, Killer Dreams, Blind Alley, Firestorm, Fatal Tide, Dead Aim, Body of Lies, The Search,* and many other novels, she lives near Atlanta, Georgia, where she is currently at work on a new novel.

Read on for a preview of

Iris Johansen's

newest novel

STALEMATE

On sale now

#1 NEW YORK TIMES BESTSELLING AUTHOR

IRIS

JOHANSEN

TAKES YOU TO THE EDGE OF SUSPENSE

STALEMATE

AN EVE DUNCAN FORENSICS THRILLER

STALEMATE

On sale now

The phone was ringing.

Ignore it, Eve told herself, her fingers moving swiftly on the skull reconstruction she'd given the name Marty. She could call whoever it was back when she was through working. The phone was set for speaker and she could pick up if it was Joe or Jane. She was getting too close to that important last step in the sculpting.

On the sixth ring the answering machine picked up.

"I need to speak to you. Answer the phone, Ms. Duncan."

She froze, her fingers stopped in midstroke. Luis Montalvo. Though she had spoken to him only twice, that faint accent was unmistakable.

"I know you're there. You haven't left that cottage in the last week." His voice became faintly mocking. "Your dedication is admirable and I understand you're brilliant at your job. I look forward to having both focused soon on my behalf." He paused. "Do pick up the phone. I'm not accustomed to being ignored. It upsets me. You don't want to upset me."

And she didn't want to pick up the phone. He might jar her out of the zone of feverish intensity she needed when she was working this close to completion. Dammit, she had hoped he wouldn't call her again after she'd turned him down when he'd phoned her over a week ago.

"I won't give up, you know."

No, he probably wouldn't. Montalvo had been polite during the first call, and even after she'd refused his offer the second time he'd phoned, he'd displayed no anger. His voice had been smooth and soft, almost regretful, yet there had been a note beneath that velvet courtesy that had puzzled her. It had made her uneasy then, but tonight it filled her with impatience. She had no *time* for this now. Marty was waiting.

She strode across the room and picked up the phone. "Montalvo, I'm very busy. You've had your answer. Don't call me again."

"Ah, how delightful to hear your voice. I knew you wouldn't be so rude as to leave me hanging on that dreadful answering device. I hate impersonal machines. I'm a man of emotion and passion and they offend me."

"I really don't want to hear what you love or hate. I don't care. I want to get off this phone and forget you exist."

"I realize that sad fact. You're absorbed in your latest reconstruction, of that boy found buried in Macon. Have you named him yet? I understand you name all the skulls you work on."

She stiffened. "How do you know that?"

"I know everything about you. I know you live with a Detective Joe Quinn of the Atlanta Police

Department. I know you have an adopted daughter, Jane MacGuire. I know you're possibly the best forensic sculptor in the world. Shall I go on?"

"That could all be public record. And how did you know about the boy murdered in Macon?"

"I have many, many contacts around the world. Do you want to know who killed him? I could find out for you."

"I don't believe you."

"Why not?"

"Because you're not even in this country. You're a scumbag of an arms peddler and you live in Colombia, where you can hide out and deal your poison to the highest bidder."

He chuckled. "I do like frankness. Very few women I know are willing to tell me the truth as they see it."

"Then I'm grateful to not be one of the women you know, you sexist bastard. If I were, I'd probably be tempted to cut your nuts off."

"Such violence, such passion. I believe we're very much alike, Ms. Duncan."

"No way." She drew a deep breath. "The answer is still no. I've no intention of coming down there and doing your reconstruction."

"You were very polite and businesslike, almost sympathetic, when I first made you the offer. The second time you were much more curt. I suppose you had Joe Quinn check me out?"

"Yes, of course. I don't deal with crooks and murderers."

"Everyone deals with whoever can make them the best bargain."

"I told you the last time that I wasn't interested in any of your fat fees."

"And I was duly impressed. I don't believe I've ever had anyone turn down a million dollars for a few days' work."

"Dirty money."

"Not true. All my cash is very well laundered."

"I thought you'd accepted that I wouldn't work for you."

"Because I didn't argue with you? I don't believe in spinning my wheels. I just go away and find another lure. It took almost a week for me to decide what that would be."

"And?"

"I'm convinced you'll be my guest in a very short time."

"Why?"

"That would spoil the surprise. I like to see a plan unfold like a beautiful night flower."

"You mentioned Joe and my adopted daughter. You touch them and I'll kill you."

"That violence again." His tone was amused. "I'd never be that stupid. That would be the trigger that would send you into the fray to take me down. I want your cooperation."

"I'm hanging up."

"Very well. I just wanted to offer you the opportunity to change your mind. It would make me happy if you would come to me for mercenary reasons. Much less stressful for all of us."

"Are you threatening me?"

"Heavens, no. You'd know it if I was doing that. There would be no question. Won't you come and make me happy and become rich in the process?"

"No."

"Too bad." He sighed. "Good night." He hung up.

Eve slowly pressed the disconnect button. He had

said he wasn't threatening her, but what else could she call it? It was subtle, but the threat was all the more chilling for the casual, understated way it was delivered. He'd been so calm when she'd turned down his offer that she'd honestly thought he'd accepted her refusal and was out of her life. It was clear she'd been wrong.

Should she call Joe and tell him Montalvo was still on the scene?

And have him think she was worried and rush home from the precinct?

She wasn't worried. She was uneasy. Montalvo had said her family was safe and she believed him. As he had perceived, any danger to them would make her angry and rebellious. He'd made no direct threat at all and he might just be trying to intimidate her into doing his job.

Maybe.

Yet he'd seemed to know entirely too much about her movements. Was she being watched?

Yes, she'd definitely tell Joe. But there was no use in alarming him right now. She'd tell him tonight when he came home for dinner. Okay, so she wanted to get back to Marty and she was afraid talking to Joe about Montalvo would keep her from doing it. She wasn't about to let Montalvo disturb her concentration on her work. That slimeball would probably enjoy the thought that he could control her to that extent. He might even call her again and try to reinforce that control. She'd be damned if she'd let him. She turned off the house phone and then her cell phone before moving back toward the reconstruction on the pedestal across the room.

Block Montalvo out of her thoughts. Think of Marty and the chance to bring him home. Think of the boy who'd been murdered and buried and left alone with no name or place.

That was better. Montalvo's words were blurring, fading away as she began to work.

Talk to me, Marty. Help me to bring you home. . . .

"Pity." Montalvo looked down at the phone. "I was hoping she'd give in to greed like a normal person. It's easy to be noble for an hour, a day, but then they start to think and perhaps dream a little. A week should have whetted her appetite and made her start making excuses why she should take the job."

"Not everyone thinks that money is the end-all of everything, Montalvo," Soldono said.

Montalvo smiled. "Almost everyone. It's unfortunate that Eve Duncan is in the minority." He rose from the carved chair at the head of the dining table. "Oh, well. One must make adjustments."

Soldono tensed. "Don't do it, Montalvo."

"She's giving me little choice. You're giving me little choice. You didn't talk to her, did you?" He shook his head. "I told you what you had to do, but you were looking for an out. I could see you scrambling frantically to avoid bringing her into the picture until time got away from you. Well, that time has come."

"Why her?" Soldono asked. "There's a fine forensic sculptor in Rio de Janeiro. Use him."

"Sanchez?" Montalvo shook his head. "Technically brilliant, but he's not what I want."

"Eve Duncan is an American citizen and she's known and respected by every police department on the planet. She turned down your money and you'll be stirring up a hornet's nest if you try to force her."

"And you wouldn't like that. The CIA tries to be very low-key these days."

"Let me try to get Sanchez for you."

"You don't understand."

"Then tell me."

He gazed musingly down at the depths of the wine in his glass. "It's a matter of passion."

"What?"

"I told Eve Duncan that I was a man of passion. It's true."

Soldono hadn't noticed any emotion in Montalvo, much less a passion. The man was brilliant and innovative, and he kept any feelings or thoughts hidden behind that faintly mocking smile. "Why Eve Duncan?" he repeated.

"She has passion, too. I've studied her file and nothing could be clearer. It's like a whirlwind spinning around her. She grew up on the streets with a drug addict for a mother and gave birth to an illegitimate child as a teenager. She turned her life around and went back to school and became a model mother. Then her daughter was kidnapped and presumably killed, but the body was never found. Instead of being crushed, the lady became a forensic sculptor and tried to bring closure to other parents by identifying the remains of their missing children."

"I know all that," Soldono said impatiently.

"You know the facts, but you've never studied Eve Duncan the way I have. I believe I may know her better than she knows herself. I know what drives her. I know what makes her tick."

"Yeah, sure." He couldn't keep the sarcasm from his tone. "Passion?"

"Don't underestimate it. Da Vinci had it. Michelangelo had it. It's the difference between art and creation. Eve Duncan has it." His tone was smooth but hard. "And that's why I have to have her. Don't try to pawn anyone else off on me."

"Find another way. You promised me that you'd—"

"And I'd keep my promise if you'd kept yours." His tone was threaded with mockery as he continued, "But since the lady is not being accommodating, I must have cooperation from someone. You can see that, can't you?"

"No."

Montalvo's smile faded. "Then your vision had better improve quickly. I told you yesterday that if I didn't get the answer I wanted, I'd move. You obviously chose to think I wasn't serious. I'll give you another four hours to persuade her, Soldono. No more, no less." He looked at his watch. "Ten tonight."

"I can't strike a bargain like that."

"Of course you can. Don't bullshit me. You do it all the time. A life for a life." He turned away. "Finish your dinner. The tiramisu is magnificent. The chef will be upset if you don't try it."

Soldono was seething with frustration as he watched Montalvo walk away. Sleek, graceful, and as dangerous as a stick of dynamite too near the flames. Bastard.

Would he do it?

Why was he even questioning it? Montalvo didn't bluff and he would carry out any threat he made in exactly the method he'd outlined.

He had four hours.

He'd hoped to find a way to stop Montalvo without involving Eve Duncan, but time had run out. But was it to his advantage to make a trade for the woman? Why not let it go? He had to be sure it was worth it.

Four hours.

He reached for his phone and quickly dialed.

"Montalvo's given me four hours. Dammit, he'll do it. How the hell am I supposed to stop him?"

Venable was silent for a moment. "It's time you offered Eve Duncan a choice."

"Some choice. Okay, I'm on it. I'll call you back when I get through." He hung up and looked in his book for Eve Duncan's phone number.

Jane called me," Joe said as he came into the cottage two hours later. "She tried to reach you but she couldn't do it. She said she'd made reservations for us at the Doubletree in Phoenix and that I was to remind you that the show is this Saturday." He smiled. "I told her there was a fairly good chance that you'd remember."

"What?" Eve tried to shift her attention away from the skull. It was like fighting her way through a thick fog. "Of course I remembered." Eve managed to tear her gaze away from Marty. "It's a very important show for Jane. I wouldn't miss it. She should know that."

"Yeah." He went over to the phone and turned it back on. "She also knows that you've been working day and night to finish that reconstruction."

"Marty is difficult." She looked back at the reconstruction of the eight-year-old boy. At least, the forensic team's estimate was eight years. "I had to practically put his splintered facial bones back together before I could begin work."

"Do we have a clue who he is yet?"

She shrugged. "You know I never look at police files before I finish the reconstruction. The Macon police have photos of children who disappeared around the time that they estimate the boy was killed. We'll see if we have a resemblance."

"DNA?"

She grimaced. "Come on. The DNA labs are so backed up with current murders that they're not going to be in any hurry to process a five-year-old cold case." She pushed the hair back from her forehead. "But if I do a good enough job I have a chance to bring him home."

"You'll do a good job," Joe said. "But not if you get so tired you lose judgment." He headed for the kitchen. "Did you eat dinner?"

"I think so . . . I don't remember."

"Then we'll assume that you didn't. I'll warm up the beef stew in the refrigerator and put some garlic bread in the oven. That means you have fifteen minutes to clean up your studio and wash up."

"I can catch something later."

"Now." He opened the refrigerator. "Scoot."

She hesitated. Montalvo. She'd meant to tell him about the call from Montalvo as soon as he came in, but it didn't seem important now. As she'd worked on the skull, everything had faded but the reality of the work itself. Marty was important. The other lost children were important. She'd tell Joe about Montalvo later. "I should finish tonight. I want to do the computer 3-D image before we leave for Phoenix."

"The boy's been dead for five years. He can wait a little while longer." He glanced at her over his shoulder. "No arguments, Eve. I let you wear yourself into the ground because you give me no choice, but not this time. You'll have a fight on your hands. I'd bet you've lost five pounds this week."

"I don't think—" She wearily shook her head.

Maybe he was right. She was exhausted and she probably had lost weight. This case had been particularly painful. She should be used to dealing with the cruelty of the monsters who killed innocent children after all these years of forensic sculpting. Yet the mindless brutality of the violence visited on this small boy had ripped aside the scar tissue. "I want to bring him home, Joe." Her lips tightened. "And I want to kill the son of a bitch who did that to him."

"I know," he said. "Give me a chance and I'll do the job for you. For that poor kid and for what his killer is doing to you." He slammed the refrigerator door. "I was hoping this damn obsession was lessening, but along comes a nasty case and you're right back where you were."

She stiffened. "This is what I do. This is what I am. Why are you so angry about it now?"

He didn't speak for a moment. "Because I'm tired. Because sometimes I can't stand to see you in pain. Because the years pass and I think the miracle will happen and it never does."

He was talking about Bonnie. She felt a ripple of shock. She couldn't remember the last time he'd spoken about her daughter. Yet Bonnie was always there, a silent presence. "I'll find her someday."

"A miracle," he repeated. "After all these years that's what it would take." He turned his back on her and moved to the stove. "Go get cleaned up. If I upset you anymore, you won't eat and I'll be defeating my purpose."

She studied him. Something was definitely wrong. His motions were jerky and that remark about Bonnie was an instant tip-off. She would have noticed earlier if she hadn't been distracted by both her work and the aftereffects of that call from

Montalvo. "I'm not the only one who's upset. What the devil is wrong with you?" She crossed her arms over her chest to keep them from shaking. "And don't tell me that you're just fed up with living here with me. If you don't want to stay with me, no one is forcing you."

"Particularly not you."

"Shut up." She tried to steady her voice. "I don't have any right to ask you to stay. I'm an emotional cripple. As you said, I'm obsessed and I'll probably remain that way for the rest of my life. Sometimes I wonder why you haven't left me before this."

He didn't look at her. "You know why."

"Joe."

"I have my own obsession. Now, get your ass in gear. We need to get some food into you." He shot her a glance. "It's okay. I'm over it. It just had to come out."

"Why now?"

"Why not?"

She hesitated, gazing at him. It wasn't over. She could sense the turbulence, the reckless energy whirling below the surface.

"You're down to ten minutes."

She tried to smile. "You used up five telling me what an obsessive wacko I am."

"Takes one to know one." He turned on the oven. "And you're my wacko."

She felt a sudden surge of warmth. He was the only man she'd ever known who could make her flit from emotion to emotion in the space of a heartbeat. She'd been angry, upset, defensive, and yet now she was feeling this powerful surge of affection. She turned away and headed down the hall. "Wackos of the world, unite."

"I only want to unite with one wacko and I fully intend to do it later tonight. After I feed you and stoke your energy level."

"Promises, promises."

She was still smiling as she stepped into the shower a few minutes later. She could feel a tingle of sexual anticipation and excitement start within her. Jesus, you'd think after all these years with Joe that sex wouldn't be this urgent. Wasn't it supposed to become merely comfortable after a while? Their coming together was just as wild and passionate as that first time. Her body was tensing, readying at the thought.

She took a deep breath and closed her eyes as the water flowed over her. She'd tell Joe about Montalvo's call over dinner, but right now she wanted to relax and forget about everything but Joe. . . .